W9-CCO-078

3 1317 00193 2046

DISCARD

F
CAR

Carroll, Gerry.

No place to hide.

$23.00   8/95

	DATE		
OCT 0 1 1995	AUG 1 9 1996		
OCT 1 6 1995	SEP 0 3 1996		
JAN 11 1996	MAY 0 9 1997		
	DEC 2 1 1999		
FEB 8 1 1996	NOV 0 9 2000		
APR 1 2 1996			

APR 2 8 1996

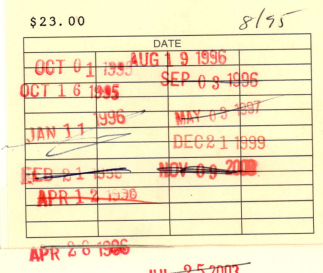

JUL 2 5 2003

APR 1   2010

FEB 16 2004

APR 1   2010

MAR 1 0 2008

BAKER & TAYLOR

Rantoul Public Library
225 S. Century Blvd.
Rantoul, Illinois 61866

No Place to Hide

Gerry Carroll's Vietnam War/Naval Aviation Trilogy

North SAR
Ghostrider One
No Place to Hide

Published by POCKET BOOKS

No Place to Hide

★ ★ ★

Gerry Carroll

POCKET BOOKS

New York   London   Toronto   Sydney   Tokyo   Singapore

This book is a work of fiction. Names, characters, places, and incidents are either products of the author's imagination or are used fictitiously. Any resemblance to actual events or locales or persons, living or dead, is entirely coincidental.

An *Original* Publication of POCKET BOOKS

 POCKET BOOKS, a division of Simon & Schuster Inc.
1230 Avenue of the Americas, New York, NY 10020

Copyright © 1995 by Gerry Carroll

All rights reserved, including the right to reproduce
this book or portions thereof in any form whatsoever.
For information address Pocket Books, 1230 Avenue
of the Americas, New York, NY 10020

Library of Congress Cataloging-in-Publication Data

Carroll, Gerry.
    No place to hide / Gerry Carroll.
        p.   cm.
    ISBN 0-671-86510-2
    1. Vietnamese Conflict, 1961–1975—Naval operations, American—
Fiction.   I. Title.
PS3553.A7639N6   1995
813'.54—dc20   94-45923
                                                                            CIP

First Pocket Books hardcover printing August 1995

10 9 8 7 6 5 4 3 2 1

POCKET and colophon are registered trademarks of
Simon & Schuster Inc.

Printed in the U.S.A.

For my wife, Debbie

I had the adventures and the fun and
I got the praise and the medals.
But she was always the one who
had the courage.

Acknowledgments

Gerry Carroll passed away shortly after finishing this novel. These are the acknowledgments he would have wanted to make:

To Paul McCarthy, his editor for all his expertise, support, patience, and especially his friendship.
To Tom Clancy for his encouragement and friendship.

Gerry's wife, Debbie Carroll, also wanted to acknowledge the support and friendship she has received:

To all the people who were true friends when I needed them the most I want to say thanks.

To my family and Gerry's family for being there whenever I need them and for all their love and support. To Paul McCarthy for helping me figure out what was going on in this business. To Tom Clancy for being Gerry's best friend and for all the support he and Wanda have given the boys and me. To Kathy, Claudia, and Mary for all their help the first week and every week since. To Vic Thomas for all the rides he provided and for being there especially for Kevin. To John Sorthorn for keeping Gerry around in lacrosse. To the Smiths for always keeping me in mind. And a special thanks to Connie for being there every day.

✫ **Contents** ✫

1968

★ ★ ★

✶ PROLOGUE ✶

Staying Behind

⋆ **Prologue** ⋆

Friday, 23 May 1969

LT. KEVIN THOMPSON LET THE LETTER FALL TO HIS LAP AND LEANED BACK in his battered Navy-issue gray desk chair. He didn't know whether to be hurt or angry or relieved as he looked out the window at the city of San Diego, shining in the late-afternoon sun. In the bay between the city and the beach outside his window, he could see several small boats moving quickly north as his fellow Navy SEAL instructors took the newest class of would-be SEALs out for their evening exercises. Their white wakes streamed out behind them as they bounced and jostled over the dim wakes left by the dozens of vessels moving about the bay.

Sailboats were luffing their way painfully slowly from nowhere in particular to somewhere else. Powered boats of all sizes were moving along at whatever pace their drivers chose, always altering course to give the right of way to the sailboaters and always mentally cursing them for being hazards to navigation. The tour boats moved back and forth giving their deckloads of tourists a close-up view of the huge gray Navy ships tied up at the quay at North Island.

Although he couldn't see them from his window, Thompson knew two carriers were there that were guaranteed to make even the most obnoxious of tourists fall silent and simply stare. One of the carriers, the one with sailors desultorily painting her sides, had just returned from a seven-month deployment to Vietnam. The other, the one with cranes steadily swinging crates and boxes of supplies aboard, was only a week away from departing for the Gulf of Tonkin and the war.

Thompson looked back at the small boats full of SEALs and

5

trainees, bouncing along toward the training area out in the Pacific. He had always loved driving those boats around, the wind and the spray in his face. But he hated the long, grueling, conditioning swim that the passengers were in for when they got to the drop-off point. He sighed. That was part of the price you had to pay, he thought, if you were going to get the job done and stay alive when it hit the fan.

Thompson picked up the letter and looked at it again. The battered, water-stained paper and the labored, almost childlike penmanship bothered him nearly as much as the message that the letter contained. He remembered the pain he'd felt when he and the others of his SEAL "action team" had been unable to find Tony Butler or any trace of him after the firefight during the last patrol a year ago. He recalled with a little pride and with some shame the screaming match he'd gotten into with the detachment commander about continuing the pullout with one of his men still missing. He remembered his commander's eyes hardening and his lips pressing into a grim line. And he remembered the feeling of a vast emptiness within as he obeyed his commander's curt order to shut up and get on the damn helicopter.

Glancing at the clock on the wall, Thompson saw that it was finally time to secure for the day. He dropped his feet to the floor and stood, stretching the kinks out of his back. After carefully folding the letter, he placed it gently in his left shirt pocket. Down the hall, he could hear the other members of the staff closing their offices and walking past his door to the exit. He waited for the distinctive sound of Senior Chief Dalton's leg cast to come thumping down the green linoleum decking. When Dalton had passed by, Thompson picked up his car keys from the desk and walked out of his office, checking as he went the locked drawers of the file cabinets standing side by side under the wall clock.

Thompson walked quickly to the exit door and looked through the wavy glass, watching Dalton as he limped across the parking lot toward his Pontiac GTO convertible. Thompson slipped his cloth garrison cap from his belt and put it on, unconsciously adjusting it until it sat rakishly low on his forehead with the little aviator's peak at the back. Pushing the door open, he trotted down the steps and across the parking lot toward Dalton's GTO.

"Hey, Senior Chief. Got a minute?"

Dalton looked up and smiled at his lieutenant. "Yes, sir. What's up?"

Thompson was suddenly unsure of himself. Dragging Dalton into this was unfair at best and illegal at worst. He decided to take it slowly. "Senior, you got time for a beer?"

Dalton grinned. "I always have time for a beer. How 'bout the MexPac in ten minutes? Last one in the door buys."

"Fair enough." Thompson turned toward his Austin-Healey as Dalton abruptly let the clutch out and left a small rooster tail of gravel as he headed for the gate. The lieutenant shook his head. It should be impossible for Dalton to drive that car with his leg in a cast, but from long experience Thompson knew that *impossible* was a word that had never entered Dalton's lexicon—that was why Thompson needed to talk to him.

As Thompson's right hand inserted the key into the ignition, his left patted his shirt pocket, checking one more time that the letter was still there.

The Mexican Village Restaurant, or "MexPac" to a generation of Navy men, sat on a beautifully manicured main street in Coronado—Orange Avenue—just south of the Naval Air Station at North Island and just north of the Naval Amphibious Base where Thompson and the West Coast SEAL teams were headquartered. With its facade a sort of dark flamingo pink, the Mexican Village looked a little odd, even standing as it did among other small businesses all decorated in what passes for normal in Southern California.

As Thompson entered the front door, he stood for a second, letting his eyes adjust from the brightness outside to the relative darkness of the restaurant's interior. He returned the bartender's wave and spotted Dalton sitting at a table along the wall, his white cast stuck out into the aisle a little way. Dalton waved an Olympia beer bottle at Thompson, who nodded and stepped up to the bar to order a couple more.

Thompson idly ran a fingernail over the edges of the mosaic tiles along the edges of the bar while he waited for the bartender to bring the two "Olys." On the ride over, he had debated further what he was going to say to Dalton, and even after he walked back to the table, he was still unsure.

Dalton watched Thompson carefully as he placed the bottles on the table and sat down. Dalton picked his up and took a sip.

The young officer nodded at Dalton's cast. "How's the leg?"

"Fine. I think I've finally learned my lesson when it comes to motorcycles." He sipped his beer and put it down. "So what's on your mind, Mr. Thompson?"

Thompson pulled the letter from his pocket and slid it across the table, carefully avoiding the wet rings left by the beer bottles. He watched Dalton's brow furrow as he picked up the letter and inspected it as if it might burn his fingers. "What's this?"

"Well, to be perfectly honest, Chief, it's a problem I have no idea how to deal with."

Thompson sat back and watched as Dalton gently unfolded the letter and began reading. Having read the letter so many times himself, Thompson watched the chief's eyes for reaction when he got to several parts that had surprised Thompson, but there was nothing other than an odd expression of growing sadness as he went on. Dalton finished the second page, glanced at Thompson, and began reading it again, this time more carefully. But there should have been some reaction.

The letter was signed by Tony Butler and was dated only a month before. Thompson had at first thought that it was a fake, but the handwriting, which he'd checked against several records he still kept in his desk, and the words and terms the writer used, suggested it was probably genuine. Although officially listed as missing in action, Butler, as far as Thompson and the rest of the action team had been concerned, was dead. Not only was Thompson totally baffled as to how to proceed, but he was also trying to deal emotionally with the grief he'd been carrying around for over a year. Up until four years ago, he'd been a leader who had inexplicably lost one of his best and most dependable men. That had been a heavy load to carry for a man so young.

Thompson had chosen Dalton to be the first with whom he'd share this because Dalton had not only been the assistant team leader but also Butler's best friend. The chief seemed to deflate as he folded the letter slowly and handed it back to Thompson. He didn't meet the lieutenant's eyes until he'd taken a long pull from his beer. He cleared his throat.

"I, um, kinda feel like switching to tequila. Olys don't seem to be cutting it all of a sudden."

Thompson bit off a sharp retort. He had been carrying this around all day and all Dalton could say was that his beer wasn't

8

strong enough. He was about to speak when Dalton let out a long sigh and looked up.

"Mr. Thompson, I got one of these, too. About a week ago. Tony told me pretty much the same things and explained how hard it had been to write at all, to make contact with the world he'd left behind. He asked that I keep the letter quiet while he tried to decide if he should write to you."

"Chief, he's not dead, for Christ's sake! He's not even *missing* anymore. We can't just keep this to ourselves."

"Yeah. I know what we're *supposed* to do, but I just couldn't bring myself to do it."

"Why?"

"Look, Lieutenant. It was his decision to stay behind with those people. He believed that they needed him or us or somebody. We armed and trained those tribesmen, and then, because some lard ass in Saigon decided that the priorities had changed, we abandoned them. We were supposed to just walk away and hope, just hope, that they could survive with half the Viet Cong in the whole damn place trying to track them down. You remember how hard we all fought to stay, and I know you remember that Agency prick telling you it was pack up and leave in three days or you'd get a court-martial." Dalton chuckled. "I also remember me and Tony pulling you off him. Good thing the commander showed up right then or your ass would still be in Portsmouth making little rocks out of big ones."

"That's beside the point, Chief. We've got a guy who's supposed to be dead or at least missing who turns out to be still living with and leading a bunch of natives and tearing up the countryside. What if somebody finds out about this and goes after him? Then it's his ass. They'll get him."

"They haven't got him yet and neither have the VC."

Thompson sat back and stared at the table. He realized abruptly that he agreed with Dalton's earlier assessment. He signaled the waitress and ordered two double tequilas.

"Okay. You tell me why we should just pretend that we never got those letters."

Dalton took a large pull from his drink and shuddered a little. He leaned forward and fixed Thompson's gaze in dead earnest. "Because he wants to stay and because it's all he's got in the whole damn world."

9

"What do you mean?"

"You know yourself that he had nobody—no mother or father or brothers or anybody. He just joined the Navy to be a part of something. When we were working up here, we all went home after the workday, and he'd go to the barracks or to a movie all by himself. He even stood alone at parties, off in a corner just watching everybody else. When we got out to that village and started working with those people, he came alive. He loved them, and you gotta admit, they took a shine to him better than they did to the rest of us. He learned to speak their language and picked up their customs almost overnight. You said yourself a couple of times that he almost seemed like one of them. I got the feeling that he's where he belongs and that he's doing something he figures is pretty important. I think we ought to just leave it be and wish him well. If we dragged him back, it would destroy him. And it wouldn't be us, you and me, that went to bring him in either. It would be a bunch of guys he wouldn't know and who don't know him. They'd treat him like some kind of freak, and Tony is a hell of a lot better man than that."

"Chief, I don't know if I can go for that. It's just not that simple."

"All right. Tell me what would be gained by dragging him back. First, we'd have to spend a lot of time and effort just finding him. Assuming we did, he'd be court-martialed and probably imprisoned. For what? For doing what we knew to be right?"

Dalton put his hands flat on the table, leaning forward to give added emphasis to his words. "We fought like hell to stay and finish the job. We all knew that it was wrong to abandon these people. Tony did something about it. He was sent in to train those people to fight their enemy and to help them do it. As far as I can see, he's still doing the original job. He made the choice—he made that very clear in those letters—we ought to respect that choice. He's got nothing to come back *to*. Let it go, Lieutenant."

Dalton sat back and watched Thompson carefully. He could see that his words had struck home, but he also knew that Thompson was torn between two responsibilities—the established one to the Navy and the ephemeral one to Tony Butler. Dalton knew that both responsibilities were equally right, and it had taken him a while to make his choice after he'd gotten his letter. At least, Thompson had had someone to share this with.

Thompson stared at the table for long minutes, twirling his now-empty glass in his hand. He didn't notice when the waitress almost silently delivered another round. Finally, he picked up the letter and looked at it, turning it over in his fingers gently. He slowly tore it into small pieces and dropped them in the ashtray. "I hope this is the right thing to do."

Dalton pushed Thompson's glass of tequila across the table. "We may never know, Mr. Thompson."

April 1975

★ ★ ★

⋆ PART 1 ⋆

Returning to War

★ 1 ★

Tuesday, 1 April 1975

Lt. Tim Boyle, USN, was going through the daily message traffic when the meeting in the conference room down the hall broke up. As one of the assistant air operations officers on the staff of the Navy's commander in chief, Pacific, he was rarely invited into such august meetings where the red security light over the door glowed in the gloom of the central passageway. To tell the truth, Boyle sort of liked it that way. He was young enough so that all he wanted to do was take care of his job, learn as much as he could, and get his tail back into the cockpit of a Navy helicopter as fast as he could. Had he been a bit more senior and better schooled in the politics of a career as a naval officer, he might have figured out how to make himself indispensable to his boss and gotten himself invited to places where he could get some "face time" with the senior officers, or "heavies," who made the decisions.

Several other young officers who worked in the partitioned office were doing all that and moving around among themselves, dropping names and talking about programs and generally doing their damnedest to make sure that the rest of their peers were suitably impressed with how important they were. Boyle, on the other hand, couldn't care less about that crap. He had learned on his last tour, as a Combat Search and Rescue helicopter pilot, what was important and what was not. Acting like a puppy to get himself noticed fell into the "not" category.

It had taken him about a month to figure out all the ins and outs of his new job at CINCPAC, and from then on he could usually have all his work done quickly and correctly. It often took

17

him less than half the morning to get all the routine work done, and he found himself looking for new projects to occupy his time. At first, the new projects kept him almost happily occupied, but it became obvious to some others around that Boyle was the guy to go to when something needed to be done, so he began to get all the leavings—all the jobs that people dumped off to concentrate on their higher-visibility interests. So Boyle stopped volunteering and occupied his extra time by taking extension courses in the vague desire of someday getting a master's degree. He was just marking time here, and as the boredom became increasingly oppressive, Boyle began to think about options outside the Navy. He hadn't spoken about them to anyone yet, but the urgings were there and growing stronger as time passed.

But he still loved flying above all else. He knew that all he had to do was not screw up and he'd go back to fleet squadron with his staff ticket punched and be quite content to be back out at sea flying a helicopter around at two o'clock in the morning in the rain and trying to find his ship. He was *very* good at being a naval aviator, but, he realized for the tenth time that week, he was absolutely abysmal at being an administrator and playing the politics game. He would always love flying, but he wasn't sure that his patience would outlast this shore-duty job.

He shook off these thoughts and turned his attention back to the messages. He initialed the one he was reading and turned to the next one, which was an unclassified summary of the situation in South Vietnam. The originator of the message, the American embassy, seemed to be putting on a brave face because the news reports that Boyle had seen recently were foretelling disaster. As he put his initial in the box, he wondered if the classified message traffic was telling a different story still. He was unaware for a minute that he had mentally drifted away from his office and was wondering how he could get his hands on the classified summaries. He had no "need to know" other than his curiosity.

A shadow fell across the message he was pretending to read and he looked up to see his boss, Cdr. Don Hickerson, standing over his desk. Boyle automatically stood.

"Good morning, Commander. What can I do for you?"

Hickerson, who had known Boyle for quite a long time, smiled at his ingenuousness. "Well, Tim, you can get us a couple of cups of coffee and come down to my office."

"Be right there, sir." Boyle closed the message board and dropped it into the communal in-basket for the others to read and headed for the coffee mess.

Five minutes later, Boyle walked into Hickerson's office carrying two steaming mugs of black coffee. Both mugs were identical except for the names painted on them. They had the crest of their old squadron, HC-17, the helicopter Combat Search and Rescue outfit, painted on one side and a picture of the squadron's aircraft, the Sikorsky HH-3A Sea King, or "Big Mutha," on the other. Most pilots had a favorite mug, and although they usually got a new one at every new command, they used one from their last sea-duty command when assigned ashore. It was one of those little attitudinal things that made many nonaviators consider the aviators cocky assholes.

Boyle glanced around Hickerson's office. He loved coming in here and seeing the plaques hanging on the wall from all the squadrons and ships Hickerson had served with. Quite a lot of history was here, Boyle always thought—not earthshaking or newspaper-headline history but the kind of history that average men get to be a part of but never receive the credit for.

Hickerson looked up and took his cup. "Thanks. Close the door and sit down."

Boyle did as directed, putting his coffee down on the corner of Hickerson's desk. The closed door seemed ominous. In the eighteen months Boyle had been assigned here at CINCPAC staff, Hickerson had only closed the door twice with Boyle—once to debrief Tim's one officer's fitness report and the other to tell him of the death in a helo crash of a mutual friend.

As Boyle sat down, Hickerson pulled out a file folder and laid it on the desk. "Tim, I understand that you and Lieutenant France have been at it again." He removed a sheet of paper from the folder. "This is a little note he sent up to his boss last night. His boss was kind enough to share it with me first thing this morning."

Boyle took the sheet and read it quickly. It was another complaint from France about Boyle, specifically about the speed with which France's proficiency flight hours were being entered into his logbook. It was at least the fourth such blast Boyle had seen in the past three months. It ended with a typical portrait of what Boyle considered to be France's brilliance—his writing skills:

For several months now, there has been repeted delays in Lt. Boyle's entry of my flight times in my Log Book. This insufficency of work has led to grevious difficulties in my keeping track of my status. Your rapid attention in this matter would be greatly appreciated.

Holding the paper by the corner as if it were covered by the germs of the plague, Boyle laid it carefully on Hickerson's desk. "What happened, Commander, is that he put his flight-time transmittal sheet in the operations in-basket last Saturday when he got back from flying and came in about oh seven forty-five Monday bitching that his time hadn't been entered yet. I explained that we have nearly a hundred logbooks to take care of and probably twenty other guys went flying last weekend, so it was a tad unreasonable for him to expect the one, single, solitary yeoman third class to have it all done fifteen minutes after we open for business. He starts yelling that taking care of logbooks was my primary function, and if I can't handle a simple job like that, I ought to think about another line of work. Then he tells me that I ought to have a duty yeoman there at all times to ensure that the operation is run properly."

"Uh-huh. And is that when you lost your temper, told him to go piss up a rope, and threw his logbook across the room?"

"Pretty much. I do believe it was just about then. Yes, sir."

"Okay. And when was it that you threatened to kick the shit out of him?"

"It wasn't a threat, Commander, it was more of a declaration. But it was right after he called me a stupid helo puke who couldn't even get his aircraft back to the ship. I kind of lost my cool there. France said he was going to see me brought up before the admiral for insubordination and stormed out. My yeomen all promised that they'd swear to any alibi I came up with if I'd let them watch me kill him."

"Tim, why didn't you tell me about this when it happened?"

"I didn't figure you needed to get involved. I mean, there can't be anybody within fifty miles of this place who'd listen to that silly son of a bitch."

"The point is, he's two years senior to you. And you treated him with a large measure of disrespect."

"But he's a lieutenant just the same as me!"

"Right. But the system says he's your superior."

"Commander, I'll admit he's senior, but I'll be damned if I'll accept 'superior.' "

"Goddamnit, this is serious! France has lodged a formal complaint with his fucking boss, you idiot!" Boyle was stunned by Hickerson's uncharacteristic vehemence. "Now you'd best get real serious, real quick. Okay?"

Boyle sat up straight and put down his coffee. He and Hickerson had been friends since Boyle had reported to Hickerson's Combat SAR detachment aboard the carrier USS *Concord*, back in 1972. There were professional limits to that friendship and Boyle realized he had just about reached them.

"Yes, sir. Sorry."

"All right. Now, first, you will seek out Mr. France and apologize to him for your conduct. You were out of line." Hickerson stared at Boyle expectantly.

"Yes, sir."

"Today."

"Aye, aye, sir. Today."

"Second, you will *personally* take care of his logbook for the remainder of the time that you are assigned the collateral duty as the logs and records officer. And you will do it with a smile."

Boyle's "yes, sir" was a little slower in coming this time, but Hickerson ignored it.

"Third, you will never speak to a fellow officer in that tone of voice again. Do you understand?"

"Yes, sir."

"Fine. Now, I managed to get this matter turned over to me. This time. I told the admiral that you would be a good little helo pilot, that you would use this as a learning experience and never let your damned Irish temper get the best of you again, at least when you're on duty. He agreed to let me deal with it, but I've got to warn you, Tim, that next time I won't be able to keep it at my level."

Boyle was beginning to feel pretty bad about this now, but then, suddenly, the image of France's supercilious face and snotty attitude came back to him and he began to get mad again. Only this time it was at the system. He wisely kept his anger bottled up.

Hickerson leaned back in his chair and picked up his coffee cup. "Okay. The ass-chewing is over. Now comes the old-uncle part. There will be no charge for part two."

Boyle picked up his cup, too. Hickerson had never had cause

to chew him out before, and Boyle's anger was rapidly being replaced by a feeling akin to humiliation. He watched as Hickerson let out a long breath and put his cup back down.

"Look, as long as you are a participant in the exercise we call life, you are going to run into people like France. The only thing that stupid bastard has going for him is the rank on his collar. Getting mad and beating the shit out of him or somebody like him will do you no good, Tim. You are going to have to grit your teeth and do your job. One of the best parts of the Navy is the fact that sooner or later you or he will transfer out and it will be over. Just remember what Walt Kelly said in the old *Pogo* comic strip: 'Don't take this too serious 'cause it ain't nohow permanent.' Okay?"

Boyle nodded glumly. "Yeah. You're right. And, Commander, I'm sorry I let you down."

Hickerson chuckled. "Tim, you haven't let me down. Your intensity and your brains are part of what make you such a good officer. You're just a little short on patience. I was just like you some years back and I had to learn to keep cool, too. Just count to ten and do your job."

Hickerson sipped the last of his coffee and pulled out another folder. "Now, is everything ready for the retirement ceremony this afternoon?"

"Yup. Everything's ready both at the parade field and at the club. I can't think of anything we've missed and neither could the master chief."

"Good. Now go finish what you were doing and I'll see you at the ceremony. And don't forget to have that chat with Lieutenant France."

"Okay, Commander." Boyle stood and headed for the door.

Hickerson swiveled his chair around and stared out the window. He hated to see a good man like Boyle at the mercy of a worthless prick like France, but Boyle had definitely overstepped the bounds by "declaring" that he'd kick France's ass. Unpleasant as the facts were, Boyle had been wrong.

What really had Hickerson angry was France's comment about Boyle's airmanship and the cheap crack about his being unable to get his aircraft back to the ship. Boyle had had some sort of an engine failure over North Vietnam on a rescue mission and had crashed, killing everyone aboard but himself. The story of his escape was already a minor legend in Naval Aviation.

Boyle had picked up another downed, and injured, pilot along the way and had finally made it to the coast with a couple of squads worth of North Vietnamese troops hot on his tail. He had been wounded holding off the enemy while the other pilot, Mike Santy, tried to inflate a one-man life raft. They'd both nearly been captured but had been snatched out just in time. The pilot of the helicopter that had made the final rescue had been Hickerson's replacement and had died of wounds during the pickup.

It was a very bad day for all concerned, but to have a clown like France, who had been no nearer the enemy than his living room TV set, denigrating Boyle's performance had been too much for Hickerson to take. He'd had a little chat with France and his boss, Commander Bailey, earlier that morning, and it had been just a bit less civil than his talk with Boyle had been. But everybody now understood *exactly* where they stood.

Hickerson sighed and sipped his now-cold coffee. He grimaced but couldn't be sure if the grimace was for the coffee or for the situation. He hoped Boyle would be able to shrug off his feelings over this, but knowing how deeply Tim felt things, he suspected that it would take a while. Hickerson had rarely seen an officer of Boyle's natural competence. He'd seen still fewer who, like Boyle, were completely unaware that they were something special—in the air *or* on the ground. The hell of it was, pricks like France seemed to spend most of their time keeping the good ones on the run. God must truly love idiots and assholes, thought Hickerson. He's made so damn many of them.

Hickerson hated days that started like this. "Shit," he said as he turned back to his desk and the endless stream of paperwork that crossed it.

The wind blew gently across the harbor bringing with it the scent of pineapples from the plantations far from Pearl Harbor. It stirred the surface of the water, making it dance and sparkle in the bright late-afternoon sun. It ruffled the bunting stretched across the front of the podium and snapped the flags held by the color guard standing off to one side. The master of ceremonies, one of the lieutenant commanders from the staff, leaned closer to the microphone and tried to force his words through the ruffling noise the wind made as it passed across the mike. Sitting in the next to last row, Lt. Tim Boyle sighed and winced to himself.

As the officer who had been tasked with setting up this retirement ceremony, Boyle had tried to convince the people at public works who owned the sound system that all they needed to do was to put a little foam rubber around the mike and the wind noise would go away. Back in his old squadron, the crewmen in the rear of the helicopters had covered their lip mikes and could talk perfectly clearly over the tremendous downwash as they stuck their heads out the cargo door to make a rescue. That solution had seemed to make a lot of sense to Boyle, but like much of what he had to deal with anymore, the sound system and the guys who put it up and took it down had remained unchanged for years, and new ideas and different approaches were, by definition, impossible.

Oh, well, he thought, all they can do is bitch about it, and since it was somebody bigger than me who ordered up the wind, maybe the chaplain ought to be the guy to answer the questions.

The emcee introduced the principal speaker, a distinguished-looking three-star admiral with several rows of ribbons and naval-aviator wings on his chest. The admiral grinned a little shyly as he strode to the podium amidst courteous applause.

The admiral began to speak in a deep baritone with just a touch of the Old South. He welcomed everyone and uttered all the obligatory bromides required for such a speech at such an occasion. Boyle was ready to tune him out and reread the program when he heard the phrase "a celebration." He glanced up in surprise— the admiral was not going to deliver the normal elegiac litany of duty stations and ships served on, jobs held, and medals earned by the retiree, but rather was beginning a sort of heroic tale of the wonders of a career as a naval aviator.

As the admiral spoke, Boyle found himself drawn in, smelling once again the salt air and the catapult steam. He could see small snatches of men moving about flight decks behind propeller-driven fighters and spanking new jets. He could see the sun on the sea and hear the roar of the engines. Boyle sat entranced, watching the no-longer-nondescript retiring commander and the three-star who was making the commander's last twenty-six years sound like something from Sir Thomas Malory.

The commander was a quiet warrior, said the admiral, one of

the many who made up the backbone of Naval Aviation. He'd been a hero and he'd been one of the men who simply followed the lead and did his job. He'd endured heartbreak and he'd been blessed with joy, each in its measure. He'd been to the gates of hell, in a sense, and he'd come home. The simple respect and admiration in the admiral's voice made it seem to Boyle that everyone and everything faded into the background, as if there were now only three people present. The admiral and his wondrous tale, the commander looking across the crowd at some far horizon, and Tim Boyle, who was hearing something special, who was getting a glimpse of the past with the long line of flags and drums and men who'd lived and sacrificed and died for an idea.

Boyle listened to the admiral and stared off across Pearl Harbor at the ships and harbor craft, coming and going, taking no note at all of the little gathering under the flags on the parade ground. The ships each had a purpose and were going about it with all the might and dignity they possessed. In the distance, hard by the shore, lay the white block of the USS *Arizona* Memorial. In its stillness it had a purpose, too, as did this little ceremony.

Boyle had no idea how long he was lost to the present, but when the people next to him stood, he did, too. The old commander was standing with the admiral at the head of the small area temporarily designated as the quarterdeck. A red carpet lay on the ground in between two rows of four officers standing at attention. At the foot of the rows of side boys was a large brass bell and an enlisted bosun's mate with one hand on the bell's ringer cord and the other holding a silver bosun's pipe on a white lanyard.

The old commander turned to the admiral, raised his hand to his hat in salute, and spoke in a firm voice, "Request permission to go ashore, sir."

The admiral returned the salute and said in a voice slightly less firm, "Permission granted, Commander. Godspeed."

The commander did a smart left face and squared his shoulders. The bosun's mate rang the bell four times, began the age-old wail on his pipe, and all the uniformed personnel present saluted. The emcee announced, "Commander, United States Navy, retired, departing," and the commander walked between the rows of saluting side boys and into the rest of his life.

It took Boyle forty-five minutes to make sure that the public-works types had broken down all the bunting and sound systems and that all the trappings were at least headed to the right destinations. He walked to his car and got in, still thinking about the little ceremony. He looked back once more at the scene, but it was as if the whole thing had never been, much like a church two hours after the wedding.

Yet something indefinable lingered there, too. Boyle looked around again slowly. He shook his head, lit a cigarette, and headed for the reception at the officers' club.

★ **2** ★

Tuesday, 1 April 1975

THE SOLDIERS SAT IN SMALL GROUPS BY THE AIRFIELD BOUNDARIES. FROM behind them the distant sounds of the sack of Danang reached them in bits and pieces carried in the stillness of the day's first light. The units following behind the front-line troops were searching the city for anything useful to the offensive, shoving aside terrified citizens and refugees from the provinces to the west and north who had fled here in the vain hope of avoiding the horrors to come.

Other troops had been rounding up enemies of the revolution who had only hours and days before been pillars of their society—teachers, policemen, clerics—anyone who represented either of the twin threats to the soldiers' ideology, education, or employment by a free government. The enemies were being marched out of the city to the west toward death in a labor battalion, or death by the execution squads, or intellectual death in the "reeducation camps."

The ordinary citizenry huddled in the doorways or by the side of the road or together in clumps with others, holding their children away from the guns and the hard-eyed squads of armed men. A few sat on the beaches and looked over the empty sea toward the ships that would never come to take them away. They had nowhere else to run. And with the relentless advance of the Communist divisions from the North, they had no place to hide.

Three days ago, the city had fallen and the soldiers at the airfield had gotten there in time to see the last plane out leave the ground with people clinging to the open stairs in the rear and hiding in the wheel wells. The soldiers who had field glasses or exceptionally good eyes could see several of the desperate fall away from the aircraft to the ground and bounce in that odd way that only the dead can. The soldiers laughed at that and mimicked the panic-stricken people who had run desperately down the runway after the big jet.

They were rested now and well fed. They had refilled their ration bags and their ammunition pouches. They had treated their wounds and refilled their ranks. They had listened to the lectures on the importance of their historic mission. They had learned of the successes elsewhere and been briefed on their next set of goals and objectives.

They had looked at their "Born in the North to Die in the South" tattoos almost without noticing them, so long had it been since they had gotten them. It had been even longer since they had seen their homes. But now the end was in sight for these soldiers and they were eager to get on with it. Down the road to the south lay the biggest objective of all, the city of Saigon, the capital of the South and the corrupt government.

It would not be long now before soldiers of the South were running, concerned only with preserving their own lives and those of their families. In places, they would hold for a little while, but the soldiers of the North would soon wash over them like a wave and move on toward the final goal. No, it would not be long now.

The sergeants and the officers came through the small knots of men and shouted them to their feet, forming them up in their squads and platoons. They turned the soldiers south once more and, with the clean sea and the morning sun to their left, set off on the last stretch of the long road to the end of their war.

★ 3 ★

Tuesday, 1 April 1975

WHEN MEGHAN BOYLE WALKED INTO THE OFFICERS' CLUB SHORTLY AFTER that evening, it didn't take her long to find her husband. He was, as usual, at the table containing the loudest and most boisterous men in the room.

It is one of the fundamental laws of the Navy that everyone gravitates to their own kind, and despite the working relationships on CINCPAC staff, off-duty club gatherings were no different. Off in one corner were the submariners, the "bubbleheads," talking about whatever it was they found to interest them. They were as a rule very clannish because most of the other communities couldn't share, or even fully understand, what they had to endure on their long and difficult patrols.

The surface-ship types, or "blackshoes" as they were called, were at a couple of large tables drawn together. They were laughing a bit more than the dour submariners but were still conducting themselves with a good deal of dignity. They were the real seamen and the faces of the older ones looked it. They knew, quietly, that they were and always would be what the Navy was about.

At the rowdy table were the aviators, the "brownshoes," who were universally considered a wild bunch and always made their best efforts to live up to their reputation, even though there wasn't all that much difference from the others.

The aviators were playing a dice game known as horse, a staple in O clubs, in order to decide who got the honor of buying the next round of drinks. Meghan stood off to one side as she watched her husband and one other lieutenant compete in the finals. The two of them took turns slamming the inverted dice cup down and

29

spilling the dice on the table to the loud encouragement of the other ten or so pilots until Tim won, forcing his rival to get up and go to the bar to pay the not inconsiderable tab.

Boyle's laughing eyes followed the loser until he spotted Meghan. With a huge grin, he got up, walked over, and kissed her quickly on the cheek.

"Hi, Meg."

"Hi, yourself. I hope you haven't lost the money you're going to take us to dinner with."

"Hell, no. That's in my wallet. Besides, I haven't had to buy a round in two weeks." Boyle showed her to a seat at one of the other tables. "Can I get you something?"

"I'd kill for a beer."

"That's what I love about you, babe, no class."

Meghan watched the aviators still left at the table as they divvied up the drinks the waitress brought, each making an exaggerated show of enjoying something somebody else had to pay for. They had begun a new game of liar's dice, which would go on for a few minutes until it was time to switch back to horse for another round.

Boyle came back and sat down, sliding Meghan's beer across the table. He sipped his own as Meghan leaned back in her chair. "So. How was your day, Tim?"

Boyle shook his head and did his best Walter Cronkite imitation. " 'What sort of day was it? A day like all days—filled with those events which shape and illuminate our times.' "

"That bad, huh?"

"Well, I don't know. I got my ass chewed for losing my cool with that slug Joe France. The retirement ceremony went almost perfectly—at least nobody's bitched at me yet. So, my net accomplishments for the day are exactly zero. Another sparkling job in defense of my homeland."

Meghan could once again sense the deep frustration that had been building up in her husband ever since the "new" had worn off his job here at CINCPAC. She knew somehow that his mood probably had little to do with the staff and more to do with him. He'd spent nearly eight months recovering from his wounds, and by then his squadron had pretty much been out of a job in that the American bombing of North Vietnam had ceased completely, the carriers had gone from the Gulf of Tonkin, at least in their combat role, and nobody was left to rescue. So after only a couple of months of his being back on flying status, the squadron had been decommissioned and its personnel scattered throughout the Navy. Since Tim had been assigned to Vietnam over two years he was sent to shore duty.

Several of the combat-experienced pilots from his old squadron had transferred early to other helicopter communities or left the Navy to try their luck at other careers. Tim had tried hard to get himself transferred into a flying job, but with the drawdown beginning throughout the military, few of those were available. He had been given the chance to serve for a couple of years on CINCPAC staff with a promise of a return to a squadron and had grudgingly taken it. He still got to fly "proficiency" flights, checking the current skills of other pilots. That totaled about four hours of flight time a month, but that was not nearly enough for him. He wanted to spend a good part of every day flying.

Even though Tim had not yet discussed it with her, Meghan was getting the feeling that he was about to decide to chuck it all and resign from the Navy. She knew he'd never do it without talking to her first, but by then it would probably be too late, and she also knew that it would be the biggest mistake of his life. They'd survive—she had an extremely well-paying job as an accountant and could find work virtually anywhere. But she was certain that, for Tim, there was no job on earth that could take the place of being a naval aviator.

She resolved to try to prevent him from doing something stupid. She'd talk to Pat Hickerson, Tim's boss's wife. If anyone could help, it would be Pat and Don Hickerson.

Meghan put on her number one smile and changed the subject. "You got a letter from Mike today."

Boyle brightened instantly. "What did he say?"

Meghan laughed. "It's addressed to you. I didn't open it. Knowing Mike, he might be writing about some exotic native girls he ran into. And since I'm his fiancée's sister, I'd rather not know. I'd hate to have to give him a false reference."

"No, he's pretty safe. He's been trapped on that ship for three weeks now. His last liberty port was Subic, and even Mike's not dumb enough to fall in love with one of those Olongapo lovelies. No matter how drunk he was."

"Speaking of my sister, Maureen's plane gets in at eleven tomorrow. Will you be able to duck out of work to meet the plane with me?''

''I suppose. Unless I'm in the brig for killing France.''

Meghan stood. ''Come on. We've got reservations for eight. We still have to change.''

Boyle looked at his watch. ''It's only five-thirty. We've still got time.''

''True. But there's other things we can do to distract ourselves at home.''

Boyle grinned. ''It is getting late, now that you mention it. Let's go.''

Far over the western horizon from the officers' club, Lt. Mike Santy was sitting at the tiny fold-down desk in his stateroom aboard the USS *Concord* as the giant aircraft carrier was heading west into a freshening wind and was preparing to launch and recover aircraft. For about the fourth time in the past few minutes, he was rereading the single sheet of paper that represented a dream come true.

The sheet of paper was a naval message that conveyed the Bureau of Personnel orders to his next duty station. They were filled with all sorts of ridiculous words like *prorep* and *delrep.* These were shorthand for some of the small details he was supposed to deal with to effect the transfer and mattered not at all to him. The one word that did matter a great deal was *difops,* which meant ''duty in a flying status involving operational or training flights.'' The transfer orders were to the Cecil Field Naval Air Station, just outside the city of Jacksonville, Florida. He would be an instructor pilot in the East Coast A-7 Fleet Replacement Squadron, commonly called the RAG.

What the orders really meant was that he'd have three more years of flying. He would be only a couple of hundred miles from his family home near Pensacola and would be able to start off his impending marriage to Maureen Collins, Meghan Boyle's sister, by being home for the first three years. All in all it was turning out to be one hell of a good day for Mike Santy.

He couldn't wait to tell Tim Boyle about his orders, but that thought brought a small twinge of guilt. He knew that Tim was trying to get orders back to a squadron, too, for when he came due for transfer in a few months, and the two had both requested assignment to Jacksonville—Boyle to the H-3 community. Santy dearly hoped that would happen.

He felt the ship shudder as the first of the aircraft was catapulted from the flight deck, directly over his head, and immediately came back to reality. He was the duty landing signals officer, or LSO, and commonly called Paddles, for the recovery that would begin as soon as all the aircraft taxiing around on the flight deck had been launched. Glancing up at the television, which was tuned to the PLAT, or flight deck camera system, he folded the message neatly in half and put it in the little cubbyhole at the top of the desk.

From the hook on the back of the door, he took down his flight-deck vest, which carried inflatable flotation bladders in case he was blown over the side. He opened the small flap and made sure that the little CO_2 bottle was firmly in the inflation valve. Santy checked his pockets to make sure he had something to write with, picked up the book in which he'd write down the pilot's landing grades and his own shorthand commentary, took one last look around the room, and headed for the LSO platform. In the fifteen or so seconds it took him to get himself ready, Santy's mind had completely forgotten about his orders, his fiancée, and everything that was irrelevant to his job and had switched over to another mode of thought entirely.

Santy climbed halfway up the small ladder that led into the catwalk beneath his post and carefully stuck his head up to check that it was safe to go onto the flight deck. He saw that all the aircraft that had been spotted back on the fantail had been taxied forward, so he climbed carefully the rest of the way into the catwalk and then up onto the deck, heading aft for the small LSO platform. He had to turn his head and screw up his eyes a couple of times to take the jostling of small blasts of jet exhaust as the winds over the deck swirled them around. It took only a few seconds before he could duck down behind the dirty white canvas windscreen on the platform, which was about a hundred feet or so forward of the stern of the ship, or "rounddown," and faced aft, looking over the wake at the incoming jets.

Santy looked around the side of the windscreen and checked the progress of the launch of the last cycle of the day. There were only two jets to go on, both A-7s from his squadron, and the deck would be clear for the recovery of the aircraft from the previous cycle. He picked up the telephonelike handset of the radio and keyed the mike switch.

"Tower, Paddles. Radio check."

"Paddles, Tower. Loud and clear. Case One recovery."

"Roger, Case One." Santy lowered the handset and checked the switches on the light controller with his left hand. "Case One" meant that the aircraft would make their approaches under procedures for clear weather in daylight. Case Two and Three were reserved for conditions of less visibility with Case Three reserved for night and instrument approach conditions.

Santy glanced again over his shoulder as he activated the wave-off and the cut lights each in turn. Both of these would give special signals to the pilots. The cut lights were only rarely used but when the wave-off lights flashed, the pilot was required to shove his throttles forward and abort his landing approach, taking the aircraft up into the pattern and trying again. Both sets of lights were working as advertised so Santy watched the arresting gear crewmen inspect the four arresting wires stretched across the deck or rather the three wires since the Number 1, or aftermost, wire had been removed while the belowdecks crewmen worked to replace a bearing in the retraction engine. Further up the deck the catapult crewmen were hustling around cleaning up their systems and waiting for the last jet to get airborne.

Santy looked up and saw the small formations of aircraft circling in the clear blue sky above the ship. The Phantoms, the most fuel critical, were lowest so that they could get aboard first. Above them, stacked all the way up above 15,000 feet, were the A-7s and the rest whose engines gave them a bit better economy. Off the starboard side of the carrier, the plane guard H-3 helicopter flew past close aboard in its tight right-hand orbit, rigged and ready for rescue should somebody have a problem and wind up in the water. Santy smiled at the ungainly looking flying machine, once again remembering Tim Boyle referring to his beloved H-3 as the "War Winnebago." He wished that Tim were still flying—Tim hadn't said it but his present job must be driving him crazy.

Santy missed having Tim around. Their friendship stretched back to the night before they'd entered flight training almost five years earlier and very soon, a month after this cruise, they'd be brothers-in-law. Neither was certain that Meghan and Maureen's parents were going to be ready to have both Boyle and Santy in the family together. Thanksgiving dinner ought to be interesting.

Behind him, the roar as the last of the A-7s came up on the power blocked out all other thoughts. He hunched his back against the canvas windscreen and closed his eyes as the acrid exhaust from the jet's engines washed over him. There was a sudden diminishing of the sound and a shudder when the catapult reached the end of the stroke and the Corsair was blasted into the air.

Opening his eyes, he glanced at the lens, the visual landing aid, to see that it had been turned on, stepped forward and checked the anemometer for the winds over the deck. Looking aft he could see the first of the Phantoms turning onto final and that the arresting gear status light was green.

The young enlisted spotter standing a couple of feet aft of Santy inspected the approaching aircraft's landing gear through his binoculars, looked at the green status light and called out, "F-4, all down, clear deck."

Santy acknowledged and waited for the Phantom pilot to visually acquire the lighted lens. It wasn't more than a few seconds. "105, Phantom, Ball. 3-point-1." The aircraft's side number was 105, it was a Phantom, had acquired the "ball" and had 3100 pounds of fuel aboard.

Santy looked at the wind indicator and transmitted his acknowledgment, telling the pilot the speed of wind over the deck, "Roger, ball, Phantom. Twenty-six knots."

The big fighter rolled out on final with the characteristic twin plumes of black-brown smoke streaming back from its tailpipes. The pilot made small corrections, flicking the wings ever so slightly to maintain his lineup. Santy could hear the engines spool up and down as the pilot jockeyed the throttles to keep himself on the glideslope and he could see the tailplanes wiggle in concert with the nose attitude. This guy was good, thought Santy, as he watched the aircraft do all the little things which kept it exactly where it should be.

The Phantom crossed the rounddown and roared past the LSO platform, and Santy followed it as it slammed down and caught a wire. The huge J-79 engines roared as the pilot shoved the throttles forward on touchdown. The procedure was to go to full power in case of a "bolter" where the tailhook missed the wires and the

35

pilot had to take it back off and try again. The absolute last thing a carrier pilot wanted was to miss the wires and not have enough power ready to take off. The jet would dribble off the end of the angled deck into the water and unless the crew was real fast with the ejection handles and real lucky, their chances of survival were not good.

The other aircraft followed in order with only one bolter—an A-6 had its hook skip the wires and it went around to try again, making a successful "trap" on the next pass. All in all, it was an excellent performance by the air wing but that was to be expected when they were in the last month of a seven-month deployment. All the LSOs had been watching for the "end of the cruise" sloppiness which could be fatal. So far, it hadn't reared its head.

The Air Boss's voice in Santy's ear warned him that he was not finished quite yet. "One to go, Paddles. The Viggie, 600, is twenty out. He may be a straight-in. He's got some engine troubles."

"Roger."

Santy looked aft for the last aircraft. The "Viggie" was the RA-5C Vigilante photo-reconnaissance aircraft. It had been designed in the '50s as a high-speed nuclear bomber but had proved a failure in that role. Somebody got the bright idea of adding a camera system and using it as the photographic eyes of the fleet. The Vigilante immediately came into its own and performed brilliantly for the rest of its career. In flight, it was also one of the most graceful looking aircraft ever built, like winged dart and at high-speed it was one of the toughest aircraft in the world for an enemy to shoot down.

But landing it aboard a carrier could be supremely difficult. The legend was that the old sailors' homes were full of ex-Vigilante pilots who, at twenty-six or so, were white-haired, walked with canes, and carried ear trumpets.

"He's at ten miles, Paddles. Everything's still running but he wants a precautionary straight-in."

"Paddles, roger."

The enlisted spotter sang out, "Got 'im. Looks okay and he's still clean."

"All right." Santy checked his wind indicator again. Still averaging about twenty-six knots. "Clean" meant that the pilot had not yet "dirtied up" by lowering his gear, flaps, and tailhook. The pilot wouldn't do that until he was much closer to the ship. If he was "dirty" that far out, it could mean that he had some hydraulic problem which necessitated lowering something by using one of the pneumatic "blow down" systems.

Santy listened on the approach control frequency as the controller guided the A-5 toward the ship. At three miles, the spotter called that the landing gear, flaps and hook were coming down and then that all the aircraft's lights showed that the various parts were all locked in place. Waiting until the Vigilante pilot was told to switch frequencies and that he was at one mile, Santy switched back to his own frequency and called the pilot.

"600, Paddles, contact. Looking good. Call the ball."

"600, Vigilante, ball. Um, two-point-oh."

"Roger, ball. Deck's steady and you have twenty-four knots now."

Santy watched carefully as the A-5 approached. The pilot was flying as smoothly as he could, trying to make as few throttle changes as he could so as to prevent overtaxing the engine. He held his breath until the jet crossed through the "burble," or the short stretch of disturbed air and stack gas caused by the ship's passage. Santy raised his left hand with the light controller and unconsciously leaned forward, willing the Vigilante across the rounddown and into the wires. He followed the aircraft as it passed him and slammed down onto the deck.

The hook caught a wire and the nose slammed down at the same time as the pilot rammed his throttles forward. The right engine responded normally but the left issued a loud *boom,* and a gout of flames and sparks flew out of the tailpipe. The aircraft rocked back on its main landing gear and the pilot retarded the throttle to idle, pulling the left one all the way back to cut-off. There was no fire. But the flight deck firefighters in their silver suits rushed up to the aircraft anyway, just in case.

"600, Paddles, no fire."

"Roj."

The Air Boss came on the radio. "600, can you taxi?"

"That's affirm, Boss."

"Okay, 600. Nice job."

"Click-click." The pilot keyed his mike button twice sending two clicking sounds over the air. It was the pilot's universal acknowledgment.

Santy handed the radio handset and the light controller to the

37

spotter and climbed up onto the flightdeck. He looked forward at the A-5 as it turned right out of the landing area and was directed toward its parking spot with the firefighters and their truck following close behind. He wondered what the Viggie crew had been assigned to take pictures of but shrugged. If it was important, he'd find out soon enough.

As he went through the hatch in the island structure which led below to the squadron ready rooms, he reviewed the Vigilante's approach, chuckling at the old story of the pilot who brought one of them back aboard on a dark and rainy night somewhere. According to the story, the approach was so hairy that not even the pilot was sure he'd made it until somebody had called him on the radio and told him to retard his throttles. The pilot did so and keyed his radio, saying, "Okay, God. I'll take over now. You never could taxi worth a damn."

⭐ **4** ⭐

Tuesday, 1 April 1975

FIVE HOURS AFTER THE VIGILANTE LANDED ABOARD THE *CONCORD*, THE photographs taken on its mission sat in a jumble with many others on a mahogany conference table in the American headquarters at Tan Son Nhut airport outside Saigon. Around the table sat the chiefs of what remained of the American military presence in the Republic of Vietnam. With the diminution of that presence came a frustrating powerlessness to do one damn thing about the disasters these photographs, and others yet to be taken, were chronicling.

This meeting had been called to assess the speed of the decline in the military situation for South Vietnam without the ofttimes confusing analyses from Washington. This afternoon there were no bureaucratic filters or delays between the staffers and the raw information. There was no analyst's caviling prose concluding that both sides of the question were equally correct and equally likely. There was no countercorroboration. There was no hedging.

There was no chance. No chance at all, to these experienced military men, that the South Vietnamese were going to be able to stop the advance of the khaki-and-green-clad mass of Communist "liberators" from the North.

A little over two weeks earlier, the North Vietnamese Army, or NVA, had driven the South Vietnamese troops, ARVNs, out of Pleiku and down Route 7B to the coast. The retreating columns of civilians and military had been harried and harassed and ambushed all the way—they'd even run afoul of expertly laid (and inexpertly cleared) minefields left by South Korean forces earlier in the war. The entire operation, ordered in the incompetence

Gerry Carroll

and panic of the ARVN generals, had been a disaster with only a little over one in three ARVN troops finally arriving on the coast at Thuy Hoa. Not even during the great North Vietnamese offensives of 1968 and 1972 had anything like this happened.

Danang had fallen three days before—the chaos and panic attendant to the final few hours before the enemy captured the place had been horrifying. The last few overloaded planes out of Danang had had people clinging to the landing gear and hiding in the baggage compartments. The ancient capital of Hue and Quang Tri and all the northern provinces were gone. There were rumors of purges, of mass executions, of wholesale confiscation of property, of concentration camps—the bringing of freedom and prosperity and the other joys of Communism had begun in earnest.

All that was truly left of the Republic of Vietnam (RVN) was the coastal plain up to about Chu Lai, a few enclaves on the coast at places like Thuy Hoa, Qui Nhon, and Nha Trang, and most of the Mekong Delta.

Lt. Cdr. Kevin Thompson looked at each photograph as it was passed around the table. These were mostly of the NVA troop concentrations north and west of Saigon. Estimates of their strength all agreed that there were seventeen divisions of regular army troops despite the Communist fiction that they were forces from the Provisional Revolutionary Government, or PRG, the new name for the old Viet Cong insurgents. The ARVNs had been inexorably pushed back until the situation was beginning to resemble the Battle of Leningrad in World War II, except that no great offensive by the good guys was going to save the day.

Thompson, a Navy SEAL, was one of the few remaining representatives of the special operations section of the military assistance command now under the umbrella of the Defense Attaché's Office (DAO). In the days of the American participation in combat in Vietnam, the murky name on the letterhead had been MAC-SOG, or Military Assistance Command Studies and Observations Group. Now all that was left were a number of CIA types, a few military officers, and a lot of Vietnamese operatives and coworkers who were about to be in deep trouble. Thompson knew that the operatives were really only a small part of the overall problem, but it was *his* part. He figured that enough brass hats and visiting delegations were around to handle the big picture.

40

When he was finished looking at it, Thompson slid each photograph to his left to Lt. (j.g.) Mark Dalton, his assistant. Dalton was a "mustang," an officer who had been promoted from the ranks. He had been with Thompson throughout Thompson's entire career except for two years, 1971–73, when Thompson had been an aide to the admiral commanding the Navy carrier force carrying out the bombing of North Vietnam. It had been Thompson who had convinced both the Navy and Dalton that he ought to be an officer.

One large photograph in particular interested both SEALs. It was of a deeply forested area well to the northwest of Saigon proper. The small circles and arrows denoting NVA units and equipment were all concentrated in the eastern part of the area, and even the routes and roads being used by the enemy seemed to be well to the east of the denser jungle. As he slid the photograph to Dalton, Thompson unobtrusively tapped his index finger on a particular spot, making sure Dalton caught on. Neither man changed expression or gave any outward sign that there was something special about the area. None of the others around the table noticed anything at all, absorbed as they were with the impending military disaster.

The senior officer at the meeting, Lew Alexander, a U.S. Army, two-star general, stood and tapped his pen on his water glass. The dull murmuring quieted quickly as everyone gave the general his full attention.

"All right, gentlemen. This is what we've got as of about five and a half hours ago. We should be getting some more imagery from Washington and CINCPAC soon, but all that will do is confirm what we have here. Comments?"

The general's deputy, a brigadier general named Toone, cleared his throat. "Well, General, strategically speaking, I'd say we're fucked."

The general looked down at his deputy and smiled resignedly. "Fine assessment, Ted. I'll bet you were a star at West Point. Anyone else?"

The general stared around the room and looked carefully at each face. They knew one subject had to be discussed, but they were all reluctant to broach the subject. The general sighed.

"Okay, I'll start. I don't see any alternative for us now. I don't think that the ARVNs can hold out more than a month. They have no chance at all to win militarily, and the other side is blowing smoke about their desire for a negotiated settlement. The ambassador is still hoping that he can get a cease-fire and maybe set up a tripartite government with the NVA, the PRG, and what's left of President Thieu's South Vietnamese government. I personally don't think that'll happen. The NVA have nothing to gain by negotiating. They're gonna win and everybody knows it except for the idiots in our Congress who still think we have all the time in the world and that the NVA are afraid of us."

The general picked up his water glass and sipped. "We're going to have to cut and run, gents. We'll need a comprehensive plan for an orderly evacuation. We can't have another mess like Danang, and we can't leave all the people who have been loyal to us for all these years. It is going to be a huge job and we'll need some help. Now, I'll get on the horn to CINCPAC and let them know what we're planning. Is there anyone who disagrees? Feel free, gentlemen. I need to know what you're thinking."

He looked around the room and saw that a few were inspecting their hands or the wet rings their glasses were leaving on the table. A few others were looking back at him in silence. He knew that they all felt the same way—despite the brave talk from the State Department and the administration, the U.S. was about to bug out for the first time in its history. It was a lousy feeling, thought the general, to have to organize a defeat. Especially when it once was not necessary.

He closed the folder on the photographs. "Unless any of you have an idea for a miracle, we'll meet back in here at oh eight hundred tomorrow. Get numbers on how many you think we'll have to pull out and any other details you can think of."

The general nodded at the brigadier, who stood and followed him from the room. The others gathered in their own small groups and began discussing their separate requirements for the operation to come.

Thompson and Dalton, by training reluctant to discuss much of what they did outside of their own kind, walked to their office. Opening the battered refrigerator, a hand-me-down from unknown generations of SEALs assigned to this job, Thompson pulled out two Cokes and handed one to Dalton.

"Well, what do you think, Mark?"

"As my grandpa used to say, 'Call in the dogs and piss on the fire, boys. This hunt's over.' "

"Yup. How many of our people do you figure we'll need to get out?"

"I started checking all that out yesterday. There aren't that many left. When the northern provinces started falling, most of them saw the handwriting on the wall and left for either Thailand or the Philippines. We still have a few down in the Delta and some here in the city, but a lot of the ones we have in the city also work for the Agency, so we'll just have to make sure that they don't fall through the cracks. I'd say we have a maximum of two hundred to evacuate, including families. There are certainly going to be a few who will decide to stay and hope that they don't get caught."

"All right, I want each of them contacted again and offered a chance. Those who are sure they want to go can start leaving immediately. I'd rather not wait until the last minute. You've seen what happened in Danang and Hue. Once the word gets out that the U.S. is leaving, there will be a major panic. Let's try to beat the rush."

"Okay. Now, how about the files?"

"We've collected all the copies in the vault down the hall. We should have time to shred them first, but, if not, they're stacked loose and in folders so all we have to do is kick over the stacks, heave in a couple of thermite grenades, and they'll burn completely. I'm worried though about any copies the Vietnamese have; they're certain to be overlooked. See if you can get them back and put them in with the others. If some miracle happens and the Vietnamese government manages to survive, we can always give the files back. But we ought to be real careful about how much is still in there when we do give them back."

Dalton nodded. "Sounds good." He stood, walked to the window, and looked out at the airfield.

He spoke the question for both of them. According to the last message they'd received from him a few months ago, Tony Butler was still out there somewhere in the area that Thompson had indicated on the photograph a few minutes before. "Do we try to contact Butler now?"

"Do you think we can?"

"I don't know, boss. We sure as hell can try."

"Yup. We owe him that much at least, even though he's always said he wants to stay. See what you can do."

43

"There are an awful lot of people who are going to get left when this war is over. There's, what, eight or ten thousand irregular troops scattered all around up in the highlands? It's going to be rough on them."

Thompson nodded slowly. "Yeah. They'll be completely surrounded by their enemies—NVA to the east and south, the Khmer Rouge to the west in Cambodia, and the Pathet Lao to the north in Laos. And there'll be not one damn thing we can do for them. They'll just have to live on the run. It will be a cold day in hell before the Congress or the people will let anybody come back here, and the NVA will never stand for a bunch of raggedy-ass insurgents running around loose out in the boondocks."

Dalton turned from the window. "Do you think they'll have any chance at all?"

"No. And neither do you. If Tony Butler doesn't come out with us, they'll get him sooner or later. When they do get him, he'll be proof to somebody that the U.S. is still hanging on here aiding the vile insurgents against the peace-loving assholes from Hanoi."

"A walking diplomatic disaster, that's our boy. Suppose he won't come out, then what?"

"We're sure as hell not going to tell anybody that he's still out there," Thompson said. "He'd become the number one target for the Agency. It's easier and safer for him to stay a ghostly legend, at least until we get him out. After all these years, he's become one of those minor mythic figures that people are almost certain don't exist. An American leading native troops in the mountains, rarely sighted and never captured? Clearly ridiculous and impossible."

Dalton laughed. "It must amuse Tony to be thought of as a spirit."

"Yeah. Well, if he won't come with us, we'll just shut up and go home. Maybe someday somebody will find out about him, but we'll both probably be retired by then, so what can they do—recall us and throw us in Leavenworth?"

"Do you figure we should have said something when we got those letters?"

"Nope. I thought you were right then. I still think so and I'm glad I decided to talk to you when I got mine. One thing I've learned in the past few years is that black and white are rare colors in this old world anymore."

Dalton stared out the window again. From their long association, Thompson knew exactly what Dalton was thinking.

He turned and stared hard at Dalton. "You will not, repeat, not, go out there and try to find him alone or without informing me first of any other cockamamy plan you may come up with. That is not a request, Mark."

Dalton chuckled. "Aye, aye, sir. You've got my word on it."

"Fair enough."

★ 5 ★

Friday, 4 April 1975

CDR. DON HICKERSON HAD BEEN LEANING BACK IN HIS CHAIR WITH HIS feet on the desk and staring at the telephone for a good five minutes before he made his decision. Dropping his feet to the floor, he picked up the receiver and dialed the number of the Boyles' residence. He wasn't certain whom he wanted to answer, Meghan or Tim. When the voice came, it was Meghan.

"Hi, Meg. This is Don Hickerson. I'd like to talk to Tim, but wait a second before you get him."

"All right." Just a touch of confusion was in her voice.

"Look, I need to take Tim with me on a little trip leaving Sunday. Pat told me about your talk with her, and I think this might help. We should be gone a couple of weeks or so, and I think he'll find it interesting. That's about all I can say over the phone right now."

In her kitchen, Meghan stared at the wall for a moment before answering. She'd been hoping that Pat Hickerson could get her husband to find something for Tim to do. It didn't need to be something upon which rested the fate of humanity, just something that would at least be a change for him, something other than shuffling reports and taking care of the routine crap. She also knew that Hickerson wouldn't let Tim get into something over his head.

Suddenly, she felt like a conspirator, going behind her husband's back like this. She wasn't sure, standing there in her bright kitchen, that she was doing the right thing. Maybe she should have let matters take their course.

"Meg? Are you still there?"

46

"Oh. Yeah, Don. Sorry about that. I was just thinking. I'll go get Tim, and if I don't see you before you all go, good luck and be careful."

"We will, Meg. Thanks." Hickerson heard her clunk the phone down on something hard and call for Tim. Her voice faded as she walked away from the receiver yelling that "your boss" was on the phone.

Hickerson and Pat had admired Meghan since the first day they'd met. She was smart and feminine and bright and funny all at the same time. She had her own career going; in fact, she probably earned more money than did her husband. Meghan knew exactly who she was and was one of those fortunate women who didn't *require* a relationship to prove her worth, much like Pat, which was why the two women had become such fast friends.

"Good afternoon, Commander. What's up?" Boyle sounded just a little out of breath.

"Hello, Tim. We have a little road trip coming up to one of the garden spots of the world. I'm going and I'll need some help. Want to come along?"

"I'd have to check with Meg."

"Fine. We'll be gone two weeks, three at the most. I can't say anything more now, but if you want to come, let me know by thirteen hundred this afternoon. Okay?"

"Yes, sir." Boyle listened to the click as Hickerson hung up.

He went into the other room and found Meg sitting on the sofa sipping a Tab.

"The commander needs me to go on a road trip for a couple of weeks. I'm going to go over and talk to him about it. Um, is that okay?"

"Where to?"

"I don't know; he couldn't tell me."

"Tim, it's your job. You don't have to ask my permission."

"I know, but I don't want to be one of those guys who forgets that there's two people in a marriage."

Meghan laughed. "You aren't ever going to have the chance to forget I'm here, sailor. Get goin', but don't take too long. We have that cookout tonight."

*   *   *

47

Fifty minutes later, Hickerson looked up at the knock on his office door. "Come in." He smiled when he saw that Tim Boyle was already halfway to the chair next to his desk.

"Well, what's the verdict?"

"I'm going. I think Meg wants me out of the way so she and her sister can run wild."

Hickerson smiled at that. "We're going to be gone for the next two, possibly three, weeks. The CINC is sending a team over to Saigon to plan for an evacuation of Americans and some Vietnamese in case the situation over there gets any worse. And it looks like it's going to. Admiral Wallace, the deputy, is heading it up, and I'm supposed to go as the helo expert."

Boyle nodded slowly. Everything he'd read for the past few days told him that Hickerson was right—it was going to get worse over there and soon. But even if all he did was sit around and shuffle plans and reports as Hickerson's assistant, it would at least be a change of scenery. He'd rather be doing something important, or at least something boring somewhere else for a while.

"When do we leave and where from?"

Hickerson laughed now. "I figured that's what you'd say. You'll probably be running the shipboard end of things, but you can handle it. We leave at oh nine-thirty Sunday from the air terminal. Showtime for the flight is oh eight-fifteen to get manifested and all that stuff. I'll bring your written orders with me. Go home and pack and meet me there on Sunday. Wear civilian clothes but bring a couple of uniforms for wearing on the ship. And, uh, if you would, please send Lieutenant Reed in here. He loves routine stuff and acting like a wheel, so I'll make him acting air ops."

Boyle was hesitant to ask a whole lot of questions. He was afraid that Hickerson would change his mind. In his growing excitement, it didn't occur to him that the commander was treating him like an equal by making that comment about Reed. He stood up and was turning for the door when Hickerson spoke again.

"Listen, Tim. One of the others on this trip is your pal, Joe France. He voiced some heavy and, in my opinion, asinine objections to your going. He seems to think that he can handle anything assigned to you and his own work, too. I don't want any trouble with him in Saigon, so you will just do your job and report to me. Furthermore you will be respectful, but you will not take any shit from either France or his boss. That will also be reported to me. Clear?"

Boyle nodded and Hickerson waved him away. Boyle left the office and walked down the passageway to his own partitioned cubicle. He quickly went through his in-basket, separating that which could wait a couple of weeks (a large pile) from that which needed earlier action (a very small stack). He walked over to Reed's desk, dropped the small stack in the in-basket, and sent Reed down to Hickerson's office. Without another word, Boyle locked his desk, grabbed his garrison hat, and walked out the door.

The small white house with all the screens stood on a long palm-lined street of identical homes stuck as an afterthought in the large naval base at Pearl Harbor, Hawaii. As he pulled into the driveway, Tim Boyle once again smiled at the mental conditioning that always seemed to take over when he was deep in thought. He had driven home from the office, making all the right turns and stops and starts, and now, as he switched off the ignition, he could remember only widely scattered details of the drive.

Boyle walked around to the rear of the house and in the back door, which led through the kitchen. Except for the times he'd lived in the various BOQs and apartments of bachelorhood, all his life he'd entered his home through the kitchen door. Even when he was a boy coming home from school, it gave him a sense of normalcy, signifying that whatever problems or crises he might have faced during the day were temporarily over and he was, for the next few hours, going to be warm and safe. But in less than forty-eight hours, in response to somebody else's crisis, he had to go far away from this little house and his wife of less than two years.

Boyle hung his keys on the rack on the wall beside the door and laid his uniform cap on top of the refrigerator. Out of long habit, he reached into the refrigerator for a beer, decided against it, and pulled out a Coke instead. He walked through the empty house to the bedroom and pulled a battered canvas aviator's kit bag down from the top of the closet. He went to his dresser and, starting with his underwear, began to pack.

*   *   *

Boyle shoved the loaded bag against the wall, shaking his head. As always he'd packed more than two men would need for this trip. Meghan was continually on his case about his packing habits, but she never really interfered. He reached back up onto the rear of the closet's top shelf and pulled down his Browning 9mm pistol. He got the cleaning kit and carried both into the kitchen. Turning on the radio, he got another Coke and sat down to begin cleaning the weapon.

Boyle spent the next little while thinking over what he would have to do on this trip, as he let a small part of his mind deal with the pistol. He was wiping off the excess oil from the slide when he heard the radio volume abruptly turned down.

"Well, well. Going hunting rats or something, are we?" His wife was standing behind him. He hadn't heard her come home.

Boyle wiped his hands on a rag and stood up. "Nope. Just my little trip with Don Hickerson."

Meghan returned his kiss with somewhat less than her usual fervor. "And why the gun?"

Boyle had been dreading this part. "We're going to Saigon, Meg. We're supposed to figure out how to evacuate the Americans and some of the Vietnamese before the city falls. My job is to help plan the helicopter part."

To cover her shock, Meghan sat in one of the chairs at the table. She hadn't figured on Tim's going there, even for a visit. The place was in chaos and Tim was going to be in the middle of it. She immediately felt a wave of Irish guilt wash over her. After all, it had been her idea to find something to get Tim out of his routine. And this sure as hell ought to accomplish that, she thought.

"You're not going to have to do anything like you did last time, are you?"

Boyle could almost feel the hard purple-pink scars on his left side just above his waist. He resisted the temptation to touch them through his shirt. He'd been shot in the back during his rescue from North Vietnam two and a half years ago. The bullet hadn't done much real damage except to Boyle's youthful faith in his immortality, but it had temporarily interrupted his career as a fleet aviator and had indirectly gotten him assigned to CINCPAC.

Boyle sensed her fear for him. "No, there'll be no flying around the countryside. It'll all be either in Saigon itself or out on the ship. There are eight of us going. Admiral Wallace, as the deputy CINCPAC, will be in charge, and Commander Hickerson will be the main planner and I'm his assistant. We're the only two helo types on the staff, so the job's ours by default."

"When are you leaving?"

"Sunday at oh nine-thirty. Gentlemen's flight. We have to be at the Air Terminal at eight-fifteen. We fly to the Philippines, Clark Air Force Base, for a short layover and then on to Tan Son Nhut."

"How long will you be gone? Don said probably a couple weeks."

"I don't know exactly, but yeah, probably about that long. By then, either the situation will be stable or it'll all be over. Come on in the other room." Boyle stood up and collected the pistol and cleaning kit. He carried them into the bedroom and stuffed the cleaning kit back in the closet and the pistol down deep in his bag.

Meghan followed him and leaned her back against his dresser. "If things get bad, will you have to stay in Saigon until the evacuation is complete?"

"Things're already pretty bad there, Meg, but I don't think so. I'm only a lieutenant, so I won't draw enough water to stay with the heavies while the press takes pictures. As it stands now, once we've got the plan squared away, I'm supposed to fly back out to the ship and coordinate the receiving end of the lift. That way, I'll get to hang around with Mike out at sea, fifty miles from the screaming and yelling."

The mention of Mike Santy seemed to divert her a little. Mike was a sort of best friend cum adopted brother to both of them. It had been Santy who had been rescued with Boyle back in October 1972. Santy had been Boyle's best man at his wedding to Meghan and was now engaged to Meghan's maid of honor, her year-younger sister, Maureen.

But the diversion didn't last long. "Even on the local news, everybody says that things are really a mess. The North Vietnamese have taken most of the country and are advancing on the capital. What happens if they take the place while you're still there?"

"Meg, that's why we're going. Our job is to get everyone out before the exits are closed off. Most of the dependents are either out already or they're about to be gone. I won't be caught in there, and even if I were, they'd let me go as soon as they found out who I am. They've got the Paris Agreements to worry about."

Meghan sighed. "Tim, don't try to snow me, okay? We both know that the front-line troops don't give a damn about the political end of things. It won't be their politburo who storms the city. It'll be just a bunch of scared soldiers running around with their rifles aimed at everybody in sight."

She was right, as usual, so there was no sense continuing to try to put a good face on it. "All right, Meg," he said softly. "I'll be careful."

"You'd better." Meghan got up.

"Where's Maureen?"

Meghan turned to his dresser and began checking the drawers to make sure that he hadn't forgotten anything. "She's taking a walk. I told her you might be going off somewhere and she decided not to be here for a while." Meghan's back was to Boyle, but he caught the odd catch in her voice. He got up and slipped his arms around her waist from behind. As soon as he did, she began to cry.

"Hey, it's not that bad."

"That's not the problem."

Confused, Boyle put his hands on her shoulders and turned her around. "Well, then, what is the problem?"

Meghan worked herself free and walked to the nightstand. She pulled out a couple of Kleenex and blew her nose, then sat on the edge of the bed looking miserable. "I, um, asked Pat Hickerson to see if Don could find something useful for you to do. I didn't figure that what you'd be doing would be to go back to that damn war. So now you're going and it's my fault."

Boyle let out a long breath. He walked over and sat next to her. He wasn't sure if he should be angry with her for her meddling, essentially behind his back, or happy that she cared enough to do it. Probably some of both.

"Meg, you did the right thing. I love you for your concern and I'm glad you know me well enough to understand. But maybe we should have talked about it first."

She nodded and sniffed some more. "You're angry."

Boyle nodded. "Yeah, I am a little. Like I said, I think we should have talked about it, even though Commander Hickerson would probably have asked me anyway. Meg, as normal as my job seems sometimes, there's all kinds of unwritten rules that sort of move things along the way they're supposed to go. One of the rules is that you don't get in the way."

"So you're angry because I meddled and not because you have to go to Vietnam." Meghan was now looking intently at him, trying to understand exactly what he was saying. This was one of those little things about the Navy that she knew she could only learn by experience—there's no book to tell you how to go.

"Yeah. Going to Vietnam is part of my job. It is, though, a hell of a lot safer now than it was last time I was there."

Meghan stood and turned to face her husband. "All right, dammit. I'm sorry I meddled and sorrier still that I did it without your knowing. But like you said, there's two of us in this marriage, and I'm doing part of my job trying to help my partner. And if there's something that needs doing, then I'm going to do it. So go ahead and be pissed, Tim Boyle, but don't ever ask me to sit around and knit doilies."

Boyle scratched his chin. This was one of those times in a marriage when everybody was right and everybody was wrong. The best thing to do right now, he figured, was to get off it. "Okay, babe. I'll shut up now. I can't argue with that. Besides, you can't knit worth a damn."

Meghan smiled and crossed her arms. "All right then. But I'm still scared about you going to Vietnam."

Boyle stood and embraced her again. "Meg, it'll be okay. Honest. All I'm supposed to do is set up an airlift."

"I know. It's just that I figured we were done with that goddamned country."

"Yeah, me, too." He just stood there with his arms around her. In the twenty-two months they'd been married, he'd been away for other trips or to various training courses, but never had he gone off for something like this. Their marriage had been almost normal even by civilian standards, and though the downside of the job had been well known to both, it had always been stuck off in some psychological closet.

Meghan had been Boyle's first visitor when he'd finally arrived in Balboa Naval Hospital in San Diego after brief stops in the hospital in Danang, Republic of Vietnam, and in the larger one in Japan. She'd come to visit every day, and when he was finally released, he found that she had moved all her "stuff" into his

53

apartment, no longer even attempting to maintain the fiction that they were not living together.

A couple of months after their wedding, when Boyle had been assigned to a two-year tour at CINCPAC headquarters, they'd set up house in a Navy duplex in Hawaii. She'd known well what it was he did when they were just dating and, later, engaged. She'd even come to meet Boyle in Hong Kong during a two-week stand-down just before he went back and got himself shot.

The back door slammed open and Maureen's voice came from the kitchen.

"You guys here?"

Boyle let her go and Meghan chuckled.

"We're in the bedroom. I'm trying to make sure that my husband, the world traveler, doesn't try to take everything he owns."

Sunday, 6 April 1975

At just about eight-fifteen, Boyle climbed out of the passenger seat of Meghan's car and pulled his bag from the backseat. He walked around to the driver's side and leaned in the open window. "Thanks, Meg. See you in a couple of weeks. If you need anything, the guys on the staff will help you. You've also got Pat Hickerson so—"

Meg cut him off with a laugh. "I know, I know. You've told me this twice already. I'm a big girl. Don't worry. Now, you—don't do anything stupid or anything heroic."

Boyle laughed, too. "Okay. I promise. Take care." He leaned in and kissed her. "I love you, babe."

"I love you, too, you dumb mick. I'll be here when you get back. See ya."

Meg put the car in gear and drove away. Boyle looked after her for a few seconds, then shouldered his bag and walked into the crowded terminal. Apparently a lot of sailors were heading for ships or stations near the flight's intermediate stops. Looking around the departure lounge, he saw no familiar faces, so he was the first of the CINCPAC staffers to arrive.

Boyle was glad Meghan hadn't stayed to await the flight's departure. They had long ago decided that whenever he had to go somewhere, Meghan would just drop him off and leave as if he were going to spend a day in the office. It avoided the clinging, weepy, wrenching scenes in the departure lounge that always made everyone squirm as if their shirts were full of spiders. Prolonging the farewell simply made everyone, principals and bystanders, feel like shit.

Boyle knew that there would inevitably be several wives snuffling in the lounge, so he dropped his bag next to the long departure desk and walked into the snack bar. He bought a large Coke and carried it out to the front steps where he sat down in the morning sun and watched planes take off and land until they called his flight.

★ 6 ★

Sunday, 6 April 1975

THE SOLDIERS WERE MOVING WESTWARD TOWARD THE HIGHLANDS. OTHER units had assumed the task of attacking down the coast roads, and the veterans of the capture of Danang and Hue were being driven in battered trucks to a rest camp for a longer period of rest and refit than they had had in the past three months.

There was an eagerness now beyond the placid acceptance of their situation they had carried with them before. Had they been troops of another culture, they might have laughed and sung a song or two. There might have been some of the soldierly banter allowed free men. But these soldiers were not permitted these things lest their iron discipline weaken.

Any sign of weakness or less than steadfast devotion to the revolution was handled quickly and surely in one of the frequent sessions of self-criticism and confession. Now that victory was at hand, none of the soldiers wanted to show any flaw that would get them transferred to a labor battalion, which would, in turn, ensure a much longer period of service before they could return home.

Word had recently come that renewed efforts were to be required of each soldier because the decision had been made in Hanoi that the timetable should be moved up so the goal for final victory was now less than two months away rather than the year it had been before. The soldiers knew that it was possible to meet the new timetable and were eager to move forward.

The enemy was falling apart faster and faster now. Resistance was rarely strong enough to delay them for long, and city after town after province was falling, almost faster than the radio could

56

announce them. There were rumors that pilots from the South were bombing their own government and then landing at airfields captured by Communist forces. Many of the soldiers had heard that entire formations of captured enemy aircraft were now being flown by Northern pilots in attacks against the crumbling enemy.

So the soldiers rode toward the west knowing that they were going to win, and soon, and that knowledge lightened their burdens. Few of these soldiers understood that their lightening by the certainty of victory was mirrored in the enemy's awareness of imminent defeat and the crushing weight of fear and panic that the knowledge was bringing them.

⭐ 7 ⭐

Monday, 7 April 1975

IN THE DIM GLOW FROM THE FLOODLIGHTS MOUNTED HIGH ON THE ISLAND structure, Lt. Mike Santy reached up and pulled the canopy of his A-7 down and unhooked the strap that kept it from being damaged by the winds that were blowing down the flight deck. He closed the canopy and locked it, double-checking that the overcenter hooks were engaged, straining to see in the lousy red light from his instrument panel. He stowed the strap and took one more look around the cockpit, making sure that there was nothing that could go flying around during the catapult shot and either jam his controls or hit him in the face.

Off to his left, the taxi director uncrossed the yellow wands that had been telling Santy to hold his brakes and began waving them in the signal to taxi forward. Santy released the brakes and let the thrust of the idling engine start the jet forward and up the deck toward the waist catapults. He glanced at the "Christmas tree" up on the island just outside the glass-enclosed "tower" where the air boss surveyed his domain. The lights were still red but were indicating five minutes to launch. Looking back down at the director, Santy saw him point his wands to Santy's left toward the next director and then switch them off.

Further up the deck Santy spotted another wand held vertically over the next director's head for a couple of seconds and followed the signals toward Catapult 3. Santy grunted to himself. He absolutely hated the farthest one outboard, Cat 4. Mechanically, there was absolutely no difference between Cat 4 and the others, Cat 3 on the waist and Cats 1 and 2 up on the bow, but Cat 4 sat closest to the deck edge and was pointed almost along the axis of the ship,

58

whereas Cat 3 was at least aimed slightly to the left of the axis so that the clearing turn that was required immediately after launch was not quite so large. After the horrendous acceleration of the catapult stroke, enough to get a thirty-ton aircraft up to 150 knots in less than two and a half seconds, the turn was just another way to get the pilot disoriented, to give him a case of the dreaded vertigo. And that, at only seventy feet from the water, invisible in the darkness, was very dangerous indeed. It was also terrifying. Of everything he did in flying, Santy hated launches from Cat 4 at night far more than anything else.

Tonight, or rather this morning, was one of those periods of dark that can only be experienced at sea. Even though first light was only forty minutes away, the night wasn't even giving a hint of the day to come. There was no moon and a cloud deck hid the stars. Beyond the flight deck of the carrier, except for the tiny artificial stars created by the running lights of the ships steaming in company with *Concord*, it was absolutely, completely, impenetrably black. Blacker than the inside of a cow. Blacker even than Captain Hook's heart.

Santy was assigned as a "yo-yo tanker." Beneath his aircraft were hung several bomblike external fuel tanks and a D-704 air-to-air refueling store. He would be launched on this cycle and assume the task of passing fuel to whatever aircraft might require it, then land with the recovery that was to begin immediately after the launch, rather than stay out until the next cycle in an hour and forty-five minutes. One way of looking at this particular mission was that one got all the thrills, the launch and the landing in the dark, without any of the boring parts such as orbiting the ship for a hundred and five long minutes sitting on a seat cushion as soft as a city street.

The director waved Santy forward and passed him off to the last one, who guided Santy's last twenty feet or so, asking for and receiving almost minuscule movements until the A-7 was correctly positioned on the catapult track. The pilot gave the thumbs-up to the sailor who held the "weight board," which indicated the total launch weight of the A-7 so that the proper amount of steam pressure could be fed into the catapult system, ensuring that the aircraft would become airborne with the correct amount of speed to continue flying.

Santy lowered the launch bar on his nose landing gear and felt the slight jolt as it engaged the catapult shuttle. The director gave the signal to take tension, and Santy shoved his throttle forward to full power and released his brakes. When in tension, the catapult is fully charged and ready to fire, and only a couple of mechanical lockouts hold everything in check. If the lockouts fail, the catapult will propel the aircraft down the deck suddenly and it is a very good idea to have your engine at full power in case an inadvertent catapult shot happens—you *might* be able to fly the jet out. But if the engine is still at idle, there is absolutely no chance of keeping it out of the water.

Santy watched the "final checkers" duck under and around his aircraft making sure that everything was properly attached, that all the safety pins had been removed, and that there were no leaks of any kind. When they were done, they hustled clear and the director passed control of the launch to the catapult officer standing just to the left of the A-7's nose. He gave Santy the full-power and turn-up signal and waited while the pilot checked everything in his cockpit one more time.

Santy's eyes moved over his instrument panel. Checking that the engine was delivering the maximum power available, that the various systems were operating within limits, and that the flaps and trim were properly set. With his right hand, Santy shoved the stick in all directions, "wiping out the cockpit," and pushed the rudder pedals to full throw in each direction, making sure that the controls were free and not binding, then centered them again. He grasped the throttle and cat grip with his left hand so that the launch stroke would not pull his hand (and the throttle) back, placed his head against the headrest of the ejection seat, and flicked on the aircraft's exterior lights with his left thumb.

The cat officer saw the lights of the A-7 come on, rechecked that the catapult track was clear, and touched the deck with his lighted wand. For a couple of long heartbeats nothing happened until the catapult fired, hurling Santy and his A-7 into the darkness beyond the deck edge.

Santy felt the acceleration cease when the catapult reached the end of its run and released his aircraft. He forced his eyes to scan the attitude and airspeed indicators as he slapped up the landing gear and turned the aircraft a little farther left to get away from the ship's path. As the jet accelerated and began to climb, he raised the flaps and retrimmed the controls. He keyed his radio: "Departure, Condor 305's airborne."

"Roger, 305."

Twenty minutes later, Santy rolled his A-7 onto the final approach course and rechecked that his landing gear, tailhook, and flaps were down and locked. As he had suspected, the short tanker flight had been completely uneventful. He had only had to top off a couple of F-4 Phantoms right after launch before he had received vectors from the radar controllers back aboard *Concord* to enter the approach pattern.

As the tanker, he was the last aircraft for this recovery and was just about to begin his descent when he was directed to "clean up and hold overhead." He raised the gear, flaps, and hook again and climbed into a three-thousand-foot orbit over the ship. He had plenty of fuel, and from this altitude he could see the first lightening of the far eastern horizon so he was in fine shape, but the cause of the delay was getting him concerned. Two of the three aircraft in the line for landing had been from his squadron, so he was hoping that something hadn't happened to them when he got the call.

"Condor 305, Approach."

"305."

"Roger. We have a fouled deck. We expect about a forty-minute delay. Say your state."

Santy looked at his fuel gauges and totaled up how much gas he had. He had just about started to dump his excess fuel from his tanker package when the call had come. As he transmitted his fuel state to the ship, he eased the A-7 into the "max conserve" attitude and airspeed.

"Approach, 305's got about two point eight."

"Approach copies, two point eight."

"And, Approach, interrogative the fouled deck." Santy just thought he'd ask.

"Stand by."

A minute later: "305, we have an F-4 with collapsed landing gear stuck in the wires. Estimating now about fifty minutes, that's five zero mikes, until clear deck."

"Roger." Santy considered his fuel. There was still no problem.

"Uh, 305, we have another A-7, Condor 310, who could use some fuel. Can you give him some? He'll be joining you shortly."

For this cycle, 310 was the squadron commanding officer's aircraft. "That's affirm, Approach, but probably not enough to get us both to the next recovery."

"Roger."

Santy reached into the small box set into his right console and pulled out his plastic-covered book of approach plates. He selected the one for Tan Son Nhut airport and looked it over, refamiliarizing himself with all the routes and altitudes he would have to fly to divert to that airport. Even though he hadn't been told to divert ashore yet, he had the feeling that that was how things were going to go.

"305, 310. I'm joining starboard."

Santy clicked his mike button twice in acknowledgment and looked over his shoulder to watch the other Corsair slide into perfect parade position, slightly below and just behind Santy's wing. The join-up was perfect, which was about what one would expect from Cdr. Nick Taylor, the CO. He was widely known as one of the best pilots in the fleet, and Santy had never had a reason to doubt that.

As soon as 310 was in, Santy concentrated on flying his own aircraft. Maintaining a good formation on Santy was Taylor's job, not the other way around.

"305, Approach. Has 310 joined yet?"

"That's affirm."

"Roger. You are to bingo to the primary divert. Your initial steer is two two five for entry into the arrival corridor. Switch to departure now."

"Roger, Condor's switching, good day." Santy switched his radio to the new frequency, waited for a couple of seconds, and keyed the mike switch.

"Condor."

Instantly, he heard Taylor's voice telling him he was on the frequency also: "Two."

"Departure, Condor 305 and 310 are with you headed two two five and level angles three."

"305, Departure. Radar contact. Climb and maintain one five thousand. Squawk three three two five."

"Roger, Condor's out of three for fifteen. Squawking three three two five." Santy spun the dials on his Identification Friend or Foe, or IFF, transponder to the proper code, or "squawk."

"Condors, primary divert advises that the only other inbound traffic is an Air Force heavy about twenty minutes behind you. No factor."

"305, roger." As Santy climbed to fifteen thousand feet, the little formation was suddenly bathed in daylight while the world below was still wreathed in darkness. The air was still and it was as if they had entered a different world. Ahead, somewhere below, was the coastline, which separated the safe and clean sea from the chaos and horror of the events in South Vietnam. Santy idly hoped that he and the skipper could spend minimum time on the ground—just a gas and go. The sooner he got back out to sea, or "feet wet," the better.

Boyle had no idea how long he'd dozed when he was awakened by someone tripping over his outstretched legs. Instantly alert, he sat up, pulled his legs back against the seat, and craned around to see up into the cockpit deck of the huge C-141 Starlifter, the "Air Force heavy" about which Santy had been informed. It was now daylight and the crew of the aircraft were moving about with a purpose. The passengers, including the one who had tripped over Boyle's legs, were sitting in their seats and fastening their seat belts.

The crew members worked their way back to the tail, checking the security of the cargo, tugging on the tie-down straps and kicking the other pieces of gear that would keep the heavy pallets from rolling forward and crushing the passengers on landing and heavy braking. Boyle idly appreciated their conscientiousness.

The loadmaster came forward again, put on his headset, and told the pilots that all was secure. He poured himself one last cup of coffee from the aluminum urn fastened to the bulkhead and sat down in his seat, sipping the almost hot coffee and looking unconcerned. Boyle rechecked his seat belt just as he heard the muted roar from the four high-mounted engines diminish still further and felt the nose of the aircraft lower to the attitude for descent. He checked the sign to see if he could still have a cigarette and, seeing that it was still off, lit up another Marlboro. He fixed his eyes on the overhead and tried to *feel* what the pilot was doing with the aircraft. Like most professional pilots, Boyle hated being a passenger in an aircraft and having no control of his fate. It was almost okay during the cruise part of a flight, but the landing was a completely different story.

The approach seemed much steeper and rougher than an aircraft of this type and size would be making. The pilots banked sharply to the right, and Boyle watched the shaft of sunlight from the small window in the passenger door to his left move across the bulkhead and disappear. A half minute later, it reappeared and began its same march across the bulkhead all over again. So, he thought, they're making a spiraling approach rather than the typical long straight-in.

He considered that. It was obvious that the pilots were using the spiral to avoid flying at a low altitude over terrain from which they might be shot at. Spiraling down directly over safe territory was normally the safest way into an airfield that was surrounded by an enemy. If the airport at Tan Son Nhut near Saigon was surrounded, then things were much worse in South Vietnam than he had been led to believe by either the newspapers or the unclassified summaries that crossed his desk.

Boyle stubbed out his cigarette and rechecked his seat belt, not that it would do him much good if this airplane got shot down. There were a few odd bumps and jolts as the 141 slammed its way through the thermal air currents rising from the fast-approaching land below. Boyle concentrated on the shaft of sunlight and tried to keep himself from wondering how well, or how badly, the pilots had done in flight training.

As he stood on the parking ramp at Tan Son Nhut air base, Boyle hardly noticed the metallic scraping sound of the turbine wheels in the C-141's engines turning in the wind, which was blowing fairly strongly across the airfield. He was struck by how deserted the place looked even though dozens of aircraft were moving around the taxiways and the airborne traffic pattern. All up and down the long flight lines were large areas where no aircraft were parked, and here and there were thirty or so hangars and other buildings that stood apparently unused, judging from the weeds that grew everywhere. Several hangars appeared to have once housed American military squadrons and were now falling into disrepair. What units were still operating from the less dilapidated buildings were South Vietnamese and were scattered sort of haphazardly among the empty areas. It was like a stadium where twenty people were trying to look like a hundred.

The admiral and his two senior aides were led to a large limousine and driven off with a motorcycle escort of South Vietnamese military police, known as White Mice because of their white helmets. Boyle noticed with a grimace of distaste that it was Joe France who held the door for the admiral and stood grinning immodestly as the cars started off. Boyle watched the little parade disappear around the corner of one of the well-kept hangars and turned back to look at the airfield.

Off to the left was a large unit of UH-1 Iroquois helicopters, known to the world as Hueys. Boyle watched as two of them turned up and taxied out together, their skids only a couple of feet from the ground. The distinctive *whop whop whop* of their rotor systems reverberated off the sides of the buildings to either side of the C-141.

Boyle was perfectly content watching the Hueys. Except for a slightly larger cargo compartment, some electronics, and a really bad paint job, they were nearly identical to the ones he'd flown in the Training Command just before he earned his wings. Like most who had flown them, Boyle deeply loved the Huey. It was a sports car compared to the big H-3s Boyle had flown in his fleet squadron, and he was certain that he could remember the procedures for starting and flying them even now.

Walking farther away, about fifty feet, from the huge 141, Boyle pulled a Marlboro out of the battered pack in his shirt pocket and lit it with a badly dented and scratched Zippo lighter. He closed the lid and ran his thumb across the rubber band wrapped around it, smiling at the old habit. Boyle had never been able to remember to zip up the small pocket on the left sleeve of his flight suit, and the Zippo was always slipping out of the pocket and falling to the deck somewhere, usually from the highest point on his helicopter as Boyle did the preflight inspection. Someone, probably his old aircraft commander Bob Watkins, had finally told him about the rubber-band trick, which provided enough friction to keep the lighter in the pocket. The Zippo had been with him for his entire career as a naval aviator, including the horrible hours of escape and evasion in North Vietnam, and it was now a sort of lucky charm, even though everybody knew that naval aviators didn't believe in such things.

Boyle stubbed out the cigarette and stuffed the filter into the pack so that it wouldn't get sucked up by somebody's engine. He walked around the nose of the C-141 and looked down the rest of the long ramp area. Off to one side were a large group of helicopters and strange-looking fixed-wing aircraft. They were all uniformly silver-gray and looked beautifully maintained in comparison with the other aircraft Boyle could see around the field. Parked in the front row next to a large green fuel truck were two A-7 Corsairs with the large letters *NC* painted on the tail. Boyle smiled at the memory—these aircraft were from the USS *Concord,* the carrier from which he had last flown, and judging from the stylized letters were from Mike Santy's squadron.

The group of people standing around them were too far away for Boyle to make out faces, but none of them had the size or Mike's distinctive stance, which made it seem as if he had a sort of relaxed tension about him. Kind of easy but ready to spring instantly. Boyle was wondering whether he had enough time to walk over and give them a message to pass to Mike when he heard Hickerson's voice calling him.

"Hey, Tim. Let's go." With a couple of glances over his shoulder at the A-7s, Boyle followed Hickerson to a blue bus that obviously once belonged to the U.S. Air Force but was now operated by a gold-toothed Vietnamese civilian. The windows of the bus were open but were covered with chicken wire to prevent the odd pedestrian from heaving a hand grenade into the bus. Boyle took this as a particularly bad sign.

As he reached down and picked up his bag, he heard an awful brogue behind him. "Well, now, Timmy me boy. And what brings you to this fair land?" He dropped the bag and turned.

Mike Santy, big as life, came around the front of the bus and stood grinning at Boyle, who for the first time in quite a while was at a loss for words.

66

★ 8 ★

Monday, 7 April 1975

SANTY LOOKED PAST HIS SURPRISED FRIEND AT HICKERSON AND NODDED. "Hi."

Boyle found his voice. "I didn't expect you to greet me, you asshole. What are you doing here?"

"The ship sent me in to see if I could restore order in this place. It's hopeless so I picked up some snakebite medicine from the Air America guys over there and we're going to go back out and get a steak or something. Seriously though, we had to divert in here because the deck got clobbered. Just a gas and go. How about you?"

"I got sort of drafted to come over with some other CINCPAC types to, um, check things out." Boyle wasn't sure whether he could tell Mike about his mission. He hadn't asked about the classification level for the trip. Santy caught the "um" and didn't press it, especially with a senior officer standing right there.

Hickerson caught it, too. He smiled at the silent byplay. "What we're here for, Lieutenant, is to plan for an evacuation should it become necessary."

Boyle shook his head at himself. "I'm sorry. Commander Hickerson, this is Mike Santy. Mike, this is my boss."

Santy shifted his obviously heavy helmet bag, and the two shook hands. "Nice to meet you, sir."

"We've met before, Mike. I was Tim's detachment commander a couple of years ago and you were in one of the A-7 squadrons on *Concord*, right?"

"Yes, sir. Still am. I'm headed for Cecil Field, near Jacksonville and the East Coast RAG."

Boyle brightened. "No shit? You got your orders? That's great, Mike."

Santy nodded. "Yeah, I wrote you about it but I don't guess you've gotten that letter yet."

"Nope. It'll be waiting back at Pearl, I suppose."

Hickerson interrupted. "Tim, we've got to be going. Our first stop will be in the Air America building for a briefing on the air picture. Why don't you catch up with us when you're done. We'll probably be departing in about an hour."

Hickerson looked at Boyle, who was obviously torn between his desire to see Santy for as long as he could and his professional sense, which was telling him that he should attend the briefing. Hickerson picked up Boyle's bag and threw it on the bus. "Don't worry, Tim. I'll make sure that you don't miss anything. It's just a situation briefing, which will probably be OBE in two hours anyway."

"Okay, Commander. Thanks." Boyle watched as Hickerson boarded the bus, which moved off in a cloud of gray smoke and clashing gears. He turned to Santy.

"How're you doing, Mike?"

"Pretty fair, actually. We're getting some flying in, but everybody's just marking time until this mess is over and we can go home. It ain't like the old days when we could do something."

"What do you mean?"

"All we're doing is flying around offshore letting the gomers know we're there. The bad part is that the gomers already know we're there and that we won't do anything without a serious provocation, so they basically don't give a shit. Other than that, it's your normal everyday deployment. How about you? Did Maureen get there okay?"

"Yeah, she arrived safe and sound last Wednesday. She and Meg have been tearing around like a couple of wild women seeing the sights and shopping. She's gonna stay with Meg at least until I get back. And you ought to be damned glad you're not married yet—you won't have to pay for all the stuff she's bought."

"How's she look?"

Boyle laughed. "You have been at sea awhile. She looks great, Mikey. She's absolutely fine and she's still madly in love with you. Which, by the way, doesn't say much for her brains."

Santy chuckled. "You're right there. Anyway, how are you? Why the civvies?"

Boyle shrugged. "I guess us imperialist warmongers aren't supposed to be here. Anyway, I'm fine. I'm glad to get the hell out of the damn office even if I had to come here to do it."

"Do I detect a small note of disgust in that statement?"

Boyle laughed a little self-consciously. "I guess. I just wish I was in a real flying job. Boring holes in the sky in a Stoof is not exactly on the cutting edge."

Santy nodded. "Come on. I'll introduce you to my skipper. He's a good guy. Used to be an A-4 pilot but he got shot like you and wound up in A-7s."

"Taylor? We met when you all came through Pearl on your way over here. He was the XO then."

"Yeah, I forgot. He took over about a month ago. Come on."

Twenty minutes later, Tim Boyle leaned against the railing on the front steps of the Air America building and watched Santy and Taylor taxi out. His eyes followed the two stubby little white-and-gray jets as they moved to the intersection of the taxiway and the runway and held short. Just a few seconds later, they taxied out onto the runway and stopped side by side awaiting their take-off clearance. Almost immediately he saw one of them move forward, accelerating down the runway, followed five seconds later by the second. The sound of the first Corsair's engine at full power didn't reach him until the second jet was just beginning to roll.

He watched both jets lift off and depart to the east, leaving brownish black trails of exhaust behind. Long after the sound of their engines had faded away, Boyle looked after them, wishing he were going along, back to the carrier and the kind of flying he loved so much.

He was thinking, too, about Mike's orders to Jacksonville. Boyle had also put in for assignment to Jax in the H-3 RAG. All the East Coast H-3s were at the Jacksonville Naval Air Station, which was ten miles east of Cecil Field where Santy was headed. It didn't occur to Boyle as he stood there looking after his friend that completely absent among the emotions he was feeling at that moment was any shred of jealousy that Santy had gotten the best set of orders he could have dreamed of.

Oh, well, he thought, maybe I'll get lucky. It would be perfect if he and Mike could once again be stationed close by each other—he'd missed that. Since Boyle had been transferred from San Diego to Hawaii, it had almost been as if part of him was missing for the first time since the two had met the night before flight training nearly five years before.

Boyle couldn't know, as he turned away to enter the building, that Mike Santy, alone in his cockpit heading out to sea, was thinking exactly the same thing.

When Boyle found him, Hickerson was standing in the passageway outside a conference room, drinking a Coke and talking with a couple of hard-eyed men in civilian clothes. Boyle walked up and stood to one side trying to appear not to be listening. Hickerson turned and pulled him closer to the trio.

"Tim Boyle, this is Mickey Harris and Frank Wheeler. They're ex-Marine helo pilots who now work for Air America. Gents, this is Tim Boyle, my assistant."

They all shook hands and smiled, mumbling the obligatory nice-ta-meechas. Harris and Wheeler turned back to Hickerson and continued talking about their supply problems, and Boyle stood by and feigned interest in their troubles, which seemed to him to be relatively minor. He glanced around the corridor and tried to see as much as he could of the headquarters of the legendary airline.

Air America was a pretty much legitimate airline contracted mostly to the American Central Intelligence Agency. The biggest part of what they did was real, legal, and aboveboard—flying passengers and cargo all over Southeast Asia—because as a civilian organization they could go where American military aircraft could not. However, another part of Air America's mission was clouded in mystery and secrecy, despite the fact that the press had been trying to make them into a cross between Terry and the Pirates and Hitler's SS in civvies.

Harris and Wheeler walked a few paces down the hall and turned into a small office, gesturing for Hickerson and Boyle to follow. Once inside, Wheeler offered each of them coffee, and as he poured from the ancient coffeemaker, Boyle took in the office.

The room had one large window looking out on the ramp and looked exactly like every other office occupied by aviators he had ever seen. On the walls were the standard group of pictures put out by the various aircraft manufacturers and the usual blackboard with the mandatory jottings in what looked like a half dozen different hands. Boyle smiled at the blackboard. It always seemed that they represented a sort of vertical scratch pad so that instead of writing things down on a yellow legal pad, some people wrote on the board to keep themselves reminded of what they were supposed to be accomplishing. Boyle himself liked the legal-pad plan, probably because he could cover it up with some other piece of business and thus put unpleasant tasks out of mind.

Of course, there was the other use for an office blackboard, the use people like Joe France put them to. France had positioned his desk and blackboard so that they could easily be seen from the passageway outside his cubicle. He liked to put everything he was doing on his board in an accountant's hand, complete with a space for "status" and another for "expected completion date," so that when his superiors passed by, they could be impressed with how organized he was. What they never seemed to notice was that the status space remained unchanged for weeks at a time, but the "expected completion date" was changed frequently as it neared. They also never noticed that the higher ranking the officer was who had given France the job, the closer the job was placed to the top of the list. It was a neat piece of theater, thought Boyle, but about twice as much trouble as just getting the damn job done in the first place.

Hickerson sat in one of the standard green ex-military chairs with which the office was furnished and placed his cup down on the desk among the dozens of rings left by other coffee cups.

"Tim, we're going boating tomorrow. These guys are going to fly us out to the *Concord* to brief the staff out there and see if we can get some sort of handle on the plan. Bring a set of khakis since we'll have to look like Navy once we get there."

"Yes, sir." Boyle wanted to ask why they couldn't be picked up by one of the helos from the carrier, but wisely decided against it. It might sound as if he didn't trust these guys. Fortunately, Wheeler answered the question anyway.

"We do most of the ship-to-shore logistics now, Tim. We had a congressional delegation over here a couple of weeks ago, and they went ballistic when they saw a couple of Navy helos parked on the ramp. Seems that Congress passed some sort of bill or resolution or something that said we aren't allowed to fly combat aircraft overland. Why those assholes figured that an antisubmarine helicopter posed a threat to the Paris Accords, I'll never know, but they got on the horn to Washington, and the fleet guys got told that they could come in here only in an emergency. So all the log flights are ours."

Boyle shook his head. "That seems a little stupid."

"That was nothing. They chewed every ass that came within a hundred yards of them and left here totally convinced that cutting military aid to the South would help the situation. Even that woman from New York, the one who wears the ugly hats and looks like the bottom of a coal barge, was there. She spent her whole time trying to find evidence to prove whatever preconceptions she brought with her. Mickey, here, flew her around and would have dropped her in the river if he wasn't afraid of all the paperwork he'd have had to do."

Harris chuckled. "Yeah, but I got her good. And that asshole aide of hers."

He saw the looks on Hickerson's and Boyle's face and explained. "I had her in a Huey taking her up the road a ways and I sort of let my arms relax, and then I got to wiggling the rudder pedals and the stick some. Got a real nice triaxial beat going as we flew along. It took about ten minutes but she got airsick and puked all over herself and her aide. Then the aide got sick and puked right back. It was great. Every time she could get her breath she started screaming at me, demanding that I land right now. Of course we were over some nasty terrain full of air currents which just happened to be on our route of flight, so I couldn't do that. We had to press on for another forty-five minutes or so until we got back here. I really felt bad for her."

Wheeler laughed as Harris finished the story. "Yeah, sure you did. Mickey picked the roughest air he could find to fly her back here. The bitch had to be helped out of the helo and just sort of fell into her limo, with Mickey holding the door and munching on a candy bar. The crewmen were gonna hose out the back of the Huey with the aide still lying in there, but the boss made us pull her out first. She was just lying there on the ramp on her face for a half hour or so, and then she finally crawled off to a taxi, probably hoping that the taxi would crash and put her out of her misery." Wheeler sighed. "I guess that'll teach them to treat helo pilots like hired help."

Hickerson laughed. "That's a hall-of-fame story."

Harris looked at the ceiling and affected his best attitude of saintliness. "I prefer to think of it as my small contribution to the noble effort to pay back the Congress for what they've done to shaft the people here."

Hickerson drained his coffee and stood. "Well, we've gotta go. We'll see you guys tomorrow. Thanks for the coffee." He nodded at the two helicopter pilots. "Or, maybe we'll see you at the Cara-velle Bar tonight."

Wheeler smiled. "Roger that. Take care of yourselves, and it's good to see you again, Don. Just hang out on the front steps and we'll scare up somebody to drive you downtown."

Boyle followed Hickerson out the door, mumbling a good-bye to the Air America pilots, who smiled and waved as he left.

Once out in the passageway, Boyle caught up with Hickerson, who was making his way to the front door of the building. Neither spoke until they were outside waiting for their ride.

Boyle looked across at the DAO compound, the former "Penta-gon East." "No briefing in there, Commander?"

"Nope. We've got all we're going to get for today. Somebody figures we've exhausted ourselves traveling here so the briefing was rescheduled. I'll fill you in later. Right now, the others are at the embassy talking to their counterparts. I figured I'd rather get the straight story from guys I trust than listen to a dog and pony from somebody I've never met."

"Have you known those guys long?"

Hickerson smiled. "Half my life, it seems. We were pretty close back in Pensacola, and we've run into each other a lot since. Mickey and I were flight instructors together once."

"What did they do, just resign and go with Air America?"

"Sort of. They're both still in the reserves. They finished their first tours here around '66 and came back to various staff jobs later. They both married Vietnamese and left active duty here rather than go back home and have to argue their way back. The company took them on because of their experience mostly, but also because their roots are here rather than back home."

Boyle frowned when Hickerson mentioned marrying Vietnam-ese nationals, and Hickerson caught it. "I know what you're think-ing, Tim. They didn't marry B-girls or hookers, although a lot of guys did. Mickey's wife is a schoolteacher and Frank's was a

73

translator on the staff. In fact, Frank's wife has advanced degrees in languages from the Sorbonne. She's smarter than you and me put together."

"What's going to happen to them if the NVA take over?"

"They're both safe and sound back in the States. They got out right after things started to go bad around here. Packed up everything they owned, grabbed the kids, and jumped on a plane headed east."

Boyle shook his head. Neither Wheeler nor Harris looked like the family type, but on the other hand, who around here did?

"How about the relatives?"

Hickerson smiled. "You mean like the legendary Asian wife with four thousand cousins?"

Boyle laughed. "Yeah."

"Most of them chose to stay. This is their home. What's left of it, that is. Here comes our ride."

The ancient jeep pulled up with a horrendous squeal of brakes. Its crusty-looking American driver waited behind his sunglasses and blue baseball cap while Boyle climbed into the back and Hickerson sat gingerly on the front seat, trying to avoid puncturing himself on the rusty springs that stuck out from the sides of the cushion.

"Where to?" asked the driver, spitting out a shred of his unlit cigar.

"Hotel Caravelle."

"Okay, Caravelle it is. Hang on."

With a great grinding of what were probably the last few gear teeth, the driver shoved the jeep into first and roared off at a frightening speed, heading down the road that led to Tu Do Street and the heart of Saigon.

Hickerson held on tightly and the driver laughed. "Don't worry, pal. You gotta drive like this or you'll get run over. Besides, with everybody on the run around here, if you slow down below about fifty, they'll strip your car for parts before you can make the next corner."

"Nice."

"Yeah. Well, at least you don't have to pay insurance here, and if you run over somebody, you don't get sued."

Boyle tried to look at the driver's face to see if he was joking, but the next turn, taken on two wheels as it was, diverted him some.

★ **9** ★

Monday, 7 April 1975

KEVIN THOMPSON AND MARK DALTON LEANED ON THE PENTHOUSE BAR IN the Hotel Caravelle. They were silently drinking and gazing out the big window toward the north, watching the flares and flashes on the far horizon as some nameless unit attacked another nameless unit. They both knew that men were dying under those flares and in those flashes, but they both knew also that it mattered not at all who was winning the fight out there tonight.

If it was a unit of South Vietnamese winning, it wouldn't slow down the NVA advance—it was very much like trying to empty the Pacific with a bucket. The NVA would soon roll over or surround or just bypass whatever brave or not-so-brave defenders were in their way. If it was the NVA winning, well, that didn't matter either, not in the long run.

Thompson and Dalton had watched the flares and flashes move inexorably closer to Saigon over the past weeks. At first, only the largest explosions would light up the night sky, but as the enemy moved closer, night after night, the horizon became progressively more illuminated until in the past week or so even tracers from individual heavy weapons could be seen on the clearer nights. Both men were well aware that the advance of the flares was a far more accurate barometer of how things were going than were the hopeful bullshit and communiqués that came from the American embassy.

Dalton signaled the bartender for another round and fished out some bills to pay for them. The bartender brought the drinks with his customary smile and nod, breaking into a large grin when Dalton told him to keep the change.

75

Thompson watched him walk back to his stool to await the next order from the few patrons who had made their way up here after their evening meals. "That guy has to be an idiot or a Viet Cong. He's the only face around here with a smile anymore."

Dalton snorted. Even a bad joke was funny tonight. "Yeah. He's probably got the only job that'll continue after the gomers get here. This place will become a mecca for Russians who'll have to make all the 'assist' visits."

"Not like us, huh?"

Dalton nodded slowly as he watched a particularly large explosion off to the northeast. "That one probably cost the taxpayers a bunch."

Thompson finished the last of his Scotch and gestured for another. "How'd we do today?"

"We've got the last of our people scheduled out of here by Thursday, and that'll be it."

"How about the records?"

"Done. Everything that needed to go is gone, and everything we need to burn is ready."

"So now what do we do?"

"We've seen all the movies and read all the books. Nobody wants to play tennis anymore, and we've bought all the stuff we can afford. So I guess we can just sit around now and wait. This is as good a place as any, I suppose."

Thompson looked around the bar. "Sounds boring."

"Yep."

"Have we heard from our friend?"

"Not yet. We sent the message six days ago, through the same channels we've been using so we should be hearing from him pretty soon."

"What are we going to do if he wants to come out?"

Dalton sipped his drink. They'd both been thinking about this part but had left it undiscussed for a week now. "We'll help him."

"You know that means somebody'll probably have to go out there."

Thompson stared out the window. Along with all the other Americans, at least most of those who worked someplace other than the embassy, he was feeling a tremendous surge of frustration, which was fast turning to rage at what was happening. No one had been able to convince the embassy that things were al-

76

most finished here. It was obvious that the official evacuation ought to have begun long before, but the ambassador had been putting up a brave front, as if all would soon be well, as if a political compromise could be achieved with Hanoi, as if reason and American logic would soon prevail. There were all sorts of theories about why the ambassador and his staff were behaving this way, some sensible and some preposterous. But to Thompson and the others the why was irrelevant.

Time was running out. And as it did, the speed of its run accelerated. No plan was going to hold up for long. Neither were the wishes nor the dreams of those who would not see.

Thompson looked at Dalton. "Are you saying that you *want* to go?"

Dalton sighed. "I guess so. He was once one of us. I figure we owe him."

Thompson took a pull from his Scotch. Dalton was right. They owed Butler the chance in exactly the same way they felt that the United States owed South Vietnam the chance to survive. The difference was that Thompson and Dalton were willing to do something meaningful. And most citizens of the United States and their elected officials were not.

"Okay. Let's figure out how we're going to do it."

Dalton looked hard at his boss. "Are you coming along?"

"I can't let you go alone. You can't read a map worth a shit."

"I won't be alone. I've got a couple of other guys who'll come."

"You don't need them now. Did you actually think I'd be able to let him go without at least trying?"

Dalton smiled a little shyly. "I guess that wasn't fair of me, was it? Or smart."

"Nope."

It was a measure of the two SEALs and their relationships, both personal and professional, that that one word carried with it sufficient admonition and professional advice to ensure that a recurrence would never happen. Dalton took it exactly as Thompson had intended it. He nodded and ordered another round.

Boyle and Hickerson had arrived earlier in the day at the same hotel, climbing shakily from the jeep. They went straight into the building, taking little note of the neo-modern 1960s decor. Receiving their keys from the front desk, they went directly to their adjoining rooms. Each took a long shower and collapsed on his bed for a couple of hours sleep, which had been very short for the past couple of days.

Shortly after five, Boyle stirred and sat on the edge of the bed at the gentle knocking on the door that connected the rooms. Before he could figure out where he was exactly, the door opened and Hickerson came in and handed Boyle a beer.

"You'll love this stuff. It's local."

Boyle grunted his thanks and sipped the beer. "Not bad. It ain't Coors, but it'll do. What's the plan?"

"There's a restaurant down the street a couple of blocks called the Guillaume Tell—that's French for William Tell. You won't believe the food. The owner is this French lady who's about forty or so and is absolutely gorgeous. Get dressed."

"Okay. What then?"

"We'll check out the club in the Brinks BOQ, and then we'll finish up in the penthouse here. We've got to make it a short night since we've got work to do tomorrow."

As he pulled on a clean shirt, Boyle asked, "If there's a BOQ here, how come we're staying in a hotel?"

"Tim, I make it a point to avoid government-furnished quarters. It's kind of a little game I play. If the Navy is going to send me somewhere where I really don't want to be, then I figure I ought to make the best of it. BOQs generally suck when it comes to comfort and privacy, so I get the boss to sign off on permissive travel orders."

Boyle buckled his belt and slipped on his shoes. By American standards, the Caravelle wasn't all that great a place, but it did beat the hell out of staying in a BOQ.

Four hours later, a little after nine, both Hickerson and Boyle were fast running out of steam as they walked into the penthouse bar. Boyle took in the scene, looking around at the fifty or so patrons all dressed in civilian clothes. It was obvious that the vast majority of them were civilians, probably from the many news organizations, some of which were headquartered in the lower floors of the Caravelle. There was an air of forced frivolity, as if everyone was trying too hard to have a good time.

Boyle followed Hickerson over to the bar, and the two found a space between several pairs of other patrons sitting on the tall stools. As Hickerson ordered drinks, Boyle turned and found himself staring into a face that seemed familiar. He frowned as he turned away until he suddenly remembered.

He turned back and touched the man's arm. "Excuse me, but would you be Kevin Thompson?"

The man started a little but recovered. "Yeah."

Boyle was taken aback at the man's coldness. "I, um . . . my name's Tim Boyle. I met you when you were the aide aboard *Concord* a couple of years ago."

Thompson brightened. "Oh, yeah. Hi. You were one of the helo guys—the one they pulled off the beach. Right?"

Boyle laughed. "Hell of a thing to be remembered for." He turned to Hickerson. "Boss, this is Kevin Thompson. He was on the ship with us."

Grinning, Hickerson leaned in and the two shook hands. "I remember. He was one of the few staff guys who didn't piss me off."

Boyle was suddenly glad he hadn't gone any further and described Thompson as a SEAL. He had the feeling that Thompson's job might not be all that openly known. The feeling was confirmed when Thompson introduced Dalton by name only, with no rank, even though it was obvious that he was military.

Thompson turned to Boyle. "How're you doing? Last time I saw you they were loading you and your buddy into a helo."

"Just ducky. The Navy was so impressed with what a good healer I was that they gave me a staff job."

Thompson chuckled. "All you have to remember is that staff jobs aren't life sentences. They just seem like it."

Boyle nodded. "That's no shit. So how are you?"

"Fine. When Admiral Welch left for Washington, his relief didn't want any snake eaters like me around, so I went back to Coronado for a while and wound up here in the DAO."

Boyle began to ask questions of the SEALs about things he had seen so far in Saigon and at Tan Son Nhut today. He listened to the frank answers and asked others questions of increasing depth. Thompson found himself enjoying talking to Boyle, idly wishing that he could have spent more time with him and some of the other aviators back when he was aboard the carrier. He began to realize that he'd missed an opportunity.

Over the SEAL's shoulder and out the window, a particularly

large flash on the horizon distracted Boyle, and Thompson turned to the window. He explained what Boyle was seeing, and the conversation took off in a new direction with the SEALs describing the military situation and Boyle and Hickerson describing how it all was being perceived back in the States. It didn't take long for everyone to realize the large disconnect between the reality of the flashing horizon and the slick words of the nightly newscasts.

Boyle found himself almost mesmerized by the battle out there. He had seen a pretty good bit of combat himself, but it had all been from the familiar cockpit of a helicopter. Pilots at least had the ability to move, so there was an illusion of some safety in what they did. But standing here watching the leading edge of an advance by an enemy with blood in his eye and no mercy in his heart was a chilling experience for Boyle. He shivered, feeling trapped all of a sudden, like the goat tied to the stake while the tiger circles out beyond the light.

Then, it occurred to him that he still had an out. He was an American and had an entire fleet assembling just over the horizon. He'd soon be back home in his own house with Meghan, thousands of miles away from all this. He'd be living in a place where the darkness didn't harbor brutal men with guns who would take everything away and give him nothing but hopelessness and intellectual death in return.

But the Vietnamese had no fleet to speak of. They had no C-5s or C-141s waiting to take them home and out of this mess. They had nowhere to run. They had no place to hide. He couldn't imagine how it must be to have absolutely no options left.

Boyle sipped at his drink and discovered that it was empty, abruptly coming back to the bar with all the light and cigarette smoke and the lousy band butchering "Proud Mary." He placed the glass on the bar and signaled for the bartender to bring another round. Hickerson and the two SEALs were talking easily, rarely noticing that Boyle had mentally slipped away for a few moments.

When the drinks came, Boyle paid the tab and sipped his beer. He found it tasteless and realized that he didn't want to be here anymore. He made his excuses, told Hickerson that he'd see him in the morning, and walked out the door to the elevators.

Thompson had watched Boyle stare out at the flares and drift away. He knew what the young aviator had been thinking and was glad to see it. He had been able to see Boyle come to understand the Vietnam of April 1975. The rest of the room was full of people, newsmen, soldiers, spooks, and lower-level diplomats who would never figure it out, who would go on with their lives and never make that breakthrough where a man could see the world through other eyes and see things with less of the distortion that ignorance brings.

Thompson turned to Hickerson. "That's a pretty good man you've got there, Don."

"Yeah, I know. And the best part is that he doesn't."

Hickerson frowned. "I've got it. There's been something bugging me for a while. Weren't you the one who went in to try and find him when he crashed in North Vietnam?"

Thompson nodded. "Yeah, I figured that was all the time ashore I was going to get for a while. But when we got in there, he was long gone from the wreck site. We thought originally that no one got out—that he was dead, too, and still in the helo, which was completely destroyed. It wasn't until later that he turned up dragging an A-7 pilot along with him."

Hickerson stuck out his hand. "I'd like to thank you for that. Tim was one of my guys, but I'd left a couple of weeks earlier."

Thompson was a little embarrassed but accepted the thanks, mumbling something about helo guys doing the same kind of thing for him if the positions were reversed.

Hickerson laughed. "I don't think Tim knows about your doing that, by the way."

"That's okay. It's not important that he does."

"Yeah, well, thanks again anyway. Now, I've gotta go turn into a pumpkin. I need more sleep than you young boys. Good night. I'll see you again, I hope." Hickerson headed out for the elevators.

Dalton looked after him. "Nice guy."

"Yup. They both are." Thompson looked at Dalton's glass. "You ready?"

"Is it your turn to buy?"

"Uh-huh."

"Then I'm ready."

*   *   *

81

Gerry Carroll

Several floors below the penthouse bar, Boyle turned away from the window in his room. He'd been watching the lights on the horizon, which reminded him of the fierce thunderstorms out in the Gulf of Mexico when he was in flight training.

He climbed into the bed and turned off the light. But it took him a long time to fall asleep.

★ 10 ★

Tuesday, 8 April 1975

ABOUT EIGHTY-FIVE MILES NORTHWEST OF TAN SON NHUT AIRPORT AND Saigon lies the first rise of the Annamite Mountains. By Alpine standards the Annamites aren't particularly impressive, but for men on the run, they will do quite nicely. The elevation in the area is less than five thousand feet, but the slopes are steep and the vegetation is heavy, so it is an excellent area in which to conceal a group of men, especially when those men can live off the land and do not require the massive amounts of equipment and support that modern armies do.

The insurgent Viet Cong had hidden themselves for years in terrain like this, choosing the right time and the right place to strike out at the Allied forces. Usually hidden by the night, they would stage quick, deadly attacks and melt back into the jungle and their highland base camps. Their goal never was to take and hold territory—they were never powerful enough to hold ground for long—but to cause the maximum destruction, confusion, and pain for their enemies.

But now, in the spring of 1975, with the help of regular troops from the People's Army of Vietnam, called the NVA by most Americans, the Viet Cong, now loftily called the Provisional Revolutionary Government of Vietnam, or PRG, had come to stay. They had brought their tanks and their supply trains and their heavy guns. They brought their promises of liberation and freedom and equality. They had brought their lists and their purges and their execution squads.

From his perch high on the slope overlooking the road that led generally southeast toward Tay Ninh, Tony Butler could see large groups of trucks headed that way, but from this distance, even

83

with the superb East German field glasses he had taken from a dead NVA artillery spotter, he couldn't tell which army was operating the trucks. They were American built, but so many had been captured by the enemy that there was no longer any point in even trying to guess who drove them now.

Concealed behind him in the brush lay fourteen members detached from the tribe of irregular fighters he had trained and led these past few years, and next to him lay another. The tribe was smaller now, less than 20 percent of the original six hundred he had begun with in 1968. But the survivors were tougher and smarter than they had once been, and the casualty rate had dropped from the statistical certainty of the earlier times to the present level of simple bad luck.

The fifteen had volunteered to accompany Butler—"But-lah" as they called him in their singsong dialect—to a rendezvous with members of the American special operations organization. When it became obvious that there was no hope of the South winning or even coming to a political settlement, the unit had taken a vote on whether to try to escape the country or stay. The vote had gone nearly unanimously in favor of staying.

The tribesmen, like most who lived in the highlands, were not ethnically Vietnamese. They had no particular loyalty to the regime in Saigon, nor was there a feeling of true kinship with the people who were about to be conquered by Hanoi. The unit had begun as mercenaries decades before, fighting for whichever army paid them, but almost always against the Communists. After the French had gone, the Americans recruited them, and they had fought just as loyally and just as fiercely as any force in the war.

But this time, when the Americans had gone, they had not taken up the fight under a new set of colors. They had continued to make life miserable for their enemies and fought against the NVA and the Viet Cong so well that they had been marked for extinction when they could ultimately be hunted down. There was no desertion or treason among these hill tribesmen. It would be a fight to the death and they all knew it, accepted it, and went on.

But Butler was different. Despite long years of living with the tribesmen, he was still an American and had an opportunity to leave. He was on his way now to a rendezvous with men who offered to get him out. The message from Saigon had come for

Butler yesterday morning through a chain of messengers nearly as tangled as the vines of the jungle.

Dalton and Thompson had specified the location of the rendezvous, in case Butler decided to come out. They'd proceed with their extraction plans unless they heard definitely from him that he was staying.

When the message had arrived, Butler spent a few moments thinking about it. He remembered his life in the United States and his service in the Navy. He remembered the bad times and the loneliness and the never-ending feeling of being the kid who was always asked last to the party or the dance or the trip to the drive-in, if he was asked at all. He remembered the conversations with his acquaintances—never friends, really—when there would be a grinning reference to something he'd not been included in. He'd laugh, too, but the laugh would be as hollow as his relationships. But none of that had been his choice.

The Navy had given him friendship without the hollowness, accomplishment with applause, a place to be without threat of loss. It had been all he'd needed until he and the other SEALs had been assigned to this small tribe of people in the beautiful green hills of Vietnam.

Thinking about the message, Butler looked around the small encampment—an anthropologist from *National Geographic* or some such would have called it a village, but in Butler's mind, it was far too impermanent to be called that. He watched these simple people going about the business of living with neither knowledge of nor concern for all the myriad things that had driven the lives of his countrymen back home. Butler saw the two elders who had brought him the message and who now waited with what could only be called placid expectancy.

Butler looked at the two men, old friends now, and shook his head. "I do not know about this. I must think."

Many times over the last seven years he'd thought about what might be happening in the States, and whether he'd made the right decision by staying, and each time, he decided all over again that he had. Much had changed though in Vietnam, and he had his sons to consider.

The elders looked at each other for a second. "Yes. But we will discuss this tonight, all of us." They walked way, leaving Butler alone with himself.

Long after the day was done, Butler and the other men of the tribe gathered around a small fire under the trees in the center of the encampment. The talk was at first desultory, each man staring into the flames, avoiding the subject, waiting for someone to broach the topic. Finally, Butler spoke.

"I have thought about this message and I have decided that I should remain here. I made my choice seven years ago and I have no reason to change it now. Even with what is happening in the country."

The oldest member of the tribe stirred the fire with a stick and cleared his throat. "But-lah, we have thought about this message also, and we have decided that you must take the opportunity and leave. You have been and will remain one of us, but there is something better for you than that which faces us. You have done us honor by remaining with us once, and you do it again by wishing to remain now. But it would be best for you to leave this place."

Butler looked around at the group. For a second, he felt that he was once again being forced to leave a home. The pain was more intense than it had been in his youth. He had selected this home. But he drove that thought away when he realized that these men wished only the best for him and knew that if he remained, he would have a future like the present, running and hiding and waiting for the day that the enemy would finally eliminate them.

Butler looked at the fire. "You are my people now. What awaits me in America is not what I want. I have found it here among you."

The old man nodded. "Yes. We know that and it honors us, but the day is coming when we will be no more. Your sons are the only future we have left to us. You must take them to America. There they can grow and learn and be safe, and when we are gone, they will still live. As long as your sons live, our tribe will live. It is important. And it is simple."

Butler let out a long sigh. Even though he was the tribe's leader and military trainer and strategist, he was not an elder, and the decisions made by the elders had to be adhered to. He could not disobey.

He stood and arched his back, trying to work out a little of the stiffness that was becoming his lot in life. He turned to the elders and searched their eyes individually. He nodded. "If I am to go, we must make plans."

Butler quickly thought through a reply to Dalton and Thompson. He was coming out, and he'd get word to them when he arrived near the rendezvous. He asked the tribesman who'd start the verbal message on its journey to request special speed from the long chain of willing messengers.

The rest of the evening was spent deciding which of the fifty or so eager volunteers would accompany Butler on his journey. The small group had left their hidden camp before dawn this morning. They had brought along Butler's two sons—small boys who were products of his marriage to one of the tribe's daughters. She had been killed two years earlier by a mine laid on a trail as she went for water for their home.

The point where Butler was to meet the Americans was forty miles or so southeast of their present position, pretty much along the road that they were observing. They could not use the road, on which they could have made the trip in only two days even on foot. They would have to take a parallel route higher up through difficult terrain, mostly double- and triple-canopy jungle.

One thing in Butler's men's favor was that the enemy had pulled nearly all of their small insurgent groups out of their traditional areas of operation and formed them into large companies and battalions. Those who were familiar with the area through which Butler's men had to travel were gone to the south to be used in the drive on Saigon. Those who were in the area now were support troops from distant parts of the country and neither knew the area nor were concerned with it. Their job was to continue to move the men and equipment south and east to support the front-line troops. Tracking down Butler's group and the others would come later, after the final victory. And someone else would do it.

Butler slid backward from the edge of the slope into the brush. He waited until the man who had gone with him had come back also, then turned to the rest of the group.

One of the older men asked, "Can we cross the road?"

"Not by day. And I am not certain that it would be best to do so."

The others nodded as they thought it over. None of them were from this area and so they were traveling blind. Everything they did was going to be by feel. Trial and error would not work for them because an error would probably mean the end of them all.

Butler looked around at his men. "If we continue along the road, we will eventually draw near to the place we must go. I think we should stay on this side of the road until we get closer. We at least know that the enemy is not behind us here, and we have somewhere to go if we run into them. On the other side of the road we would have to cross through them to reach safety."

The others nodded in agreement and stood. Without another word, they put themselves in their marching order and set off to the southeast, careful to begin with the proper spacing. In the center of the column were Butler and the two boys, who even at the ages of six and five were experienced jungle travelers, already hardened to the difficulties and trained in survival in hostile environments.

As they started off, Butler looked at the backs of the men with whom he had lived and worked for so long. His new resolve to meet his old comrades and get himself and his sons out to a life where they had a realistic chance to see the age of sixteen was not quite as firm as it had been the previous evening. He knew that this was the only intelligent thing for him to do, but intelligence and loyalty were not always compatible.

Lt. Mike Santy flattened himself against the bulkhead as several red-shirted sailors dashed past him and ran on down the passageway heading aft. He looked carefully to see if any more of the *Concord*'s Nucleus Fire Party were coming. Above his head, the 1MC, or shipboard PA system, blared again, "Fire, fire, fire. There is a fire in compartment two dash one fifty dash twenty lima. Supply storeroom. Away the Nucleus Fire Party."

He wondered what the supplies in compartment 2-150-20L were for as he turned for the ladder that led up to the O3 level and his squadron ready room. If they were lucky, it might be some brussels sprouts. If the fire was serious, Damage Control Central would call away more fire teams instead of the quick-response NFP. As he climbed the ladder, he remembered with a grimace the week of fire-fighting training he and every man, regardless of rank or job title, received before they went to sea in the Navy. After a couple of disastrous fires at sea aboard aircraft carriers, it was realized that many lives could have been saved had *everyone* been trained to fight fires at sea. On a ship that carried 3.5 million gallons of jet fuel, 3,300 tons of bombs, nearly 100 aircraft, and untold amounts of flammable supplies, fire could get out of hand quickly. Besides, Santy thought as he opened the ready room door, where the hell can you run to when the ship's on fire?

Santy was almost to the coffeepot in the corner when he heard his commanding officer's voice greeting him cheerfully. "Well, good morning, Mike. Come on over here. Have I got a deal for you."

Santy filled his cup and approached the CO's chair warily. Like everybody else in the squadron, and all over the ship for that matter, Santy thought the sun rose and set on Cdr. Nick Taylor, the new CO of VA-19, short for Light Attack Squadron Nineteen. The phrase "Have I got a deal for you" was sort of a way of saying, "You're about to get screwed, so bend over."

"Listen, Skipper, it's not fair that I should get all the good deals. You should spread them out to some of the younger guys. Give *them* a chance to excel. I'm perfectly happy staying mired in my mediocrity. Besides, I have to go get a haircut. That'll probably take me the rest of the week." Santy plopped down in the high-backed chair next to Taylor.

The CO leaned back and assumed an air of imperial dignity. "Yes, We've thought about all that. Even though We don't believe in showing favorites, We're going to give you this one last chance to impress Us before you transfer out."

Santy sighed. "All right. What is it this time?"

"You are going to be the Air Wing Thirty-three representative to the CINCPAC team which is coming aboard."

"What is this team supposed to be coming here for, if I may be so bold?"

"You'll find that out when they get here and brief us."

"When are they coming?"

Taylor looked up at the PLAT television system, which showed every landing and takeoff from the ship. On the screen was an F-4 coming in for an approach, and to the left of the Phantom, Taylor could see a Huey orbiting out in Starboard Delta, the helicopter holding area. "I'd say in about fifteen minutes. They're in that Huey out there. The early group, that is. I imagine the heavies will be here in time for lunch."

Santy groaned. "Come on, Skipper. Why me?"

Taylor looked at Santy in all seriousness. "First of all, you're available—you've only got three months max left around here and your relief is already on board. But even if you weren't, Mike, I'd have to make you available. The other reason, the real no-shit reason, is that you're the best I have. I know that you'll do the job right and that we can rely on you to make a smart decision without consulting us if you have to."

"Yes, sir. But who's 'we'?"

"CAG, the captain, and me."

When you got told that you were considered the best choice for something, by your entire chain of command, it was hard to find an argument "Hell, Skipper. You don't even leave me any room for whining about it."

"I know. Now, get your tail up to flight deck control so you can meet your new coworkers. You'll have permissive travel orders so you can go where you need to. Pick 'em up from the SDO when you're ready to leave."

Santy stood. "Does that mean I get to go ashore, like maybe into Saigon?"

"Yeah, if you have to. But don't be too eager to go in there, Mike. I hear the liberty is getting a little dangerous, and you're too short to take any chances. Just let me know what you're doing."

"Okay, sir. See ya later."

Taylor watched the young man leave the room and smiled after him. He opened the folder on his lap and reread the orders he'd just signed for Santy. He got up, favoring the leg that had almost ended his career, and dropped the orders on the duty officer's desk, asking him to make sure that they remained handy to give to Santy when he had to leave the ship.

With a grimace of distaste, he looked at the endless pile of paperwork sitting in his box in the rear of the room and decided that it could wait. He headed for Maintenance Control to see how the squadron's aircraft were holding up.

Tim Boyle climbed out of the copilot's, or left, seat of the UH-1H Huey helicopter as Wheeler rolled the throttle to idle. From the compartment behind the pilots, Hickerson stepped down followed by Lt. Joe France and his boss, Cdr. George Bailey. Boyle reached back into the cockpit and made sure that the lap belt and shoulder harness were securely fastened over the seat so that they wouldn't fly around and interfere with Wheeler's controls on his trip back to Tan Son Nhut, waved good-bye, and closed and locked the door. He looked in the back for his bag but saw that Hickerson had already taken it and was heading for the large hatch in the side of the island structure.

As Boyle walked clear of the rotor arc, he looked back at the gray Air America helo and smiled. It had been a real pleasure to fly it this morning, even if only as a copilot and only during the cruise part of the forty-five-minute flight. It had been better still to see the USS *Concord* again. The last time he'd been on this flight deck, he'd been in a stretcher getting loaded into an H-3 for his trip to the Danang hospital and home. In fact, he thought, it was from the same spot on which he'd just landed.

He watched as Wheeler rolled the throttle back on and set the engine rpm. The yellow-shirted landing signalman, or LSE, squatted and looked under the Huey making sure that no tie-downs were attached to the skids, then gave Wheeler the launch signal. The Huey moved crisply up to a five-foot hover and stabilized for a moment while the pilot checked his gauges. Then the nose dipped sharply and the Huey was gone.

Boyle turned to the hatch and followed Hickerson and the others down a ladder and into the maze of passageways and compartments that made up the interior of the giant warship.

The four visitors were led forward along one of the main passageways, "I-95 Starboard," until they came to the "flag" spaces where the admiral commanding the task group and his staff lurked when they were aboard. Boyle always thought of staffs "lurking" rather than living aboard ship. It was one of those small personal things that aviators do even when they are on a staff. It makes them feel that they are not really part of the problem.

The *Concord*'s operations officer handed each a key to a stateroom and told them that the first meeting would be in forty minutes down in CVIC, the carrier's intelligence center, and that they could use the time to get settled in and changed. He left no doubt that *change* meant into a proper uniform.

Boyle found his room a little farther forward, close to his old ready room, but resisted the temptation to change quickly and go there to see who occupied it now. He shoved his key in the lock, entered, and flicked on the light, almost unconsciously taking in the sparse soullessness of the room. It was painted in the standard ugly light and dark green like every other room he'd ever seen on the ship. The green linoleum floor was equally ugly with large splashes of dried floor wax in the corners. It was obvious that whatever sailors had last cleaned, or "field dayed," the room had not had their hearts in it.

He threw his bag down on the lower bunk and sat next to it. As he took in the entire room, with its little white sink and its well-used furniture and the marks on the walls where some previous occupant had taped a poster or two, he smiled. It almost felt like home.

★ **11** ★

Tuesday, 8 April 1975

BOYLE WAS ADJUSTING HIS "GIG LINE," MAKING SURE THAT THE LINE OF his uniform shirt buttons was perfectly aligned with his belt buckle and the fly of his pants. As he always did, he smiled, remembering the Marine drill instructor back in Pensacola who'd once made Mike Santy do push-ups for fifteen minutes when he said the word *pants*.

The gunny had screamed something about "only girls wear pants. In the Navy men wear trousers." Unfortunately for Boyle, he'd snickered when Santy was ordered to "assume the position," and he had been overheard by the gunny. In the blink of an eye, he was down next to Santy matching him push-up for push-up. A quarter of an hour later, arms feeling like lead weights, Santy and Boyle had vowed never to let the word *trousers* cross their lips again. It wasn't much of a rebellion, but it at least was something.

He looked at his watch and saw that it had been nearly an hour since he'd arrived aboard. It annoyed him a little that he hadn't been able to call Santy or even let him know he was here. When he'd arrived in the room, he'd sort of mentally drifted off, thinking about how glad he was to be back aboard a carrier and wishing he'd never left. By the time he had come back to the present, he had lost nearly half an hour and so had to rush through his unpacking and digging out his uniform. He hoped the briefing wouldn't take too long so he could go find Mike.

Boyle looked himself over one more time and left the room, headed for the carrier's secure briefing area in the intelligence center. He entered the I-95 Port passageway and walked forward, carefully stepping over the kneeknockers and dodging around sailors headed in the other direction. He turned into the tiny passageway that led into CVIC, noticing that the deck still had the yellow linoleum tiles centered in the blue. The passageway had been called the Yellow Brick Road long before Boyle had ever come aboard the ship and probably would be until the day she was decommissioned.

He knocked on the door and waited for somebody inside to electrically unlock it. He heard the buzz and click of the lock, opened the door, and waved to the sailor standing by the desk. The sailor didn't challenge him, so whatever was going on in the briefing area must not have been too secret.

Boyle walked into the interior room and looked around for a seat. He found one in the last row, but before he could sit down, Commander Hickerson called him to the front row where he could no longer be anonymous.

"No hiding in the back, Tim. We're going to be introduced to the assembled throng."

Boyle nodded and looked around the room for familiar faces other than the ones from the CINCPAC team. He didn't recognize anyone from the ship, staff, or air wing, but that was not surprising. He'd been away over two years and in that time probably 80 percent of the men aboard the ship had been replaced in the normal routine of transfer.

He was looking at the familiar walls and the posters and charts that hung there. Many of them were the same as they had been two and a half years before as he'd been briefed for his last mission. It gave him a chill when he remembered all that had happened because of that flight. But that was followed almost immediately by a sense of completeness, as if by coming back to this room he'd closed a circle. He was wondering about that when he felt himself shoved roughly to one side in his chair. The shove was followed by a familiar voice.

"Move over, asshole. Let a real pilot sit down." Santy was, as usual, grinning.

"Hi, Mike. Didn't they tell you that you seagoing lowlifes are supposed to sit in the back of the bus?"

Santy chuckled. "Yeah, well, I'm now attached to you staff pogues so I get to sit here in the stratosphere. I must admit that you guys smell better than we do, which is probably because you haven't been showering with JP-5.''

"You mean they still haven't fixed that leak?"

"Hell, no. But they figure that if they tell us often enough that there's no jet fuel in the fresh water, we'll believe it."

"So how did you get assigned to us?"

"It appears that I am the only officer aboard capable of dealing with you guys and making sure you don't steal the silverware. Actually, since I'm due to roll out of here, I'm getting to be an extra. So Skipper Taylor gave me the job."

Santy looked around conspiratorially and asked, "So when do we get our secret decoder rings and cyanide pills?"

"What?"

"Yeah. This is a secret mission, right? You know, cloaks and daggers and mysterious women in smoky bars."

Boyle chuckled. "C'mon, Mike. The last guy in the world I'd play Terry and the Pirates with is you. It would take you about half an hour to start World War Two all over again. This is just a simple planning team. There ain't no spies here."

As Boyle spoke, Admiral Wallace entered the room and at someone's "Attention on deck," everyone stood. Wallace called, "Carry on," and everyone sat again. Several staffers, including Joe France and his boss, Commander Bailey, arranged the easel and the rest of the briefing materials, most of which were stamped "Secret."

Santy took one of the copies and showed the stamp to Boyle. Looking smug, Santy leaned closer and whispered, "Okay, I told you this was gonna be a secret mission, but don't worry, Tim, I'll behave."

Boyle doubted it.

Much later that evening, Santy and Boyle were sitting in the dirty-shirt wardroom, munching popcorn and waiting for the movie to start. The movie was *The Wild Bunch,* sort of a cult favorite with the officers attached to the *Concord.* Every week it would be shown without sound so that the assembled officers in the wardroom could provide the dialogue and the sound effects. Years before, when Boyle had been aboard, he and Santy excelled at taking the part of the Mexican general. Boyle was eagerly looking forward to the carryings-on.

But what they were discussing was the assignments they'd received at the briefing earlier. They were to form part of a small briefing team that would go from ship to ship, making sure everyone was singing from the same songbook when the evacuation began. Santy had taken less than a minute to decide that Lt. Joe France was an asshole and was now wondering how come Boyle hadn't shoved him down a flight of stairs yet.

Boyle leaned back in his chair. "Well, mostly because Commander Hickerson has ordered me to watch my step around him. But the real reason is that if he fell down some stairs, everyone would know it was me who did it."

"He seemed pretty impressed with himself. I noticed that he was the only one who was wearing his ribbons."

"Yeah. He's one of the great jerks of Western civilization all right, but I've quit worrying about him so you should, too."

"I'm not worried about him. He's just a pain in the ass. What I'm worried about are all these helicopter rides we're going to have to take."

"Why? Helos are perfectly safe."

"The hell they are. They can't really fly—they just vibrate so bad that the earth rejects 'em. Besides, we're going to have to be hoisted up and down on some skinny little cable that hasn't been load-checked in God knows how long. The decks will probably be pitching and they'll smash us off a gun mount or something. The pilots will probably be myopic drunks and the ships' deck crews will all be rejects from the Army."

Boyle chuckled. This was Santy's way of dealing with something that was unknown and a little scary. Being hoisted on and off a small ship's deck because it was too small to land on was a completely routine operation that was done hundreds of times every day throughout the Navy. There were incredibly few incidents and it was considered far safer and more effective than the old method of highlining between ships.

Santy, like many fixed-wing-only pilots, didn't understand helicopters. They seemed an aerodynamic impossibility. There was even a widespread prejudice that helo pilots were second-rate, that if they were any good, they'd be flying jets. Thus, riding in the back of a machine they didn't understand, being flown by pilots whom they looked down upon, made many jet jocks nervous. This didn't always square with reality or the reputations of individual pilots such as Boyle, who was widely regarded as one of the best, but the inbred prejudice was difficult to overcome.

Boyle, for his part, absolutely hated riding in the back of helicopters. Flying in the back of fixed-wing was bad enough, but a ride in a helo was sheer torture for him. He needed to see the gauges, to have his hands near the controls, to be able in some way to affect his fate. But, the last thing he needed to do right now was to tell Mike that. It might be fun to watch him sweat, but he was too good a friend.

"Don't worry, Mike. They've got good helicopters and the pilots are all pros. You don't think I'd let you go with somebody second-rate, do you?"

Santy shook his head. "No, I guess not. But I wish it were you doing the flying." He sighed. "You want some more popcorn? I'd better get it before the line gets too long."

"Yeah, thanks." Boyle handed Santy his small paper bag and lit up a cigarette. He looked around the wardroom and at the gathering crowd. His mind wandered to the task ahead of the CINCPAC team. A daunting number of ships were gathering from all over the Pacific. Amphibious ships, destroyers, and auxiliaries of every type and class were coming to take station offshore from South Vietnam, just over the horizon from the coast. The next few days were going to be very interesting, he thought.

★ PART 2 ★

The Enemy Advances

✵ PART 2 ✵

The Enemy Advances

★ **12** ★

Friday, 18 April 1975

THE SOLDIERS ARRAYED THEMSELVES ONCE AGAIN IN THEIR SQUADS AND platoons alongside the road. It struck a few of them as ironic that they had been driven to the places for rest and refit, but now that they were headed back into action they would walk the long miles to wherever they would be employed. Most simply accepted it and waited for the trucks.

The past weeks had been good for the soldiers. They had regained the strength that had been so severely depleted during the long months of marching down from the North and of fighting for the larger towns in the highlands of the South. They had been fed well, but at first the richness of the captured American rations, after the near starvation of much of the past months, had caused some of their systems to rebel for a little while. But they soon got used to it and they began to put back a little of the weight they'd lost.

They had also taken advantage of the time to heal. Many had brought wounds and illness with them to the rest areas, where they had finally been properly treated by the doctors. Even the doctors from the South, now working as virtual slaves, had worked diligently to make them all well again. No one had had the courage to say it aloud, but the doctors from the South seemed more capable and more effective than those of the Northern army. None of the political cadre appeared to have noticed that many of the soldiers often arranged things so that when they reported for treatment, it was with one of the Southern doctors.

There had been entertainment for them also. Several troupes of actors had visited them and put on the plays that had so often

101

delighted the soldiers before. The plays were about the revolution of course and the hard road ahead before the country could be reunited. The soldiers stayed most attentive during these performances, and no one seemed to feel that they paid any undue attention to the female actors. In an egalitarian army such as theirs, that would have been unseemly and the subject of a long and embarrassing self-criticism session.

But now, standing by the road and preparing to march back into battle, the soldiers put all that behind them. There were enemies to be killed and towns and villages to subdue. There was a war to be won.

Soon, the sergeants and the junior officers began to lead them in their thousands down the road to the southeast toward a place called Xuan Loc and beyond that Saigon, the capital of the enemy.

★ **13** ★

Friday, 18 April 1975

C<small>DR</small>. D<small>ON</small> H<small>ICKERSON</small> <small>WAS STANDING IN THE CATWALK OUTSIDE THE</small> ATO shack leaning his forearms on the rail and watching the plane-guard helicopter fly its seemingly endless racetrack pattern off the starboard side of the carrier, always ready to launch a rescue effort in case an accident happened on launch or recovery or with one of the helos. The big H-3 would fly up alongside and turn outbound just short of the bow. About a mile out, it would turn right again and fly back toward the stern, turning inbound even with the fantail and finally turning once more to parallel the ship's course close aboard. Hickerson idly tried to figure out how many miles he must have flown out there in plane guard during his career and could only estimate that it must be well over a hundred thousand miles at seventy knots and between one hundred fifty and three hundred feet from the water, day and night. Virtually every mile of that had been boring as hell, too.

Hickerson glanced up and watched a flight of four A-7 Corsairs fly high over the carrier as they entered the landing pattern. The carrier would land its fixed-wing aircraft first so that later, when the Air America Hueys came out to pick up him and the rest of the team, the helos could easily be brought aboard.

Hickerson let his eyes drop back to the sea below as he thought about the events of the past ten days or so. They had been more tiring and difficult for Hickerson than any of his days at CINCPAC. He and the team had gone from ship to ship and carrier to carrier briefing the ships' companies and sometimes the air wing officers on the best guess for an effective plan that everybody concerned had been able to come up with. Surprisingly, there had been little

103

of the meddling that people like to do by inserting their own little changes that make them feel as if they'd been one of the queen bees rather than merely one of the workers. Everyone had accepted his role in it and only asked questions about the details.

The team had split up into smaller groups to brief the smaller ships like the destroyers and the amphibs. The admiral had been smart enough to make sure that that pompous ass Lieutenant France and his boss, Commander Bailey, did not go out on the smaller briefing missions. Nothing had been said, at least in Hickerson's presence, but it seemed that the two were being kept close by so that they wouldn't screw things up. Hickerson had to admire the admiral's style. Neither France nor Bailey suspected that the admiral didn't have full confidence in them. He made it appear that their contributions were much more important close at hand. The two almost strutted around in Admiral Wallace's wake, sitting in on the higher level meetings and briefings, sort of glorying in their seats along the walls of the throne room. All the while, Hickerson, Boyle, and the others had been out doing the work.

When Hickerson thought of Boyle, he smiled almost reflexively. Boyle and his buddy, Mike Santy, had proved so adept at the briefings and solving problems on the fly that the admiral and Hickerson had sent them out together for the past six days to various of the smaller combatants. They had done a superb job, and the staff had received almost universal compliments on their performance. The thing that Hickerson was most proud of was that Admiral Wallace had made the two his personal fire brigade, dispatching them to trouble spots throughout the armada of ships assembling off the coast of South Vietnam.

They'd even been ferried to the ships carrying the Marine Corps helos that had completed the textbook evacuation of Phnom Penh, Cambodia, two days before, so that they could get as many as possible of the lessons learned while they were still fresh. They had gotten back to the *Concord* late yesterday afternoon, and had a complete and surprisingly insightful report ready for the admiral within a half hour of their return. The admiral had been so impressed that he simply put an endorsement on the report and had it passed up the chain of command.

The only cloud on this was that Boyle and Santy had made themselves indispensable to the CINCPAC team and the admiral had decided that they would now be full-fledged members of the team ashore. Hickerson had quietly planned from the outset that Boyle would be one of the men safely positioned out on the ships. He was a bit hesitant to admit it to himself, but Hickerson strongly suspected that he was being too overprotective of Tim by treating him a lot like a little brother and not the extremely capable naval officer that he truly was.

Originally, Hickerson had brought him along to get him away from a job that was steadily eroding his professional enthusiasm and to get him a little face time with Admiral Wallace, but his performance had been so good that Boyle had become a key player in the effort.

Hickerson wasn't sure how he really felt about that. There was some pride that one of his young lions from his old Combat Search and Rescue detachment was doing so well. There was a bit of worry for him for the same reason—one of the young lions was standing into danger because of a decision that Hickerson had made.

He was also aware that there might be just a touch of envy in there also. Boyle was in the springtime of his naval career while Hickerson was now fast approaching the autumn of his. Hickerson, the naval aviator and naval officer, had been almost entirely molded and shaped by service in the Vietnam War. He was a warrior and knew that another of the historic times for warriors was passing now and quickly. Soon the administrators and the bean counters and the clerks would once again reaffirm their culture and take over the Navy as they always did as soon as the shooting stopped from the latest war. The clerks, like Bailey and his fair-haired boy, France, would bring their sheaves of paper and their studies and their colorless stolidity back to the bland and uniform offices of the command structure. The warriors, like Hickerson, would soon lose their place and be again relegated to the fine print in the history books. They would be sent far away from the halls of power and influence. They would be patronized and their counsel carefully ignored.

Boyle, on the other hand, was young enough to have a place in the return of the new Navy. He was a combat-experienced officer, but he had not yet gotten himself locked onto any one of the unchangeable paths of his future. He still had his options and it would be up to him how far those paths would take him. He would not be pigeonholed for a few years yet, and if he stayed in the Navy and kept his nose clean and picked his fights, he could go very far indeed.

But if he kept kicking over the shit can when he was convinced he was right and either the system or the members of it were wrong, he would wind up retiring long before his talents and usefulness were exhausted.

Hickerson sighed and turned for the short ladder that led to the ATO shack. He knew that if he could spend the rest of his career being nothing more than a pilot aboard a carrier and avoiding the carpeted offices of shore duty, he would gladly stay in the Navy until he was a hundred and six.

Tim Boyle reached into the small closet in his stateroom and pulled out a set of civilian clothes. Now that he and the rest of the team were about to head back to Saigon, he could no longer wear his uniform. The Air America helos were due to pick up their passengers, or "fax" as they were called in Navy jargon, in less than an hour, and he was supposed to rendezvous with the others in the air transport officer's shack fifteen minutes before that. On the top of the room's ceiling, which was the flight deck, the first of the jets landing from the last cycle slammed down and ran out the arresting wire. The sound of the engines directly overhead blocked out all sound until the jet stopped and the pilot pulled the throttles back to idle.

Boyle pulled the plastic off the shirt and pants he'd worn aboard and looked carefully at them, inspecting them for damage done by the ship's laundry. All the buttons and things seemed to be present, so he stripped off his uniform and began to dress. The clothes smelled a little like jet fuel, which brought back memories.

The *Concord,* like most other conventionally fueled carriers, always seemed to have fuel mixed in with the fresh water. The captains of the ships and their fuels officers always swore that it was impossible for this to happen, but everything always smelled like a gas station.

The ships' laundries were manned largely by young, low-ranking sailors borrowed, or TAD, from the squadrons and never really seemed to have their hearts in their work, which wasn't surprising since they had to work in a hot, smelly place below the waterline and were separated for ninety long days from not only their friends but also the jobs they had joined the Navy to perform.

Mike Santy had been telling Boyle that the *Concord* was now equipped with the latest computer-controlled laundry technology. The sailors down there now could select the precise spot on the seat of a pair of pants that they wanted the buttons automatically ripped from the shirts to be shot through. Santy swore that the new zipper destroyer had revolutionized the system and that the label mixer now ensured that no one would get back the same clothes he had sent down.

Boyle was tucking in his shirt when the phone rang. In the past ten days that had usually meant that he was being summoned to another long, boring, and redundant planning session. He briefly debated whether to ignore it but reached over and picked it up.

"Lieutenant Boyle."

"Hi, Tim. You about ready to go?" It was Mike Santy.

"Just about. I'm finishing packing now."

"I'll be right there." Santy hung up and Boyle cursed. Mike had the laughter back in his voice as he always did at the prospect of a new challenge. Boyle tried to talk him out of going, but Santy refused to stay behind because, he said, he was now part of the CINCPAC team and major events would be going on and he wasn't going to miss them if he had a chance. He also figured that he and Tim could have some fun if they ever got any time off.

No matter what objections Boyle raised, Santy waved them away. He had the bit between his teeth and would not be persuaded. What was bothering Boyle was that even though he himself was on this trip essentially by choice, he didn't want Santy to have to share the risks. He wasn't sure if his reluctance was because of fear for his friend or something else. Mike was perfectly capable of taking care of himself—he'd proved that often enough—but Boyle didn't want to have to worry about Mike in addition to himself. Maybe that was it, he thought, maybe I just don't want to feel responsible if something bad happens.

Mike had been able to point out sound military reasons to justify his presence on the team. In fact, Admiral Wallace had been glad to have him stay on the team a while longer, which effectively overrode Boyle's objections. What Tim finally realized was that Santy had decided that he ought to be with his best friend and that was going to be that, and it truly pissed Boyle off because he definitely did not want to be the reason Mike was going. It was probably pretty dumb, Boyle thought, that it was somehow all right for him to be running around the mess that was Saigon but it was not all right for Mike to be there.

Thinking over the situation, Boyle finished packing with a lot more vehemence than the job required.

Less than three minutes later, he opened the door at Santy's knock and went back to tying his shoes. Santy dropped his bag on the floor and himself into a chair next to one of the desks.

Boyle looked up. Santy had on a pair of jeans and a polo shirt.

"Well, you look like every other American walking around Saigon these days. You'll blend right into the scenery."

"I considered wearing a white suit with a Panama hat and a cigar, but I thought that the Sidney Greenstreet look might be conspicuous. You know how the honeys always go for that here in the mysterious East. How can you be a successful spy when you have a dozen girls hanging on your gun arm?"

Another jet slammed down on the deck above, and Boyle waited until the sound had died down. "We're not spies. I keep telling you that. And you shouldn't be doing this."

Santy sat forward on his chair and looked hard at his friend. "Yes I should and I don't want any more shit from you, okay? It's my choice and you don't have a say, so please shut the fuck up about it, goddamnit." He knew well that if their positions had been reversed, Boyle would be doing the same thing.

Boyle shook his head disgustedly. "You're a dumbass, Mike, you really are. And you're never going to make it as a spy."

"Look, dammit. If I want to be a spy, I'll be a spy. We have to wear civvies and be careful who we talk to, right? We have to go to secret meetings and talk about operations and cases, right? I'll never get another chance to do this stuff, so just leave it alone, okay?"

In spite of himself, Boyle laughed. "All right, Smilin' Jack. Just remember to eat everything you read and always sit in a dark corner."

Boyle reached into the small safe, took out his Browning 9mm and two spare magazines, and put them into his bag.

Santy watched him carefully place it between layers of clothes. "Hey, Tim, I was just kidding. Are we really supposed to have one of them with us?"

"No, I just carry it around to make a bulge in my pants. Look, it's like I've been trying to tell you. Most everybody in there has a pistol somewhere on him. It's not like there's all sorts of gun battles going on in the streets, but you never know."

Santy looked worried. "I don't have one. Maybe I can check a .45 out from the squadron."

"No. You don't want to rely on those shitty Navy-issue pistols which were made back in World War One. We'll get a pistol from the Air America guys. If there's anything that there is a lot of in Saigon, it's loose weaponry."

Another jet landed. Boyle used the interval to zip up his bag and sit down on the bed. He pulled out a cigarette and lit up. Santy shook his head. "When are you going to quit those things?"

"You and Meg. I wish you two would get off my back about smoking. Hell, even Maureen gives me shit about it. She's going to be your wife so I suggested that she bust your balls and not mine. She said that she was using me for practice. So stand by, pal. You're getting a world-class nagger."

Santy laughed. "Meg never nagged you."

"Mike, old friend, it's against the Woman's Code to nag before the wedding, but just about the time you roll over from consummating the union, it starts."

Santy looked at Boyle in alarm. Boyle shook his head. "I'm kidding, Mike. Meg only nags me about stuff she should."

Santy pretended to relax. All the guys in his squadron had been busting his chops with dire warnings about connubial bliss, and a part of him was worried about it. He was entering the last phase of his bachelorhood wherein marriage begins to be a little bit scary. He sighed and stood.

"Come on. Let's go. I've got to check out with the SDO."

Boyle threw the strap of his bag over his shoulder. "Okay. I've got to stop by and drop off my key to the room."

Cdr. Nick Taylor dropped his helmet and the bag that contained all his charts and checklists on the ready room chair. He pinched his nostrils shut and blew, releasing the pressure in his ears from the flight and breathing 100 percent oxygen for the past 110 minutes, wiggling his jaw getting the last little bits of pressure out. He was unfastening the chest strap on his torso harness when Boyle and Santy walked in.

Santy grinned as he walked past. "Hi, Skipper. Bye, Skipper."

"Hold it."

Santy stopped and turned. "Aye, aye, sir. I'm holding as ordered."

"When are you leaving?"

"The helos will be here in about a half hour. We have to muster with the ATO in about fifteen minutes."

"All right. Get your orders signed and come back over here." Taylor looked at Boyle. "You, too. I have some words of wisdom for you."

Taylor pulled off the rest of his flight gear and dropped it in the chair. When Santy came back over, Taylor motioned both young pilots into seats in the front row and pulled around the large ammo box the squadron used as a burn bag and sat on it facing Boyle and Santy. He pulled out a Marlboro and lit it.

Boyle looked over at Santy. "Don't you want to tell him he ought to quit?"

Santy elbowed Boyle hard in the upper arm. Taylor looked at the two and chuckled. It was good to have a best friend like these two did, but Taylor's old squadron mates and buddies were scattered all over the Navy and throughout the world. When one is the commanding officer of a squadron, it is sometimes a lonely thing in that there is little closeness with one's peers since, at that level, everyone has far greater responsibility and far less idle time than he did when he was young like Mike and his friend here. Taylor envied them just a little.

He sighed. "Okay, knock it off. Now, you guys are not going on a sight-seeing trip here. Tim, you've been out here for the last several days so it won't be the same as it was when you first arrived in Saigon. What I'm trying to say is, watch your asses. Things are getting pretty crazy in there lately. Stay out of crowds and don't go exploring. Stay away from the bars and stick around where the embassy guys are."

Taylor paused and scratched his head. Boyle started to speak, to ask that Taylor keep Mike here on the ship, but held back. The decision had been made, and asking Taylor to override it would be wrong. While Boyle was making up his mind, Taylor spoke again in dead earnest.

"Look, Mike, you're only assigned to these guys temporarily and you really belong to us, so if things start to fall apart too fast, I'm giving you an order to consider your temporary duty revoked and to get your ass on an airplane headed out. I don't really give a shit where it's going to as long as it's away. If it's Singapore or Bangkok or the Philippines or Bumfuck, Egypt, I don't care, just get the hell out of there and we'll figure out how to get you back here later."

Taylor turned to Boyle. "Tim, I have no authority to give you any orders, but I'd like to ask that you do the same thing. There are a bunch of people who are going to have to stay till the bitter end, but you aren't on that list. I can order Mike to go, but I suspect he'll probably stay around as long as you do. I would appreciate it if you decided to beat feet someplace early and took this clown with you. Don't wait too long because when the last plane or helo is gone, there won't be another for years. If you miss it, you're screwed because there will be no mechanism to help you. Nobody in the U.S. government is going to put anything on the line for you, and there won't be anything the Navy can do either. Do you understand me?"

Both Boyle and Santy nodded and said, "Yes, sir," almost in unison.

Taylor stood. "Good luck to you both. Don't do anything dumb." He picked up his flight gear and left the room, leaving both young men sitting in the seats staring at the wall.

Santy finally spoke. "That certainly throws some more cold water on this trip."

"Yeah, but he's right. In case I haven't made myself clear lately, that's a mighty bad place, Mike, and I've got to admit it scares me some."

Santy looked over at his friend. "To be honest, me, too, Tim. Here's the deal. If either one of us decides that it's time to go, we both go. No arguments. Okay?"

Boyle nodded. "Okay, it's a deal." He got up, grabbed his bag, and headed for the door. Santy folded his orders, shoved them in his bag, and followed. He didn't pause to take a last long look around the ready room. In truth, it never occurred to him.

★ **14** ★

Friday, 18 April 1975

LT. CDR. KEVIN THOMPSON SLID THE RECONNAISSANCE PHOTOGRAPHS TO Dalton, looking carefully at only a few of them. Most of the other people at the conference table showed nothing more than the most cursory interest in them. There was little point in studying them because they were the same as yesterday's, only worse. South Vietnam, the part controlled by the government anyway, was now about half the size of Connecticut and shrinking fast.

The photographs that Thompson and Dalton looked at carefully were the ones showing the area west and northwest of Saigon. Except for large divisional troop concentrations drawing closer to the South Vietnamese stronghold around Xuan Loc, there seemed to be only smaller company- or battalion-size formations in the area. Both men were hoping that Tony Butler and his small group were still undetected in their march into the area, but no word had come from him since the message that he wanted to come out and that he would let them know when he had arrived in the vicinity of the pickup point.

Thompson and Dalton had been like caged bears since the reply to their offer had come. With the major parts of their routine work finished, they had had far too much time left. The strain of waiting for word from Butler was wearing on them, and for the first time in years they had argued. It was about something absolutely trivial, the proper format for a funding report, but it had surprised both of them. Now that the strain on both men was out in the open, the two SEALs simply acknowledged it and pressed on, but were careful to think before they spoke.

The awareness did nothing, however, to make the waiting any easier.

Major General Alexander and his deputy, Brigadier General Toone, entered the room from the small door that led to their offices. Alexander was carrying a single folder and Toone carried a disgusted expression. With no preamble, Alexander got right to it.

"You've all had a chance to see the latest recon photos and the intelligence summaries. I just got off the horn with the embassy, and they're sending over the latest cables between the secretary of state and the embassy here. They should be here in a couple of minutes. In the meanwhile, is there anything new since yesterday that I should know about? I'd prefer good news like somebody telling me that the NVA has decided to forget the whole thing and go home, but even if it ain't that good, let's hear it."

Toone cleared his throat. "I've got the final assessment from the evacuation of Phnom Penh. The Marine helos went in, picked everybody up, and got the hell out. They took no fire and had no problems. According to the report, it was a 'milk run.' Unfortunately, the wrong people are looking at that and saying that it will be the same here when we have to go."

Alexander sat back in his seat. "The last report I had says that the embassy figures we have at least ninety days before an evacuation will be required. Does anyone here agree with that?"

He took in the expressions of surprise and disgust on the faces in the room. "I didn't think so. I'm beginning to get the feeling that most of them don't believe it either. Personally, I doubt if we have *nine* days. I told them that, but what the hell, I'm only a soldier and not a diplomat so I obviously always look at the dark side."

He leaned forward and addressed the senior Air Force member of the staff. "Harry, how are we doing?"

"Fine, sir, all things considered. We've been sending full planes out but many of them are carrying only Vietnamese. There have been some press reports that we're flying out loads of hookers and B-girls, but it's not true. Certainly some of them are getting on the planes, but we're not conducting the 'whore-lift' we've been accused of. Mostly, the passengers are low-level employees or government officials. We're also getting out dependents of American personnel. They should be completely gone in the next day or so, we hope."

Alexander asked, "Okay, what about the big airlift that's the main plan? Can you do it?"

There had been in place for quite a while a plan that had four options. The easiest was a controlled exodus by large military and civilian chartered aircraft. The next two options concerned a mixture of a sealift from the Cap St. Jacques Peninsula and an airlift from Tan Son Nhut airport. The last option, Option 4, was an evacuation by helicopter that had been added almost as an afterthought. When the plans had originally been made, a rapid collapse of the South had not seriously been considered.

"In our view, the plan as stated is not going to work. If the NVA get close enough, they can shell the Tan Son Nhut airfield and runways, which will preclude heavy aircraft from operating there. Unless the ARVNs suddenly decide to hold out, the NVA will probably take Vung Tau and Cap St. Jacques. If either or both of those things happen, we're in trouble. To be honest, General, I'm certain that we'll wind up going with an evacuation by helicopter and not the orderly multi-plane operation everybody's figuring on."

Alexander nodded, but before he could speak the door behind him opened and a gray-haired sergeant came in and handed him a folder. The general opened it and scanned the first few pages, his expression clouding as he read. He closed the folder and handed it to Toone, leaning back in his chair and letting out a long sigh.

"Gents, those are the cables between the State Department and the embassy. Some people at State are talking about evacuating two hundred thousand people. Can you believe it? Two hundred fucking thousand people! The goddamn embassy is telling State to hold on because if they give the order to start the evacuation, it will cause panic in South Vietnam. Jesus Christ! Panic, he says! What do you call a million refugees?" Alexander's voice rose as he spoke and his face began to turn a deep red.

Toone placed his hand on Alexander's forearm and spoke up. "We all know that we'll never get that many out. Judging from these cables from Washington, they know it, too, at least a few of them do. Washington is going to set up a multi-agency system to handle the evacuees. Isn't that nice. None of that is going to be worth a shit because the whole thing is predicated on their ninety days. I strongly suggest, gentlemen, that anyone who works for

114

you who is not absolutely critical to your efforts be shipped out of here immediately."

One of the other Army officers, a major, spoke up. "I agree, sir. I'll have my people heading out by tomorrow. But I have another problem. We still have tons of ammunition and other supplies coming in for the ARVNs. What do we do with it all?"

"Can you get it out where it's needed?"

"Not anywhere near the quantities needed and not quickly enough."

Toone thought a moment. "Okay. Put it all close to where the ARVN trucks can get at it, call their headquarters, and tell them where it is. If they want it, they can come get it—that's their problem. I don't want any of our people out making deliveries."

"Yes, sir. That makes a bunch more people I can send out now. We have been running the 'black flights,' getting out a lot of the intelligence operatives who will be most at risk from the NVA. We haven't been telling the government about them and so far they haven't caught on. So we're still looking good there."

Alexander grunted and spoke again to the whole group. "Okay. Admiral Wallace and the rest of the CINCPAC team will be coming back in shortly. As you know, they've been out getting everybody offshore on the same page in case we had to go with Option Four. When they left, it was more possible than probable that we'd have to use a helo evac. Now, we're all agreed that it's more probable than possible. We'll reconvene in here in an hour to discuss what Wallace and his team have for us. In the meantime, let's go around the table and get all the particulars out."

Thompson listened as the meeting got down to details. He was thinking about one of the truly veteran newsmen, a friend, he'd talked to yesterday evening. The man had been half-loaded at the Caravelle Bar and had told Thompson that he was leaving this morning because he was totally sick of the whole mess. Ever since a C-5A attempting to fly a load of orphans, mostly under ten years old, and some nonessential American-embassy personnel, had crashed on takeoff two weeks earlier, the newsman had spent most of his time in the bar. He had gone out to the wreckage and had seen the bodies, some seemingly small enough to fit in his coat pocket, loaded five and ten to a litter as the rescue personnel worked. He had turned and walked away and, much later, found his way to his office.

That night, and for most nights since, he had taken a seat at the bar and stayed until it closed. To Thompson, it seemed that the very life had gone out of the man, who normally was one of the most boisterous and fun people left in the city.

Yesterday, he had told Thompson of the many men from both the embassy and the intelligence units who had come by his office, some in tears, begging him to get the word back to America about what was happening in Vietnam. They were all frustrated by the complete blindness and sheer stupidity of higher officials in either recognizing the crisis or in taking some sort of action. The bottom line, said the newsman, was that the higher civilian officials weren't particularly blind or stupid, at least not any more than the average government employee. It was just that, for some unfathomable reason, they were simply *refusing* to accept that the end was at hand. The newsman said that attitude was going to cost lives and he wanted no further part in this disaster, so he was about to be gone.

Thompson was shaken out of his thoughts by Alexander's voice. He looked up in surprise. "Yes, sir? Sorry."

Alexander smiled a little. "Commander, we're all a little distracted lately. I was saying that since we need to concentrate on Option Four, we're going to revisit the entire plan and check it all again. I'm assigning you to get with the Marines and Air America and find out how many landing zones we'll need and whether there are any other acceptable ones than the ones we already have."

"Yes, sir. How many people are we to plan for?"

Alexander looked down at the table for a second. "I don't think that we'll be limited by numbers, Commander. I think we're going to be limited by time."

Thompson and Dalton were sitting on the ramp outside the Air America building when the Hueys carrying the CINCPAC team arrived. They watched them shut down and most of the passengers walk toward their ground transportation. Admiral Wallace climbed into his vehicle, followed by several others. Most of the remainder got in a van that quickly followed Wallace's car, leaving two men standing around the helicopters talking to the pilots. Thompson and Dalton rose and walked over to the group.

Tim Boyle turned and smiled warmly. "Hi, Kevin, Mark. How are you doing?"

Thompson shrugged and nodded at the Air America pilots. "Just ducky. We need to talk to these guys when they're done."

"Okay. We were just leaving."

"No. Don't let me run you off. There's nothing secret about this."

Boyle smiled again. "Good. I'd rather stay around out here than sit in on the meeting they're having in there." He gestured toward the DAO building. "I'm so sick and tired of meetings and briefings that I'm going to lose it if I have to sit in on another one."

Thompson chuckled and looked at Santy. "Don't I know you?"

Santy stuck out a hand. "I believe you do. I'm Mike Santy. I was on *Concord* when you were the aide. Actually, I still am."

Thompson introduced Dalton and turned toward the Air America pilots, who were just finishing their postflight inspections. Just as he was about to speak, an almost gentle whooshing sound was followed by a loud explosion a hundred yards away. Before anyone could react, several more explosions happened slightly closer. Thompson yelled, "Rockets," and took off for the space between two large hangars.

Boyle and Santy stood frozen for an extra second or so, then sprinted after the SEALs and the two Air America pilots. Several more explosions erupted from the tarmac before they made it to the bunkers dug into the ground between the hangars. Santy and Boyle dove for the door and collided as they went through it.

Boyle picked himself up and moved to the rear of the small sandbagged bunker followed by Santy, who sat next to him cursing and holding his left knee.

"You all right?"

"Yeah. We have to work on our timing." Santy looked at the door as several more rockets hit the airfield. He looked for Thompson.

"What the fuck's going on?"

"Those were NVA 122-millimeter rockets. The gomers are letting us know they're out there. Every so often for the past few days, they've fired a few salvos at the airfield just to keep us off balance." Thompson stopped speaking as several more blasts shook the bunker, causing sand and loose dirt to filter down. Santy cursed as a stream of debris dropped down the back of his neck. He tried to stand but ran his head into one of the overhead beams and dropped back onto Boyle's lap.

Boyle helped him up to a sitting position. "You okay?"

Santy was leaning over holding his hands on the top of his head. "I think so. I smashed my head on the goddamn beams. It hurts like a bitch." He looked over at Boyle. "Is it always like this in here?"

"Nope. At least it wasn't when I left last week. I told you not to come in with us, you dumb shit."

Thompson chuckled at the two. They reminded him of himself and Dalton. "The gomers can do this because there really isn't anything the ARVNs can do about it. All their good units have been moved out of the city to try and stop the NVA advance. There's a big fight going on at Xuan Loc and the ARVNs are holding, but the NVA are coming at us from three sides, north, south, and west. It's just a matter of time."

Boyle looked at the door. "If my geography serves, there are only three sides that they can come from. The east is mostly water."

"That's about right, Tim. They've even got a division coming at us from the Delta."

Dalton got up and moved to the entrance. He peered out and then stepped through. He was gone for a few seconds and then stuck his head back in. "I think it's all clear. Looks like the bastards have had their fun for a while."

Everyone got up and walked out into the sunlight, brushing the dust and sand from their clothes. Outside they were met with an odd sort of picture. Everything in their immediate vicinity was just as they'd left it. All the aircraft on the line were intact; even the Hueys that had just landed were sitting unscathed with the long main rotor tie-down lines hanging loosely from the ends of the blades, which were gently rocking against their droop stops.

Several crash trucks roared down the taxiway headed for what appeared to be a huge fire farther up the flight line. The small group walked out near the taxiway and looked to see where the trucks were going. Two or three hundred yards up the ramp, several Vietnamese Air Force helicopters were burning, at least two CH-47 Chinooks and a couple of Hueys, but the biggest fire was from two C-119 Flying Boxcars, which had apparently collided while taxiing. In reality, the only way anyone could tell what

118

type of aircraft were burning was by the two distinctive twin-boomed tails of the 119s.

As the small group of Americans watched, a large explosion went off within the fire, sending burning chunks of aircraft flying in all directions and a huge black-and-yellow ball of flame and smoke skyward. One of the larger pieces of burning wreckage landed squarely on an ambulance that was rushing up to help.

The ambulance swerved back and forth a couple of times before it ran head-on into the side of one of the crash trucks. Even from this distance the Americans could see bodies scatter in all directions as the firefighters ran from the new disaster. The foam nozzle of the fire truck began spraying in an apparently random pattern as the operator either was injured or had fled. Two figures ran from the front doors of the ambulance, surprisingly spry for men who had just been through the wreck they had. The two got about fifty yards away and fell down in a heap, for the moment completely ignored by those who were still trying to fight the fire.

The Americans watched without speaking as several more trucks went past them up the taxiway toward the conflagration. They drove up to the fire and stopped with tires squealing on either side of the truck that had been hit by the ambulance. Men in silver fire suits dashed toward the truck and ambulance, pulling open doors and peering in to see if anyone was trapped inside. One man emerged from the rear of the ambulance carrying a limp figure over his shoulder, which he lugged over to the other two members of the ambulance crew, who were lying mostly inert on the grass next to the taxiway.

Large streams of white suppressant foam issued from the turrets of the newly arrived crash trucks and began to blanket the fire. In only a minute or two the smoke began to change from black to gray as the foam did its work.

Abruptly, the Americans became aware of a horrible stench, like burning flesh, as the gentle breeze carried toward them from the fire.

"Jesus Christ," said Dalton as he walked away, back toward the Air America flight line.

The others, nearly gagging, followed, concentrating on breathing through their mouths. Thompson coughed. "What the hell? Somebody must be cooking in there."

Boyle glanced at him. "Yeah, maybe. But that foam is made

119

from cow's blood. It really stinks when it hits a fire. I hope that's all it was."

In the lee of a hangar, the smell wasn't too bad, or maybe they were all just getting used to it. The two Air America pilots went over to their aircraft, tied down the rotors, and began a thorough inspection. Santy and Boyle pulled their bags out of the back of one of the helos, called their thanks to the pilots, and walked back to where Thompson and Dalton were standing.

"You guys need a lift into town?"

Boyle answered, "No. We'll wait out here for the heavies. But I believe we'll stay pretty close to that bunker."

Dalton chuckled. "Okay. We'll see you guys later. Maybe at the hotel." The two SEALs walked away.

Santy looked at the slowly shrinking pillar of smoke. "You were right, Timmy. This place is fucked up."

Boyle pulled out a cigarette and lit it. "I wish just once you'd listen to me when I tell you something."

Santy plopped down next to his bag. "No, you don't. If I ever listened to you, you'd have nothing to whine about. I'm doing you a favor."

Boyle sat down, too. "Terrific. I'm overwhelmed with your consideration."

★ 15 ★

Saturday, 19 April 1975

TONY BUTLER LOOKED DOWN FROM THE ESCARPMENT AT THE PLAIN BELOW. It was not much of an escarpment really, more of a sharp rise from the surrounding terrain. It wasn't much of a plain that he was looking at either—mostly rice paddies broken by occasional clumps of trees. Everywhere below were small streams and rivulets that flowed toward the river in the far distance. Butler figured he was about eighteen miles west of the river and still twenty miles from the pickup point he'd sent to Dalton.

The traveling had been much slower than he'd anticipated. The enemy seemed to be everywhere, forcing the small group to spend much more care and time in scouting ahead. One night, they had almost blundered straight into an NVA rest camp in the midst of a rain shower, and it had taken then five hours to get clear of the camp and the pickets the enemy had set out for security. How they'd gotten as close to the camp as they had without being detected, Butler had no idea, but it had been such a near thing— one of the group had had his hand stepped on by a picket walking by—that the group had spent an extra half day hiding in the deeper forest to get their composure back.

The ability of his men to move stealthily enough to make a mistake like that and recover from it completely undetected came as no surprise to Butler. Stealth and cunning had been the only things that had kept what was left of his little army alive for the past seven years or so. There had once been enough of them to routinely cause chaos for the North Vietnamese and their Viet Cong surrogates, but it was not long before the Communists tired of the disruption and the losses even though none of them had

121

been overwhelming. The final blow had been the harassing attacks that Butler's force and others had made when the Communists launched their Spring Offensive in 1972.

The small forces had struck at supply lines and headquarters areas, killing the leadership and destroying essential matériel that had caused the postponement of a few attacks, the cancellations of others, and disorder in the carefully planned timetable. Prisoners were taken, information was extracted from them in novel and universally fatal ways, and the information passed on to the Allied commanders.

When the Spring Offensive had been crushed, like all the others, the enemy had retreated into the hinterlands to regroup and await the departure of the Americans. While they had time, the Communists put it to use hunting down the small irregular units throughout the highlands and western Vietnam. There were no sanctuaries for the irregulars and they were gradually and inevitably exterminated.

There was no one to protect them or help them or even care about them. The South Vietnamese didn't consider them countrymen, much less allies, so they let the hunt continue. They had their own concerns.

The Americans who had trained and equipped and led them were gone, forced to leave by the changing priorities of a democratic nation. As far as Butler knew, he was the only American left.

He had long ago made his choice and had never had cause to doubt that choice very seriously. He almost relished the hardships of life on the run in a wilderness, leading what he now considered his people. He had married and begun a family. He had been accepted and had gradually assumed a position of leadership within the group as opposed to his position of leadership external to the group when he had been one of the American SEALs assigned to them.

Nothing had ever been said, but the group deeply respected his choice to stay with them. They were not concerned with his motives and had never raised the question with him. It simply did them honor that a man from what they murkily understood to be a magic land of fabulous wealth and wizardry would choose to be a part of them, to turn his back on paradise, to choose them.

They were quietly pleased by the obvious pride he took in their acceptance of him.

When Butler's wife had been killed, they stood with him sharing his grief and, as was their custom, making his two boys sons of the entire tribe, never lacking for affection nor guidance nor attention. The boys were growing well and Butler was proud of them.

Last month had come the next-to-last massacre. The enemy had boxed them in a small valley southwest of the famed A Shau Valley, site of so many battles and so much pain earlier in the war, pounding them with heavy weapons and murdering them indiscriminately with no regard for age or sex. The remnants had fled southward, higher into the rugged hills and mountains. They all knew that there was no real hope for them, but they still refused to surrender to the xenophobic armies of the North. And now they understood that to get Butler and his sons to freedom was going to be their last small victory.

It would be one that would never be known outside the group, but as long as they had left to live, they would know, and the knowledge, the certainty, that some small fragment of them and their history would survive would sustain them. They would disappear in the last massacre but they would not be completely forgotten. Someone would know, and that was all they asked, now near the end of things.

Butler watched as the last of a small convoy of trucks passed beneath him. There were longer and longer gaps in what had been only a few days before a seemingly endless line of convoys moving south and east. The convoys had been appearing to be more and more lax as time went on. They moved almost carelessly by day, and their spacing and poor air-defense discipline told him that the threat from South Vietnamese aircraft was almost nil.

Fewer and fewer aircraft had been overhead of late, and he couldn't remember the last time he'd heard either the large thumps of bombs detonating in the distance or the bangs and coughs of antiaircraft fire. He had hoped that the VNAF would at least make a token attack here and there, which Butler could use as some sort of cover.

But the absence of air activity had its good points also. It meant that the front lines were farther and farther away, confirming his suspicions that the troops they were now attempting to move through were second-rate support troops. He chided himself silently for assuming that sort of thing. Even the dregs of the NVA could end their hopes if they made another mistake like that last one and blundered into another camp.

Butler shuddered involuntarily at what could have happened. He checked the area he had been lying in for any sign that he'd ever been there and crawled back from the edge. Silently, he gestured to his men and led the way down the rough slope. They would be at the bottom, still concealed in the trees, by nightfall. Then, they would cross the road below and strike out for the south. They would be leaving the last little bit of the highlands behind and would have to traverse flat ground.

The prospect frightened them, but they silently followed Butler down the slope, keeping the boys in the center and their attention on the journey before them.

Santy followed Boyle into the room at the Hotel Caravelle and dropped his bag on the bed nearest the door. He looked around and scowled a little. "Well, Mr. Hilton's got nothing to fear from this place. Neither do Mr. Holiday or Mr. Ramada."

Boyle laughed as he opened the drapes and the window. He turned away and began unpacking. "That's for sure. But on the other hand I'll bet you can get some real good deals on real estate around here."

Santy walked over to the window and looked out. Below in the street were hundreds of Vietnamese riding bicycles, pedicabs, motorbikes, and every other sort of conveyance one could think of except horses and buggies. Mixed in with the crowds were small family-sized knots of refugees either moving purposefully along with their shoulders hunched and their heads down or gazing about them in wonder. It was easy, thought Santy, to tell the ones straight from the countryside from the ones who had been near civilization before.

"This is really pretty grim, Timmy. What are they all going to do when the commies get here?"

"Same thing they always do, I guess, try to survive."

Santy leaned against the window frame. "Y'know, from up here it doesn't look much different from Singapore or Hong Kong or any other place in Asia. I've always wondered what it must be like to be one of them. Do they want the same things as we do? Do they feel the same way about things as we do? Are they afraid of things like we are? Do they have the same anything or the same everything?"

Boyle came over and stood looking down. He looked at his friend and was about to make a flippant answer, but he saw that Mike was dead serious. Boyle didn't know what to say—he'd asked himself the same questions many times before but had never found an answer. It was one of those nagging large questions that one wonders about but can never really entirely figure out. "I don't know, Mike. I imagine they're not much different from us, but I don't know."

"This is the first time I've ever been in Vietnam except for the times I landed at Danang. Most of the time I've been four miles overhead passing by on the way to blow something up. You kind of think of the place as deserted mostly, like you're bombing things instead of people. Looking at this puts a different light on it."

"Regrets, Mike?"

Santy shook his head. "No, not really. Not about the fighting or anything. I'm just thinking that I should have learned more about this place than where the targets were or where the safe ejection areas were. Now, it's all going to be gone and I won't get the chance."

"Y'know, that's a feeling a lot of people around here are getting lately."

Santy sighed and moved away from the window. "Well, I guess we should go get a beer or four and talk about that."

"Yup. We've got an hour or so before Commander Hickerson gets back, so let's hit the bar."

As Santy and Boyle were leaving their room, Cdr. Don Hickerson was walking around the grounds of the U.S. embassy a few blocks to the northwest on wide, tree-lined Thong-Nhut Street. He looked at the ornate concrete wall surrounding the embassy and remembered seeing the pictures of the place when the Viet Cong sappers had blown a hole in the wall and attacked the embassy during the Tet Offensive in January 1968. He remembered the film of the bodies by the fountain and the Americans in civilian clothes, trying to kill the sappers, firing their weapons *into* the windows from the outside.

The attack had accomplished nothing more than causing the deaths of virtually all of the attackers and had been only a minor inconvenience for the Americans in Saigon. But the images on American television had begun the galvanization of the antiwar efforts. The people back home had been led to believe that the war, after three and a half years of American presence in strength, was nearly won. The people couldn't understand how an enemy that was supposed to be on the ropes could mount such an attack and penetrate to the very heart of the American presence. Followed immediately by the countrywide attacks by other Viet Cong and main-force NVA units, the attack in the embassy had begun the destruction of the crucial American public support for the war. It had led directly to the decision by President Johnson not to seek or accept another term and indirectly to the societal chaos of the next two years.

Hickerson leaned against the wall and looked around the courtyard, a fairly quiet oasis in the city of Saigon. He could see a tall tamarind tree, really quite a beautiful thing, sitting quietly by the parking lot in the courtyard providing shade and rest for the birds. He knew that if there were to be helicopter operations from this courtyard, the only area big enough to handle the Marine Corps CH-53s, the tree would have to go. He realized, somewhat sourly, that the tree and its imminent destruction could be a perfect parable for this situation.

But, on the other hand, he thought, it might not.

Hickerson shook his head and continued his walk around the embassy grounds. At one point, he looked out through the heavy iron front gate and could see dozens of Vietnamese camping across the street. Several of the embassy staffers had pointed them out and commented that they hoped to go with the Americans when, not if, they pulled out. A staffer had remarked that the secrecy with which the planning for an evacuation had been carried out seemed not to have worked. At least, he said, they weren't out there in thousands clambering over the wall and causing the Marines to have to shoot them. If that happened, things could turn into a massacre instantly and that would be the final tragedy for the American effort that had begun with such noble purpose so many years before. Hickerson had politely agreed with the staffer but had held back the thought that the real tragedy was that the Americans, after so much effort and pain, were going to have to leave in the first damn place.

Hickerson went back into the building and made his way up to the roof. Walking around the edge, he surveyed the grounds from above, which only confirmed his earlier judgment that only one CH-53 was going to fit at a time. He paced off the roof and noted that the area was only big enough for one CH-46 or Huey at a time to land and load up. A 53 could not operate from the roof, and it would be a waste of time and effort to mix the 46s and Hueys into the lineup for the courtyard.

He looked around at the adjacent rooftops and saw that they wouldn't be much use since the area surrounding the buildings could not be secured, and unless there could be some sort of crowd control, the panicky evacuees would mob the aircraft, preventing anyone from getting out. But just two landing zones, one here on the roof and one below, were not going to be able to handle the numbers of people expected. He was thinking about alternatives as he climbed down the stairs to the ground floor. The only other option was to use the airport, but if the enemy had its capture as one of his main objectives, even that was going to be difficult.

What his inspection of the embassy told him, in its most basic terms, was that the evacuation of Saigon was going to be one of the biggest clusterfucks in modern military history. On the other hand, he thought, if it were going to be easy, then anyone could do it.

Boyle and Santy were sitting with Thompson and Dalton at a small table next to one of the larger windows in the Hotel Caravelle's penthouse bar. On the northern horizon things seemed to be relatively quiet this evening—at least there were none of the large flashes of light that there had been the last time Boyle had been in here.

As Dalton got up to buy the next round since he had just lost at horse, Boyle looked around the bar. The band was playing just as badly as they had been two weeks earlier, and "Proud Mary" was still only recognizable by the chorus. The room was just as full as it had been nearly two weeks earlier even though so many people had been leaving the city. Boyle had mentioned that to Thompson, who had chuckled a little grimly.

"Well, Tim, either the remaining people have nowhere else to go or the hard-core drinkers are the only ones staying. Offhand, I'd say it was the latter."

Dalton returned with the beers and sat down. He pointed to a couple of men at the bar who seemed to be somewhat the worse for their time in here this evening. "Those two are really getting themselves shit-faced. They seem to have totally pissed off everyone around them, and I'm somewhat ashamed to admit that they even got to me." He looked at Thompson. "Don't worry, boss. I'll let 'em live."

Boyle looked at the two. He hadn't noticed them earlier since they were at the darker inside end of the bar and he hadn't really paid much attention. As the larger of the two turned around to survey the room, Boyle started. It was Joe France who was looking somewhat malevolently around, and next to him, leaning his elbows on the bar, was Cdr. George Bailey, his boss. Boyle watched France weave a little as he stood and finally turned back to the bar. Above the noise of the band, Boyle could hear France yell for the bartender, using some rather nasty adjectives.

Santy poked Boyle. "Excuse me, Mr. Boyle, sir. But aren't those two clowns from our staff?"

"Yup. They seem to be enjoying themselves. At least, they're behaving true to form."

"Shouldn't we do something?"

Boyle looked Santy straight in the eye. "Fuck 'em," was all he said.

Santy nodded. "Well, that seems to be a definite plan." He picked up the dice cup and slid it over to Dalton. "It's your honor. Bring 'em out."

Dalton grinned and took the cup. "I'll wait a while and let my luck build up again."

Boyle asked Thompson what had happened to the battle that they'd been watching the last time he was in here. Thompson said that the ARVNs had lost it and were now digging in closer to the city. Things had been pretty quiet for the last two days, but it was the lull before the storm. Boyle nodded and looked out at the lights of the docks down by the river. Even now, ships were unloading large cargoes of equipment that would probably be captured even before the ARVNs could get it unpacked, much less delivered to the front-line units. He sighed.

Suddenly, there was a crash and several shouts from the bar. Boyle spun around in time to see France and Bailey squaring off against two other, smaller patrons who were, from the length of their hair, civilians. The two civilians stood facing France and Bailey calmly as France said something to them. Judging from France's expression, it was not a nice thing, but the civilians didn't say a word nor did they make any move. That, thought Boyle, was not a good sign for France.

"Do you think we should break it up?" Santy asked.

"No. I think we should wait a minute or two." Boyle turned to Thompson. "Who are those guys?"

Thompson took a pull from his beer. "The blond one is a correspondent from one of the newsmagazines and the other one is his photographer. They've been here for years and I've never seen either one of them do anything violent."

Boyle looked at the forearms on the correspondent, which reminded him of Popeye's. "Okay. If France and Bailey look like they're going to win, Mike, we'll go over and help the newsguys."

Thompson looked at Santy questioningly and Mike shrugged. "Seems that they have gotten themselves on Tim's shit list, and I've observed that that's a bad place to be."

The four continued to exchange words until suddenly France tried to shove the correspondent. His hand never got to the man's shoulder before the correspondent had landed two hard punches to France's midriff and a nifty right cross to his chin. France spun halfway around and collapsed in a heap, holding his middle. Boyle didn't see what happened exactly, but less than a second later Bailey landed on top of France.

Santy looked at Boyle, grinning. "O-kay. Can we go help them now?"

Boyle got to his feet. "Of course. It's our duty to help our brother officers when in need. Especially two fine men like them." He turned to Thompson. "We'll be back in a minute."

Boyle weaved his way through the crowd and walked up to the correspondent, who saw him coming and stood warily with his fists at waist level. Boyle stuck out a hand. "Thanks. I've been wanting to do that for months. I'd like to buy you a beer once we get these guys out of here, if that's all right with you. The correspondent laughed and shook Boyle's hand.

Squatting, Boyle waited until Santy had gotten Bailey to his feet, then grabbed France by the shoulders and helped him up. They led the two staggering men to the elevators and supported them until the car arrived. As the doors opened, Don Hickerson stepped out and took in the scene, looking archly at Boyle.

Before he could ask, Boyle spoke. "Boss, honest to God, I didn't do it. But I wish I had. We'll be right back up." He and Santy maneuvered their charges into the elevator. Santy fished around in Bailey's pocket until he found his room key. Boyle did the same with France and pushed the button for their floor.

Once off the elevator, France began mumbling curses at the correspondent, threatening loudly all the terrible things he was going to do to him once he got his hands on him. Boyle grunted in acknowledgment and half-carried and half-dragged France down the hall and, after nearly dropping him at the door as he tried to fit the key into the lock, into his room. As they passed the bathroom, France reached out and grabbed the doorjamb, mumbling something that sounded ominously like "puke."

Boyle helped him into the bathroom and held his shoulders while he threw up violently several times. Finally, France sort of collapsed to one side between the toilet and the bathtub. Boyle flushed the toilet, glad that France had at least good enough aim to avoid repainting the room. He got one of the bath towels, wet it under the tap, and cleaned France up.

Hauling the now semiconscious man to his feet, Boyle got him onto the bed. He pulled off his shoes and carefully removed his stained shirt, throwing it into the bathtub and running water over it. He went back into the main room and cracked open the window.

France lay on the bed mumbling while Boyle inspected the side of his face for serious damage. The punch had landed squarely between the point of the jaw and the lower lip, but he hadn't been spitting blood and his teeth all seemed to be in place. Boyle carefully felt around the area, making sure that nothing was obviously broken or displaced. As for France's stomach, he hadn't vomited any blood, so there was probably no internal damage, but just to be sure, Boyle pocketed the room key so he could check on France once more before he turned in himself. Boyle turned out the light and waited until France's breathing quieted and evened out. He looked down at the still form and pulled a blanket over him.

As he opened the door, he looked back at France's form. "Good night, Joe. You poor dumb bastard."

He pulled the door closed and walked down the hall to the elevator.

★ 16 ★

Sunday, 20 April 1975

TIM BOYLE CONSULTED THE CHART ON HIS LAP AS MICKEY HARRIS CIRCLED the building slowly and carefully. Boyle took in the rooftop and the streets surrounding the high-rise. Actually, it wasn't a high-rise in the sense of a New York or Los Angeles high-rise. It was simply a building higher than the rest in the immediate area.

Boyle and Harris were scouting Saigon for rooftop landing zones, or LZs, which needed to be only large enough to fit one of the Air America Hueys. The plan was that when the proper signal was given, should ground transport such as buses and cars be unable to get through, the evacuees, either American citizens or selected Vietnamese, would make their way to one of these buildings where the Hueys could load up to fourteen passengers per trip. The evacuees would then be flown to larger LZs, which would be able to handle the larger helicopters such as Marine H-46s or 53s. If the evacuation was to be carried out by a massive airlift using fixed-wing transports, the people would simply be dropped off in a secure area near the aircraft. But if it was to be Option 4, the Marine helos would fly them directly to the ships assembling offshore.

So Harris and Boyle had taken off an hour ago on the second of their inspection flights of the morning. They had a list of buildings that were close to concentrations of potential evacuees and that were little threatened by the hordes of people who wanted to flee the country. The chart Boyle was holding had each of the possible rooftops clearly marked. They had so far found only three suitable buildings since most either had large obstructions that would preclude landing or were apparently not strong enough to support the weight of the Huey and its passengers. Several buildings that looked as if they would be vulnerable to enemy fire from higher buildings nearby were eliminated, too.

Off to the west, Boyle could see the other Huey with Hickerson and Wheeler aboard doing the same thing in another sector. And down on the ground, other teams were moving about the city trying to find the safest routes to the airport and the embassy for the buses that were part of another contingency plan. On the whole, Boyle was having a great deal of fun flying around at relatively low altitudes checking out the scenery. It beat the hell out of sitting in a windowless conference room listening to the elephants discuss plans while Boyle and the other lower-ranking rodents sat there and pretended to be awake.

"Okay, Tim, your turn." Harris took his hands off the controls and held them out straight in front of him.

"I've got it." Boyle leaned forward and placed his hands gently on the stick and collective and rested the toes of his shoes on the rudder pedals. Harris slid the chart off Boyle's lap and consulted it, paying no further attention to the actual flying of the helicopter. This pleased Boyle immensely since he had apparently proved his abilities to Harris enough that he considered Boyle a copilot rather than one of the usual "visiting firemen" who just wanted to sit in front and feel like a pilot.

Boyle had forgotten, over the past four years or so, how much fun flying the Huey really was. It was a quick, nimble sports car compared to the big H-3s he'd flown in the fleet. This one was an H model, which had essentially the same power plant and rotor system as the L models he had flown in advanced helicopter flight training at Ellyson Field back in Pensacola.

He hadn't flown any helicopter for nearly two years, but the touch had returned quickly—it had taken about five minutes to get the feel of the increased responsiveness, and after ten minutes or so, he wasn't even thinking about the mechanics of flight at all. He was just being a pilot, the one thing he had always wanted to be.

Only a small part of him could feel the steady vertical beat of the Huey's two-bladed main rotor system, which bounced him up and down gently in the dark green armored seat. When he turned, he wasn't conscious of the distinctive *whop whop whop* that the Huey always made. He wasn't aware that his right thumb was incessantly pressing and releasing the force trim button, constantly changing the trim reference point for the stick and smoothing out the flight. He didn't feel his left hand slightly increase the collective pitch as he banked the aircraft and reduce it again when he leveled it back out. He didn't know that his eyes glanced in at the instruments about once every three seconds, checking that all the systems were operating normally and that he was keeping the Huey in perfectly balanced flight.

He wasn't even giving that much of his attention to where the aircraft was going, although he was certainly giving it everything it presently required.

With just a touch of shame, Boyle was wondering how he could ever have been dumb enough to allow himself to think seriously about leaving Naval Aviation. Back in Hawaii, his flying was restricted to being a check pilot, sitting in the hot and smelly cockpit of a C-1 or an S-2 as aging senior officers droned around the landing pattern getting in their required proficiency flight time every month. Most often, the flights were always the same: two hours in length, which by the use of a "heavy pencil" would often become two and a half or three hours when the proficiency pilots filled out the postflight paperwork.

These pilots, no longer assigned to "operational" billets, or jobs, needed to accrue one hundred hours every year with a monthly four-hour minimum to maintain their flight pay. Boyle and a couple of other junior pilots got assigned to the "pit," a loose collection of available bodies who would go flying whenever required but mostly always when there was something better for them to do. For the most part, the proficiency pilots, who would never again occupy a seat in a fleet squadron, no longer cared about keeping their skills particularly sharp; they just wanted to keep their pay coming. Boyle would very professionally give them their annual instrument check flights, which led to many of them asking specifically for another examiner on their next check ride. But his main job in the air was to fly in the other seat and do his best to keep them from flying into the ground or forgetting the engine run-ups or raising the flaps too soon after takeoff. Or taking off without the tower's clearance or buzzing the beach or putting the damn thing into a spin when practicing single-engine procedures.

Boyle couldn't help from laughing to himself at how far away all that seemed just then. Here he was out flying a mission to which there was a real purpose. It was not one of the "day dick-arounds," or DDAs, back at Pearl. Not only was he doing something useful, but it was a gorgeous day and he was enjoying himself immensely. His laugh activated the intercom system and Harris looked over quizzically.

"What's so funny?"

"Not a damn thing, Mickey. I'm just having fun."

Harris smiled. "Been a while, huh?" When Boyle laughed again, he continued, "Okay. Come right some. I think our next possibility is over there about four blocks."

Boyle eased the Huey to the right and climbed up to five hundred feet so that they could do a careful orbit and look over the immediate surroundings before they went down and took a look at the specific rooftop. Since Harris was one of the pilots who would have to fly the actual pickups, it was more important that he get the best look at the LZ and the surrounding area. Boyle set up for a right-hand orbit and rolled so that Harris could look down on the area. Boyle could see it by looking across the cockpit, still keeping his eye on the instruments.

Down below, the streets surrounding the building were teeming with people. Two narrow streams of motorbikes, pedicabs, and bicycles were moving in the center of the narrow street in front of the building and herds of pedestrians on either sidewalk. Smoke from the small fires of street vendors trailed gently up to the level of the rooftops before it was carried away into the general layer of smog above the city.

On the other three sides of the building were other structures of roughly equal height, separated by narrow alleys. Boyle got one look down into one of the alleys and saw literally dozens of little lean-tos built by those who couldn't find better shelter and had to live exposed to the chaos of the city.

"Okay, Tim, it doesn't look real promising, but make a low pass and we'll see what the roof's like."

Boyle descended to fifty feet or so over the rooftops and lined up with the specific building marked on the chart. He slowed the helo down to a fast air-taxi and kept it steady through the turbulence caused by the gentle breeze flowing up and around the city. As the building got nearer, he could see that the roof sagged, and large spots of bare wood showed through the black tar covering

135

the roof. Boyle wouldn't even think of walking around up there, much less landing a helicopter on it.

"Mickey, I think we can cross that one off."

"Yeah, even if the roof was okay, I wouldn't recommend it because of the number of people in the streets. As soon as the locals see a bunch of Caucasians going in the front door carrying their American Touristers, it won't take them long to figure out what's going on. I'd hate to see a bunch of our guys fighting their way up the stairs. We'll pass on this one." Harris made an X on the chart.

"Okay, the next one is down by the racetrack. Come left and line up with that bend in the river. The track'll be about a mile on the nose."

Boyle looked out the windshield and picked out the racetrack, banking the Huey as he did. For some reason he glanced down and to the left at the buildings they'd just flown over and saw a figure step out of one of the rooftop doorways and raise what looked like a weapon.

He let out an involuntary "Shit!" and hauled up on the collective. He rolled the Huey over into a steep bank to put the tail of the helicopter toward the gun and got the thing climbing as fast as it would go. Before Harris could ask what the hell he was doing, they felt several thumps in the belly of the Huey. The radio console between the pilots exploded into flying pieces of plastic, and two holes magically appeared in Boyle's side of the windshield.

Harris grabbed the controls. "I got it. You all right?"

"Yeah. Some asshole popped out on that roof we were looking at and opened up on us." Boyle took his hands off the controls and reached down for the pocket checklist that was a digest of the larger "Dash 1" flight manual. He scanned the gauges for some sign of trouble but saw nothing out of the ordinary.

"I don't see anything wrong. How's it flying?"

"Fine so far, but I think we'll call it a day."

"Good plan."

Boyle looked down at the lower console and inspected the damage. Most of the radio panels were intact, but the FM communications set and the low-frequency navigation radio were pretty chewed up. The VHF comm panel looked fine. He pressed the radio switch on the stick to try it out, calling Wheeler.

"157, this is 154. How do you read?"

"Loud and clear." Well, at least they could communicate. Boyle pressed the switch again.

"157, we took some hits from one of the buildings down there. We seem to be okay, but we're heading home." Boyle looked out to his left for the other Huey and quickly found it. "And, uh, we're at your eight o'clock for about two miles, level one five hundred."

"Roger, we're on the way." Boyle watched as the other Huey swung around and began to climb to rendezvous. He rechecked the instruments and reassured himself that none of them were making a slow creep toward the red lines. He began to relax.

Harris looked over and grinned. "Bet you didn't figure on that."

"Hell, no. I'm just a tourist. Does that kind of thing happen often?"

"Nope. At least not in the city. But what the hell can you expect with the place falling apart like it is? You want to switch up tower freq? It's button four."

Boyle called the other helo. "157, go button four." He heard two clicks of acknowledgment and rotated the channel selector, waiting for the accustomed channelizer tone to stop.

"Tower, this is Air America 154. We took some ground fire and are heading back for a precautionary landing in company with 157."

The controller spoke amazingly good English for a local, but he'd probably been up there since the war started back in '64. "Roger, 154. There is no reported traffic at this time. Are you declaring an emergency?"

Boyle looked over at Harris, who shook his head. It is a point of pride with most pilots that they avoid declaring emergencies unnecessarily and causing all the crash trucks and ambulances to run out to them with sirens and lights on. Besides, a great deal of paperwork can often be involved.

"That's a negative, Tower. Request landing on the taxiway abeam the company hangar."

The tower controller seemed disappointed. It must be a boring shift, thought Boyle. "Okay, 154, you are cleared into the control zone for landing as requested. The winds are three forty at five knots gusting to fifteen, and the altimeter is two nine point nine nine. Cleared to land."

Boyle glanced at the window in his altimeter and spun the knob to the proper setting. It was higher than when they took off, so the high-pressure area must be moving closer. "Roger, two niner niner niner. Cleared to land."

Boyle pulled out the landing checklist, which was considerably shorter than the one in either the H-3 or the C-1s and S-2s he'd flown lately. He heard a loud whine followed by a distinct metallic thump from somewhere in the rear of the helicopter and heard Harris speak the words that all flight crews hate. "Oh, shit."

Boyle looked over and saw that Harris's left leg was nearly straight out on the rudder pedal. "What's 'oh shit.' "

Harris lowered the nose and accelerated to seventy knots. "We've just lost the goddamn tail rotor."

The words sent an automatic chill through Boyle. He put his feet on the pedals to see if his worked, but he had the same response as Harris. He cursed.

The tail rotor was one of the crucial parts of a helicopter, compensating for the torque of the main rotor and controlling the heading of the aircraft. In the H-3, tail-rotor problems were among the most serious problems a pilot could have. They nearly always resulted in at least a hard landing and aircraft damage. In the extreme, they could lead to a crash and serious injuries for the crew. The aircraft hadn't pitched down so the tail rotor was still there, but Harris couldn't control it. That was bad, but not as bad as it could have been. Boyle was trying to remember the procedure in the Huey when Harris spoke up.

"Okay, we're at seventy knots and it's still flying kinda all right. We'll have to run it on the taxiway. Tell the tower and tell them to roll the trucks."

Boyle looked out ahead at the airfield. He'd have chosen to run it on the grass next to the taxiway where the helo would slide easier. Also, it had always seemed to him that crashing on grass was preferable to crashing on pavement. He said so to Harris.

"Normally I would, but the ground out there is pretty uneven. I'd hate to dig in a skid and roll it up in a ball." That was logic Boyle could understand. He keyed the radio.

"Tower, 154 has lost tail-rotor authority. We're going to make a running landing on the taxiway abeam the company hangar."

"Roger, 154. Are you declaring an emergency?" Even though the guy had to ask, it seemed like a stupid question to Boyle.

138

But then the controller wasn't strapped into the machine with the problem.

"That's affirm, Tower. 154's declaring an emergency."

"Roger, 154. The crash equipment is on the way."

Off to the left, Boyle could see the other Huey flying loosely alongside. Wheeler came on the radio and told them that the tail rotor was still in place but windmilling slowly. Boyle rogered and reached over to lock Harris's shoulder harness, double-checking his own. He told the pilot that as far as he could see, they were all set for landing.

Out ahead the taxiway was about a half mile away and about two hundred feet below them. Boyle checked the heading indicator and saw that the wind was coming almost straight down the taxiway, so at least Harris wouldn't have to worry about a crosswind. As the ground got closer, Boyle placed his shoulders squarely against the seat and retightened his shoulder straps until they hurt.

The Huey is equipped with metal runners, called skids, instead of wheels, so the normal way to land one is to come to about a five-foot hover and then air-taxi to wherever one wants to go, finally setting it down vertically. If the aircraft for some reason is overweight or the meteorological conditions are such that the helicopter does not have enough power to hover, the pilot will approach the ground with a little forward velocity and then gently slide the aircraft along the ground for a few feet on landing. But with a tail-rotor failure the pilot can't control the heading of the aircraft except for allowing it to "weather-vane." Unfortunately, this takes a great deal more forward velocity that he would use for a normal running landing.

The helo must be touched down with the skids pointing exactly in the direction of travel. If the aircraft is coming down at an angle, there is a good chance that it will tip over with the rotor blades striking the ground and shattering, throwing heavy chunks of metal great distances in all directions. If that happens, the safest place to be is *inside* the aircraft.

Harris brought the aircraft down as carefully as he could, avoiding sudden large power changes that would cause yawing motion that he would be unable to compensate for. The airspeed was riveted on seventy knots, exactly what the book prescribed for an approach. He had it lined up with the yellow line down the center of the taxiway and was gently flicking the stick to keep it that way.

To Boyle, the asphalt became more and more defined as they descended. The grass alongside became a blur, and the crash truck belched black smoke as the Huey passed over and the driver stomped on the accelerator to follow. Boyle resisted the temptation to stare at the asphalt and looked out ahead to get a better feeling for their altitude.

The skids touched the surface of the taxiway and began the long, loud grinding slide along the pavement. Harris smoothly reduced the collective, allowing the friction of the skids to slow the forward momentum and the weight to be gradually transferred from the rotor blades to the skids.

Boyle glanced at the airspeed indicator and saw it drop past forty knots, below which the indicator lost some of its accuracy. Harris reduced collective more quickly now, and Boyle felt the deceleration increase, pressing him forward into the shoulder straps. He let out a breath in relief—they had it made now.

They were traveling less than fifteen knots when the left skid dug into a small pothole in the pavement. At the last instant, Boyle had seen it, but before he could say anything, the aircraft rocked forward and to the left, the rotor blades coming within a couple of feet of the ground. Harris had hauled the stick back to the right rear and held the collective down all the way.

The Huey seemed to teeter on the point of the left skid for what seemed to Boyle like about an hour and a half before it slowly fell back to a normal attitude, with a loud wham. When the rocking stopped, Harris had already rolled the throttle off and secured the fuel switches. He cut the battery switch as he released his harness. Boyle released his and waited for the rotor to slow down before he opened the door and climbed out.

He walked around to the tail and helped Harris open the drive-shaft cover, looking for what caused the failure. They inspected the shaft until they got to the forty-two-degree gearbox at the base of the vertical tail. There was oil dripping from the tail boom and a large hole in the side of the gearbox.

Harris pulled out a cigarette and lit it. "There it is. He didn't hit anything else important, but the lucky little bastard sure got the gearbox dead square. He was probably aiming at the cockpit and didn't lead us enough."

140

"What a shame."

"Yeah, if the gomers had ever learned how to shoot, there wouldn't be a flyable helicopter left within a thousand miles of here."

Boyle pulled out a cigarette, too, and was surprised by how much his hand was shaking from the postadrenaline reaction. He turned around and walked over to the grass and sat down. He watched Harris dismiss the crash crews with thanks and smiled at their obvious disappointment that they hadn't crashed and given them a chance to do their jobs. Harris walked over and sat down next to him.

"Nice job, Mickey."

Harris chuckled. "You know, I can't wait to get the hell out of this place. I'm tired of people shooting at me."

Boyle nodded. He was wondering what Meghan was going to say when she found out about this little adventure. He resolved to swear to Mike Santy to secrecy. There'd be time to tell her all about it later, like when he was sixty or so and retired.

★ 17 ★

Sunday, 20 April 1975

KEVIN THOMPSON REREAD THE MESSAGE AND THEN LOOKED BACK DOWN at the chart spread out on his desk. Mark Dalton was looking over his shoulder and trying to figure out how the hell they were going to get to the spot marked by an X far to the north-northwest of Saigon.

The message that Thompson held was not the original that had been dispatched by Tony Butler, but Thompson hoped that it was close. It had been given verbally to the first in a chain of messengers until it finally reached a place that had a radio. It was then transmitted using a simple code to a receiver here in the DAO building, where it finally had been put down on paper.

Thompson was no longer able to ask for a retransmission because the people who had sent this message followed it up by clearing all the other, routine, traffic they had to send and had then bugged out. The final transmission from them had stated that the enemy were less than a kilometer away and appeared to be preparing to attack the small encampment. They had said that they were going to relocate and try to reestablish contact with their superiors in the CIA-led organization, but they had not been heard from since. They had missed three scheduled check-ins, and all attempts to raise them had been unsuccessful.

It was possible that they were still free but moving too fast to set up and reestablish contact. It was also possible that they had been forced to destroy their equipment to prevent the enemy from capturing it and were legging it as fast as they could toward Saigon or somewhere where they could effect an escape.

It was possible that they might make it. Thompson thought that it was also possible that pigs could fly.

The CIA had taken a helicopter out there to look for them, but all of the planned rendezvous areas had either been empty or already overrun by the NVA. Even the CIA was beginning to understand that there was little hope for their communications people. Two Americans had been out there with the comm station, and unless they turned up quickly, they were certain to be left behind when the evacuation was carried out. Thompson stifled a shudder at what certainly lay in store for those men if they were captured.

Now, he and Dalton were here in their comfortable and well-lighted office, planning to go out there themselves.

"How far do you make it?" asked Dalton.

Thompson took a piece of paper and laid it on the chart, its edge running between Tan Son Nhut and the small X. He marked the edge even with both places and swung the paper around so that the two marks were lined up with the scale on the bottom margin of the chart.

"About forty-five miles. That's the straight shot."

"How do we get in there? HALO?" Dalton was referring to a "high-altitude, low-opening" parachute drop, which was one of the more effective means of covert insertion used by the special-ops types. What he didn't know was that most of the pilots who flew the aircraft that they dropped from considered them suicidal idiots for jumping out of a perfectly good, nonburning airplane at twenty-five thousand feet or so and pulling their rip cords around a thousand feet from the ground. To the pilots with their admittedly narrow point of view, it seemed kind of risky to play chicken with the earth. They always felt that by the time you figured out that your parachute hadn't opened, you would have just about a second to say "Shit!" before you became part of the local ecology.

Thompson sighed. "No. That won't work. We don't have enough time to set up the drop properly, and I don't think we could find an aircraft to do the job. The other problem is that the way things are out there, we could easily be jumping right into the gomers' headquarters—we just have no idea who's where.

"We'll have to go in on the ground. I figure we'll need to make a detour down here to the southwest and then swing around this way, back up to the northeast. We'll be making a big V on the way in."

"Swell. How do we get out?"

Thompson used his pencil to point out routes on the chart. "We can head south for the Saigon River along here and grab a boat, or we can head southeast for the coast somewhere around here past Vung Tau. Or, we can get really brave and head west for Thailand through Cambodia."

Dalton grunted. "Yeah. Right through a whole country full of those Khmer Rouge assholes. Maybe we can hitchhike."

"I wouldn't want to have to try that either."

"Well, if we're fast enough, maybe we can get somebody to fly out and pick us up. Like those Air America guys."

"Maybe. But they'll probably be real busy. It's for sure that we won't be able to get a U.S. military helo to come out that far. No, Mark, I believe we'll have to plan on taking the low road both ways."

"If we have to go that way, we'll have to leave real soon, like tomorrow. The way I see it we'll have to be back in Saigon no later than the second of May. Unless a miracle happens, the ARVNs will be just about done by then. Leaving tomorrow will give us a couple of extra days to allow for problems or detours."

Thompson scratched his jaw. "Yeah, but we've got a shitload of work to do. I think we ought to wait until tomorrow night. That'll give us time to get everything we need and still get a good night's rest first."

Dalton nodded slowly and looked Thompson dead in the eye. "Are we going to tell anyone what we're doing? I mean, I'd hate to get left behind without somebody knowing where we went off to."

"Yeah, I agree. We'll have to tell at least General Toone, and I'd like to tell the Air America guys."

"Okay, but I'd feel better if we had somebody from the Navy who knew also. None of those others are from the same family, if you know what I mean."

"All right, who?"

"How about those guys from the CINCPAC? You knew them all before, right? They seem like pretty good people."

Thompson nodded and stood up, carefully folding the chart.

"They are. Anyway, I'll go see Toone while you start getting our gear together. See you back here in half an hour."

"Okay. But what if Toone says we can't go?"

Thompson looked at Dalton. "I don't even want to think about that."

General Toone called Thompson into his office as soon as he heard his knock. It surprised Thompson a little because up to now the general, as the number two in the DAO, always had more work than he had time for, and Thompson was used to waiting up to fifteen minutes to see the general if he came in without an appointment.

Toone looked over his half-glasses and up at the SEAL. "Hello, Kevin. What's up? You don't look too cheery."

Thompson suddenly felt a little abashed, as if his plan were now somehow diminished in the presence of Toone, who, in a way, represented the big picture. In contrast to the size of the human tragedy befalling South Vietnam and the concomitant societal disaster it had long been causing back at home, the problems of one SEAL, "missing" for nearly eight years, and two quixotic old comrades determined to go "rescue" him seemed almost trifling now.

Thompson had been wondering exactly how he was going to explain his plan to Toone. He wondered how he was going to explain just what Butler was doing out there, alive no less. But standing here and looking at Toone's face, far older than its years, and aware of the respect that he and everyone else around here felt for the man, Thompson knew that bullshit would not do.

"Well, General, it's like this. Mark Dalton and I would like to go out into the boonies for a few days and bring in a Navy SEAL who has been listed as missing in action for eight years. That's it in a nutshell, sir."

Toone stared at the younger man for several long seconds, and then let out a long sigh. Despite his first thought that this was a bad joke, Toone knew that Thompson was being deadly serious. He removed his glasses and sat back in his chair, putting his feet on the desk. "Sit down, Kevin."

Thompson did so and waited for Toone to continue. It took a few seconds and when it came, it was surprisingly calm. "You'll pardon me if I think that what you just told me needs a wee bit of explanation.''

Thompson leaned forward and told the general the entire story, from the day the SEAL team had been formed to their assignment to Vietnam and the decision to pull them out. He related the story of the mission on which Butler had been lost and presumed killed. He told of the letters both he and Dalton had received years before, of the contact they had maintained since, and of the decision they'd made to honor Butler's choice and keep their silence. He left nothing out, not even Dalton's desire to go after Butler all by himself if that's what it took.

When Thompson was finished, Toone stared out his window for a long minute or two. Finally, he turned back and looked at Thompson, with a touch of sadness in his expression. "Is there any chance that I can talk you out of this?"

"No, sir, I don't think so."

"You know that I can order you not to go."

"Yes, sir. But I hope you don't." That wasn't strictly true, thought Thompson. Now that I'm actually doing something instead of thinking about it, I almost wish you *would* forbid us to go.

"I'm not sure that I could give you that order. Not that I'm not in a position to and not that it wouldn't be the strictly prudent military thing for me to do. It's just that I don't think *I* could give you that order."

"I don't understand, General."

Toone nodded. He took a cigar out of his top desk drawer and carefully prepared it and lit it with a black Zippo he fished from his fatigue pocket.

"Kevin, back in '66 I was a midgrade major assigned to the Studies and Observations Group detachments up in I Corps." He pronounced it "Eye Corps."

"We were operating with the Nung tribesmen from a camp near Khe Sanh, and I was in charge of sending out some of the teams who did the recon of the Trail over the fence in eastern Laos. I had an entire six-man team disappear once. We put them in and they disappeared in the first half hour. They never made their first radio check-in and we never found a thing. Not even a scrap of cloth." Toone inspected the end of his cigar.

"That's always bothered me. I think probably more than anything that's ever happened to me. There's times when I dream of

146

going back out there and finding those guys alive. It'll never happen, but I wish it would."

He turned and looked back at Thompson. "You understand that we have no assets to dedicate to helping you. We can't wait for you, and when we leave, that's going to be it for a while, like years."

"Yes, sir. We figure we've got fourteen days. We should be back long before then, but we've allowed some slack in the time."

"Show me where you're going."

Thompson walked to the wall chart and pointed to the area where Butler was supposed to be. "Right about here, General."

Toone nodded. The place was west of the two large arrows depicting the enemy lines of approach toward Saigon. If Thompson and Dalton planned this all right and could stay away from the enemy, they should be able to get back in time—that is, before there were no more Americans left in Saigon.

"You said you're figuring that we have two weeks left, but I'll be honest. I don't think you've got that much time, Kevin. This is not for dissemination, but President Thieu is about to resign, maybe as soon as tomorrow. The embassy believes that the Communists will stop and negotiate, but they're whistling in the wind. By the time the government figures out how to use the phones, the operators will all be NVA. I expect that we've got no more than ten days, Kevin, and if I were you, I'd plan on less than that."

"Okay, sir. That's going to cut it kind of fine, but I think we can make it."

"Who else were you going to tell about this? I mean, you surely aren't going out there without telling somebody other than me. If you're smart, it would be somebody wearing Navy blue."

Thompson looked up quickly, surprised that the general could see so much in this. "Yes, sir. We've got a couple of those CINC-PAC guys who'll know. We'll leave them a copy of the chart just in case."

Toone pulled a piece of paper from his desk drawer and wrote something. When he was finished, he folded the paper in half and slid it across the desk toward Thompson. "That's authorization for you to draw whatever equipment you're going to need. I'd like you to set up some sort of a communications plan and keep me informed. I'll fix it with the radio room here to copy down what

147

you send and pass it to me. Maybe you should use those CINCPAC friends of yours as the couriers, they have the clearances. That way, I won't have to send copies of anything anywhere."

"Yes, sir. That's a good idea. Thanks."

"Okay, Kevin. Get going. I wish you luck. But most of all I wish you wouldn't go."

"Yes, sir. I know. But I have to at least try."

Toone reached out his hand and Thompson shook it. Without another word, the younger man turned and left the office. The general sat back down in his chair and turned to look out the window again. He was there for quite a few minutes before he got up and walked to the small hidden door between his office and the boss's. He knocked discreetly and listened for a moment. He pushed the door open and stepped into General Alexander's office.

Pouring himself a cup of coffee, he sat down in the chair next to Alexander's desk. He looked up at his increasingly harassed superior. "Well, Lew, you were right. They were up to something." He filled Alexander in on his conversation with Thompson, omitting nothing.

When he was finished, Alexander nodded. "Did you try to stop him?"

"No, sir. I couldn't do that. If you want me to, I'll call him back and send him in here."

Alexander chuckled. "Nope. I'm not going to do it either. They're big boys and if anyone knows how to pull off something like this, it's them. I'd really rather that they not go, but I think I understand why they feel they have to. If they pull it off, then they'll be able to look back on all this a little easier than we will."

"All right, Lew. I'll get back to work. And, uh, I'll keep you posted."

"Thanks. Don't forget that we've got that damn meeting at the embassy at seventeen-thirty."

"No, sir, General, sir. I'd never forget a high-powered gathering like that. It might not look good on my record and I might miss something important, like maybe the fact that we're in deep shit here."

Alexander laughed and threw a pencil at his old friend, but it bounced harmlessly off the closed door.

Thompson walked back into his office and found Dalton staring out the window at the airfield. He joined him and looked out at the scene of several crash trucks surrounding one of the Air America Hueys on the taxiway.

Dalton looked over. "Well, what did he say?"

"Nothing really. He tried to talk me out of it but not very hard. He doesn't want us to go, but I think he understands why we are. He gave me this." Thompson handed Dalton the authorization order.

"This is nice. But we'd probably have stolen what we couldn't draw anyway."

"He knows that. He probably figured he'd give us as much help as he could, and that's it right there."

Dalton smiled. "There's been times when we've gotten less help."

"That's for sure."

"So what else did he say?"

Thompson told Dalton the story of Toone and the recon team. When he was finished, Dalton grunted. "Sounds rough. Did he lay any 'requirements' on us?"

"Just the comm checks. He wants us to keep him posted on our progress. He even advised us to make sure that we let somebody from the Navy know."

Dalton pointed out the window at the Huey, now deserted by the crash trucks and surrounded by maintenance types who were tying down the main rotor and installing the ground handling wheels in preparation for towing. "That helo guy, Boyle, just got out of that one, and I think Hickerson was in the other which landed just a couple of minutes ago."

"Okay, let's go get 'em and fill them in."

Dalton walked to the desk and folded the chart. He stuck it in the desk drawer and locked it. As they left the office, they unconsciously looked around, making sure that they'd left nothing classified lying about. Even in a highly secure building such as this, old habits died hard.

★ **18** ★

Sunday, 20 April 1975

I<small>T WAS AFTER NINE THAT EVENING WHEN</small> B<small>OYLE</small> <small>WALKED INTO THE HOTEL</small> room, collapsed on the bed, and kicked off his shoes. He let out a long sigh followed by a quiet curse.

Mike Santy sat in the chair across the room, next to the open window. He put down the newspaper he'd been reading and looked at Boyle's prostrate form.

"Rough day at the office, dear?"

Boyle grunted. "Well, if you count getting shot down as a rough day, then, yeah, you could say that. Do we have any beer or did you drink it all?"

Santy reached into the cooler next to his chair and handed Boyle an almost cold beer. "Would you like to explain 'shot down'? Like by a girl or like by the bad guys?"

Boyle explained what had happened during his flight, spicing up the account with as much humor as he could.

Santy reached for his own beer. "I told you those goddamned helos aren't safe."

"Well, at least I got an emergency-procedures refresher. I'd forgotten how loud a Huey can be as it scrapes its way along the ground. I'll bet we sanded the skids down to nothing."

"How come you're back so late? Did you get dinner?"

"No dinner yet and I'm starved. It's after curfew so we'll have to hustle something up here in the hotel." Boyle sipped his beer. "The reason I'm back late is that I was helping Thompson and Dalton get ready for a little trip out into the boonies."

Santy leaned forward in his chair. "Say again? Into the boonies? Isn't it a little late for those guys to go out looking for intell? I

150

mean, all you have to do is look out at the horizon and see the smoke and the fires. If you can't figure out where the gomers are that way, you have a serious problem.''

Boyle briefly filled Santy in on the SEALs' plan and as much as he knew about Butler. When he was finished, Santy got up and walked to the window. He was silent long enough that Boyle got up and fetched another beer.

Santy turned back from the window and looked at Boyle. He cleared his throat. ''That kinda reinforces your faith in people, doesn't it?''

''Yup, that it does. You, ah, want to go scare up some chow?''

''Let's go up to the Penthouse. If we can't find any real food, we can always stuff ourselves with peanuts and popcorn.''

Boyle pulled open the door. ''Right now, I'd even eat that lousy chicken adobo they make on the ship.''

Cdr. Don Hickerson sat on the couch in Mickey Harris's apartment off Tu Do Street. He was leaning back against the cushions with his feet up on the rattan coffee table and sipping his drink. It was Old Bushmill's Irish whiskey and water. He watched Harris pace the room, drinking almost as unthinkingly as he breathed. It struck Hickerson that this was a vastly different Mickey Harris than the one he'd flown with years before in Pensacola. Indeed, it was a vastly different Harris from the one he'd seen when he'd passed through Saigon only a year ago.

Once they'd left Tan Son Nhut air base this evening, Hickerson watched Harris's tough-guy pilot mask start gradually to slip as the distance from the airfield and the flight line grew. The difference in him away from aircraft and schedules and the bustle of his job was subtle, almost manifesting itself to Hickerson as a feeling rather than a certainty based on observation. There seemed to be a desperation about him, as if he felt that the time he spent away from the job was wasted. As if he were somehow smaller than he was in the increasingly frenetic pace of the Air America operations.

Once in the spacious apartment, Harris had poured them drinks immediately, heading for the small wet bar even before he'd given Hickerson the grand tour. As Harris poured the drinks, Hickerson looked around the apartment. There were none of the small things that one would expect in a place where a family of four had lived.

Even the pictures on the wall were of the standard anonymous-apartment type—prints of lesser-known artists' work, signifying nothing, not even the owner's taste. The room, while approximately tasteful, could only be described as soulless. Even a velvet print of the famous *Dogs Playing Poker* would have added something.

Hickerson took his drink and followed Harris into the small kitchen. They cobbled a meal together and sat down at the counter to eat. The conversation was limited to the mundane rememberings of times past, of mutual friends now gone along the various paths of the rest of their lives, and to the larger issues that avoided the precipices of things close to the heart.

After dinner, with the dishes done and the kitchen once again looking like a poster, the two went into the living room and got comfortable, talking easily as old friends do. But Hickerson watched Harris polish off his drinks quickly, always returning to the bar for another just as the last sip in the previous one went down. He'd always offer Hickerson another in a sort of detached way as if it were part of a ritual that interfered with his own drinking. For his part, Hickerson nursed his drinks, making sure that he mixed them himself, making them progressively lighter as the evening wore on.

All the while Harris chattered on about the war, the evils of working for a civilian contractor, and his perceptions of what had gone wrong here in Vietnam. It dawned on Hickerson slowly that Harris had been here for nearly eight years and was obviously at the end of his effectiveness.

When Harris took a break to pour himself another drink, Hickerson spoke quietly. "Mickey, you ought to go home. Now. You don't need this anymore. You've got a family."

Over at the bar, Harris's shoulders sagged a little bit and then straightened again, as if by a conscious act of will. He turned back and faced Hickerson. "I don't have a home, Don. No place to go. When I leave here, it'll be just some other place they need a pilot. Some other dead end."

"What about your wife?"

Harris smiled bitterly. "She and I lost whatever we had long ago, if we ever had it in the first place. She's out of this mess now and she's free. She'll do fine in the States—she's a smart lady—and she sure doesn't need a beat-up and drunken old pilot around. No, it's better if I find another flying job somewhere and

152

stay out of her life. We've already worked it out that as soon as she gets her citizenship papers, we'll get a quiet divorce and we'll go our own ways."

Hickerson looked at the floor. "But what about you, Mick? Look at you. You're drinking way too much and you're just . . . I don't know, you're just sort of existing. You can't do this forever. You're gonna run out of outfits like Air America sooner or later. Then where'll you be?"

"Flying's all I know, Don. I was a lousy administrator in the Marines and everyone knew it. Nobody shed a tear when I got out, especially me. This Air America stuff suits me fine. It's simple. No rules. I just get my ass into a helo every day and fly until they run out of things for me to do. Then I come home and wait until the next day to do it again. When they close it down here, I'll find another job somewhere else."

Hickerson spoke quietly. "Mickey, you're better than that. You're selling yourself short."

Harris looked Hickerson full in the eye. "Am I? What does the warrior do when he hasn't got a war? Hang up the guns and retire to an easy chair in Miami? Wear a suit and punch a time clock? No thanks, Don, I've thought about this a lot. There's nothing else for me. I'll do all right. Maybe someday it'll be time, but not just yet."

Harris looked at his watch and stood. "It's almost nine-thirty. We're already past curfew, but I've got a pass. It works less well as the night goes on though. So, come on, I'll get you back to the Caravelle."

Hickerson wanted to talk more, but it was obvious that he'd touched a nerve. He stood and put on his jacket. There'll be more time for me to try to help Mickey, he thought. But how much?

Ten minutes later, as Hickerson watched Harris drive away from the front of the hotel, it struck him that Harris was only thirty-six years old. Tonight, his eyes had looked seventy.

Several miles away from the Hotel Caravelle, Lt. Cdr. Kevin Thompson lay on his bed staring at the ceiling in the darkness. He had tried to get himself to sleep, but the mission was keeping him awake. He was running the plan and the preparations through for about the fortieth time in the past few hours. Several times, he'd gotten up from the bed and dug into his pack, checking to see that something he'd suddenly remembered he would need was really there. The item invariably was in the accustomed place in the pack, and Thompson would curse himself for being so worried and return to bed only to repeat the process several minutes later. Finally, he'd taken the entire bundle apart and repacked it, convincing himself that he was not, in fact, losing his touch.

He began to try to run one of the more boring and tedious of the Navy training manuals through his mind. After a few minutes, he was able to concentrate exclusively on it, numbing his mind and finally drifting off to sleep. His last thought as he went under was that at least the manual he was replaying was irrelevant to tomorrow's mission, but then, most of the manuals were.

✴ PART 3 ✴

No Getting Out

✳ **19** ✳

Friday, 25 April 1975

MARINE 1ST LT. BOB DUNN CLIMBED UP ONTO THE FLIGHT DECK OF THE old aircraft carrier USS *Madison* and looked down the deck at the long line of Sikorsky CH-53 helicopters. All around them Marine maintenance men were bustling about doing the daily inspections and dozens of routine maintenance chores that were required to keep these huge green helos operable.

Other Marines were laying on coats of the special paint, called IR paint, which was supposed to reduce the heat signature of the helo and make it less susceptible to detection by the seeker heads of the NVA's SA-7 infrared antiaircraft missiles. The normal high-gloss paint that squadrons liked to keep as shiny as possible reflected the light from the sun, providing a nice little beacon for the Grail, as the Americans called the Soviet-built SA-7. When fired by the operator, a job that took almost as much skill as sweeping a floor, the little shoulder-fired missile popped out of its launcher and streaked into the sky looking for a nice warm target against which to detonate its small explosive charge.

The aircraft exhaust was the primary source of heat, and the engineers back in the States were working hard to disguise it and had designed the first, albeit crude, countermeasure. But a completely effective suppressor system was probably years away from the fleet, so the only defenses available to the crews were magnesium decoy flares fired out the windows from a Very pistol and wild evasive maneuvers. The paint was of some help, but it was more of a psychological aid than a true countermeasure. The rule was that the best way to avoid getting shot down by a Grail was to fly as low as possible and to be fortunate enough to see the little bastard launched in the first place.

As Dunn walked aft toward the fantail, he glanced up at the bridge and saw that the captain of the *Madison,* Captain Guy, was as usual glowering down at the travesty that operational necessity had made of his carrier. It was no secret to anyone on the ship that Guy absolutely hated to have his attack carrier turned into a helicopter landing platform.

The standard Navy air wing that the *Madison* normally carried had been off-loaded in the Philippines and the Marine helos flown aboard. The other two carriers would provide whatever fixed-wing combat support might be required for the evacuation. Since the *Madison* was an old *Essex*-class carrier of World War II vintage, she had temporarily lost her air wing while the newer, bigger carriers such as *Concord* and *Shiloh* kept theirs.

Captain Guy had been furious that he, an old fighter pilot, should have his ship, his pride and joy and his ticket to admiral's stars, relegated to the role of supporting a bunch of goddamned Marines and their stupid helicopters. Guy had missed no opportunity to pick on the Marines and had petulantly done everything he could to make their stay as miserable and as aggravating as possible. He had effectively limited their opportunities to fly and exercise their aircraft and systems. He had made supply service as slow as possible by demanding that all transactions be done with the exquisite precision paperwork of a career bureaucrat, and he had done everything he could to find fault with the performance of every Marine, however lowly. In short, he was acting very much like a five-year-old.

It was an absolutely pathetic way for a captain in the United States Navy to act, thought Dunn, but what the hell could you expect from a man who believed that the only men worthy of wearing the Wings of Gold flew fighters.

Dunn walked aft to the fantail and stood behind a large group of Marines who were practicing with their weapons by shooting at a sort of wooden Maltese cross being dragged across the surface of the sea by a line attached to a stanchion in the jet shop three decks down. The cross, or "spar," threw up a huge froth of white water as the various rounds splashed around it. Some of the crewmen were firing their .50-caliber machine guns, and several of the pilots were taking advantage of the lulls to blaze away with the pistols they carried in their flight gear.

Dunn chuckled at the hoots and catcalls the enlisted men let out whenever one of the pilots missed the target, which was quite often. It is a long-standing tradition in the military that enlisted men enjoy few things more than watching their officers have difficulty like that. There usually is nothing malicious about it. It reinforces the idea that despite the necessary separation of the two classes, there are things that each group does well that when combined make the whole unit succeed. An officer who reacts poorly to some friendly harassment from his troops is, in their eyes, a lesser leader. One who shows good humor and gives as good as he gets soon earns the deeper respect, which in bad times may be the difference between success and failure.

Suddenly, Dunn got one of those full and complete feelings that come on a man when he realizes somewhere deep down that he is *exactly* where he ought to be and doing *exactly* what he ought to be doing with his life. He looked at the backs of the Marines, shirtless and well-tanned in the noonday sun. The Marines were young, strong, and professional, and he secretly hoped that he was just like them. He smiled again and turned away, walking back up the deck against the warm breeze toward his helicopter, which was parked off to the side of the landing area.

He slowly walked around the huge 53, letting his hand gently brush along its aluminum skin. He looked at the immense rotor blades tied back against the sides, and the tail folded over in the stowed position. The painters had finished with it, and the dull flat paint, although still Marine green, seemed rougher than the old smooth enamel that had been so unceremoniously covered. He looked up on the sides and saw that the black soot from the exhaust had been cleaned off but still stained the new paint job. Up in the cockpit he could see the young plane captain sitting in the pilot's seat as he performed some small task on the instrument panel. The Marine finally sat back in the seat, placed his hands on the controls, and thrust his chin forward, no doubt imagining himself as one of the pilots roaring off on some dangerous mission. Just for a moment, Dunn watched the plane captain and then turned and walked the other way.

He was stepping around the nose of another helo when he met

his commanding officer, Lt. Col. Greg Miller, who was apparently out on the same type of walk in the sun that Dunn was.

Miller was an old-time Marine who had learned his trade when flying helicopters was a new and truly dangerous profession. He had survived when one in three of his peers had not and was still at it when another third had given it up. He was the kind of leader whom other men would unhesitatingly follow into hell if that's what he thought the mission required. Miller was tough, profane, irascible, loud, and brash. He was compassionate, fair, articulate, smart, and respected by everyone who knew him. He was also a brilliant pilot.

Miller grinned at Dunn past an unlit cigar. "Mornin', Bob. How're you doing?"

"Couldn't be better, Skipper. Unless of course I was home."

Miller grunted. "Did you get ashore in Singapore?" A few days earlier, the ship had pulled in for a port visit but had been hastily ordered back to sea again twenty-four hours later. About half of the crew and members of the Marine squadron had managed to get ashore for some well-earned liberty before they were rounded up and sent back to the ship.

"Yes, sir. I got off on the first liberty boat and it was really looking like a good place to be. How about you?"

"I got stuck in another goddamn planning conference and only got ashore long enough to eat dinner before the shore patrol tapped me on the shoulder."

"Do you think we'll have to go in and evacuate Saigon?"

"I'm sure of it, even though others are saying that the new government will be able to negotiate with the bad guys now that Thieu has resigned. And I don't think it'll be a milk run like Phnom Penh was."

Dunn nodded. The squadron had participated in Operation Eagle Pull, the helicopter evacuation of the Cambodian capital. They'd gotten all pumped up to fight their way in and out, but not a shot had been fired, at least nobody had taken any hits, and it had been nothing more than a round-trip flight on a sunny day.

Miller looked up at the nose of the 53. "Well, I'll see you later. Don't forget the training meeting at nineteen hundred."

"No, sir. I'd hate to miss a lecture on the blade-fold system."

The old CO laughed and walked off. Dunn headed for the bow and the ladder that led below to his room. He looked out at the sparkling blue sea and was glad he was a Marine and normally stationed ashore. At least there he could get a beer after work.

Lt. Cdr. Kevin Thompson nosed the sampan up against the bank of the small tributary and jumped out onto the ground. He held the bow while Dalton clambered up from the stern and began handing the packs out. Dalton was especially careful to keep the weapons away from the water as he climbed out and helped pull the thin boat free of the water and into the brush away from the edge. The two men carefully erased the traces of their presence and backed into the brush until they were completely hidden from the view of any passerby.

Dalton pulled the Velcro cover off his watch and checked the time. It was just past five P.M. and they'd been paddling all day against the sullen current of the narrow little waterway that eventually flowed into the Saigon River and on to the sea. He recovered the watch and flexed his fingers and forearms. Paddling all day was a form of physical exercise that he had become quite unused to in the months he had been assigned to his job in Saigon. Thompson was doing the same, and when their eyes met, they both laughed soundlessly.

Thompson pulled out his copy of the map from the plastic bag and unfolded it. He inspected the long route he and Dalton had been forced to take by constant detours around what they suspected were enemy units. Even if the groups of people had not been the enemy, the two SEALs would have avoided them anyway—turning in two Caucasians would go a long way in proving someone's loyalty to the revolution.

The two had moved quickly at first, but as time and the distance from the relative security of their billets at the DAO increased, their pace became more careful and controlled. For the first couple of days, they had been almost boyish in their enthusiasm, so long had they been held hostage by their job requirements, which mandated that they shuffle papers and sit in on the endless meetings and planning sessions. They were also eager to be going out to attempt to finally deal with something that had lain within them like a lump of stone since they'd been forced to leave their small band of native soldiers so long ago.

But as the time went on and they passed deeper into the territory behind the necessary confusion of the "front lines," their excitement was gradually replaced by a professional wariness and tension. Their experience and training took over, forcing them to be aware of every sound, every bit of disturbed earth, the flight of every small animal from their passing. In fact as the time passed, Thompson and Dalton moved more like those animals than like men. From the very beginning, stealth and surprise had been the most effective weapons of the SEALs and the other special-warfare types. They had been rigorously, almost brutally, trained in these skills which they had used to such great effect in their prior tours, and the old tricks and techniques returned quickly.

They were getting tired, but at least it was a tired that came from action.

Dalton broke out the small radio, checked it over carefully, and turned it on. He watched Thompson write down the coordinates on a small bit of paper and concentrated for a moment or two, getting the sequence of numbers and words straight in his mind. He didn't want to make a mistake and make the transmission any longer than absolutely necessary. The NVA were almost certainly not going to be able to locate them by their radio direction-finding equipment, but there was no sense in taking chances.

As Dalton made his transmission, Thompson listened and folded his map, replacing it in the plastic bag. As they waited for the reply, the two pulled out a couple of candy bars and began munching them. They would need the energy for their three or four hours of travel that evening. Dalton adjusted the small earphones of the radio—somehow they always made his ears itch as if the sounds themselves were an irritant.

In the communications room of the DAO Compound, Tim Boyle removed his earphones and leaned back in the chair next to the radio operator. The operator sent the acknowledgment and turned to the message he'd copied down. Boyle waited as patiently as he could, forcing himself not to look over the man's shoulder as the operator deciphered the near-gibberish of Dalton's report. After what seemed like at least half an hour but was probably less than four minutes, the operator handed the sheet of paper to Boyle without a word and went back to making a smooth copy of Dalton's message for the files.

Boyle idly wondered why the hell the operator was doing that when it was obvious that the files were going to be destroyed in a matter of days, if not hours, anyway. Boyle looked over the message and, with a bit of relief, saw nothing unusual in it. The position given showed some progress, but just how much he couldn't tell until he consulted the chart he, Santy, and Hickerson were keeping in their temporary office. The SEALs had had nothing extraordinary happen as was evidenced by the complete lack of amplifying information—had there been something worth reporting it would have been included. Silence meant normalcy.

Boyle folded the message form and stuck it in his shirt pocket. He picked up the earphones and pulled out the small form over which he and Hickerson had labored for nearly two hours. He handed the paper to the radio operator.

"Here's the new one, Alan. Send them this, please."

The operator looked over the message and began to speak intently into his microphone. Boyle listened as the message went out carefully, almost languidly. There was no concern that the enemy would be able to locate this transmitter. They had it surrounded anyway.

The operator finished and both men listened to the hiss of the carrier wave, waiting for Dalton's acknowledgment. It came in a few seconds with no request for a repeat. Boyle sighed and put down the headphones again. He stood and thanked the operator and left the room, making sure that the door was closed securely after him. He climbed the steps to the corridor above and headed for the front door of the embassy, past the long line of increasingly frantic Vietnamese people trying to get the necessary paperwork that would enable them to be taken along in the evacuation.

Once outside, Boyle found his vehicle and steered it out of the embassy compound, careful not to block the gates so that the few Marines of the embassy security detachment could continue to control the large mob of people camping outside.

Boyle was momentarily ashamed of himself, as he always seemed to be anymore, that the worried faces of the people outside the gate affected him less and less as he drove through them. It wasn't that he didn't care, he told himself, it was just that he had only so much concern to go around, and right now he had more things to worry himself about than he had time or strength to put on the list.

*   *   *

Dalton handed the slip of paper to Thompson as he tapped out the acknowledgment to the radio operator back in Saigon. He lowered the radio antenna and carefully repacked the radio for travel. When he was finished and once again ready to move out, he looked up at Thompson, who was looking at his chart through the plastic cover.

"Well? What do you think?"

"I believe we can do it, Mark. We'll just have to step it out some more and maybe take a few more chances."

Dalton nodded grimly. "Yeah, I guess so. But I gotta tell ya, I'd rather be taking chances a little closer to Saigon than out here."

"I heard that. Let's eat now and move out in ten minutes."

The two pulled out some more high-energy food from their packs and ate it slowly, washing it down with water they mixed with their own form of Kool-Aid. The Kool-Aid, mixed with lots of sugar and repackaged securely, not only made the taste of the water more palatable but also provided a little extra energy. As they drank, they thought of the ominous words in the message they'd just received.

Essentially, the message told them that things in South Vietnam were falling apart at an even faster rate than before. Even the embassy was beginning to see that little time was left, and the evacuation was expected to begin in no more than seven days. The message also told the two SEALs that they could plan on no help from anybody in Saigon once the evacuation began. It was up to them, the message said, to decide whether to press on with their mission or to turn back. Basically, they were being told that if they wanted to pull this off, they'd best get their asses in gear and pick up the pace.

This trip was about to turn into a race, and if the SEALs lost, the prize for second place was not going to be pleasant.

Or survivable.

✴ **20** ✴

Saturday, 26 April 1975

THE SOLDIERS LAY IN THEIR HOLES AND HUNKERED BELOW GROUND LEVEL. *The artillery rounds burst all around them with no discernible pattern. A few would go long, bursting in their rear, at the same time that a few more would detonate in the trees to either side. There were a few smaller explosions among the holes from some of the heavier mortars still operated by the South Vietnamese Army, but these were wildly inaccurate and getting killed by one was purely a matter of chance.*

The soldiers had dug their holes quickly but with great care when the first artillery rounds had begun to fall and had improved them, digging deeper and throwing the earth out and forming it into small berms around the holes to stop shrapnel from tearing into whatever body part they might inadvertently expose as they shifted their positions to get more comfortable.

Even if they did not know the proper word, it struck the older veterans as ironic that they were now in the same sort of position that the Americans had once been in—lying in fighting holes and waiting out the impersonal assault from the blind, emotionless killers of the enemy's mortars. It was as if they had become that which they once fought—an army that was moved by truck down easily mined roads. They had become a force that was concentrated as opposed to their dispersed and shadowy existence earlier in the war.

Behind them lay the ruins of the last major defensive position in the ARVNs, Xuan Loc, although the soldiers knew it only as another obstacle in the long series of assaults moving toward Sai-

165

gon. The Southerners had fought gallantly, if not brilliantly, and had shown that some of them were as effective and as tough and as professional as any soldiers on earth. It had been a relatively long battle, unusual in that the NVA's tactics had been almost conventional and the Southerners had made them pay for every inch of ground gained.

When the soldiers finally broke through after heavy casualties, the Southerners had retreated grudgingly, with little of the wild panic that had characterized their earlier defeats farther north. They had pulled back to defensive positions from which they would use all their heavy weapons to delay the onslaught, but their artillery fire had grown progressively less effective until it was now little more than a loud annoyance.

Up ahead, the soldiers knew that there were other units, just like theirs, that were moving out to the sides in order to flank the enemy's new positions, and when the artillery fire slackened and finally ceased, the soldiers would climb from their holes and move out once again down the road for a few miles until the guns of the enemy's next defensive position opened fire.

But that fire would be less effective than this had been because of the losses that the flanking units had inflicted on the defenders. The replacements would be that much less experienced and well-trained, and they would be that much more poorly coordinated. So the delay would be shorter and the ground gained would be larger and the cost would be smaller.

The only constant in all this was that the Southerners never seemed to run out of ammunition or equipment.

After a time, the artillery fire slackened and the lieutenants and sergeants blew their whistles. The soldiers climbed stiffly from their holes and looked about them, each man looking to see if the other members of their platoons were able to answer the call. Most were gratified to see that their close comrades were standing nearby looking about them also. This sort of action had become so commonplace that there were none of the nervous grins one would expect from men who had just survived a terrifying experience.

There was just a matter-of-fact weariness on their faces as they went about their duties, checking their weapons for dirt and putting their packs back on.

Even those who had lost members of their units in the past few minutes, to unfortunately accurate shells, merely glanced at what was left of their comrades and moved off to rejoin the formations for the road ahead. After all these years of struggle and suffering, the deaths of a few more men meant little.

Except to the dead.

⋆ **21** ⋆

Saturday, 26 April 1975

LT. TIM BOYLE HANDED THE MESSAGE FORM TO HICKERSON AND STOOD looking over his boss's shoulder as he placed it on the battered gray metal desk and read it. Hickerson pulled over the tactical pilotage chart and made a small mark at the position that Dalton had transmitted. He looked carefully at the terrain between that point and the square that indicated the area in which the SEALs were to rendezvous with Butler. He pulled across another chart that indicated the positions of the enemy forces closing in on Saigon. He nodded to himself in satisfaction and tapped his finger on the SEALs' position.

"Looks like they'll be able to make better progress now. The terrain looks like it will be easier going. They should be able to link up tomorrow, but they still have a long way to go to get out of there and not a whole lot of time to do it. Did you send them the updated assessment of the situation?"

Boyle nodded. "Yeah. They acknowledged, but that was about all we got, which is the good news, I guess."

Hickerson looked up. "And the bad news?"

"The way I see it, boss, is that they're fucked. I'd hoped the going wouldn't be so tough or the time so short, but now, if they had a goddamn jeep and clear roads, they wouldn't be able to make it out."

"Any suggestions?"

"Yeah, let's you and me go get 'em and fly them out."

Hickerson chuckled. "Well, for your information only, Mickey Harris has already agreed to do that if necessary. He's managed to wangle the schedule so he can be close by in case we need him."

168

"That's good. Mickey's a good man."

Hickerson nodded slowly. "Yeah, he is."

Boyle caught an odd note in Hickerson's voice. "Commander, is everything okay with him?"

Hickerson looked at the younger man. He'd told no one about the experience he'd had in Harris's apartment the other night. He suddenly felt the need to share the burden with somebody else, but he wasn't sure why. After a few seconds, he made up his mind. He leaned back in his chair and put his feet up on the desk.

"To answer your question, Tim, yes and no. On the outside he's fine. He can fly and do his job and all that stuff. Hell, he's still the best pilot within a thousand miles. But inside, it's like, I don't know. Like he's a hundred years old."

Boyle thought about the times he'd worked with Harris over here and especially about their flight that could easily have ended in a fireball at the airport fence. "What do you mean? I didn't know him before we came over here, but he seems pretty sharp to me."

Hickerson sighed. "Tim, there's a lot of guys around like Mickey. They've found a place here, flying in the middle of a mess like this, and they're a little afraid, no, a *lot* afraid, of what their lives will be like when this is all over. In many ways, they're like the cowboys of the Old West—they're rootless and almost nameless. They'll fly until the job goes away, and they'll move on to another one just like it in some crummy little corner of the world, and they'll keep at it until they get too old and their skills and value decay. Then, they drink themselves to death or they get themselves killed flying some piece of shit airplane somewhere. They have no future, only a past and a present, which becomes the past at a faster and faster rate than they realize until its all over for them. Finally, one day, they're gone. And nobody remembers that they were ever here except a bunch of old guys in a bar in north Florida or Arizona or some such.

"Mickey's smarter than most. I think he knows all that, but I don't think he can figure out how to get off this particular tread-mill. But once we get us all out of here, I'm going to do what I can to help him. He deserves better than this."

Boyle had listened in rapt silence. He'd looked at men like Harris as sort of legendary figures, embodying as they did all the experience and mystery and adventure he could imagine. Listening to the other side, he began to see these men as they truly were—slightly better than average guys but with their halos askew.

Hickerson dropped his feet to the floor, emphatically breaking the mood. "Well, enough about that. I've got to get over to Air America Operations. I'm going flying with him. I figure you and Mike have been having too much fun, so I'm going to have some myself. We're going to do a check of the routes in and out of the city for the Marines. Where is Mike anyway?"

"He said he was going to go over and 'supervise' the setup of the positions for the landing-zone controllers. He found out that their call sign is going to be 'Alamo,' and Mike figured he'd go see why. What he's probably doing is catching rays on the rooftop. Anyway, he's due back in a few minutes."

Hickerson folded up the chart on the desk and handed it to Boyle. "Maybe it's time you two caught a helo out of here to the ships. You don't seem to have all that much to do around here anymore, and you'd be two fewer things I'd have to worry about. Whatever's left to do here isn't going to take three of us."

"Are you suggesting or telling, boss?"

Hickerson laughed. "More like hinting, Tim. We'll talk more about this when I get back."

Boyle nodded. "Okay, but I'm really not sure I want to go, and I sure as hell don't want to leave and have that silly son of a bitch France changing all the plans we've made."

"Good point. I hadn't thought of that. Well, I'll see you later." Hickerson pulled on a borrowed leather flight jacket and left, leaving Boyle to stand and stare out the window.

Boyle never knew how long he stood there staring through the glass at the little corner of the airfield he could see between the buildings across the street. He was thinking about Hickerson's description of Mickey Harris and the life he was leading. As he considered things, it dawned on him that, for him, flying was probably just as important as it was for Harris, but for entirely different reasons.

For Harris, flying was all he knew and, at least right now, was the only option he had. Boyle allowed himself to try to feel the sense of doom and hopelessness that might bring to a man—to have a fleeting sort of external thing be the driver of his life, to feel that nothing else could provide that little daily reinforcement of the idea that he was a valuable member of the human race. To have to seek it in a lousy little war-torn shithole of a place like Vietnam. Boyle shuddered at that thought when he realized how terrifying it must be.

Boyle, on the other hand, loved flying because it was what he did best and what he had always wanted, but the difference was that he had other things, too, such as Meghan and a career, that made him more than simply a pilot. Many times he had considered himself nothing more than that, and at other times he had even *wanted* to be nothing more than that. But he had learned somewhere that there was more to life—that many other things could give him that little reinforcement.

He watched a South Vietnamese C-119 gunship taxi by and found himself unconsciously looking over the aircraft, judging it professionally for signs of wear, breakdown, or poor maintenance, wondering if the darker exhaust from the starboard engine was a sign of potential problems for the crew.

He realized suddenly that he was never going to be happy if he left the profession he loved and quit the Navy. He couldn't imagine himself doing anything else and enjoying it. Maybe that was the difference between him and Harris. Although they both did essentially the same thing, at least Boyle got to fly for something bigger than he was.

He turned away from the window and put away the chart and messages lying on the desk. He left the office, carefully making sure that everything was securely locked. He lit a cigarette as he walked down the front steps of the building and turned down the street toward the areas being prepared for the helicopter operations.

Far to the west of Tan Son Nhut airport, Tony Butler was feeling his son's forehead. The little boy had a slight fever from something, but other than being a little sluggish, he seemed pretty normal. Moving his hand down slightly and caressing the trusting little face, Butler cursed quietly because he didn't even have an aspirin to give the boy to bring down the fever. He shook his head at the cruelty of the past few years.

Any medicine that this little band ever received from the South Vietnamese government had always been issued after the expiration date printed on the package and was always far too little to

171

have a lasting effect on the tribe's health even if it had been top of the line. The bastards in Saigon and the provincial capitals had always taken things like the medicine and sold it, rather than giving it to the people who desperately needed it. For about the ten-thousandth time, Butler wondered why these tribesmen had stayed so loyal all these years to people who considered them less important than the goddamned water buffalo they used to work the rice paddies.

Butler stood and walked over to the group of tribesmen, who were eating the small rations of rice they were allotted each day. He squatted and took his portion and those of the boys. As he turned to carry the food to them, his eye caught on the long, jagged scar on the arm of one of the men squatting around the cooking pot, and he remembered the day the man had received that wound during one of the numberless firefights with the enemy.

Butler felt a wave of frustration when he also remembered the man waiting four hours for a South Vietnamese doctor to finish giving school physicals to the province chief's family before he got around to treating the wound. He had sewed up the long slash with maximum haste, minimum concern, and no anesthesia.

As Butler sat down on the ground and handed the small tins of food to his sons, he realized that the greatest moment of his life was going to be when he had these two boys safely out of this country and on their way to a place where they could get a goddamn lousy aspirin without having to take it from the pockets of a dead soldier.

Completely out of habit, Don Hickerson reached down with his left hand and rechecked that his shoulder harness was locked. He went over the last couple of items on the checklist while Mickey Harris received taxi clearance from the ground controller at the airport.

"Comin' up," Harris said as he lifted the Huey into a five-foot hover.

Both pilots checked the instruments, and Hickerson looked out the window in his door to see if anybody was coming the other way. Only a Vietnamese Air Force Huey was hover-taxiing toward the taxiway, but several other aircraft were using the main runway. None of them, though, would be a factor. "Clear left. We've got a Huey coming out of the VNAF line and going the same way we are.''

Harris glanced across the cockpit and saw the VNAF helicopter. ''Got him. I didn't hear him call for taxi, but that's pretty normal around here lately. Everybody seems to do whatever the hell they want, like the rules don't apply anymore.'' Harris looked over the instrument panel again. ''Gauges're good. Comin' left.''

Hickerson watched the VNAF helo continue its taxi out, far faster than he should have been going. ''Only as fast as a man can walk'' was the old phrase that every Navy pilot learns on about his second hour in flight school. This VNAF guy was moving about as fast as a man could spring, thought Hickerson.

Harris moved the Huey out onto the taxiway and spun it around ninety degrees into the wind. Hickerson watched the VNAF helo enter the taxiway, move a little way closer to them, and stop, finally spinning 180 degrees and pointing its tail toward the Americans.

Hickerson pressed the intercom foot switch. ''Looks like that clown is going the other way. He's clear.''

Harris nodded and keyed the radio. ''Tower, Air America 189 is ready to go southeast departure.''

The tower came back in the odd singsong way that many non-English-speaking controllers have when they give clearances in English. ''Rojah, wan-uh eight-uh nine. The altimeter is two nine point nine-uh wan. Wind is southeast at ten knots. You are cleared to depart. Call when you are clear.''

''Roger, Tower, 189's cleared to go. Two niner niner one.''

Harris rechecked his instruments and pulled in the collective, gently beginning to lower the nose as he did. ''Okay. Here we go.''

Hickerson glanced at the instrument panel and then back out to the side. He only had time to yell, ''Look out!'' as the VNAF helicopter struck the rotor system, rolling the Huey on its right side and forcing the suddenly almost bladeless aircraft to slam into the ground on its side.

A few minutes earlier, Tim Boyle had easily found Mike Santy among the crowd of Americans standing around one of the landing zones in the DAO compound at the airport. This one was at the tennis court, which lately hadn't seen very much of the spirited competition of the old days of the American presence in

Vietnam. Santy was sort of looking over the shoulders of the men, who were consulting clipboards and what looked to be blueprints of the buildings. Occasionally, one would point to a rooftop, and the pages on the clipboards would all be shuffled in unison and the charts would all be referred to with great seriousness.

Boyle walked up behind Santy and peered over his shoulder. "Have you got this whole operation sorted out yet, Mike?"

One of the group, a Marine captain named Zeigler, laughed. "I don't know how we ever got along without him, Tim. He's pointed out all sorts of things which we would have missed, like for instance we probably can't plan on landing a C-141 on the tennis court."

Santy laughed, too. "I proved beyond a shadow of a doubt that the problem has nothing to do with the fact that the pavement isn't big enough. The real problem is that the Air Force guys wouldn't understand the markings. They'd do better on a golf course."

Boyle gestured over his shoulder with his thumb. "C'mon, genius, we've got to have a talk." He looked at Zeigler. "If you guys don't mind, I need Mike to help me plan the defense of the bars in Olongapo. See ya."

Zeigler waved and turned away. Santy followed Boyle off toward the Air America building. When he was about fifty feet away, he turned and called, "Hey, Ziggy, if you need any more help, just give me a call. I'm always ready to help the jarheads." He waited until Zeigler gave him the expected raised middle finger before he turned again and caught up with Boyle.

"What's up, Tim?"

"Nothin' much. Hickerson says we should get our stuff together and think about getting out to the ship. He says that our part here is pretty much done and it's only a matter of a few days before the whole thing will be over. You've got all the Tacair plans agreed upon and all the briefings finished. I've pretty much done all my spear-carrying. It's going to be up to the Marines and the embassy now."

"Did he tell us to go or did he just sort of present the option?"

"He said he was just hinting, but I think he was really letting me know that he'd be real pleased if we got out of here most skosh."

"You agree?"

"Yeah, I guess. It does make sense from his point of view."

"So why do I get the feeling that you don't want to go?"

Boyle shook his head. "I kinda don't. Maybe because it's not completely over yet and I'm afraid I'll feel shitty about it, like maybe I ran out on something."

"Like on Thompson and Dalton?"

Boyle sighed. "Yeah. There's them, too. But that's only part of it. I hate to cut and run just because things don't look so hot." He sighed again. "I don't know."

Santy stopped and turned to Boyle. "Like maybe you're having trouble looking the locals in the eye? Like maybe you're the guy at the Alamo who *didn't* cross the line?"

Boyle hung his head for a few seconds, staring at the ground and gathering his thoughts. He looked back up at Santy, and a mixture of pain and anger was in his eyes. "Mike, you and I both had a part in this war. We fought it and we lost a bunch of good people we knew. Now here we are, not even two years later watching these people who depended on us for help about to lose everything they have—families, homes, jobs, and even their lives in a lot of cases. All *we* have to do is get on an airplane and in twenty minutes we're on the way back to a nice safe life with all the comforts these people will never even see. Hell, most of 'em can't even imagine the stuff we have right in our own apartments. In six months, this place will be back in the last century again living with the same bullshit they've suffered for a thousand years. They won't even be able to walk the fucking dog without permission."

Boyle looked up at the sky, his shoulders heaving with barely suppressed emotion. "Goddamnit, Mike. They had a shot at freedom, at a real future, at something better than living in the Stone Age. We promised to help them get it and keep it and we lost fifty some thousand good men who believed that we were here for a reason. All because some chickenshit guys in suits didn't have the balls to let us do the job. Now, back home the people have shoved this place and all the little folks off in some corner like their crazy old uncle who might embarrass the family. It's just not fair that we're running out on these people after all the promises and commitments we as a people made to them. We just declared victory and hauled ass. This sucks. It's, I dunno, it's dishonorable."

Santy nodded gently. He felt pretty much the same way. He

175

suddenly remembered something his father had said to him years earlier when Santy had decided that he'd rather play baseball one afternoon instead of mowing the next-door neighbor's lawn as he had promised.

"My dad told me once that if a man didn't keep his word, he wasn't much of a man. I guess that doesn't apply to presidents and congresses and countries and such. But you're right, Timmy. This sucks."

"So what do we do about it?"

"What? You and me?"

"Yeah."

"We put our tail between our legs and get on the fucking airplane."

"Thompson and Dalton didn't."

Santy nodded. "Yeah, that's true. But they have a reason. We don't. We can't go around rescuing the whole damn country, Tim. The problem is just a little bigger than us."

Boyle nodded. "I know, and that's the damn problem. I've never given up on anything in my life and I just can't now either."

"Yeah. I can't give it up either, dammit."

Santy felt a sort of vague relief that his friend felt just as powerless and defeated as he had. But on the other hand, he would have been surprised if Tim hadn't. He wondered what it would be like to have the chance to do something about all this. No matter how small. He thought about the SEALs all alone and way out on their chosen limb.

He'd been just as involved as Boyle in the saga of the two SEALs so far. He'd stood the communications watches in shifts with Boyle and Hickerson and had allowed himself to become just as concerned. The reason he could so easily tell what Boyle was thinking was that he was thinking the same way himself.

"So what's the latest?"

Boyle shrugged. "They're getting close to the area, but so far it's been kind of slow going. They're moving away from the river area now so it should speed things up. Once they pick up their guy, getting out might be easier than going in. At least, they'll be going with the river instead of against it."

"Yeah, but it's still going to take a while."

"Hickerson says that he's set it up with Mickey Harris to try a helo pickup if it becomes necessary. I thought that should have been the plan from the start, but I guess stealth works just as good as speed, and Hickerson reminded me that the Air America helos have the main evacuation as mission priority."

"Did you tell Hickerson that you, meaning we, want to stay until Thompson and Dalton get out?"

"No, but he knew. I did suggest that he and I go get 'em. He didn't seem all that wild about the idea."

"So what do we do?"

"Do you want to get out of here?"

"Of course not. Why would I want to leave a place that's about to be overrun by bad little people with lots of guns who have an ego problem because they're short and who probably are still pissed off at me for bombing the old homestead back north? No, I'd love to stay. Maybe I can sell them some T-shirts or postcards or something. Hell, I'll bet there are some great deals available on real estate right now."

"So you want to go."

"I didn't say that. I'm going where you're going. I was merely doing my job and pointing out that certain courses of action have inherent dangers. What I haven't said is that you have never been smart enough to think of that."

Boyle grunted. "Yeah, you're right. When the boss gets back, we'll tell him we'll leave."

Santy raised his eyes heavenward and extended his arms out from his shoulders. "Thank you, Lord, for finally giving this dumb son of a bitch, your servant, a shot of common sense." He looked back at Boyle. "Even if it does hurt."

They started to walk away quickly, then gradually slowed and stopped.

Santy smiled a little. "You can't do it, can you? You know how dumb and dangerous it is to stay, but you can't leave. In spite of everything we talked about and agreed on."

"Yeah. And it's not just Thompson and Dalton, it's these people. I haven't done enough."

"Don't count on me holding you back anymore, Tim. I knew you'd change your mind, and I wanted you to, but I had to try."

"Hickerson will take some persuading." Boyle laughed. "But we'll gang up on him."

The two rounded the corner of the Air America building and walked out onto the ramp. They could see an Air America Huey lift up and move out toward the taxiway. Boyle vaguely pointed to it. "That's Hickerson now. He should be back in a couple of hours or so. Let's go get something to eat."

Santy nodded and, as all pilots would, kept his eyes on the helo. He and Boyle watched the Huey smoothly maneuver out onto the taxiway and stop. The noise from the rotors was loud enough that they didn't hear that of the VNAF helo, which would only have been partially in view anyway, had they even noticed it.

They watched as Harris began his takeoff, just starting to gain altitude, maybe five feet or so, when a brown blur approached from their left and struck the Air America helo's rotor system, sending chunks of rotor blades flying in all directions, like large ugly confetti.

Time seemed to slow down for them. It felt as if someone had thrown a lever on a carnival ride. They stood rooted for a second, only beginning to feel the emotions of horror and shock as the silver Air America Huey seemed to partially disintegrate, rolling to the right and toward the ground. The brown VNAF helo continued straight ahead for a few feet before it slowly nosed over and struck the ground nearly inverted, forty feet or so from the crumpled fuselage of the Air America Huey.

Before the highest-flying pieces of the helicopters had begun their downward arcs toward the earth, Boyle and Santy were running as hard as they could toward the wreckage.

★ 22 ★

Saturday, 26 April 1975

IN THE STRANGE SILENCE THAT FOLLOWS EVENTS LIKE THE HELICOPTERS' crashing, as if the entire world momentarily pauses at the abrupt interruption in its measured progression, the only sounds were the rapid footfalls of Boyle and Santy as they sprinted across the tarmac toward the wreckage. But neither one was aware of it— for them, there was no thought, there was no personal fear, there was only action that needed to be taken. It would be years before they remembered that silence, but the emotions they felt now would always be close by.

Santy was slightly faster and reached the Air America helo first. Running around to the nose of the Huey, he peered in through the ragged hole that had only seconds before been the front windshield and instrument panel. His adrenaline masked the visceral reaction as he looked down at what was left of Mickey Harris.

One of the rotor blades, torn completely in half by the collision, had slammed through the right side of the cockpit and into Harris's torso, nearly cutting him and his seat in two. His right hand, attached only to the lower half of the arm, still grasped the stick, and his left hand was around the collective pitch lever, which was at the full upper level of travel. The thought struck Santy that Harris had continued to try to fly the Huey even after he was effectively dead.

Hanging in the left seat, which was now the upper one, Don Hickerson slumped against the torn leading edge of the rotor blade, which had apparently stopped just short of hitting him, too. He was covered in blood and was at least unconscious.

179

Boyle's voice came from just over Santy's shoulder. "Jesus Christ. Is he still alive?"

Santy climbed into the cockpit, unaware that he had scraped his leg on a jagged piece of metal. He put his fingers on Hickerson's throat and felt a pulse.

"Yeah, he's alive, but I don't know how bad he's hurt. I don't know if we should try to move him. Where's the fucking crash crew?"

Boyle looked over his shoulder and didn't see any fire trucks or ambulances coming yet. He climbed in beside Santy. "I don't know, but I smell an awful lot of fuel. This thing may go up anytime, Mike. I think we have to get him out."

"Yeah, shit, you're right. Okay, you get his shoulders and I'll release his harness."

"See if his legs are free first." Boyle maneuvered himself around, cursing as he jabbed his back on something sharp.

"They're okay, but the right one looks broken."

Boyle reached around, grabbed the handle on the left side of the seat, and unlocked the shoulder straps, allowing Hickerson's weight to move his torso forward a little. The lap belt still held the lower part of his body close to the seat. Boyle reached around behind Hickerson and grasped him as tightly as he could. "Okay, I've got him."

Santy shifted his left foot to a firmer spot and reached for the buckle in Hickerson's lap. "Hold his shoulders back some. He's doubled over the buckle."

Boyle pulled upward on the surprisingly heavy form. "How's that?"

"I can get it now. Are you ready?"

When Boyle grunted, Santy pulled up on the latch and caught Hickerson's hips as they fell away from the seat when the harness released. He grasped the limp form around the upper thighs and began to back out through the huge hole in the nose. "All right. His legs are clear. You still okay?"

Boyle tried to twist around while Santy pulled on the lower part of the body, but his foot caught under the seat frame. "Shit. I'm stuck. Can you hold him up here?"

Santy let the legs down gently and shifted his grip upward. "Okay. I got him."

Boyle let go and maneuvered his foot free, reestablishing his hold and allowing Santy to guide Hickerson's form clear of the wreckage.

The two carried him well clear of the Huey and laid him on the grass. Boyle stood up and started to walk back to the wreck, but Santy's voice stopped him. "Mickey's dead, Tim. One of the blades hit him."

Boyle froze, remembering Hickerson's words only—what?—ninety minutes before. Shaking off the thought, he asked, "Was there anyone in the back?"

"I don't know. I didn't see anyone."

"I'll check." Boyle trotted over to the wreck and looked back into the cockpit. For the first time, he got a look at what had happened to Harris. Fighting back a sudden nausea, he tore his eyes away and leaned in, looking past the pilots' seats and into the rear cabin. The cabin was a disordered jumble of equipment, but, to Boyle's great relief, there were no passengers or crewmen. He was backing out through the cockpit again when he heard an almost sultry *whurrrumph* followed by a huge ball of black smoke and yellow flame from the hulk of the VNAF Huey. He could feel the blast of heat from the fire through what was left of the cabin roof.

Suddenly, he looked down at the ground between the wrecks and saw that the flames were spreading toward him at a furious pace. He turned and ran toward Santy, who was struggling to get Hickerson's form farther away from the fire. Grabbing Hickerson's lower legs, Boyle helped Santy move Hickerson across the taxiway and lay him down on the ramp. Kneeling next to Hickerson, Boyle turned back just in time to see the flames reach the Air America Huey, which immediately caught fire with a roar.

Boyle looked back to see Santy staring at him, and the expression on his face was a mixture of fear, relief, and concern. "Almost got your ass that time, Timmy."

Boyle nodded. "Yeah." He looked over Santy's shoulder at the small herd of emergency vehicles far across the airfield but fast approaching. "Here comes the cavalry."

The two young aviators turned their attention to Hickerson, who was beginning to stir. Santy pulled off his shirt and wiped as much of the blood off Hickerson's face as he could, feeling the skull for damage. Finding none, he gradually felt his way down the body, checking for more broken bones while Boyle held the

181

fractured right leg immobile. Santy had finished inspecting the shoulders and arms and was halfway down the right side of the rib cage when Hickerson groaned at his touch.

Santy quickly finished and looked up at Boyle. "Aside from his leg, I think he's got a couple of broken ribs. He's breathing okay and his pulse is strong, but he'll have a concussion for sure."

Boyle nodded. Santy had once been a volunteer firefighter while he was in college, so he should know something about this sort of thing. Even though Boyle had been a rescue pilot, he had never been really trained in anything other than applying bandages and recognizing bottles of aspirin. His job had been to drive the helo while the crewmen in the back took care of the rescuees. He looked at the burning wrecks.

"I wonder, what the hell happened?"

Someone else would have thought Boyle was an idiot for asking that question, especially since he'd *seen* the two helos collide less than a hundred yards away. Santy knew automatically that the question was really about why two aircraft had hit each other on a clear day when both had only moments before been hovering in full view of each other. The question was aimed more at the mistake that led to the event than the event itself.

"I don't know. Maybe somebody took off on somebody else's clearance. Whatever."

There was a sudden screeching of brakes and the footfalls of men running up from behind Boyle. He turned and saw several Air America men piling out of a small ex-Army jeep. In the lead was Frank Wheeler, followed by a group of grease-stained ground crewmen.

Wheeler peered over Boyle's shoulder at Hickerson's form on the ground and looked up at the burning wreckage. He started toward it, but Boyle jumped up and grabbed him by the arms. "Frank! Stay back. There's nothing you can do. It's over."

Wheeler shook off Boyle's grasp and spun around, staring uncomprehendingly at the younger man.

Boyle softened his tone. "He never knew what hit him, Frank. He was dead before the fire started. We checked." The little lie and the words about every pilot's greatest fear—being trapped in a burning airplane—seemed to deflate Wheeler, who turned back and stared at the burning wreckage.

The crash crew roared up and began putting the foul-smelling suppressant foam on the wreckage. The fire quickly diminished until only light gray smoke streamed up from the twisted metal. Soon even that was gone, leaving a cloud dissipating in the wind and two piles of wreckage, incongruously covered with a snow-like whiteness.

Wheeler watched the firefighters go about their work, spraying down everything that could possibly reignite. Several men in silver heat-reflective suits began to approach the wreckage in the vain hope of finding survivors. Wheeler spoke over his shoulder. "How 'bout the people in the other one?"

"No chance. It came down on its back and buried itself. All we had time for was to get Don out before the whole thing went up." Boyle put his hand on Wheeler's shoulder. "I'm sorry, man."

"Yeah. Me, too." Wheeler turned back and knelt beside Hickerson. He looked carefully at the unconscious face. He looked back up at Santy. "How's he?"

"Beat up pretty good. His leg's broken and I think a couple of ribs, too. I've no idea about any other internal injuries, but we've got to get him to a hospital."

Wheeler stood and walked quickly over to the commander of the crash crew. They began speaking in high-volume Vietnamese, complete with great amounts of hand-waving and gesticulating. After a moment, the Vietnamese commander stomped over to one of the ambulances and yelled at the driver, pointing at the small group of Americans surrounding Hickerson. The expression on his face as he watched the driver back around was one of distaste. Wheeler walked over and pulled the back doors of the ambulance open, allowing the two Vietnamese crewmen to jump down and pull out the gurney.

Santy stood back and watched as the crewmen, Wheeler, and Boyle maneuvered Hickerson's form onto the gurney, strapped him to it, and put him in the back of the ambulance. Wheeler climbed back out and closed the doors, but Boyle stayed inside and shouted at Santy to find the admiral and fill him in. Santy waved and followed the ambulance with his eyes as it sped away, disappearing around the corner of one of the hangars with the pitiful wail from its siren fading away.

Wheeler spoke to a couple of the Air America mechanics and climbed into the battered jeep, motioning Santy to get in the other seat.

Gerry Carroll

Santy climbed in and Wheeler started the engine, shoved it in gear, and let out the clutch too quickly. The jeep bucked forward and stalled. Wheeler pounded the steering wheel with a string of curses and started the engine again. This time he got under way successfully and headed off in the same direction as the ambulance had. He was still cursing, but Santy couldn't tell specifically at what. The first turn nearly threw Santy out the open right side of the jeep, and he grabbed the windshield frame and the back of Wheeler's seat to stay aboard.

"Jesus Christ. Easy, Frank. We don't need to get the beds next to Don. Slow down."

Wheeler let off the accelerator a little and got to a more reasonable speed. "Stupid bastard," he shouted.

Santy took his eyes off a fast-approaching bus and looked over. "Who?"

"That crash-crew prick. He said the ambulance was for the Vietnamese in the other helo. I had to convince him that one live American needed it more than four or five dead Vietnamese."

"How'd you convince him?"

"No problem. I told him I'd cut off his balls and feed 'em to my dog if he didn't give me the ambulance right now. I told him I could find out where he lived and that he couldn't run far enough or fast enough."

Santy smiled. "And he bought that?"

Wheeler pulled his shirt up and showed the handle of an extremely large bowie knife protruding from his waistband. "I showed him this. What you might call your basic hard sell. He bought it."

When Admiral Wallace strode into the small waiting room in the Seventh-Day Adventist Hospital, Boyle, Santy, and Wheeler were drinking their umpteenth cups of lousy coffee and rapidly running out of cigarettes. Santy was idly lecturing Boyle on the evils of tobacco and Boyle was pleasantly ignoring it.

Boyle looked up and saw the admiral approach, followed by Joe France and his boss, Commander Bailey. Boyle stood as did Santy, followed by Wheeler.

"Good morning, Tim. How is he?"

"The doctor says he's in fair shape considering. He's got a broken leg, some splintered ribs, a cracked skull, a concussion,

184

and"—Boyle glanced at the clock—"he should be coming out of surgery in a minute or two. His spleen was ruptured so they had to remove it. That's what the surgery is for. Outside of that he's fine."

Wallace nodded. "What happened?"

"I don't know for sure, Admiral. The VNAF helo collided with him and Mickey Harris and rolled them into the dirt. The VNAF landed inverted and caught fire after a couple of minutes. Harris was dead, and Mike and I couldn't get him out. The VNAF crew didn't have a chance. As to why it happened, I don't know."

"Any more of that coffee around?"

"Yes, sir. It's down the hall. I'll get you some."

Wallace held up a hand. "Wait a sec." He turned to Bailey and France. "You guys want some?" They both nodded.

The admiral turned to Santy. "Lieutenant, why don't you make a coffee run. Get some for everyone and take Commander Bailey and Mr. France with you. There's something I need to speak to Tim about so take your time. Thanks."

The three moved off, Bailey and France trying hard to hide their pique at being left out of something, or at least having Boyle involved in something that they weren't.

Wallace led Boyle down the hall a short distance and stopped by a window, only the inside half of which was clean. Wallace took out a cigarette, looked around, and put it back with a sigh. "Tim, first of all, I'm going to have my wife go over to Pat Hickerson's and tell her about this. I don't want the chaplain in his dress blues walking up the driveway. As I understand it, your wife and Pat are pretty close, so I'd appreciate it if she went along. Okay?"

"Yes, sir. But that'll be up to Meg, although I can't imagine her not going."

"Okay. When I leave here, I'll make the call. Now to another matter."

Boyle watched Wallace look down the hall before he began. "As you know, and as I've discovered with General Alexander, Don was taking care of some small but extremely important, um, details. For reasons you are no doubt aware of, I'd prefer not to leave them in the hands of Commander Bailey and Lieutenant France. You are therefore the next in line. If he already hasn't, Don Hickerson was about to tell you to go back out to the fleet.

Now, that was at my orders because I didn't want any extra people wandering around getting lost in the shuffle. I need you now to keep a handle on things here as far as Don's responsibilities went. I also need you to keep an eye on the other little situation."

Wallace stared at Boyle to make sure he got the point. It could only be the "mission" of Thompson and Dalton. Boyle stared back in what he hoped was a professionally confident way. "Yes, sir. I can do that."

"I know you can, Tim. Now, I'll tell you your orders. Since the situation is so fluid, I will leave it up to your discretion as to how you handle it. Do what you think best, but keep me informed. You are to brook no interference from anyone, especially from members of our staff. *You* are in charge and no one else. Clear?"

"Yes, sir."

"Okay. There isn't a lot of time left. When you decide to leave is pretty much up to you, but in no case are you to wait for the last helo. When the evacuation starts, you leave, understand?"

"Yes, sir."

"Good. Ah, here comes our coffee."

Wallace moved past Boyle and accepted the cup from Bailey. Santy handed one to Boyle. Wallace looked at Santy for a moment and turned back to Boyle. "Tim, keep Mr. Santy with you. Two heads are better than one. I have to go. Please arrange for Commander Hickerson to be moved out to the *Concord* as soon as he can be moved. Keep me informed."

Wallace turned back to Bailey and France and led them slowly toward the door. Boyle stood there and listened to Wallace's fading voice assign them to investigate and report on the circumstances of the crash and injury to an active duty naval officer. Boyle couldn't be sure, but he thought he actually saw Bailey's face light up with pleasure at an assignment that was obviously so important. Boyle shook his head.

At his shoulder, Mike Santy watched the three leave before he turned to his friend. "And may I ask what it is you're going to keep me with you for? I get nervous when admirals refer to me as 'mister.' "

"I'm not exactly sure, Mike. It seems we now have an official job which is a little vague. The bottom line is that we're not going back to the ship just yet."

"Uh-huh. And when are we?"

"Mike, when you see me sprinting toward a helo, you might want to tag along."

"Oh, good. That helps. I've always loved firm plans."

Early that evening, Boyle and Santy rode over to Tan Son Nhut airport in the ambulance with Hickerson's semiconscious form. With them in the ambulance were two Vietnamese nurses and one Navy flight surgeon still in his flight suit.

The nurses couldn't have been more different from each other. One was older, somewhere in her late thirties, and was coldly professional, speaking only when directly addressed and then only to the flight surgeon through the other nurse.

The other was in her early twenties and very frightened. She hovered over Hickerson, doing and redoing in an obvious effort to keep herself busy as they drove through the dark streets of the capital, passing only the periodic four- or five-man patrols of the ARVN military police enforcing the increasingly early curfew. The one time one of these patrols stopped them to make sure that they were not some terrorists or criminal gang merely using a military vehicle for cover, the young nurse had almost cowered in the corner behind Santy, hiding behind his broad shoulders until the MPs let them proceed.

The older nurse, however, had not been intimidated by the soldiers and their posturing and their guns and had slapped away their hands as they reached to check under Hickerson's sheets. She had leaped between them and her patient and bullied the soldiers back out the door until they shouted what sounded like curses at her and slammed the door, pounding on the side and yelling for the driver to proceed. It struck Boyle that no expression of triumph was on her face at the small victory—she only bent down and inspected Hickerson for any signs of disturbance from their paws. She is one formidable lady, even if she is only about five foot two, thought Boyle.

The drive continued on out the long road to the airport with Boyle sitting against the wall watching, Santy trying to comfort the younger nurse and the flight surgeon and the older nurse bending over Hickerson. At one point, the older nurse caught Boyle watching her and her expression softened, just for a moment, before it was once again hidden behind the professional mask.

187

Once they arrived at the airport, the ambulance went directly to a darker area near the Air America hangar where a Marine Corps H-46 was waiting. The ambulance backed up to the rear ramp, and Boyle and Santy helped carry Hickerson aboard. They walked back out and led the ambulance off to the side, well clear of the rotor arc and far enough away that Boyle felt comfortable lighting up a cigarette.

Leaning against the side of the ambulance, they watched and listened to the helo engines start and the rotors engage with that odd rushing clatter so characteristic of the H-46. The crewman did a fast walk around marked only by the splash of his flashlight on the various parts of the helo as he checked them. The crewman climbed back aboard, closed the lower half of the personnel door, and stood there as the 46 taxied a short distance away and lifted into a hover. The exterior lights came on suddenly and the helo climbed away, turning to the southeast, toward the ships waiting offshore.

Boyle dropped the stub of his cigarette and crushed it out with his boot. He turned to Santy, who was staring off into the darkness. "You ready to go?"

"Yup. Let's see if these folks will drop us off at the hotel." He spoke to the younger nurse, who nodded and turned to the older one, speaking rapidly in Vietnamese. Boyle tried to make some sense of what she said but couldn't figure out whether or not she was telling or asking.

The young nurse turned back and told Santy they'd be delighted to drop them off, and everybody climbed back into the ambulance. Boyle got in the front where there was at least a seat designed for an upright human and didn't notice when Santy didn't argue and held the door for the young nurse as he climbed in the back after her.

✮ **23** ✮

Saturday, 26 April 1975

BOYLE AND SANTY TOOK THEIR BEERS AND GENTLY SHOVED THEIR WAY back through the thick crowd at the bar in the hotel. They found an unoccupied table near the window and sat down. Santy took a long pull from his bottle and leaned back in the chair.

"That tastes good."

Boyle nodded slowly, looking over the crowd at the bar. "That it does, Mike. Do you think we should have gotten a couple more? That crowd is murder."

"Nope. These are going to put me to sleep most skosh."

Boyle arched an eyebrow at his friend. "Tell me something, Mr. Smooth, were those serious moves I saw you putting on that young nurse? You seemed pretty eager to protect her from the MPs."

Santy shook his head. "Hell, no. I'm almost married. You don't screw around in front of your future bother-in-law." There was none of the expected humor in the statement.

Santy was silent for a moment and then he looked out the window and spoke more gently. "Her name's Tran. She's only twenty."

Boyle was struck by the strange tone. He started to say something but stopped when he realized what Santy was saying in those two short sentences. He had then what was probably the same thought that was running through his friend's head—"these people" now had a face and a name.

Instead of feeling the tragedy of South Vietnam in a sort of historical sense, as if it were something in a book or a television documentary, the two young aviators, especially Santy, would

189

now feel it as if it were happening to someone just like them, like one of their own countrymen. And in a sense it was.

Boyle remained silent and watched his friend think. When he had something to say, Mike would open up, and from long experience, Boyle knew that this was not the moment to interrupt him. He just sat back and watched the wheels turn.

After a few more minutes, Mike leaned forward and rested his arms on the table. "She's scared shitless about what's going to happen when the bad guys get here. She says that her father and most of her family either worked for the government or were military officers. The word is out, Tim. She says that when the Communists get here, the first thing they're going to do is round up people like them and ship them off to some 'reeducation' camp if they don't shoot them first. They're just regular folks and can't get out, so they're screwed. I offered to try and let her go out on the helo, but she said she couldn't leave her family."

Boyle, knowing that Santy was leading up to something, quietly inspected the wet rings his beer bottle was leaving on the table. He thought for a minute and then looked at Santy, who was off in a different world, staring blankly into the middle distance. His forehead was furrowed and the new dark circles under his eyes made him look like a mad scientist.

"Okay, Mike. What're you thinking?"

"Well, I was thinking that it's pretty shitty that housekeepers and B-girls are getting out while good people like her don't have a chance. I was just wondering if there's something that can be done about that."

"And is there a plan yet?"

Santy shook his head slowly. "Nope. I'm just kicking around the problem right now. I don't have a plan."

"Yes, you have. Now all we have to do is figure out what and how."

"We?"

"Mike, you said earlier that we can't save the whole country. Well, maybe the best we can do is to save a little piece of it. Maybe we can do something for that little nurse."

"What exactly?"

"Well, why don't we stick her and a couple of her family members on one of the Air Force C-141s going out of here?"

"We have to get the visas or exit permits or whatever the hell paperwork done and then get her on one of the lists. Do we have time?"

"Not for all that shit. But why don't we just round 'em up, drive 'em to the airport, and just stick 'em on an eastbound C-141?"

"That simple?"

"Why the hell not? This place is so fucked up nobody'll notice a couple of extra people leaving."

"I hate to bring this up, but wasn't it you who said we have to tuck our tails between our legs and get on the plane?"

"Nope, that was you. And we will. Just like good little American boys. Right after we get the nurse and her clan on one, too."

Boyle stood and Santy asked, "Where are you going?"

Boyle gestured to the crowd at the bar. "I'm going to see if I can find that newsguy Mickey Harris introduced us to last week—Callahan."

"Why him? What are you going to do, issue a press release?"

Boyle laughed. "No, you asshole. Callahan seems just as pissed off about what's happening as we are. He speaks Vietnamese, and even though Tran is okay in English, Callahan can make sure there's no misunderstanding. Besides, he's been here forever and should know a few tricks."

Santy turned and looked out the window at the ever more rapidly approaching war, flickering and flashing in the darkness. "I hope he knows a bunch of them because I don't think we have a lot of time."

Two hours later, Boyle, Santy, and Callahan sat on the hard wooden benches in the small waiting room in the Seventh-Day Adventist Hospital. Callahan was quietly telling the younger pair stories from his long experience in Vietnam, a few of them dating back to the days when the place was called French Indochina.

The newsman was one of those rare treasures of which his profession was seeing increasingly fewer lately. He had a true belief in the ethics of his profession and an insatiable desire to actually learn about things beyond the trivial, hysterical, and fatuous, which was all that would be required for a fifteen-hundred-word article or a thirty-second on-camera appearance. Liam Callahan believed that truth was more important than selling papers and ratings. A half dozen of his pieces over the years had been

191

in the running for the Pulitzer, and two had won it, which he considered nice but not particularly important.

He'd been pulled out of Vietnam twice and given larger, more visible, and more prestigious assignments but always wound up back in Asia. He was a short, round, brilliant American mick. He was far from pretty and would never make it as an anchorman or be able to put on a Brooks Brothers suit and mingle with those at the National Press Club.

Boyle and Santy had liked him immediately when Harris had brought him over to their table one evening. Their natural reserve around the press had evaporated quickly as they all talked. But more important was the fact that Harris had told them that he could be trusted. That had been enough.

Somewhere during Callahan's first-person account of the march and brutal battle from LZ Xray to LZ Albany during the battles around Pleiku in 1965, Boyle and Santy realized that the older nurse, the supervisor who had ridden in the ambulance to the airport with Hickerson earlier, was standing across the room listening. Callahan stopped his story and walked over to the nurse, speaking rapidly in Vietnamese.

The nurse never changed her expression as she glanced over at Boyle and Santy and curtly interrupted Callahan several times. When Callahan wound down, she was silent for a moment, staring thoughtfully at something high on the far wall. She then fired off some more rapid-fire Vietnamese and spun around, leaving the room in a great cloud of dignity.

Santy looked at Boyle for a second and then back to Callahan. "Well?"

"She said she'd go get your young lady and we could put the question to her ourselves. I got the feeling that she thinks it's a good idea. I'll tell you one thing though, I'd hate to cross that lady."

"Yeah, but if it was me stuck in this hospital, she'd be the one I'd want taking care of me."

"You got that right." Callahan picked up his lukewarm coffee and turned to face both young men. "Now, listen. All we can do here is offer the opportunity. No matter how good an idea it might seem, we can't kidnap the kid and shove her on a plane. Rescues don't always work. Got it?"

They nodded and Callahan continued, "One more thing. I'm

192

only a reporter. My job is to tell the story of the fall of Saigon, not to be a part of it. I'll do what I can, but don't expect me to run the show or to get you guys out of trouble if you put your foot in it. You two started this and you two'll have to finish it. I don't come along with the deal here."

Santy smiled. "We understand. Just like that reporter who was with the First Cav in the Ia Drang Valley. What was his name?" He looked at Boyle. "You ought to know, Tim. It was some little Irish guy."

Callahan shook his head. "Fuck you, Mike," he said with resignation.

With nothing more to say just then, the three were silent for a moment until the door opened and the supervisor stepped in, followed by Tran, who was doing her best to hide behind her supervisor.

The older nurse gently placed her hand on Tran's shoulder and steered her close to the three Americans. It was clear that she didn't want to be the center of attention.

Callahan stepped forward and spoke gently in Vietnamese, occasionally pointing to one or the other of the young Americans, who were doing their best to look unthreatening. Given their size relative to hers, it was a difficult task.

At one point, Callahan sighed and rubbed his hand over his face in a mixture of sadness and frustration. Boyle asked, "Problems, Liam?"

"Yeah. She doesn't have a real high opinion of Americans just now. I think she's afraid that you guys want to take her home and make a slave or a prostitute out of her. She's heard all sorts of stories about that. Hell, I don't know, maybe some are even true."

Boyle looked at the young girl and stepped forward. Pulling out his wallet, he removed a picture of Meghan and held it out, telling Tran who she was. Santy pulled out his picture of Maureen and handed it over. Callahan showed the girl the pictures and spoke again to Tran. The older nurse inspected the photo over Tran's shoulder and spoke earnestly to her, gesturing toward the young pilots.

The three spoke for several minutes in rapid Vietnamese, making Boyle and Santy feel as if they were watching a game of Australian-rules football—they could see the action but had absolutely no idea what was happening. After a while, the conversation turned to abrupt statements and a series of nods and monosyllables. Then there was silence for a full minute while all eyes were on Tran, who was staring at the floor.

She looked up and stared at each of them for a long moment and then nodded, setting her chin in a mannerism that reminded Boyle of Meg when she had come to a decision. She spoke for a few seconds in an almost little-girlish voice. All the while, she looked straight into Santy's eyes with a sort of defiance that belied her tone. Callahan let out a long sigh and turned.

"She says that she thinks she can trust you and would very much like our help in getting her family out of Vietnam. She is afraid of the danger and she knows that there is not a lot of time. The boss here says that she must finish this shift since the hospital is pretty short-handed, but she'll be available in three hours. If we come back then, we can start planning this whole deal. I asked the boss here if she wants to go, and she said that she will be more useful staying than trying to start over in a new country. Somehow I think that the gomers are going to have a hell of a time with her. Serves 'em right."

Callahan turned back and spoke again to the two nurses, then headed for the door. "Let's go. We've got some things to do in the next three hours."

Boyle and Santy followed, but before they got to the door, the older nurse's voice, in perfect English, stopped them. "Thank you, gentlemen. What you are doing is a noble and decent thing. I am grateful, and when Tran is a bit older, she will feel as I do. But right now she is afraid. Please bear that in mind."

She turned to Callahan, actually smiling a little. "You're damned right they're going to have their hands full, Mr. Callahan. Good night, gentlemen. And thank you." The nurse disappeared through the ward door, leaving the three Americans open-mouthed.

As they walked out the door of the hospital and got into the car, Callahan said with a great deal of reverence, "I'll bet that if we come back here in five or ten years, that lady will be running the whole hospital."

"Hospital, nothing. More likely the whole damn country."

★ 24 ★

Sunday, 27 April 1975

KEVIN THOMPSON AND MARK DALTON LAY CONCEALED IN THE SCRUB about five yards back from the road. They'd been lying there for the better part of an hour waiting for the traffic to slow down. And in the early-morning darkness, they were also waiting for their hearts to slow down.

Less than a minute before, one of the seemingly endless stream of marching NVA soldiers had left his file and stepped off the road to urinate. He had stood less than ten feet from Dalton's right shoulder and blithely gone about his business, staring idly at the trees overhanging the road. Dalton and Thompson had lain there more still than the logs of the dead trees that littered the first fifty yards of the scrub until the soldier had tucked himself back together and rejoined the column, hustling to catch up with his mates, who had passed around the far bend in the road.

Thompson felt Dalton's elbow press his, and he raised his head and looked to his right across Dalton's broad back. About one hundred yards away, what seemed to be the end of the long column of NVA made the turn in the road. Unlike those who had been farther toward the front of the column, the soldiers at the rear were marching in that mind-dead way that soldiers have as they switch everything off and only use those parts of their bodies and brains actually necessary for following the back of the man ahead of them.

Those at the front had to be more alert, searching alongside the road for potential ambush and the road itself for the mines that both sides were wont to place. Toward the middle, the need for vigilance was smaller but still present as the soldiers half-listened

195

for the shouts and commands of those up front, but still they would have time to gather themselves for a fight if the men at the point walked into one.

But at the rear, all that was required was measured and constant movement. No concentrated thought, no special awareness, no sweaty palms on the rifle stock, no intense searching of the surroundings—just the dull, brute endurance it took to get from rest stop to rest stop.

Off to the left, or south, Thompson could hear the engines of the last trucks move off into silence. To the right, neither man could hear engines of more trucks approaching, so these last few soldiers should be the end of the column, at least for the moment. Dalton slid his leg up under himself and began a slow crawl to the right as Thompson raised himself on his elbows and pushed his rifle closer to a firing position. He watched Dalton ease his way a little closer to the road.

Dalton waited until the last man in the column had turned the bend to the left, listened for approaching vehicles, and sprinted across the road, diving silently behind a bush on the far side. Thompson watched him lie still for a moment and then peer back up the road for any approaching stragglers. He raised his hand slightly and motioned Thompson across.

Thompson took a deep breath and got a firmer grip on his weapon. He mentally counted to three, then rose and sprinted across the road, doing his best to avoid stepping in any damp spots and leaving footprints. He flopped down beside Dalton and looked back the way he had come. From what he could see, they had left no obvious trace behind; their tracks were sufficiently blurred so that they would become noticeable only to someone looking specifically for signs of an enemy. They had left no debris, such as C-ration cans or cigarette butts, on the other side, so the enemy shouldn't pick up their trail easily.

This was the last major road they would have to cross before their rendezvous with Tony Butler. One at a time, the two SEALs slid farther back into the scrub, covering each other and keeping their weapons pointed at the greatest threat—the road. When they were finally far enough away that they could no longer see any part of the road, they stood up and moved more quickly until they finally felt relatively secure. They found a small clump of trees and used it for concealment.

⋆ **24** ⋆

Dalton slid his pack to the ground and leaned back on it. "Well, what do you think?"

Thompson was looking back the way they had come and answered over his shoulder, "I think the little bastards figure the war's all over but the shouting. Seems to me they're getting pretty bold now. It wasn't too long ago that they'd be trying to conceal themselves and their equipment well before this time of the morning. Now, it looks like they don't really give a shit about their attacks or even artillery spotters."

"Yeah, I think so, too. But at least they're not quite as alert as they used to be. Either that or the guys who're passing by now ain't the varsity."

Dalton pulled the folded map from its plastic bag and laid it on the ground. Thompson eased over and stared down as Dalton oriented himself with the map. "I think we're about here, boss. If Tony is where he said he's gonna be, we've got about ten klicks to go. From what this map says, we need to go almost due west from here. Maybe, um, two hundred seventy-five degrees."

Thompson nodded slowly and reached for the radio. "Okay. I'll phone it in."

Dalton watched over Thompson's shoulder as he wrote down the map coordinates of their position and jotted the jumble of numbers and letters that would make up the situation report, or "sitrep." The thought struck him that it hadn't taken long for the two of them to get back some of their fieldcraft.

The only problem, he thought as he massaged his aching knees, was that they couldn't get back their youth.

While Thompson and Dalton were finishing their radio transmission, Tony Butler lay shivering under two of the sleeping mats his men had carried as part of their meager store of personal equipment. He was having another bout of a recurrent fever that had been plaguing him for the past eighteen months. The fever was not malaria, he was certain of that, but when it struck, it was just as incapacitating but lasted less than a day, usually. The attacks had been coming with greater frequency lately and were beginning to be more and more vicious, although Butler only knew this from others since he was completely out of his head during the largest part of the attacks.

Butler looked to one side and saw his two sons were being

amused by one of the other men in the small group. They were being shown some sleight-of-hand trick and were laughing delightedly as all children will when confronted with something magical and mysterious. But they were laughing quietly as if a full measure of delight would bring the enemy down on them.

Butler looked back up at the dark sky and wondered at the unfairness of it. In most of the world, the boys would be squealing and shouting happily at the tricks they were being shown. They'd be calling loudly for more and would wind up pulling at the magic hands and trying to figure out the trick. To have to look over their shoulder and wonder who heard them or where the bad people were would be as foreign to them as the language his two sons were speaking.

Butler tried to remember his own youth, what little there had been of it. He'd never known his father, who had been killed in Korea, and his mother, a sad, quiet woman who had an air of defeat about her like a shroud in the only picture he'd had of her, had died of tuberculosis when he was about three. He'd been raised for a little while by his maternal grandparents, but even that had been taken from him by the time he was eight. A succession of foster homes, a lonely and undistinguished career in school, and finally the prospect of the draft had led him to enlist in the Navy.

Although he'd never understand it this way, Butler had sought challenge after challenge in the Navy until he began to prove himself to Tony Butler: It was when he'd applied for the SEALs and been accepted that he actually found someplace he'd belonged. And when he'd come to Vietnam and been assigned to the little hamlet full of people whose society was just as pummeled as Tony Butler's life, he'd found a home.

And now that home was going away, too. All that would be left of it for him were his two sons and memories of these past seven years, at once the most difficult and the happiest time of his life.

Butler threw off the mats and tried to get to his feet. One of the other men left the small, smokeless cooking fire, came over to him, and helped him sit on a log by the fire. The two boys left their playmate and came over, standing next to him and looking carefully at his face. Butler put out his hands and gently stroked their faces, forcing a smile of reassurance. He pulled them both down on the log so that they could sit on either side of him, and he put his arms around their thin shoulders, feeling their boniness.

He wished he'd been able to give them a decent diet, but their life on the run had made that impossible. That was almost over now. In a couple of days, he and they would be on their way to a place where there were no bad people hiding in every bush, or waiting around the next bend in the trail. In a couple of days, these boys would have a life and a future. In a day or so, they would at least have a chance.

The man who had tended the fire handed Butler a plate of food. What it was didn't really matter much, it was just a sort of slub-gum made up of whatever the small group could find or trap. He ate ravenously at first, but his shrunken stomach filled quickly and he gave the rest to his sons, careful to make them use their own implements. The man tending the fire stayed close just long enough to make sure Butler could handle things and then moved away.

Butler looked around the small clearing and noticed that the scouts hadn't returned. He dimly remembered that they'd gone out toward the rendezvous point and would guide Thompson and Dalton here when the two SEALs arrived there. There had been no word from them, but the thought that they might not come or that they might be caught in the attempt had not worried him at all.

In Butler's tiny little universe, those two old friends were as dependable as gravity.

Seated in the left, or copilot's, seat of the huge CH-53 helicopter, Marine 1st Lt. Bob Dunn looked out ahead and saw the coast of South Vietnam, bright and beautiful in the early-morning sun, slide underneath the lead helo. The two aircraft were headed to Tan Son Nhut airport to drop off an additional fifteen or so Marines whose job it would be to help coordinate operations around the DAO compound at the airport.

The lead aircraft was flown by the squadron skipper, Lt. Col. Greg Miller, with one of the other junior officers, Tom McGee, flying as copilot. Even though Dunn and McGee were aircraft commanders, or HACs, in their own right, Miller had decided to take this opportunity to give the younger men a chance to get a feel for the routes they were going to have to fly under much more

199

difficult conditions in a couple of days. He had several other flights scheduled to come in later on and had doubled up the HACs for the flights. Dunn liked the idea. At least somebody in each crew would have seen the place before.

Dunn's pilot for the morning was the squadron maintenance officer, Maj. Jim Lawson. He was sitting in his seat affecting complete calm while Dunn did the flying. Dunn knew that Lawson was paying attention to everything going on—his attitude was simply an old aviator's trick to make Dunn think he wasn't being evaluated.

Dunn did a little S-turn to space his aircraft a little farther behind and out to the side of the lead. He rechecked his altitude, 7,200 feet, and looked at the sectional chart clipped to his kneeboard to make sure that he was to the right of the penciled line that led toward Saigon.

The actual route in during the evacuation was dead on the line and at 6,500 feet heading in (Route Michigan), with another corridor at 5,500 feet heading back out (Route Ohio). Since these were the only two aircraft on this mission, the skipper had decided to vary the routes and altitudes slightly so as to throw off any enemy gunners who might either have a grudge against the Americans or been tipped off to the plan, or both.

As the helos flew past Cap St. Jacques on their right, Dunn could see several pillars of smoke, which rose only a hundred feet or so before they were blown eastward by the freshening breeze. Vung Tau, on the cape, had been designated an embarkation point for seaborne evacuation, but judging from the number of fires down there, that route was effectively closed. That thought simply added to the seriousness of what Dunn and the crews of the two 53s were about this morning.

★ 25 ★

Sunday, 27 April 1975

IT WAS A LITTLE AFTER EIGHT IN THE MORNING WHEN THE TELEPHONE NEXT to Meghan Boyle's bed rang. At first, she had no idea what the noise was, but after sitting up and looking for fire trucks and elevators, she figured out that it was the phone and picked it up. The voice on the other end was crisp and businesslike.

"Meg, good morning. Sorry to wake you. It's Betty Wallace."

Meghan leaned back against the headboard, trying to figure out what Betty could possibly want this early on a Sunday morning.

"Hi, Betty. What's up?"

"I need your help. Everything's okay, but we have to go see Pat Hickerson this morning. Don was in a helicopter accident. He's not badly hurt and he'll be fine, but since you're Pat's closest friend on the staff, I thought you'd like to be there."

"Of course." Betty's statement had carried all the necessary details for Meg. First, there had been an accident. Second, it did *not* involve Tim. Third, the accident had not killed anyone she knew. Fourth, the one involved whom she did know would survive. Navy wives, especially those married to aviators, have to live with the constant burning knowledge that something could happen at any moment, when the husbands are out flying from carriers or a foreign base.

"Okay, Meg. I'll be there in thirty minutes. If you have some coffee ready, it'll take me about one cup to fill you in."

"I'll be ready, Betty. See you in half an hour."

Meghan got up and went into the kitchen and put on the coffee-pot, also making herself a cup of instant coffee while she waited for the percolator to do its thing. As she watched the coffee pop

201

up through the little glass top, she allowed herself to think about what she had to do.

Meghan tried to recall whether she'd ever heard about Don Hickerson either crashing or being shot down before. If it had happened, his wife, Pat, would be much more able to deal with this. If not, then the visit she and Betty Wallace were about to make was going to be far more difficult.

Meghan thought back to the horrible days when she herself had gone through the fires of hell. Tim had crashed in North Vietnam and was initially listed as missing in action. Tim's father's voice on the telephone telling her of the crash carried with it the faint hope that he had survived, but it was obvious that the officers who had gone to the parents' home had not carried a great deal of optimism. It was two days later when another call came—this time telling her that Tim had been rescued but was wounded.

The second call had created one kind of worry that was much more specific than the first. When Tim was briefly listed as MIA, she could visualize him intact, either captured by the enemy or fleeing through the woods toward rescue of some sort. The fear was there, but it had no definition. She could worry, but helping him was up to his fellow professionals—he was in an arena that she could never enter.

When the second call came, the image changed to Tim, unconscious, wrapped in huge bandages, and lying on a bed of pain. He was hooked up to every machine known to man while concerned doctors and nurses huddled around and spoke in muted tones. Now, the worry had entered *her* area of responsibility. Her fiancé, the love of her life, her *mate,* was hurt, and it was her job to help him get well. She never really believed the good reports of his condition she received until he had finally arrived in Balboa Naval Hospital in San Diego and she could go in and see for herself—to look in his eyes and see life and the prospect of much more to come. Sitting on the edge of the bed and crying in relief, in joy, and in anger that would never find expression was her catharsis.

Meghan smiled when she remembered that she wouldn't even believe Mike Santy, who had been with Tim—on the ground in North Vietnam, through the rescue, and for the initial time in the hospital. Santy had received lesser injuries and had come home three days before Tim arrived. He swore that Tim was going to be fine and had made the mistake of smiling when it was obvious that she didn't fully accept it. She'd hauled off and belted him and then dissolved into tears because she'd lashed out at the man who was Tim's best friend, and hers, really. Santy just held her and let her cry, understanding in that dim way peculiar to males that she needed to see for herself that Tim was all right.

"Who was that on the phone, Meg?" Meghan hadn't heard Maureen get up or come into the kitchen.

"Mornin', Moe. Coffee's almost done." Meghan got up, pulled a cup down from the cupboard, and filled one for her sister and refilled her own. "That was Betty Wallace, the admiral's wife. There was an accident and Don Hickerson was injured. Betty and I have to go over to Pat's house and be with her for a while. At least, until she gets over the shock of it, or whatever it is she has to get over. I suppose the shrinks have a name for it."

Maureen sat at the table across from Meghan. "Was he hurt badly?"

"I don't think so. Betty didn't say exactly, but she seemed reasonably normal. What I mean is, you can tell from someone's voice how things are. Betty didn't seem particularly upset."

"It's not her husband who's hurt."

Meghan looked up with steel in her eyes. "It could have been." She instantly regretted her tone. "I'm sorry, Moe. What I mean is that Navy wives feel just as strongly for the safety of the other wives' husbands as the pilots do for their friends. If Don were really in bad shape, Betty would never be able to hide it."

Maureen nodded. "And what can happen to one can just as easily happen to another, right?"

"That's about it, Moe."

"Well, we'd better get ready."

"We?"

"Uh-huh. You're going to need some help, too, big sister. And since I'm almost a Navy wife, I'd better get started learning my job."

By the time Betty Wallace arrived, Meghan was rooting through her closet trying to find the right pair of shoes. Maureen was blow-drying her hair and would be ready in a couple of minutes. Meghan smiled a little as she remembered all the times she and Maureen had dashed madly around the house getting ready for dates, much to the amusement of their father and younger brothers.

At the knock on the front door, Meghan called from the bedroom, "Come on in, Betty. It's open."

A few seconds later, Betty Wallace appeared at the bedroom door, holding a cup of coffee.

Meghan glanced over. "Where are we in the process? Has Pat been told yet?"

"No. Keith called me from the embassy in Saigon in the middle of the night and told me to intercept the chaplain before he received the message and charged over to Pat's. Keith was all admiralish about it, but he figures Pat doesn't need to see a staff car pull up. It'll be easier on her if it's us, especially since Don's going to be fine. He called me again right before I came over here and confirmed it."

Betty followed Meghan into the kitchen and declined her offer of another cup of coffee. Maureen walked in and Meghan made the introductions and then asked, "What the hell happened?"

Betty shrugged slightly, not ready to go into all the details then. "Apparently, Don was flying some sort of logistics flight and they had a midair with a Vietnamese helo."

A chill went through Meghan—Tim had promised! She knew perfectly well that if Hickerson had been out flying, so had Tim. She had the thought that if the dumb mick survived this little trip, she was going to kill him. She looked up into Betty's eyes and was suddenly aware that Betty Wallace knew *exactly* what she was thinking.

The small amount of silent communication ended when Betty stood. "Well. Are we ready?"

"I suppose. We can walk. It's only a block or so."

Ten minutes later, all three women drew deep breaths and squared their shoulders as they heard Pat Hickerson's footsteps come down the short hall and approach the front door. Pat pulled it open and saw her visitors. The expression on her face went from sleepy confusion to a smile of welcome when she registered who was standing on her porch. And then, the realization that two Navy wives, even good friends, don't appear on one's porch without calling first, at least not early on a Sunday morning, struck her. In the instant before Betty could reach and touch Pat's arm in reassurance, Meghan saw comprehension strike her, followed by soul-searing fear.

Betty spoke quickly. "Pat, Don's okay. There was an accident, but he's okay."

Pat sagged against the doorjamb—it was obvious she didn't believe it. Betty Wallace steered her into the house and sat her on the living room couch. Meghan sat next to her and took her hand while Maureen tried to blend into the wallpaper. She had the thought that she was getting a graduate course in being a Navy wife. She also hoped that this morning would be the only time she'd ever be involved in a moment like this.

All the while Betty kept speaking, trying to break through the wall that fear puts between the mind and the heart.

"Pat, I spoke to Keith not even an hour ago. Don is beat-up, but he's going to be perfectly fine real soon. Honestly."

Pat looked up through the beginnings of tears while Meghan put her arm around her shoulders. "What happened?"

"Apparently Don was out helping to scout for landing sites in the city and another helo collided with them."

"He was flying? But he said he wouldn't have to do that."

"I don't know the whys and wherefores, but you can chew him out when he gets home in a week or so. The important thing is that he's going to be fine."

"How badly is he hurt? Did he get burned?"

"No. No burns. Not unless the ashtray spilled on him."

Pat smiled a little at the small joke, and Meghan could see that she was now dealing with it, getting over the shock. She had her mind on the practical. Asking the question that most helicopter pilots' wives always ask near the front, about the burns. They know that you can neither eject nor bail out of a helicopter. When it goes down, so does the crew. The trick is managing how hard you hit the ground.

Betty sat down on the chair facing the couch. She pulled a sheet of paper out of her purse and handed it over. It was the naval message form that reported Don Hickerson's medical condition and, as usual, was incomprehensible to someone outside the medical profession. It was full of long words and references to diagnoses by number. Pat read it and put it down.

"What the hell does this all mean?"

"What it means is he's got some broken ribs and a broken leg, a nice concussion, and they had to take out his spleen. He's back aboard the ship and locked up in sick bay. He went through the surgery very well, and as soon as he's more comfortable, they're going to fly him off to the Philippines and then home. Keith says it'll be no more than a week before you can, quote, 'punch the dumb son of a bitch in the nose for scaring the shit out of you.' He says you've earned the right.''

Pat closed her eyes and hid her face in her hands. She began to sob quietly and Meghan pulled her head down on her shoulder. Meghan looked up and saw Maureen gesture toward the kitchen. While gently rocking Pat, Meghan nodded and Maureen left the room to attempt the often difficult task of finding the makings for coffee in another woman's kitchen.

After a moment, Pat heard the clatter of cups in the kitchen and sat up. Sniffing and wiping her eyes on her housecoat sleeve, she stood to go make the coffee, but Meghan held her down. "Moe can handle that. You just sit here awhile.''

Betty handed over a small unopened packet of Kleenex, smiling a little shyly. "Be prepared. I learned that from an Eagle Scout once.''

Pat took the Kleenex with a small smile and blew her nose. "I'm okay. Can you tell me any more of what happened?''

Betty Wallace nodded. "Yeah. He was flying with the Air America people looking for landing sites for the evacuation. They were just taking off when a Vietnamese Air Force helo ran into them. Both aircraft crashed.'' Betty looked hard at Meghan. "It seems that Tim and another pilot from the *Concord,* named Sandy or something, pulled him out right before the helo caught fire.''

At the mention of Tim's name Meghan froze. For a moment, she didn't know whether to be proud that Tim had apparently saved Don Hickerson's life or furious with him for apparently risking his own. She put that off for the moment. She was just about to speak when she heard Maureen's voice from the doorway. "Betty, could that name have been Santy instead of Sandy?''

"The connection wasn't all that good. It could have been. Keith did say that he was a friend of Tim's who is TAD from the ship. Why, do you know him?''

Meghan smiled. "Mike Santy is Maureen's fiancé. He's like Tim's brother, and if Tim is involved in something, it's a sure bet that Mike isn't far away.''

206

Betty nodded. "Anyway, Pat, they took Don to the hospital and then flew him out to the ship. Keith said that he's awake and alert and sore as hell. As soon as he can walk up to the radio room, he'll call by a phone patch."

"How about the rest of the crew?"

"I don't know, and to be honest, Pat, I didn't ask."

Pat nodded and leaned back on the couch, looking up at the ceiling for a while. Meghan and Betty remained silent, thinking that they were very glad that the news had not been worse. The spell was broken by Pat's teenage son, who walked in from the kitchen.

"Good morning, ladies."

Meghan looked at the young man, now almost finished with high school. He was tall and handsome, just like his father, but had an amazing insouciance that would never allow him to survive professionally if he were to follow his father into the Navy. He'd decided to be a marine biologist, and Meghan was vaguely glad for that.

The young man's expression clouded as he looked at each of the three women in the room. He walked over and sat down on the couch next to his mother. "What happened, Mom? Is Dad all right?"

Pat put her arm around his broad shoulders. "Yes, Kyle. Your dad's all right. He was in a helicopter crash and he's beat-up a little. But there's no permanent damage and he'll be home soon."

Kyle stood up and squared his shoulders. "All right, then. I'll go help that pretty lady in the kitchen with the coffee."

As he walked from the room, acting as best he could like the man around the house that his mother needed right now, Betty cleared her throat and stood, looking out the front window into the past when her son had done exactly the same thing for her. Keith had managed to get himself declared missing for a day when his F9F went down over the Cascade mountains. They'd found him merrily sitting in his makeshift camp next to a logging road, and all was well. But Betty had never forgotten how in that crisis her son had suddenly ceased being a little boy and had become almost a man. She remembered the swell of pride she'd felt. But she also remembered the wrenching sense of loss that the pride had carried with it.

Gerry Carroll

Certain that she was totally back in control, Betty turned back to Pat. "That's quite a young man you have there, Pat."

Pat grinned a little. "Yes, he is."

Two hours later, Meghan and Maureen sat at home on the porch of the small bungalow. Meghan was waiting for the two aspirin she'd taken to kick in and do something about the pounding headache she'd gotten at Pat's house.

After a few minutes, Maureen spoke as she looked out over the Pacific.

"Meg, does that stuff happen very often?"

"You mean having to sit with your friends when something happens to their husbands? No. Not very."

"I'm not even married yet and I'm afraid of having to do it again. What would it have been like if Pat's husband had been killed?"

"It would have been ten times worse."

Meghan looked over at her sister. "Moe, don't worry. It doesn't happen often anymore. If you allow yourself to dwell on it, you'll drive yourself crazy. You just pretend that he's got a normal job, just like everyone else, and carry on."

"It doesn't seem fair, Meg, that the wives have to sit home and worry and take care of running the family while the men are out flying and having fun."

Meghan laughed a little. "Look, it's not fair. But you have to understand that what they do isn't all fun. Mostly it's work. They tell their sea stories, but you'll find out that the stories are about one-tenth of one percent of their time. The rest of it is just as aggravating and boring as the things that a wife has to deal with."

"Yeah, but how are you supposed to deal with it for twenty years? Shouldn't there come a time when you have a normal marriage?"

"Think about this. If they were normal men, we wouldn't be hanging around with them. If you marry a good one, like Mike or Tim, the marriage is fine and a hell of a lot of fun. It all evens out."

"Don't you sometimes wish Tim would get out?"

"Yes and no. Yes, because it would make things easier on me. And no, because, if he did, he'd begin to die inside and he wouldn't be the maniac I fell in love with. Someday, when he

208

retires, we'll probably have a plain old average life, but then he'll be ready for it. Right now it would drive him up a wall. Just being here on shore duty is making him feel trapped.''

"I can see that after the wedding, my phone bill is going to be ridiculous with me calling you every five minutes for advice.''

"You'd better. But think of poor Mom and Dad—they're going to have two of them in the family. Neither one of their daughters married a doctor or a lawyer. How will they ever hold their heads up at the club?''

Maureen laughed. "Dad is proud as hell, bragging all over the place, and Mom is starting to say things like, 'Anybody can be a lawyer these days.' ''

Meghan chuckled and got to her feet. "These aspirins are beginning to work. Want to go to the beach?''

"Okay. Let's get some lunch first.''

Meghan followed her sister into the house. She smiled to herself as she thought of just how much fun being married to Mike was going to be for Maureen. Marriage to Tim certainly was, even when he went off and tried to be a hero.

She was going to have to work on that, she thought.

★ **26** ★

Sunday, 27 April 1975

TIM BOYLE WAS JUST FINISHING HIS SHOWER WHEN SANTY CAME INTO THE hotel bathroom, waving his hands in a vain attempt to clear the steam, which filled the entire room.

"Jesus Christ, Timmy, you got something against leaving some hot water for the rest of the world?"

"Nope, just against leaving it for you. Hand me my towel, would you?"

"Here you go. And if it's not too much trouble, you can hurry up now. We've got visitors."

"Who? What time is it?"

"Almost nine. It's your boy Joe France and his boss. They're here to conduct the investigation. They sure look official, too. They've got notebooks and clipboards and Number 2 pencils and all that good stuff."

"They ain't my boys, Mike."

"Sure they are. They're from the same staff as you."

Boyle grunted. "All right, go divert their attention while I shave."

Santy paused before he pulled open the door. "Whatever you say. But I don't think the good Commander Bailey will be pleased having to wait while a mere lieutenant shaves. He probably expected us to be standing at parade rest waiting for his call."

"Fuck 'im."

"No thanks. He's not my type. Talks too much."

When Boyle walked out of the bathroom about ten minutes later, Bailey was sitting on the small couch with his papers scattered across what passed for a coffee table. Joe France was seated in one of the desk chairs next to the table, and Santy was stretched out on his bed with his hands behind his head gazing innocently at the two visitors.

Boyle stifled a grin. That was the expression Mike always assumed when he was deliberately annoying someone.

Boyle sat on the other bed. "Good morning, Commander. What can we do for you?"

Bailey looked at Boyle for a long three seconds before he dropped his eyes to his notebook, theatrically reminding himself of his purpose. When he looked up at Boyle again, it was as if Bailey were looking at a total stranger, perhaps one who had just crawled out from under a rock.

"We are here, Lieutenant, as part of the investigation ordered by Admiral Wallace of the circumstances surrounding the injuries to Commander Donald Hickerson, U.S. Navy, occurring on Saturday, twenty-six April, 1975, at Tan Son Nhut airport, Republic of Vietnam." Bailey looked at both Boyle and Santy to see if they understood and was surprised to see them glance at each other. He didn't like the look.

"Something wrong, Lieutenant, um, Santy?"

"Are you tape-recording this interview, sir?"

"No."

"Well, if you're not recording it, it seems a little silly for you to be laying on all the legal crap. I mean, if anyone knows when and where this all happened, it's me and Tim. It's not like we were out getting a couple of hot dogs."

Bailey's tone got even icier. "Lieutenant, I have been directed to conduct this investigation and I will do so in the way I see fit. You, on the other hand, will simply answer the questions. Clear?"

Santy sighed and nodded.

"Is that clear, Lieutenant?"

"Yes, sir." A barely perceptible pause. "Commander."

Bailey was not at all certain about Santy's tone but decided to let it pass for now. "All right, in your own words, tell me what happened, and please be specific."

Santy told the entire story, then Bailey asked Boyle to do the same. Bailey seemed surprised when their accounts left him nothing to pick on. He asked question after question of both young men, and his frown deepened as they answered as accurately as they could. Finally, Boyle sat up and, after glancing at France, who was being extremely interested in Bailey's notes, asked, "Is there something specific you're looking for, Commander? We've been around the block on this at least three times now and nothing's changed."

"I'm just trying to get the facts straight and you two are the only witnesses I can use, so your accounts will have to do."

France spoke for the first time. "Commander, um, it seems to me that we've gotten about all we came for here. There are other things we need to check on, and time's getting a little short."

Bailey fixed France with a withering gaze. "We've gotten what we need when I say we have, Lieutenant."

Santy, seeing France shrink from Bailey, spoke up. "Okay, then, one more time. The VNAF helo hit the Air America helo, which landed in the dirt on its right side. the VNAF bird came down inverted and caught fire. Tim and I pulled Commander Hickerson out, but we couldn't do anything for the other pilot, who was extremely dead. The Air America aircraft caught fire and burned up. End of story. Commander, I don't see what the hell else you could be looking for."

"Why was Hickerson flying with Air America?"

Boyle answered, barely keeping the surprise out of his voice. *Didn't this dumbass know what was going on? Where the hell has he been these past weeks?* "He was scouting for LZs and checking the evacuation routes. Just like we've been doing for a week."

"Under whose orders?"

Santy had caught the tone of Boyle's answer. "Under Admiral Wallace's orders. We've all—by that I mean Tim and me and Hickerson—been under his orders from the start. Haven't you?"

Bailey ignored that. "Do you have copies of those orders? I'll check Hickerson's later."

Boyle stood up and went to his briefcase. "Of course, Commander. Let me get them for you." Santy kept his face straight. There *weren't* any written orders. Never had been. What was Tim up to?

Boyle made a show of rooting around in his briefcase. "Damn. I would have sworn I put them in here." He snapped his fingers and turned to Santy. "I remember. We gave them to your skipper, Mike. Did you get 'em back?"

Santy looked pained. "No. I clean forgot to pick them up from

212

him before we left." He turned to Bailey. "I'm sorry, Commander, it's my fault. I left them on the ship. But we can get you a copy as soon as we go back aboard. Or maybe you can get a copy from Admiral Wallace himself."

Bailey couldn't drop the subject fast enough. "No. No. That's all right. We'll get copies when we get back to the ship."

The phone broke the silence, which threatened to become quite thick, as Bailey tried to figure out a new tack. Boyle and Santy both were glad of the interruption.

Santy answered and listened for nearly thirty seconds. "Okay. Fifteen minutes." He hung up and looked back expectantly at Bailey.

Bailey scowled. "Who was that?"

"Tim and I have a meeting to go to. They're sending a car for us. We've got be down there in fifteen minutes." Santy figured that repeating what he'd said on the phone might let Bailey know that as far as the two younger men were concerned, the interview was over.

"You'll be free to go when I say you are, do you understand?"

Boyle watched as the back of Santy's neck got extremely red. From all their years together, he knew that this was a very bad sign. He briefly considered intervening but decided to let it go. After all, he thought, hadn't Hickerson expressly forbidden him to get into it with Bailey and France? Besides, this was going to be fun to watch.

"Commander, we have a job to do. The job has a whole lot more priority than answering your stupid fucking questions. We intend to do that job." Not bad, thought Boyle, Mike was almost civil.

"I'm giving you an order, *Mister* Santy. You will remain here until I release you."

Santy sighed and walked over to the coffee table and began gathering up Bailey's papers. "What are you doing?" asked France, speaking for only the second time.

"Simple. I'm throwing you two the fuck out of here."

France's jaw worked a little. "We're here on official business," he protested, but without much feeling.

"Check the regs, Joe. A hotel room, that's this place, rented by a naval person, that's us, is not a military installation of any kind. Personnel, that's us again, are not required to permit official per-

213

sons, that's you, to either enter or remain without a warrant, which you ain't got. So get your lightweight ass out the door. Now."

Bailey recovered his poise a little. "I'm your superior officer. You will do what I tell you."

Santy smiled, but not in a way that would indicate a great deal of warmth and friendliness. "You're half-right. You *are* senior to me but you're not in my chain of command. We get our orders directly from Admiral Wallace, and, *Commander,* you don't draw enough water to countermand him. So kindly get out. And if you don't like it, go see the admiral."

Santy ushered the now furious commander out the door. France followed and stood in the doorway watching Bailey stomp toward the elevators. France looked back at Santy and Boyle. "I'm sorry. He gets wound up sometimes and I can't turn him off. I'm sorry, Tim." He turned and followed his boss.

As he pushed the door closed, Boyle could hear Bailey say something about this not being the last they'd hear about it. Santy came back over and sat on the bed. "Christ. What a pair."

"That's for sure. I must admit that I'm impressed with the way you handled them. My legendary tact and diplomacy are obviously rubbing off on you."

Santy laughed. Boyle was the one who usually used the Attila the Hun approach while it was Santy who always tried to be nice first. "It just seemed that it was getting to be a colossal waste of time. The other thing that bothers me is that it feels like they were trying to find out something that they can use against somebody. I don't like those games."

"Yeah. But remember that it was just Bailey busting our balls. Even France could see what he was doing. It's typical though. Bailey's always competing with the other commanders on the staff, and France is his star pupil. I've told you about how France and I don't exactly see eye to eye, but I think Hickerson and Bailey have the same problem."

"So that's how come all the questions about why Hickerson was in the Huey. Oh, yeah, nice work on the written-orders question, by the way."

"Thanks. We'll cover that with the admiral next time we see him. But I think we ought to watch our step around those two."

"Yeah. They're probably still pissed about us putting them to bed the other night. We shoulda left 'em for the wolves."

Boyle leaned back against his pillow. "Yep. So who's coming in fifteen minutes?"

"Nobody."

"Umm, okay, then who was that on the phone?"

"Callahan. He said he'd like to meet us for breakfast in the restaurant, but he had some stuff to do first. He's going to call back in fifteen minutes."

"Nice work, Mikey. I like that."

"Thought you would."

An hour and ten minutes later, Boyle, Santy, and Liam Callahan were finishing their breakfasts, which were considerably more meager than they had been when Boyle had first arrived in Saigon. The coffee was still good though and the two pilots were savoring it.

Callahan put down his napkin and leaned back in his chair. He regarded his plate with some regret and looked at Boyle. "Not much of a breakfast, huh?"

"It's okay really. All us aviators need for breakfast is a cup of coffee, a Snickers bar, and a cigarette, and then we're good to go."

Callahan nodded and pulled an envelope from his jacket pocket and pushed it across the table. "Here's the exit visas or travel permits or whatever the hell they're calling them now. There's enough for Tran and her immediate family and a couple of extras."

Boyle fanned out the visas and inspected them. He slid them over to Santy, who looked at them as if he actually had a clue what they said. "Are they real?"

Callahan chuckled. "Ah, my son, what is reality? They feel real, they look real, so they must be real, right?"

Santy shook his head. "What I mean is, if they're not real, will they fool the cops?"

"Probably not if they get hauled down to the station and inspected carefully. But their purpose is just to get Tran and all onto the airport. There aren't any more civilian airlines flying in and out, so the immigration people shouldn't have a chance to look them over. Our Air Force guys don't give a shit what the paper says anyway. They're just coming in here, dropping off whatever useless cargo they have anymore, then loading up and taking off. There's always going to be the chance of getting nabbed, but I don't think it's too likely. The hard part is going to be rounding them all up. Have you figured that out yet?''

Boyle and Santy looked at each other and then back to Callahan. Now that they were faced with the practicalities of getting Tran's family on a plane headed out, they realized that their idea might be just a little bit more difficult than they'd figured on. They looked to Callahan like college sophomores waiting for the professor to demystify the fall of Rome.

Callahan looked at each of their faces and grunted. ''That's what I thought. Look, I've said it before. It ain't my job to be a player in any of this. I'm just the guy who writes it up. I got you the damned paperwork and I went and translated the hard part for you with Tran and her boss. That's about as far as I'm going to go, okay? Tran speaks English well enough so you don't need me. Understand?''

Santy looked pained. ''Hey, Liam. No problem. You've been a tremendous help and we understand your position. You have to keep a clear head and you can't let anything come between you and objectivity. The gang down at the press club would be horrified. You can't get involved and help save some poor girl from whatever is going to happen when the commies get here. Don't concern yourself with that stuff. It's definitely not your problem. Really. We understand that you have to live by your rules. You've no choice.''

Boyle nodded. ''Yeah, all we need for you to do is hook us up with somebody who knows the town and can interpret with the locals for us if we need it. Then you can just walk away from the whole thing with a clear conscience. Piece o' cake, right?''

Callahan was trapped and he knew it. His damn quixotic Irish nature had roped him into this, and now he was stuck. *Again.*

He sighed. ''Someday, I'm gonna learn. Okay, what's next?''

Boyle and Santy grinned and leaned forward. For the next half hour, the three kicked around their plan. None of them said it, but in the back of each of their minds was a growing doubt that it was going to work.

Callahan sat at the table for a while after Boyle and Santy had gone, drinking another cup of coffee and remembering a time in his life when things were as black and white as they were for

Boyle and Santy. With a bit of surprise, he found that he envied them some.

After they left Callahan in the restaurant, Boyle and Santy made their way to the DAO compound at the airport and, after showing what seemed to be half the Marine Corps their identification, finally arrived in the communications room, which was full of more activity than either man had ever seen in there before. The two walked up behind the operator who maintained the listening watch at the radio that was constantly tuned to the frequency that Dalton and Thompson used.

The operator glanced up, saw them, and unsmilingly handed them a clipboard, immediately returning to concentrate on the radio. Boyle looked at the top sheet of paper and quickly inspected the ones underneath. He'd seen them all before, so the only new one was the one on top. He read it quickly, then went over it again. When he looked at Santy, his face had lost much of its color.

"What happened?" Santy didn't wait for an answer but grabbed the clipboard and read the flimsy piece of paper. Essentially, it said that the two SEALs were holed up less than two miles from the rendezvous point and were going to wait for darkness before attempting to move in. The original plan was for the meeting to take place by noon today, but as the SEALs had begun to close in on the spot, they'd heard a great deal of small arms fire up ahead. They had no idea who was shooting at whom, but they could not go any farther until they had gotten some idea of where the enemy was. And that couldn't be done safely during the day in unfamiliar territory unless they were very careful. That was going to take time. And time was fast running out.

"Shit," was about all Santy could muster.

"Yeah. We have to go track down one of the heavies and tell them about this. Unless something happens a lot quicker than tonight, those guys are going to get left."

★ 27 ★

Sunday, 27 April 1975

KEVIN THOMPSON PACKED UP THE RADIO AND TOOK A DRINK OF WATER from his canteen. The gunfire off to the west was only sporadic now—a single shot followed by a long silence followed by another shot or two. Ten minutes ago the volume of fire had been intense, as if two entire platoons of men were engaged in a firefight. Thompson looked up at Mark Dalton's dirt-streaked face.

"Sounds like the winners are finishing off the losers out there."

"Yeah, all the fire now is coming from AK-47s. I thought I heard some M-16s and at least one M-60 in there while the fight was on."

Thompson looked at the map. "I make us right here, and the firefight ought to be right in here somewhere." He pointed at a small bowl surrounded by low hills. "That puts it about dead in between us and where Tony's supposed to be."

"We can't stay here, boss. We're running out of time."

"We ought to ease our way around to the north and west and try coming in from that way. If that was Tony's bunch and if they're still alive, they'll try to pull back the way they came, to the northward, and we can still meet up with them. If it wasn't Tony, then they'll have heard the firefight and be lying low up that way. They'll certainly have scouts out."

"Yeah, all the NVA have been moving either south or eastward. They'll probably press on now that the firefight's over." Dalton scratched his chin. "Unless whoever was involved in there is from a unit whose job it is to comb the area for ARVN stragglers."

"Could be. Well, we either pack it in right now and head back for the coast or we press on."

218

Even though Thompson felt the need to at least acknowledge the choices, there was no question about what they would do. The two SEALs gathered their gear and headed off, cautiously, to the northwest.

Four miles from where Thompson and Dalton quietly picked their way through the bush, Tony Butler lay facing downhill with his rifle aimed along the small deer trail that was the only entrance to the small clearing. The worst part of his attack of fever was behind him now. His mind was alert, but he'd needed assistance to get himself over here to a covered position.

Behind him, the other members of his party, including his sons, lay concealed in the underbrush just outside the clearing. Butler looked over his shoulder at the clearing and saw with satisfaction that in less than a minute after the gunfire to the south had erupted, the group was hidden and virtually every sign that they had been in the clearing had been removed. A good tracker would pick up sign relatively easily, but on a quick inspection, the clearing would look exactly like any other.

Butler smiled sadly at the sudden memory of the long months in other small camps and clearings in between the periodic efforts of the North Vietnamese to either exterminate the local tribes or to "educate" them and bring them into the Communist fold. Both objectives seemed to have the same result. Those few tribes that had gone under had lost either their lives or their identity, which, to Butler, was probably the same thing in the long run.

The long periods of peace as the war had moved off somewhere else had been pleasant for Butler. Almost idyllic in a Joseph Conrad kind of way—at least that was the way that Butler thought of them. He had read *Lord Jim* years ago in school and had become so fascinated that, over time, he'd read everything that Conrad had written. He'd scrupulously avoided reading any other fiction in his life and had only once wondered if any other writers could stir his imagination as had Conrad. But then he'd decided that he really didn't *need* to find out. He was happy with what he had, and as always with Tony Butler, that had been enough.

Butler turned his attention back to the trail and waited patiently for the men who had gone out as scouts to return. He knew that they would have been so widely scattered that whoever was doing the shooting could not have gotten them all, and it should only be a matter of time before one of them came up the trail with a report. He felt more than saw the disposition of his small group, spread into small but effective interlocking fields of fire. If the worst happened, the single alternate escape route would be covered, at least long enough for the boys to be gotten to safety. Well, maybe not *to* safety, thought Butler, but at least *toward* safety.

The sun was nearly at its highest point in the sky, judging from the angle of the small spots of light in the deer trail, when Butler heard a rustle in the bush just around a little bend in the trail. With difficulty but still silently, he moved his rifle to his shoulder and forced himself to remember to aim low. He'd had a hell of a time with that when he'd first entered SEAL training, and he'd created a little mantra for himself whenever his target was at all lower than the muzzle of his weapon. He wished momentarily that he had a grenade or two to throw first.

An agonizing minute later, Butler saw a figure ease its way around the bend holding his rifle vertically with one hand on the forestock. He stopped in full view so that there would be no question of identity and waited for Butler's low whistle before he leaned forward and trotted the rest of the way into the clearing. He slid to a stop and lay down next to Butler, facing back the way he'd come.

Butler glanced at the man, who seemed unwounded. "The firing?"

"It was a small group of men from the Southerners' army. The Communists ambushed them and shot them down. They then executed all the wounded and hunted those few who escaped until they caught them. Those they killed also, as if for sport. Then they marched away to the south." He spat. "Those people are evil."

The word he used could mean "evil" or "bad" or "not nice" depending on the context, and Butler smiled as he thought of the NVA as simply "not nice." There seemed to be a lot of "not nice" people around here lately.

"You saw no sign of the Americans?"

"None. Tomason and Mahk are too smart to be taken by such as those." He spat derisively again in the general direction of the firefight. The names were the closest the tribesmen had ever been able to come to Thompson's and Dalton's names. Thompson got the more respectful use of his last name since he'd been the officer.

Butler hid his relief. He couldn't admit, even to himself, how fearful he had been that the firefight had involved Thompson and Dalton. His old friends were the last hope for his sons.

"And our men?"

The scout smiled, showing surprisingly white teeth. "We, too, are too smart for those lice. Our men are still waiting, but we moved slightly to make sure that we would meet the Americans. To stay hidden, Tomason will have to travel around to the north, and our men are across his path. It will not be long now."

Butler nodded and struggled to his feet, standing away from the brush and swaying as he waited for a sudden light-headedness to go away. He signaled to the rest of his band, who appeared from their hiding places and began to reestablish the camp.

By the time the conference door opened, Boyle and Santy had been sitting in the anteroom for nearly thirty minutes. After five, they had begun to wish that it was a dentist's waiting room because there they'd at least have some dog-eared *National Geographic*s or *Reader's Digest*s to thumb through. There might even be a Norman Rockwell print in a fake-wood frame to ponder. This room in the DAO headquarters building was as bare and cold and boring as a taxman's heart, and neither young man was particularly adept at simply sitting in one place and waiting.

So, despite the fact that they had some at least moderately bad news to deliver, they were relieved when they were finally admitted to the conference room. Only three men were in there, Admiral Wallace, General Alexander, and his number two, General Toone. Boyle was struck with the idea that this was as close to the old-time councils of war as he would probably ever see—three gray-haired and battle-scarred warrior kings planning their troop dispositions for some great battle on the moor in the morning. These men—maybe it was their bearing or perhaps the expression in their eyes—but these men had the clash of steel about them.

Wallace smiled wearily. "Good morning, gents. Sit down. I just got a report from the fleet. Don Hickerson is safely aboard the *Concord* and doing fine. He's already complaining about the food in sick bay." He waited for Boyle and Santy to digest this and give the obligatory nod of approval at the news before he continued.

"What have you got for us this morning?"

Boyle handed across a copy of the message from Thompson.

221

"Just this, Admiral." The two young men waited until all three heavies had read it.

Alexander shook his head. "That's not good. They haven't even gotten to their objective and now we'll have another delay. We're going to have to make some alternate plans here." Santy thought he saw a sidelong glance pass between Alexander and Wallace, who picked up the conversation.

Turning to Boyle, the admiral leaned back in his chair. "Tim, how much time do you have in the Huey?"

"Uh, I don't know exactly, Admiral, maybe a hundred hours counting what I've gotten here. Maybe a little less. I've flown about twenty or so in the past week."

"Do you have your civilian tickets?"

"Yes, sir. My dad made me go take the FAA's Military Competency Exam right after I got my wings. They gave me all sorts of stuff—single-engine land, commercial, helo, and instrument ratings."

"So you're legally rated to fly commercially as a pilot-in-command in helicopters by the FAA?"

"Yes, sir. I've even got a current Class 1 medical. I just don't have the sign-offs in specific aircraft."

"Okay. How about you, Mike?"

"Single- and multiengine land. Commercial and instrument and a Class 1. No helos."

Boyle and Santy exchanged glances. What the hell was this about?

Wallace smiled. "Here's the deal. With Jim Hickerson gone, we don't have anyone who can go retrieve our two wandering boys out there if we need to. I can only ask, not order or direct, that you take his place. I know that this wasn't in the plan when you volunteered to come over here, but I don't see that we have a choice now."

Though this was almost the same suggestion he'd made to Hickerson earlier, Boyle suddenly had the feeling that he was on a train headed quickly downhill without brakes. "There's nobody else? How about Wheeler or the Marines?"

Toone sat forward with his forearms resting on the table. "Wheeler and the other Air America pilots have got a lot of other things they *have* to do, which, frankly, are of higher priority. Their orders come from levels higher than us. As for the Marines, can you imagine the response back home if we were to dedicate our active forces to what would easily be perceived as a combat mission? Besides, we're going to need every one of the Marine helos for the evacuation.''

Wallace spoke gently. "Tim, and you, too, Mike, we are aware of the circumstances of your last combat mission. If you choose not to go, there will be no further discussion or repercussions, now or ever, from anyone. You have my word. I will tell you that this is an option we have to pursue. If it's not going to be available, then we have other decisions to make. Okay?"

Boyle looked at Santy for a long moment until Mike shrugged slightly, deferring the decision to Boyle.

"Admiral, I think we all knew that it was going to come down to this. Frankly, sir, I don't see any other options at all. Those guys are too far away to get back here in less than three days, and I'm not sure that they could make it at all judging from the situation maps we just saw downstairs."

"Does that mean you'll try to get them if it comes down to that?"

"Yes, sir. I'll go."

"We'll go," Santy said, elbowing Boyle.

Wallace looked at the two of them and smiled sadly. "Okay. When we're finished here, go see Frank Wheeler. He'll get you set up. But before you do anything, you will inform me. Now get this straight—there will be no cavalry charges. If there is not a better than average chance of success, you will not make any attempt to go out there. Is that clear?"

Both pilots spoke in unison. "Yes, sir."

"All right. Now to another matter. I understand that you had a visit from Commander Bailey and Lieutenant France this morning. I further understand that the interview did not go particularly well, correct?"

Santy refused to look guilty. "That's right, Admiral."

Wallace took one of Alexander's cigars out of the humidor next to the water pitcher in the center of the table. "Don't concern yourselves about it. He won't bother you anymore. Once I informed him that you all have been operating under my express orders, a written copy of which, by the way, will be in your CO's hands by tonight, Mr. Santy, Commander Bailey is taking the investigation in another direction. Now, unless you have something else for us, you can go see Wheeler, and make sure to bring all messages from Thompson and Dalton to us as soon as they arrive."

"Aye, aye, Admiral," said Boyle as the two stood and left the conference room. Outside the door, they stepped aside as a small group of harried staffers moved into the room carrying what looked like a large pile of charts. Boyle was glad he was too junior to have to sit through a briefing like that was going to be.

"Well, numbnuts, you did it again." Santy was not smiling as he spoke.

"Did what again?"

"Volunteered."

Boyle sighed. "I guess so. But I figured that if it was me out there, Thompson would be coming after me."

Santy nodded. "He did, you know."

"What?"

"Tim, when you crashed that time up north, Thompson volunteered to go in and look for survivors. They launched a helo and some A-7s for RESCAPs, went in, and checked out the wreck and the immediate area. Thompson and one other guy jumped out and searched the site before the gomers came up the hill and made them beat feet."

"Are you serious? I mean, I knew that they came looking, but I didn't know it was Thompson who was on the ground."

"Now you do."

"Well, all the more reason for me to go then. But you sure as hell don't have to."

"Yeah, I do. First, the guy Thompson went after that time was my best friend—you. And second, you'll need somebody to do the navigating and switch-flipping and seat-warming. I also don't want to be around if Bailey and France get another wild hair. That's the end of that discussion."

"Okay, then. Let's go see Frank Wheeler."

When the two pilots walked in, Wheeler was sitting in his office glumly going through Mickey Harris's desk. A cardboard box on the top contained a few items, including photos of Mickey's wife, his pilot's logbooks, and at least three framed citations for decorations he'd won as a Marine. There were a couple of chipped squadron coffee cups and Mickey's old squadron baseball cap.

Next to the desk was a round gray wastepaper basket filled to overflowing with other stuff that Wheeler didn't consider worth keeping.

Wheeler looked up as the two came in. He smiled a little and held up the baseball cap. "Not much to send home, is it? Not a hell of a lot to mark a man's passing."

Neither Boyle nor Santy answered. They'd each had to go through a close friend's gear after he'd been killed and knew that absolutely no words on earth could ease the pain of performing that singularly tragic act.

Wheeler carefully placed the cap in the box and put a sealed envelope on top. Folding over the flaps, he picked up a roll of tape and carefully and deliberately sealed the box.

"Do you two know anybody in the Marine squadrons in the fleet out there?"

Santy nodded. "Yeah, a couple of guys."

"I'd like to ask you to see if you can get this box to a Lieutenant Colonel Greg Miller, the CO of HMM-848 aboard the *Madison*. He was an old squadron mate of Mickey's. He'll know what to do with this. I'm afraid to trust it to normal channels, especially now that the mail is, um, a little slow."

Santy took the box. "Okay, Frank, we'll see to it."

Wheeler stood and walked over to his own desk. "Thanks, Mike. Now, Admiral Wallace said that I should fix you guys up with some company ID and some other paperwork. I don't suppose that you brought your civilian licenses with you."

Boyle grinned and pulled out his wallet. "I have no idea why I carry this around, but here you go." He handed over a worn and creased white card.

Wheeler shook his head. "Just don't keep any old girlfriends' phone numbers in there. My wife found one once and made my life miserable for a week." He noted the license numbers on a form and signed it at the bottom, then he folded it twice, stuck it in a small leatherette holder, and gave it and the license back. As he did, he looked at Santy with a raised eyebrow.

Santy shrugged. "Sorry. I don't have my Eagle Scout card either."

Wheeler chuckled a little and wrote something on a form similar to Boyle's, folding it and handing it over. "That's okay. You're

225

listed as a crewman. You don't need a license for that. Just a strong back and weak mind.''

Boyle put the holder in his pocket. "So what are we supposed to do?"

"Those papers make you Air America employees. You're supposed to be civilians. They'll work okay here in Saigon, but I don't think anybody out in the weeds right now is going to give much of a shit about the niceties. If the bad guys get you, you'll be just another round-eyed American. I'd suggest that around here you just be who you are and only use those IDs when you're in the aircraft.

"We have a spare company helo available in the next hangar. It's in good shape, in fact, I turned it up myself yesterday. If you have to go out there, we can have it out on the ramp in less than twenty minutes, but that could change real fast. If you want to test-fly it, we can schedule it for later on today, like around three.''

Boyle and Santy stood. "Okay, Frank. We'll come back later. Is it okay if we go over and have a look at our trusty steed?"

"Sure, Tim." Wheeler reached behind his head to a metal bookshelf and tossed a thick binder to Boyle. "That's extracts from the NATOPS manual for your aircraft. It's an E model and a little different from the one you flew with Mickey. The only major differences are a smaller cabin and a little bit less power. The procedures are pretty much the same."

Boyle caught the book, stuck it under his arm, and turned for the door. Wheeler's voice followed him. "Oh, yeah. I almost forgot. Liam Callahan called here looking for you about a half hour ago. He says to meet him at the hotel for lunch around twelve-thirty."

"Thanks, Frank. We'll try not to hurt your Huey."

Wheeler laughed. "Hell, we don't have the pilots left to fly it anyway. When the bad guys get here, we'd just have to burn it. But don't hurt yourselves with the damn thing."

As they walked out, Santy turned to Boyle. "You tried to deny it, but I knew we were going to be spies, and now here we are, working for Air America."

✯ **28** ✯

Sunday, 27 April 1975

LIAM CALLAHAN STOOD LOOKING UP AT THE TALL APARTMENT BUILDING on one of the side streets of Saigon about halfway between the Presidential Palace and the old Chinese district of Cholon. The building, six stories tall, was surrounded by buildings at least one entire story taller and probably one entire generation newer. Even the ones across the narrow, crowded little street seemed to look down on this decrepit structure. It looked, he thought, like a wizened old woman at a fashion show.

Callahan squared his shoulders, walked up the two steps of the building, and entered the foyer, waiting for his eyes to adjust to the sudden relative darkness after the bright sunlight on the street. He stood still for a moment, and when he thought he had adjusted, he moved toward the stairs only to trip over somebody lying on the floor. A string of loud and nearly incoherent Vietnamese, echoed immediately by at least two other voices, told him he'd managed to step on one of the innumerable families of refugees that crowded the city almost to overflowing lately.

He managed to make them understand that he apologized and barely held his temper enough to refrain from telling them that if they weren't lying in the middle of the passageway, they probably wouldn't get stepped on. As his eyes further adjusted, he could see that there were five of them—a mother, three children under five, and one young man with no legs. Liam realized sourly that the one he'd stepped on had, of course, been the legless one.

The young man wore the remnants of an ARVN uniform with the insignia of a lieutenant on the collar. Callahan apologized again, more softly and sincerely this time, and carefully edged his way to the foot of the steps. He climbed them slowly, his mind filled with the tragedy he'd just seen in the foyer. The accent of the family showed him that they were from the northern part of South Vietnam, which was now under the domination of the NVA. They'd obviously fled here to Saigon to avoid the purges of intellectuals, clerics, government officials, and military officers that were being carried out with great determination and glee by the victors. As a military officer, the legless man in the foyer was doomed to a reeducation camp or death depending upon the whim of whoever ultimately captured him. And when he was captured, his family had no one to support them.

The young man had fought for his country, which was very shortly to cease to exist. There would be no pension for him. There would be no veterans employment program or G.I. Bill to give him a start on another career. There would be no VA hospital physical-rehabilitation program to teach him how to stand like the man he had once been. The absolute best he could hope for was for the victors to ignore him and allow him to eke out some living selling pencils on the street. Hell, thought Callahan, the poor bastard won't even be able to make it as a black marketeer.

As Callahan continued to climb the creaking steps toward the top floor, he felt like sitting down and simply crying. He'd loved Vietnam when he had first come here early in the war as a sort of junior war correspondent. He'd loved the people and their simple ways before this war and the American presence and even previous wars here had ripped their agrarian society from the slow passage of the generations and dumped it forcefully and with no preparation square in the middle of the twentieth century. He'd been amazingly successful, beyond his wildest dreams, in that his "dispatches"—he called them that for his whole career, feeling very Kiplingesque—had won him award after award, which all sat gathering dust in his parents' attic. They'd won him several promotions to various "desks" in his organization, and they'd won him two divorces. He'd been assigned to all the mysterious cities of the Far East, but every time he'd managed to get himself reassigned back to Saigon.

Callahan had often wondered if he was any different from some of the men who flew for Air America or inhabited the various cubicles in the CIA offices. He certainly hoped so. At times, he felt he had more purpose.

When he finally reached the top floor of the building, he checked again the small slip of paper upon which he'd written the address. He walked to the end of the small hallway and knocked gently on the door. He waited a moment and knocked again, more loudly this time.

The door opened slightly and Callahan could see part of a head through the gap and one eye regarding him. The eye blinked a couple of times and then the owner stepped back, pulling the door open and gesturing for Callahan to enter.

"I am glad that you could come, Mr. Callahan," said Tran as she closed the door behind him. "My father is a stubborn man and will not listen to us women. He feels that he knows the situation far better than we ever could. He is convinced that because he is retired, no harm will come to him when the enemy arrives. He says that this is his home and he will not leave it."

"And you, Tran? What will you do?"

"I do not know."

Callahan sighed. "All right. I'll talk to him. Does your father speak English?"

"Yes. Better than I speak it. He was attached to General Westmoreland's staff before he was wounded." She stepped down the hall toward the front room. "He is in here."

Callahan stepped into the room, which would have been called a parlor in America in the thirties. It was decorated with truly beautiful wicker furniture and was so neatly kept that Callahan desired to stay in the doorway so as not to cause any clutter. An older man seated in a large chair was regarding him carefully. He had a large book on his lap and half-glasses perched on the end of his nose. One leg was stretched out on a hassock, and his left hand, which lay on the book, was missing two fingers.

Tran walked over and placed her hand on her father's shoulder and introduced Callahan. She referred to her father as "General."

The old man nodded regally and told Callahan to sit down and make himself comfortable as Tran smiled and left the two men alone.

The old man smiled at Callahan and reached for a cigar. "So, Mr. Callahan, you have come to talk me into leaving my country. Is that so?"

Callahan chuckled. "Yes, I have, General. Tran called me an hour or so ago and said that you were being stubborn. I thought that since I was used to dealing with stubborn American officers, I might have a try at dealing with a stubborn Vietnamese officer. So here I am."

"I remember you, Mr. Callahan. Your reputation is above those of your countrymen. You covered some of our battles in the First Military Region when I was assigned there. You were one of the few American journalists who seemed to realize that the Vietnamese were fighting the war, too."

Callahan nodded. "And the Koreans. And the Australians."

"Yes. They were gallant allies and excellent soldiers."

The two were silent for a moment—simply remembering. Then the general sighed. "I have told Tran that I'll not be leaving with her. My place is here."

Callahan shook his head sadly. "General, your place is with your family. I don't believe that Tran will go unless you do. For what my opinion is worth, Tran deserves a better chance than she and the rest of your family will have here. But when the NVA get here, you will be taken from them. And as the family of a former general in the Southern army, they will be treated as if they do not exist. They will not be allowed to have any of the benefits of the revolution because they did not share the sacrifice to make it succeed."

Callahan watched the old man look down at his wounded hand and gently flex the remaining fingers. "General, you've paid the price. You've given all you can for your country, but in a matter of days your country will no longer exist except as a memory in those who are fortunate enough to leave. That, at least, is something better than a bullet in the back of the head or a slow death working in a reeducation camp."

The general looked at Callahan and opened his mouth to speak, but closed it again. The reporter knew suddenly that he'd been about to say that Callahan could not know what it was like to have your country destroyed and your way of life taken away. Callahan said it for him. "Yes, sir. This is not my country and I perhaps do not understand how you feel. But since I am not Vietnamese, I can look at the situation with more detachment. It does not make sense to me that you would stay here and condemn your family simply because of your loyalty to what once was. To me, *that* would be a bad decision. You fought to keep your people free. You have left good men and I imagine many friends on battlefields all over this country for that idea. You don't seem to be the type to give up, so why start now when you can keep on resisting? You can go to America or Thailand or wherever. You can make sure that Tran and your sons keep that freedom."

The old man looked sharply at Callahan. "My sons are dead, Mr. Callahan."

"I'm sorry, General, I did not know. When Tran told me about her family, she mentioned brothers. I made an assumption and a poor one. Forgive me. But that is all the more reason for you to get Tran out. And you know she will not leave without you."

"One of my sons had a wife and a son of his own. Would it be possible to take them, too?"

"I don't know if there is time. But we can try."

The old man sighed. "All right, Mr. Callahan, you have made your case. I must think about it. Where can I reach you?"

Callahan stood. "Tran knows how to contact me. I spend much of my time in the Hotel Caravelle. I will wait for your call, General, but I don't think you have more than twenty-four hours."

"Very well, Mr. Callahan. I will call you soon. And thank you."

Callahan nodded and walked back down the hall to the front door. Tran came out of one of the rooms and followed him to the door. She pulled it open and looked at him questioningly.

"I don't know, Tran. It's up to him. He's a proud man."

"Aren't you all?"

Boyle and Santy walked around the silver-gray Air America Huey checking over the forty or fifty small items on the preflight inspection. Actually, Boyle was doing the checking and Santy was looking over his shoulder. Boyle was explaining each item and its connection to safe flight, surprised at how quickly all he had learned about this helicopter at Ellyson Field near Pensacola was coming back. On the few flights he'd flown with Mickey Harris, Boyle had not been invited to help with this walk-around and so had not really been able to poke and prod and get back into the systems. He was once again comfortable with the cockpit routine and with the Huey's somewhat skittish handling in comparison with the big H-3s he'd flown in his last fleet tour.

Boyle opened the tail-rotor driveshaft covers and inspected the bearings and the little strips of heat-sensitive tape, explaining to Santy that the tape would indicate that the bearings were running hot, which could be caused by poor maintenance or a slight mis-alignment. Heat would melt the tape and show that the shafting was about to fail. He made sure that Santy understood that this was one of the truly bad things that could befall helicopter pilots.

Santy nodded knowingly. So far this was about the fifteenth bad thing they'd looked for. They hadn't found any yet, but the sheer number simply reinforced Santy's long-held belief that helicopter pilots were congenitally crazy. He remembered that old saying that helos weren't really aircraft—they were loose collections of thousands of spare parts flying in close formation.

Finishing with the shafting, they closed the covers and made sure that the dzus fittings were secure. Boyle then popped open a small door in the side of the Huey and made sure that the collective accumulator and battery were as they should be, closed and fastened the door, and with practiced ease, climbed up onto the top of the helo. Santy followed with a great deal more care until the two stood on either side of the rotor system. He watched as Boyle yanked and pushed on the various tubes and linkages and bearings and stabilizer bars. He was struck by the sheer complexity of the system even after Boyle explained what everything did.

When he remarked that there sure seemed to be a lot of parts up here, Boyle laughed. "This is nothing. You ought to see the H-2. There are five hundred and four moving parts on the rotor system of that baby. One hundred and twenty-six per blade. And any one of them can break at any time. However, this system is designed for rough handling. About the only thing you can't do in a Huey is put in a control movement when the head is unloaded, like when you go over a ridge and shove the nose down. Like one of those weightless moments when you go over a big hump in the road in your car."

"Then what happens?"

"You get into what they call 'mast bumping.' Which means the rotor head and blades come off."

"What about the Jesus nut?"

Boyle patted the huge nut at the top of the rotor mast, which held everything together. "The J-nut is very democratic. It goes with the majority of the other parts—up and away."

"You can't get it down safely. No bailout either."

"Nope. In a nutshell, your ass is grass. If you're lucky, the blades will come through the cockpit and kill you. If you're not, you get to sit in the seat and watch the ground come up and hit you in the face."

"Tim, no offense, but I really don't need to be hearing this shit."

"Yeah, you do. It'll help your career."

"How the hell is knowing that the fucking rotor head can come off going to help my career?"

"Professional knowledge. Now you can sit around the ready room and expound on the mysteries of rotary-wing flight. You'll be a star."

Santy laughed. "My skipper says that helicopter time in your logbook is like having syphilis in your medical record. I can see why."

Twenty minutes later, Boyle eased the helo into a gentle climb and banked out over the city. From this altitude he could see the smoke from a half dozen large battles rising from several points of the compass. Sitting to Boyle's left, in the copilot's seat, Mike Santy had a tactical pilotage chart, or TPC, spread out and was making marks generally where the smoke was coming from. If they were going to go after Thompson and Dalton, the route they took would have to avoid those areas or it would be a very short flight indeed. Boyle flew in a wide circle, easily varying his altitude and airspeed, trying to avoid being predictable for anyone on the ground with a gun.

"Make it quick, Mike. I don't want to make another orbit after this one."

"Just about got it all down here. It's matching up pretty close to the situation maps back in the DAO." He made another couple of ticks and folded the chart away. Pulling out a street map of Saigon, he moved it around until he had oriented himself against what was in front of the Huey.

"Okay, ease your way a little to the right of the Caravelle and hook a left at the second intersection."

"Roj."

Boyle let the helo down until it was fairly level with the higher rooftops of the city. He and Santy both kept their heads and eyes moving, scanning the rooftops for people like the guy who had hit the Huey that Boyle and Harris had been flying last week. Boyle was surprised when he realized that it *had* only been seven days since that flight. It struck him even harder when he realized how much had happened in that time.

Santy watched the Hotel Caravelle go by on the left and looked down, counting the intersections. "Okay, turn here and go down about four blocks. Callahan said that the building is the fifth one down on the left. It's supposed to be shorter than the others."

Boyle let his eyes scan the gauges and then go back out to the rooftops on either side, still looking for one of those elusive sonsabitches with a gun to pop out and blaze away at him. He had the brief thought that there seemed to be a hell of a lot more places for bad guys to hide in a city than in the open country that he was used to flying over. Next to him, Santy was looking at the same things, but he was thinking about how few safe landing places there were in case something happened to that maze of metal parts on top of the helo.

"Okay, Tim. There it is." Santy pointed to the building that Callahan had described for them at lunch. "Looks kinda tight."

"Yeah." Boyle looked at the rooftop. At lunch, Callahan had suggested that Boyle take a look at the rooftop in case there was a problem getting Tran and her family to the airport by road. The thought was that it might be possible to pick them off the roof as was planned for the larger groups at their evacuation points throughout the city.

A large square on this roof appeared to be the top of the central stairwell. A small brick wall ran around the edge, and at least four clotheslines stretched across. Boyle shook his head. "Mike, count the bricks in the wall. I know I can't land this thing with both skids on the roof itself, but if the wall isn't too high, I might be able to get one skid on. Tran will have to do something about those clotheslines. With them like they are, there's no chance at all."

Santy nodded and wrote down a number on his kneeboard. "I make it about eight bricks with a flatter layer on top. Looks to be about three feet high, but I can't tell. I have nothing to scale it to."

"Shit. That'll be real tight. If we can get a skid over the wall, I might be able to do this like a slope landing except half the rotor system will be in ground effect and half won't."

"And that's not good, right?"

"I'd rather get a tetanus shot in my eye."

"That's not good."

Boyle pulled up and around, looking at the adjacent buildings and their roofs. "I think it might be a better plan to see if we can get Tran and all onto one of the roofs next door. All we'd have to worry about there is whether the roof will be strong enough to support the weight. But that we can handle." He wiggled his butt in the seat. "Okay. Let's go take one more look at the evacuation routes."

Boyle leveled the helo and headed out over the river. At one of the piers was a medium-sized cargo ship with its decks jammed with people. The lines heading from the pier to the gangway stretched at least a quarter of a mile. Off to the right, the river wound along for a way then widened out and led to the open sea where the American fleet lay. Off to the left, columns of smoke rose from the green earth as the last remnants of the ARVN soldiers tried to hold off the enemy drive.

The distance between the smoke and the center of the city was a hell of a lot shorter then the distance from the city to the open sea.

★ 29 ★

Monday, 28 April 1975

IN THE DISTANCE, THE SOLDIERS COULD SEE THE CITY CLEARLY NOW. THEY were squatting on a small knoll listening to their lieutenant brief them yet again on the glorious victory they were about to achieve and the usual need for completely rededicating themselves to the cause and for the obligatory sacrifice.

The soldiers kept their eyes on their lieutenant, but their minds were not on the cause or the revolution. These men had survived long, hard months and years of campaigning. Many of them had tattoos that said, "Born in the North to Die in the South." For untold thousands of their comrades, that blue-inked prophecy had come true in some forgotten patch of jungle or on the barbed wire surrounding an equally forgotten firebase or quietly in a damp and dark underground hospital or in any of a thousand unimportant places.

The minds of these soldiers were on survival. The war was all but over, and none of them wanted to be the last hero of the revolution to die in the fight. Even though the enemy resistance was crumbling, the bullets and shell fragments were completely unaware of it, and unlike soldiers, these deadly bits of metal would move at the same speed regardless of the proximity to the end of the fighting.

The city in the distance could not hold out for more than a day or two now. Off to the west of the city, the last effective Southern divisions were now surrounded and could no longer influence the outcome. Headquarters was rumored to have ordered a massive artillery barrage against the city to take place sometime the next day. The soldiers squatting on the knoll were perfectly willing to

236

wait until the dust of that settled before setting off on the last great push that their lieutenant was now exhorting them about.

The lieutenant was new to the small unit. He had arrived only two days ago and assumed command after ther previous lieutenant had been gravely wounded by a surprise artillery attack. Listening to his nearly hysterical briefing, the soldiers dearly missed their old leader, who would simply have laid out the plan and the objectives for the upcoming battle, mixing in the barest minimum of mandatory political context before he dismissed them and sent them off to see to their weapons and to their souls. The soldiers wondered idly whether this man's harangue was directed at them or at himself. Probably at himself, they concluded, since, as he was now saying, this was going to be his first major action with them. In truth, it would be his first action of any kind with them, but the soldiers wisely let that pass without comment.

Just when the soldiers thought they were about to be let go, the lieutenant pulled a map from his case and spread it on the ground. He pointed to arrows and marks that represented the grand victories won. He regaled the soldiers with accounts of the heroism of men like them who had served so gloriously.

At this the soldiers began to squirm and look sidelong at each other. The men whom the lieutenant was praising to the heavens were the very men whom he was now commanding. It was astonishing that he did not know this, they thought. Had they been in the service of another political system, they would probably have been able to talk about the thoughts they were all having at that moment. Could this man possibly be as stupid as he seemed? Was it possible that he truly believed all that he was telling them?

When the lieutenant at last wore down and had emptied his bunker of patriotic fervor, at least for the moment, he dismissed them. He strode off with his back straight and his left hand resting very professionally on the case hanging from his shoulder. The soldiers shuffled over to the packs and sat down without a word.

✬ 30 ✬

Monday, 28 April 1975

LT. CDR. KEVIN THOMPSON SLIPPED QUIETLY AROUND THE STAND OF bamboo. Behind him, Mark Dalton kept his weapon trained on the man hiding alongside the trail. This was the area, within five hundred meters or so, where they were to meet Tony Butler, but their natural caution made them look things over before exposing themselves, and the man beside the trail, although well hidden, seemed to be a problem. Neither SEAL could tell who the man was or to whom he belonged, but given the firefight that had taken place yesterday, neither man wanted to take a chance.

It had taken them all of yesterday afternoon and most of last night to make their way to this place, at the foot of a small rise in the forest and well away from the roads. Neither man had spoken of it, but the firefight they'd heard the day before had scared them as few things in their careers had. It brought home to them just how chancy this present enterprise was. At one point they had nearly stumbled into several armed men who, they supposed, were from the unit that had engaged in the firefight. The SEALs went to ground and lay sweating.

When one is engaged in something dangerous and does it for a living, one learns to concentrate on the matter at hand and to shut out all thought of failure. Pilots of crippled aircraft, for example, will concentrate on getting the aircraft safely on the ground, filling their minds with airspeeds, control corrections, emergency procedures, and mental pictures of affected systems. They will review options, constantly updating them as they approach the runway, instantly discarding those that are no longer relevant. As long as there is something to do, some action that has to be taken, the mind can be diverted from thoughts of the pile of flaming wreckage that the aircraft may soon become.

It is in the long stretches of relatively stable miles and minutes before the aircraft gets close to the airfield or carrier that the fear lurks. With nothing to divert itself with, the mind will engage in its favorite pastime of creating horrible images of the results of failure.

So it was for Thompson and Dalton. As they lay in hiding, giving what they hoped was enough time for the victors of the firefight to finish up their work (the SEALs supposed) of searching the immediate area for still-surviving losers, then deciding on a new plan, and finally gathering themselves to go on to whatever was next for them, Dalton and Thompson had to remain undiverted. They heard every sound that the forest made, every rustle of a leaf, every footfall of every creature, every beat of their own hearts against the moist earth.

They heard sounds, too, that existed only in their minds. They heard the sounds of the enemy moving closer. They heard the shouts of discovery as one of them was discovered. And they heard the clamor as the rest of the enemy rushed over to surround them. Worst, they lay there knowing that they would never hear the shots that would kill them.

It was probably the longest hour of their lives, but once they could move on, it was forgotten and would only be remembered with a shiver, and a quick change of mental subject.

Now, as they moved to surround the figure just off the trail, the fears were gone, disappearing in action and in the complete concentration required to move and yet be more silent than silence itself.

Thompson eased forward until he was only a couple of feet from the edge of the bamboo thicket. He looked carefully at the ground, searching for and finding a spot that would give him solid footing as he shifted his weight to that spot and popped out with his weapon trained on the man beside the trail. Finding such a spot, he placed his right boot on it and gradually placed more and more weight on the leg, trying to *feel* whatever was underneath his boot and the dead leaves.

He was nearly ready to make his move when he felt something cold and hard behind his left ear. It touched him gently at first, but there was no doubt about what it was or why it was there.

Thompson froze, debating whether he could make some surprise move and bring his weapon to bear. He tried to use his peripheral vision to see who had placed the rifle muzzle against his head but couldn't get his eyes around that far.

Suddenly but silently a small brown hand reached out and grasped the forestock of Thompson's weapon, pulling on it slowly but insistently. Thompson resisted at first, but a hard jab behind his ear made him think better of it and he released his grasp, making sure to keep his hands in sight. The two stood like that for a few seconds until Thompson heard a rustle from the other side of the thicket and then a low whistle.

He heard a chuckle from the man behind him. "You are getting old, Tomason. You were the one who taught me how to do this."

Thompson felt the pressure from the rifle leave his head and turned around slowly, still keeping his hands in view. As he turned, Thompson was astonished that his knees still worked at all. The man stepped back and lowered his weapon, grinning through stained teeth. It was a man from the tribe with whom Butler had stayed. Thompson felt like an idiot—coming all this way and he couldn't remember the man's name. At least, he still remembered the basic dialect.

He was saved from embarrassment as Dalton came around the thicket followed by the man who had been sitting beside the trail, obviously as a decoy.

"Well, boss, it appears that we're just a tad rusty."

"Yup." *Khe*—that was the man's name. Thompson turned and retrieved his weapon.

"Khe, here, had me cold. He was just waiting for us to sneak up on the decoy."

"As I recall, that's a trick we showed them."

"Khe mentioned that already."

Dalton turned to his ex-captor. "Where is Butler?"

The other native smiled and pointed to the west. "Not far. Come."

In the communications room in the DAO compound, Santy handed the message to Boyle. "Well, they've hooked up with Butler's men. Now all they've gotta do is get Butler and get out."

Boyle nodded as he read the transcript of Thompson's latest message. "Let's check the chart."

The two pilots left the communications room and walked to the office they'd dumped their gear in. Boyle opened the TPC chart he'd kept of Thompson's progress and consulted the message. Tracing his forefinger down from the grid marks at the top and then across from the ones on the left edge, he made a mark with a pencil. "Okay, he's right about there as of what, a half hour ago?"

"Yeah, something like that."

Boyle shook his head. "There's no way, Mike. No way at all."

Santy sighed and dropped his tail on the edge of the desk. "Shit."

Both men were silent for a moment, thinking over the implications of the distance from Thompson's position to Saigon.

Boyle broke the silence. "I guess it's time to go see the man."

Admiral Wallace nearly exploded out of the conference room when he heard that Boyle and Santy were waiting. "Come in, come in. What have you got?"

The admiral moved a pile of reports from in front of his place and Santy spread the chart on the table. "Thompson's right here, sir. They've met up with the scouts with no problems, and they're on the way to meet the main group. Apparently, the main group is hiding only about a kilometer or so from where they were when they sent this message. But, and it's a big but, sir, the area is crawling with squads of NVA and whoever else is looking for ARVN stragglers. They say it will take them at least three days to get back here at best speed, which ain't gonna be much."

Wallace slumped into a chair. "Fuck," he said wearily, "I don't think we even have *one* day, gents. By the time our wandering boys get their tails back here, General Giap and his NVA troopies will be selling souvenirs to each other on street corners."

"Yes, sir. When we passed by the embassy this morning, the place was surrounded by Vietnamese civilians. It looks like they figure it's about over, too."

Wallace looked up, his brow furrowed. "I haven't been by the embassy since early yesterday, and when I was, there were only a few people camping out. Most of them were in line to get paperwork to enter the U.S."

Boyle shook his head. "Admiral, there aren't enough clerks in the whole Far East to handle paperwork for that mob. They're acting pretty peaceful though. So far, anyway."

"That'll change when the helos start showing up."

Boyle looked at Santy. "Are the helos due soon?"

"No. The decision hasn't been officially made yet, but it better come soon. The road to Cap St. Jacques is cut now so the convoys can't get through to Vung Tau, which means that the only way out by ship is from the Saigon docks."

Wallace smiled a little. "You've noticed, I trust, that the enemy is shelling the suburbs already, and the bastards can start shelling the airport seriously anytime now. When they do, that'll be the end of it for the Air Force transports. When that happens, Washington'll give the word to go with the helos. I hear that the ambassador is still resisting the evacuation, something about not wanting to start a panic."

Santy groaned. "Panic? Is he kidding?"

"Unfortunately not. He's still grasping at straws. He believes that the NVA will actually stop right in the middle of a final push for a certain victory and negotiate a peaceful settlement, giving up what they've wanted for years. I've heard that he sent a cable to Washington last night that said that the NVA won't make a direct attack on Saigon."

The admiral paused and took a sip of coffee. "Lots of these State Department guys are like the ambassador. They believed in this country's government and in the word of our government. The problem is usually that our government's word depends on the will of Congress, and Congresses and agendas change. Right now, Congress has nothing to do with honor or duty or integrity. It no longer gives a shit about Vietnam and what happens to these people. They've decided that, agreements and commitments and treaties be damned, we, as a people, are gone."

Wallace glanced at the two younger men with a little embarrassment and then looked back down at the chart. "Sit down, gents. What do you think about this?"

Boyle sat in a chair at the admiral's right. "I think we can get him out if he can find us a clear area."

"Where exactly?"

"That's up to him. We know where he is down to a half mile or so. We can get that close and he can guide us the rest of the way in."

"Are you gonna have enough fuel to get back out?"

"Yes, sir. If we don't have a long delay. It'll be about a forty-five-minute flight each way. That'll give us about another forty-five minutes loiter time."

"And if you can't land here and need to go out to the fleet?"

"Then we'll have no loiter time at all to speak of, and when we get out to the fleet, we'll need an immediate landing."

The admiral scratched his chin. "Can you make it to Thailand if you have to?"

"It'd be close. There wouldn't be any room for error."

"There's no way at all for me to give you an escort of any kind, you know."

"There'll be an Air Force C-130 up, won't there? We can use that for comm relay."

Santy spoke up. "There'll be an E-2 up, too, right? Those fleet weenies can't wipe their ass without an E-2. We can use him for radar following."

Wallace smiled a little at Santy's joke and rubbed his eyes. "Okay. You're not to go anywhere until the C-130 is up, and that won't be until the word is given for the evacuation to start. Do not, repeat not, go until you talk to me. Clear?"

"Clear, Admiral."

"You got anything else for me?"

"No sir."

"All right, then. Keep me informed about anything that happens. No matter what."

Before the two pilots had gotten out of the room, Wallace was once again buried in his pile of reports. Boyle looked at Santy and shook his head. "Fleet weenies, huh? I wouldn't mind being one of them right about now."

"Yeah, me, too. Actually, I'd really rather be on Pensacola Beach, knocking back a couple of cold ones at the Tiki or Dirty Joe's."

Tony Butler saw his men come around the bend in the little trail followed by the much larger forms of Kevin Thompson and Mark Dalton. Still weak from his bout with the fever, he got painfully to his feet and stepped into the open.

Butler didn't know what to feel at that moment. He opened his mouth to call out, but no words came to him. It had been seven years since he'd seen these two men who had once been simultaneously his leaders, his comrades, his friends, and his only fam-

243

ily. For the early parts of those years, Butler had had many sleepless nights as he at first vaguely regretted not only his staying behind but also the way he had done it. But in the morning, when the village was awake and the sun shone, his purpose was always renewed when he saw how much needed to be done for these people. In the activity came at least temporary justification.

His regrets never left him and had eventually led to a morose sort of guilt, which in turn had driven him to send the first two letters—they'd represented a sort of confessional for him, although he would never understand it that way. It was long months before he'd received a reply from Dalton, and in that letter had come the forgiveness that he didn't know he so desperately needed.

From then on, contact had been sporadic at best, but he'd always tried to keep Dalton (directly) and Thompson (indirectly) informed, to let them know that he was alive, if not exactly prosperous.

Now, as the two men approached him, he couldn't find the words. He wanted to run and embrace them as if he were marooned on Mars and they had come to rescue him. He wanted to hide his head in shame for having deserted from their unit. He wanted to cry when he thought that these two old friends had risked everything just to come help him. He wanted to stare at the sky and thank whatever God there might truly be that such men existed.

But he did none of these things. He simply stood there in the tiny clearing with his hands limply at his sides and his shoulders slightly slumped and watched Thompson and Dalton walk up to him.

They stopped within arm's length and their guides eased away. For a long moment there was complete silence until finally Dalton shifted the tobacco he was chewing to his cheek, spat on the ground, and grinned at Butler.

"Jesus H. Christ, Tony, you look like shit."

Butler smiled a little crookedly and then stuck out his hand, his eyes beginning to well. Dalton struck his hand away and embraced him. Thompson joined in, and in that instant the awkwardness disappeared for all three.

Dalton stepped back and looked around the clearing. He approached each man and shook hands. He knew them all, but they all looked a hundred years older than they had once. Even the young ones had faces that were lined and creased.

Butler called for the two boys, who walked forward from their place of hiding slowly and shyly, holding each other's hand. They came up and stood on either side of their father, looking up at the tall Americans. Butler placed his hands on their shoulders and introduced them, the older one first.

"Lieutenant Dalton, Commander Thompson, these are my sons. Their American names are Mark and Kevin."

Six hours later, Boyle and Santy were standing in Frank Wheeler's office as Wheeler dumped file after file into a large cardboard box. When they had left the admiral, they'd gone to the communications room and drafted a message to be sent to Thompson and Dalton. They'd then tracked down Callahan and told him that they were ready to move on his call.

After checking their Huey, they'd come straight here and had walked into what Santy referred to as the "Great File Inferno of '75." Except for periodic checks with the communications room to see if Thompson had answered their message, the two had stayed near the airfield. Thus far, all that they'd gotten was the acknowledgment that their message had been received. So, to keep themselves busy, they'd joined in helping the Air America guys burn everything that could help the NVA when they got here.

All over the area, small fires sent a cloud of dense white into the still and humid air, and even the normal smells of an airport were hidden by that of burning paper. Santy had heard the rumor that a couple of Army officers were burning a large store of genuine American currency and wanted to go see if he could help them stoke the fires, but Boyle convinced him that it was truly only a rumor. Aside from Santy's near gold strike, the high point of the afternoon had come when they managed to get the box of Mickey Harris's effects onto one of the Marine helicopters that landed to drop off several Marines, who hustled off to the DAO compound.

It was just after seven when the telephone rang and Wheeler answered. He listened for a second or two and hung up. He looked at Boyle.

"That was the comm center over at the DAO. There's a message for you." Wheeler grinned. "Go on over. I can finish this up, but I do have a couple of bottles of Jack Daniel's I may need help with later."

Boyle had his hand on the doorknob when the building shook and the sound of flying glass filled the air. Before the second round hit, all three were out the door and sprinting for the hangar.

★ 31 ★

Monday, 28 April 1975

As WHEELER, BOYLE, AND SANTY RAN TOWARD THE HANGAR, THE BAR-
rage was already moving away from their area of the airport and
toward the runways. Several large gouts of reddish dirt and dust
flew up near the main runways and taxiways. Here and there
aircraft, mostly Vietnamese, were taxiing quickly to the areas that
were not under imminent threat of exploding.

On the runway a U.S. Air Force C-141 lifted off just as two
rounds hit the concrete behind it. The aircraft banked sharply
around toward the southeast and climbed as steeply as its load
and abused engines would allow. The three pilots watched carefully as the 141 sped away, scanning the sky behind it for some
sign of the deadly little one-man SA-7 missiles the NVA used.
As if in disappointment, the NVA barrage stopped when the big
American cargo plane was out of range.

When the 141 was just a dot on the far horizon, Boyle looked
back at the airport. Several ambulances sped past along the taxiway, and at least four small fires were burning across the field
among the ARVN and VNAF facilities. Closer by, the DAO compound and the Air America buildings didn't seem to be visibly
damaged. Their largest concern, the hangar sheltering the helicopters, was untouched.

Just in case, all three pilots walked into the hangar and did a
fast check of the line of Hueys sitting well away from the door
with their rotor blades tied down fore and aft and the ground
handling wheels in place. Three of them had tow bars hooked to
the rings on the skids in readiness for a quick pullout and launch.
Boyle looked around for the tow tractor and found it sitting be-

hind the door. He figured that in an emergency, he could have his Huey airborne from the hangar in less than five minutes. If his was the first one pulled out, that is—he could add three or four minutes if it was the second.

Boyle walked outside the hangar and sat on the bumper of a Follow Me jeep. He pulled out a cigarette and lit it, staring across the airfield at the small columns of smoke and listening to the silence. Wheeler came up and sat next to him.

"Got another one of those?"

Boyle handed over the pack and his lighter. Wheeler took one and lit it, inspecting the rubber bands around the Zippo. He smiled at the small touch that marked Boyle as a military flier. He handed the cigarettes and lighter back. "Well, Tim, it looks like the gomers are sending us a message."

"Yeah. No more free rides out of here. At least not in the big jets."

"The Air Force'll probably try a couple more times to get in and out, but that'll be it. They don't need to be losing any more of their jets. Especially after that C-5 crashed with all the babies on board. If we can't protect the airport anymore, we're fucked."

Santy sat down on the other side of Boyle. "Near as I can tell, we've been fucked for quite a while."

Wheeler nodded. "That's true."

"I heard this morning that there are something like thirty thousand people trying to leave. There's no way we can get that many out. That's about two thousand helo trips using only 53s, even if you stacked 'em five deep in the back."

Wheeler took a drag from his cigarette and flicked away the ash. "How are things in town? I haven't been in there since Sunday."

Santy sighed. "Kinda looks like Times Square on New Year's. There's people everywhere, especially around the embassy. All the merchants are selling whatever they have left as fast as they can. Seems silly when you figure that the money's not going to be any good pretty soon."

"You buy anything?"

"No. I don't want any souvenirs of this."

Boyle crushed out his cigarette and stood. Behind them, they heard fast-approaching footsteps and turned to see one of the other Air America pilots jogging up to them. He stopped in front of Wheeler. "Frank, one of those rocket rounds just hit at the gate and killed two Marines. We're supposed to seal off the compound in case the NVA attack. There's a meeting in the DAO building in ten minutes for all senior officers, which includes you, Frank, since you're our head helo type."

Wheeler nodded. "Okay, Sam, I'll be there. Thanks." He turned to Boyle and Santy. "I'll see you guys later. You might want to stick close."

Liam Callahan cursed at the telephone. It was taking forever lately to get a local call through. He listened to the various clicks and hisses and heard the ghost of another conversation between two Vietnamese women who were arguing about where they should keep their chickens to hide them from the Northerners. The woman had nearly figured it all out or at least come to some sort of agreement when the phone on the other end began to ring. It was answered quickly and the women's solution to the chicken crisis was lost to him forever.

The voice spoke gruffly. "Air 'merica Operations."

"Yeah, this is Liam Callahan. I'm trying to find either Tim Boyle or Mike Santy. They're those Navy guys who should be hanging around with Frank Wheeler somewhere in your helo shop."

"Yeah, they're down the hall. Stand by a minute."

Callahan waited for a minute or two, listening carefully for the faint voices of the two women, then heard the phone picked up.

"Boyle."

"Hi, Tim. Listen, we have a problem with Tran. The streets are so jammed with people that I don't think we can get her either to the embassy or to the airport by car. I'm sure that we couldn't get them through the gates of the embassy even if we could get that far."

"What's happening back there?"

"It's a mess. There's all sorts of people running around in packs stopping cars and buses. It's pretty dangerous."

"Can you get to them?"

"I think so. I can try, anyway."

"Fair enough. Does Tran have a phone?"

"Yeah. The service is pretty shitty though. Ma Bell would shoot somebody over it, but it does work."

"Okay. If we can't drive her out here, then we can try and pick her off the roof. How many of 'em are there?"

"Counting me, there'll be six. Last I heard, they were all assembled in Tran's apartment."

"All right. Get down to her place and call me from there. Mike or I or somebody will be right by this phone. As soon as we hear from you, Mike and I will come pick you up. We'll put her on a Marine helo out to the ships."

"No Air Force?"

"They just shelled the place again. Frank Wheeler says that there might be a couple more 141s in here, but I wouldn't bet on it. The heavies're having a big powwow right now. I'll do what I can to get her on a 53. But whatever happens, we'll get her out."

"Okay, Tim. I'll call you when we're ready. It should take me about an hour."

"All right. But just in case the phone system finally craps out, if we haven't heard from you, we'll be overhead the building in two hours. If you don't think the roof is strong enough to support a helo, go to the next roof if you can. And listen, Liam, be careful, okay?"

"Tim, cowardice is my middle name. See ya." Callahan hung up, leaving Boyle holding a dead phone and staring out the window.

Santy and Boyle looked into Frank Wheeler's office and found that he still hadn't returned from the meeting at the DAO compound. Figuring that they'd better be prepared, they walked over to the hangar and rounded up a couple of helpers to pull their Huey out onto the flight line. While Santy helped return the tow tractor to the hangar, Boyle did the preflight walk-around, even though they'd checked the helicopter carefully less than ninety minutes before.

Boyle was climbing up to inspect the rotor head when Santy came back and stood on the ground looking up at him. "Christ, Timmy. Didn't we do this a little while ago? I mean, if we have to wait for another two hours, will we have to do another preflight?"

Boyle lifted one of the rotor blades with his back and checked a droopstop. "Not really, but I figured I'd get a little more caressing in. Helos are temperamental, you know. If you don't tell 'em you love 'em often enough, they'll do something to scare the hell out of you."

"Is that another bad thing? That's about the hundredth bad thing you've told me. Is there *anything* good that can happen?"

Boyle climbed down. "Yeah."

Santy waited for a couple of seconds, staring at his friend. He couldn't stand it. "Well, what, for instance?"

"It's really good if none of the bad shit happens."

"Oh. Silly me. What could I have been thinking?"

"It's typical. You jet guys just don't understand the intricacies of true flight. There's a lot more to it than going fast. We helo pilots are real genuine aviators while jet types are mere pukes. Anybody can fly a jet."

Santy chuckled at the old argument. He and Tim had been saying things like these to each other for years, ever since flight school. They'd even gotten Meghan and Maureen involved, and they were sure that their children would probably carry on the tradition, which, on the whole, was going to be a pretty good thing.

"Okay, Rotorhead, let's go see if the SEALs have checked in in the last half hour."

Liam Callahan made his way carefully down the narrow street to the building where Tran and her family lived. He had been able to get a ride with one of the pedicabs only about halfway from his office in the hotel and had had to walk the rest of the way. It had been a while since he'd had to walk that far, and he resolved to try to get himself into better condition.

Once, earlier in the war, he could march with the young soldiers up and down hills and stay with the best of them. Now, on the far side of forty, he could feel the additional effort his legs had to put out. Maybe I could stand to lose a few pounds, too, he thought.

The streets were a mess, reminding him of Calcutta where the crowds were often so large that one couldn't walk fifty feet in less than five minutes. There were people everywhere, moving slowly with no apparent destination. He'd had to give up on the pedicab when even a vehicle as small as that couldn't go any farther.

As he approached the building, he reviewed the brief conversation he'd had with Tran's father less than an hour ago. The old man had been brusque, saying that the family had decided to leave and was now planning things in the way of what he had once been—a soldier used to order and timing and preparation.

251

He had everything ready, he'd said. All the important family papers had been gathered and the family had each been allotted one small suitcase to take whatever treasured personal items they chose. Clothes had been kept to a minimum to save space, and the family was now prepared to leave. Callahan suspected that the general had put his family into an almost feverish preparation so that whatever feelings they might have about leaving their homeland, probably forever, would be buried in activity.

Callahan climbed the steps and entered the building, being careful this time to let his eyes adjust to the darkness before moving far from the door. He didn't want to step on the legless veteran again. After a half minute or so, Callahan saw that the entryway was empty, as if the veteran and his family had never existed. There was nothing left behind. He had the odd thought that in New York, a family like the veteran's would have left considerable garbage in their wake.

Callahan climbed the stairs to Tran's apartment and knocked softly. The door was instantly pulled open by a woman who turned and walked down the short hallway to the front room. The newsman followed, peeking into each room as he passed and finding them empty.

"Mr. Callahan, welcome. We are ready to go." The general spoke firmly.

Callahan looked around the room. There seemed to be quite a crowd, all seated on the sofa and the floor. The general, his wife, Tran, a woman holding a small boy, and the legless veteran and his family—ten of them in all. The general stood and made the introductions—the woman and small boy were indeed the wife and son of the general's son.

The surprise was the legless veteran. "Mr. Callahan, this is Lieutenant Vu Van Minh. He was a platoon commander in my old regiment. He was wounded in the battles in the spring of 1972 and lived near Pleiku until the enemy came. He fled to the city. I would like him and his family to accompany us."

Callahan nodded and spoke to Minh. "Weren't you living in the entryway?"

Minh smiled. "Yes, until last night. We had stopped in there only an hour before you came here." Callahan was glad that Minh left out the part about being stepped on by an American oaf. "The

252

general came down to go shopping and saw me. He remembered me and invited me into his home."

The last was said proudly, with a noticeable lift of the chin. And justifiably so, thought Callahan. To be remembered by a general who had had thousands of other men under his command said a lot for this former junior officer. It also said a lot for the general.

Callahan scratched his chin, looking from Minh to the general. "I don't know how much room there will be in the helicopter, but I suppose we can make two trips if necessary."

"Only one, Mr. Callahan. By the time the helicopter returned, there would be fifty people on the roof trying to get on board. The city is filled with more than refugees. There are deserters from our army and even a few of the enemy also. All of them are armed. There have been several gun battles in the street already in the last day or so. People are becoming completely lawless and they will fight to go on the helicopter."

Callahan surveyed the group. He couldn't remember what the capacity of a Huey was, but somewhere between seven and ten passengers. If it was one of the ones with a small cabin, it would be a tight fit.

"All right, General. I'll have to talk to the pilots. They are expecting only six, including me. May I use the telephone?"

"Certainly."

Callahan picked up the receiver, hoping that the system was still working. He heard the dial tone amid a louder hiss of static, and with a sigh he dialed the numbers.

Mike Santy heard the phone ringing in the now-unoccupied office. Everyone at Air America headquarters was out trying to accomplish the last few things they could before the evacuation began. Many of them were trying to get to their homes to pack whatever they could; most of these had been working nearly around the clock for the past few days, and they were certain that this was their last chance.

Others were loading aircraft and pulling them out of the hangars. The word had come down that the fixed-wing aircraft were going to be flown to Thailand later that evening, but the helicopters were to stay to do whatever they could when the evacuation began. An air of gloom and defeat was around and the heavy feeling that the evacuation was only hours away.

253

Santy picked up the phone and heard Callahan's voice faintly on the other end. The newsman was almost shouting to make himself heard, and Santy closed his eyes and covered his other ear to try to make out whatever it was Callahan was saying. He was sure he heard something about "eleven" and "soon" before the connection was broken and the phone went dead. After the noise on the line, it was almost as if the aircraft movements outside the open window were being done in complete silence.

Santy stared at the telephone for a moment or two and gently replaced the receiver in the cradle. That act had an odd feeling of finality to it. He felt as if he was hanging up on Vietnam itself. He sighed, looked around the office, and went to find Tim Boyle.

He found him sitting on the steps of the building. He was smoking a cigarette and watching the Air America people move the aircraft around.

"Liam just called. They're all set to go. I couldn't make it all out, but I think he said that there'd be nine of them and they need to go soon. I think I got most of what he wanted to tell me, but the phones died so I couldn't follow up."

Boyle turned to him. "Eleven? We should be able to carry that many. But if not, we can make two trips."

"Okay. We make two trips. Was there anything from Thompson?"

"Basically an 'ops normal' report. We're to expect a new pickup point from them this evening. The one they had picked out was too small and had too much slope to it. I drafted a message for them to get a move on and find someplace fast. I don't think he knows how close to the end we are here."

Boyle stood and brushed off the seat of his pants. "You ready for this?"

"I guess. The sooner we go the sooner we get back."

They had taken about five steps when they heard Wheeler calling them. They turned and saw him hustling toward them with Admiral Wallace. The admiral's longer legs got him there first.

"I'm glad I found you so easily. I've been ordered to go out to the ship for a meeting. I need you guys to take me there."

Boyle and Santy looked at each other. Flying out to the ship, waiting for the meeting to end, and then flying back here was going to take hours. Hours that Tran and her family didn't have.

Wallace caught the look. "Something wrong, Tim?"

✯ **32** ✯

Monday, 28 April 1975

CALLAHAN LISTENED FOR A FEW SECONDS AND THEN JIGGLED THE BUTTONS in the cradle. Hearing nothing at all, not even the static, he hung up the telephone and looked at the general.

"That's it for the phone, but I think they got the message, General. I told them that we'd be waiting on the roof in thirty minutes."

"Very well. I have some good whiskey in the other room. Would you care to assist me in a small act of defiance, Mr. Callahan?"

Callahan listened for a moment to the faint thumps from the artillery across the river. "Why not?"

Admiral Wallace waited for a moment for Boyle to answer his question. When nothing came forth, he took off his sunglasses and stared at the young man in one of those moves that always let subordinates know that the superior is serious. "Is something wrong, Mr. Boyle?"

Boyle glanced at Santy and then looked back at Wallace. "Um, well, sir, we kind of have another commitment."

Wallace stepped closer. "Thompson and Dalton? Are they ready for pickup? Why didn't you tell me earlier?"

Santy shook his head. "No, sir. We have to wait for the SEALs to get to a safe area before we can go, and that probably won't be until the morning. What Tim means is that we're supposed to be picking up a Vietnamese family and flying them here to the airport."

"When?"

"We're supposed to be overhead in thirty minutes."

255

"Overhead where?"

Boyle found his voice. "Downtown, Admiral. They're stuck in their building and we'll have to pick them off the roof."

Wallace's jaw flexed several times as he looked from Boyle to Santy and back again. "Let me get this straight. You two have decided to start your own taxi service. Boyle's Rooftop Livery, is that it? Who authorized this?" He looked at Wheeler. "You, Frank?"

Wheeler opened his mouth to speak but Boyle beat him to it. "Sir, we hadn't told Frank about it yet, but we were going to." Boyle figured that wasn't really an untruth—they were going to tell Wheeler if they ran into him before they took off. "We figured that since we had plenty of time before we had to go after Thompson, we could just zip over, pick up these folks, and be back here in less than an hour."

"Well, CINCPAC says that I've got to get out to the ship most skosh and you are the only available people who can get me there. All the other Air America crews are committed. So what do we do, *gentlemen?*"

Both Boyle and Santy knew what they wanted to do, but saying so didn't seem to be a particularly wise move just now. They remained silent.

Wallace put his sunglasses back on. "Okay then, decision's made. You can get these people after you get me to the ship. With a little luck, that'll be this evening well before sunset. If not, they can wait until tomorrow. If you're gone after Thompson and his band of merry men, they can take their chances with everybody else. Okay? Let's go." Wallace began to walk away.

Santy nearly saluted but remembered just in time that, among other things, he was in civilian clothes. Boyle pulled a piece of paper and a pen from his shirt pocket. He scribbled some numbers on it and handed it to Wheeler. "Frank, could you try and call this number for us. Ask for Liam Callahan and let him know that we'll be there but late. Tell him that he'll know we're there when he hears us hovering over the roof. There'll be no doubt that it's us."

Wallace stopped cold. He took a long breath and let it out slowly as he turned around. He took off his sunglasses again. "Lieutenant Boyle, is that Liam Callahan as in Liam Callahan the news guy? How did he get involved?"

Uh-oh, thought Boyle. "Yes, sir. Liam is helping us with this family. We only asked him along as a translator, but he could do a lot of stuff we couldn't so he sorta took the lead."

"Translator for who?"

Santy jumped in. "Admiral, this is all my fault. The family is that of one of the nurses who took care of Commander Hickerson. She's only twenty and she's scared shitless of what's going to happen here. I thought it was a lousy deal that she got stuck here while a bunch of B-girls get to fly out courtesy of Uncle Sam, so I convinced Tim and then we got Liam to help us. It'll be Tran, that's the nurse, her folks and her brother's widow and one or two children, and maybe a couple of others. Plus Callahan."

"Where's he?"

"He's over at Tran's place holding everybody's hand. He was going to drive 'em here and Tim and I were going to see that they got on a helo now that the Air Force can't use the runways anymore."

Wallace considered the two young officers. The initial anger he'd felt toward them waned as he heard their story, told with complete ingenuousness. He looked from one to the other—two young men, both of whom had already seen the worst this war could offer, both of whom had already been wounded fighting it, both of whom had already nearly given everything for what they believed to be their duty. And here they were, far from home and the safety that the rest of the Navy now considered the norm. They stood easily in the sunlight, with artillery fire and battles and disaster all around, looking him dead in the eye, not as subordinates but as fellow warriors.

He looked at their open, determined, and unapologetic expressions and knew that, even though the necessary flight to the ship was going to screw things up for them, they were, by God, still going to do everything they could to get that family out. He knew that failure was the one thing they were determined would not result.

Wallace cleared his throat. He turned and looked at the silver H-1. "Tim, how many people can that Huey hold?"

"I don't know, sir. It depends on the gross weight."

"Could you take, say, Callahan and the Vietnamese plus me and my aide plus Mike and yourself?"

257

Wheeler spoke. "Yes, sir, I think so. It's got a full bag of fuel so it wouldn't exactly handle like a Porsche, but you could do it."

"Well, let's go, then. But I'm a lousy passenger, so I'd like to sit in the copilot's seat."

Boyle and Santy looked at each other and grinned. "Aye, aye, sir," they said almost in chorus.

Callahan drained the last of the glass of Bushmill's and savored the taste. He'd always loved Bushmill's in that odd way the Irish have. The flavor brings back memories of the land of their ancestors, even for those who have never seen the place or walked its green hills. Callahan had learned to drink Bushmill's from his grandfather in the warm spring evenings in Boston when the two would sit on the old man's front stoop and Liam would listen to all the stories, told in the delightful soft brogue. He would listen to his grandfather sing the old songs and found that he had a pretty fair tenor himself. Years later, on an assignment to Ireland, Callahan was not surprised when he discovered that the country looked and felt exactly like the whiskey had tasted.

It was a wonder to him that the general could have gotten this stuff here, but he was glad the old man had. They'd gone into the small kitchen and broken out the bottle and glasses and poured a generous measure for each. Before they drank, the general remembered the lieutenant in the front room, so they'd gone in, helped him to the kitchen, and poured him one, too.

They'd each had one drink, and with an expression of mild loss, the general had poured the rest of the whiskey down the sink. Six unopened bottles remained in the cupboard, so the general handed two each to Callahan and the lieutenant, keeping two for himself. He said he couldn't bear to pour it all out, and he wasn't about to let the enemy have it.

Callahan smiled inwardly at that. He checked his watch and looked at the old man. "It's time to go, General. The helicopter should be here shortly."

The general stood and nodded. "If they received your message clearly. In any event, we can wait on the roof just as easily as we can down here. If you will help the lieutenant, I will get the rest." He left the room carrying the two bottles of Bushmill's.

Callahan waited until the general had the rest of the group moving out of the apartment with their luggage, then walked over, turned, and squatted in front of the legless man, who sat some-what awkwardly in one of the straight-backed kitchen chairs. After a few seconds of weight-shifting and silent cursing, Callahan managed to get himself to his feet again, carrying the lieutenant piggyback. As he walked out the front door of the apartment into the hallway, Tran closed the door and locked it as if she were merely going to work.

She looked at the newsman. "Can you manage all right?"

He smiled. "No problem, but I would appreciate it if we could hurry up there."

Tran turned and led the way to the stairway to the roof. By the time Callahan had gotten to the top, his legs were almost com-pletely numb. He needed help to put the lieutenant down and then stand up again. Bracing his rear end against the outside wall of the stairwell, he bent over with his hands on his knees, trying to catch his breath.

"Mr. Callahan, could you come over here for a moment?"

Straightening up, Callahan walked over to where the general stood in the center of the roof. As he did, each step seemed oddly springy. He watched the general hop up and down on the roof and could feel each impact in his own legs.

"This roof seems weak, don't you think?"

"Yes, it does, General, and one of the pilots who's coming has warned me it might be a problem. Do you think that it can support the weight of a helicopter?"

"I don't know, but if it can't and the helicopter breaks through, we'll never be able to get it back out. That means we'll all be stuck here."

Callahan looked around. The building next door was about fif-teen feet higher but much newer. Its roof should therefore be stronger, assuming of course, that the building codes, if any, had been enforced.

"Okay, General, why don't we try to get onto that roof?"

The old man scratched his chin with his good hand. "It would be better for us if we went directly up there rather than going all the way down to the street and then back up through that build-ing. By the time we got to the roof we would have attracted a crowd of others who would all try to get on the helicopter with us."

The general's face clouded for a second and he looked di-

259

rectly at Callahan. "What I just said sounds very callous, doesn't it?"

"General, in other circumstances it would. But we both know that your responsibility is now to your family. You must do what is necessary for them and not concern yourself with that which you can't control. I imagine there will be a time for those concerns, but the time is not now." Callahan smiled. "Now, let's figure out how we're going to get up on that roof."

Tim Boyle rolled the throttle up to the maximum and then adjusted the rpm with the small black switch under his left thumb. He spoke over the intercom. "Okay. Looks like we're all set. Everybody strapped in?"

He heard three affirmatives from the admiral in the seat to his left and from Mike Santy and the admiral's aide, Lt. Lou Bonnett, in the back. Bonnett was a "blackshoe," or surface-warfare officer, whose first tour had been in destroyers. He hadn't gotten to ride around in aircraft much until he was assigned to Wallace's staff and now couldn't get enough of it. When Wallace had filled him in on the extra stop this flight was going to make, he'd grinned like a teenager going to the dance.

Boyle keyed the radio. "Tan Son Nhut Tower, Air America 181 to lift from the Air America ramp for direct flight to the east."

The tower's reply came back instantly. "Roger, 181, you are cleared to depart to the east. The altimeter is two nine point nine two. Winds are light and variable generally from the north. Are you going to return?"

That's an odd question from a tower controller, thought Boyle. On second thought, the controller was going to have to stay here while others made it out ahead of the enemy. "That's affirmative, Tower. One eight one will return prior to sundown."

"Roger, 181, have a safe flight."

Boyle clicked the mike switch twice in acknowledgment and eased the Huey into a hover. He did a fast check of the engine instruments and pushed forward on the stick with his right hand while simultaneously pulling up on the collective lever with his left and correcting for the yaw with his feet on the rudder pedals.

The Huey moved forward across the ground for a few yards before it shuddered and began to climb away from the ground. Boyle's eye constantly switched between the view out the wind-

shield and the instruments as he gently banked the aircraft to the right and leveled off to three hundred feet, well above the tops of the buildings in the city.

Wallace looked around at the horizon and saw the columns of smoke rising from nearly all points of the compass. The situation maps he'd been seeing for the past few days couldn't give him the truth of what was about to befall this city. On the map, neat and tidy little symbols and arrows of many colors all represented events and people and units and plans, but they were just that— symbols. The smoke and the little dots of people moving around on the ground below were reality. The maps gave one an almost divine view of the world, but looking out the windshield of this Huey gave him the human view. He wasn't sure which view he preferred, he thought. Maybe neither.

Boyle guided the Huey out over the river and turned south, counting city blocks in his mind until he was almost certain that he had the right area. Santy was squatting in the door behind him squinting into the airstream and trying to see Tran's building. "Come right about five degrees, Tim. I think it's that shorter one at twelve-thirty and a half mile."

"Yeah. Looks like it. I'm going to do a high fly-by just north so we can see if they're on the roof. No sense making a low pass and giving it away."

Boyle steadied the aircraft and watched as the building came up low on the right side. He looked carefully but couldn't see anyone on the roof. "Mike?"

"Nobody home, Tim. The clotheslines are still up. Make another pass."

"Comin' left."

Tran and Callahan had taken almost ten minutes to find a ladder that would be of some help climbing the fifteen feet or so to the neighboring rooftop. They maneuvered it against the wall of the other building and found it to be about four feet too short. When Callahan placed his weight on the first rung, there was a cracking sound and the right side of the ladder broke through the rooftop.

Tran's father ran back down the stairs and returned with a board, which they placed under the feet of the ladder. Callahan climbed the ladder to the top and grabbed the edge of the other building. With much huffing and puffing, he pulled himself over

261

and flopped down flat on the black tar of the roof. Once he had regained his strength, he leaned over and beckoned the others to come up.

Tran was first, and once she was up, they sent the other women and children up. When they got to the top of the ladder, Tran and Callahan reached down and pulled them the rest of the way up and over. The general followed the women, grimacing in pain as he nearly fell, and Callahan grabbed his damaged arm. With a struggle, he made it, too, lying gasping on the roof.

Callahan climbed back over the wall and felt for the top rung of the ladder. He found it and carefully made his way back down to the roof of Tran's building. He walked over to the legless lieutenant and sat down next to him.

"Well, Lieutenant, looks like you're next."

The man avoided Callahan's eyes and simply nodded.

"What's wrong?"

"Seeing you all go up there reminds me of how useless I am going to be, even in America."

Callahan rounded on him. "Well, if nothing else, we can always hire you out as a paperweight. That's one of the good things about America—there's a place for everybody. Even wounded lieutenants."

The man looked at Callahan in surprise, and after a second he began to laugh. It was the first time the newsman had seen any real animation in his face at all. "Come on." Callahan maneuvered him up on his back and half-walked and half-staggered to the foot of the ladder. He struggled with each rung, making himself think that each one he climbed was one less he had to go. He stopped every second rung and gathered himself for the next two. Finally he reached the top of the ladder and felt the lieutenant's weight lifted off him as those above pulled him up.

Callahan rested for a few minutes and then struggled up himself, flopping down on the roof and reaching for a cigarette. He lit it and just sat there as he watched the others gather themselves and their meager belongings together in the shade of a small lean-to someone had built next to the stairwell. Tran came over and smiled at him. "If you didn't smoke, you wouldn't be so tired."

"Jesus Christ. You're gonna get along just fine in America." He grinned as she pulled him to his feet.

★ **33** ★

Monday, 28 April 1975

LT. CDR. KEVIN THOMPSON SPREAD THE CONTENTS OF HIS SMALL PACK of medical supplies on the ground in front of him. While everyone waited for the food to be cooked, he was holding an informal sick call. They'd brought along as much extra food and medicine as they could carry, which they intended to leave with the tribe when they left. It was a kind of penance, Thompson thought, first for leaving these people seven years before and now for taking the last American away.

Thompson remembered doing this long ago with the corpsman assigned to their SEAL team. The corpsman had always looked forward to this ritual as the one thing he could do in the war to actually help people instead of killing them. Thompson, as the team leader, had found that he felt the same way and never missed an opportunity to assist the corpsman. Now, he was once again sitting on the ground, trying to do some good, trying his best to recall everything the corpsman, now finishing medical school in Virginia, had so patiently taught him.

The small boys who'd come as a surprise to the SEALs, were the first to go through what little medical inspection Thompson could provide, and he found them in surprisingly good shape. They were small, but that could well be genetic. They were well nourished in comparison with the rest of the small group, and that was certainly because of the near-veneration that the tribe had always given its young. They seemed bright and eager, but behind the eyes lay a wariness that came from spending their entire short lives on the run. As he dismissed them, Thompson fervently hoped that they could get these two kids back to

263

America where they'd at least have a chance. Butler had always been a private man, and it was in character for him not to have mentioned his sons in his sporadic messages over the years.

Thompson knew, somewhere deep down, that when Butler returned, he would probably have to face disciplinary hearings for what could be called desertion by some. The Navy might call it "missing movement," or failing to go with one's unit when it was transferred from one place to another, but that would probably be the least of the charges. It would not be pleasant for Butler and he knew it. It might lead to some time in the brig, which would leave the boys at the mercy of the courts. As the men of the tribe began to come over to Thompson, he resolved to see that the boys weren't left to the mercy of the child welfare system. After they'd run and hid all their lives from men whose only interest was in killing them, being left to a bunch of well-meaning bureaucrats whose ostensible interest was in "what's best for them" didn't seem like that much of an improvement.

A few paces away, Dalton was helping prepare the food. Some of the rations that he and Thompson had contributed were now mixed in a pot with bits of food that the members of Butler's group had foraged from the land and a few of the more legendary spices that they always seemed to have stuffed away somewhere, even when they traveled the lightest. The resulting "gumbo" would have given American military nutritionists the vapors.

Butler sat off to one side and watched his two old friends and the men who had come along to protect him and his sons. He had feared that they would be reticent when they all met and that it would take some time for the natural barriers built by seven years of different experiences to break down. He was pleased almost to tears when the reunion had the feeling of family about it. Butler looked around the small camp and thought of the future.

He knew the Navy wouldn't throw a party or a parade in his honor when he returned to the States. He would be somewhat of an embarrassment to them—he was pretty certain that no one had ever deserted from the SEALs before. The very nature of an elite unit like the SEALs precluded such things, and offenses were treated harshly, more so than in other units. There were the rigidly codified lists of allowable punishments for every offense, and the official penalties were fair and understood by all concerned. But the unofficial sanctions put on by one's peers were often far harder to endure. He wondered whether his fellow SEALs would understand what he had done and, more importantly, why.

Their opinion mattered, maybe even a lot, but Butler suddenly realized that what the Navy thought or what it might do to him was really secondary. He thought of the future his sons would have with their father in prison. He remembered his life as a ward of the state and wondered what he could do to help them escape that fate. He knew he could rely on Thompson and Dalton, but he wondered how much of an effect they could have on his sons' future. As he looked around the small encampment, he knew only one thing with certainty—his sons must have a better future than the one they faced here.

Butler watched as Thompson repacked his small medical bag and handed it to one of the tribesmen. Butler remembered all the times when he would have traded a year of his life for the things in that bag. He knew that lacking them had most probably already cost him at least a few years.

Thompson walked over and picked up the radio. He raised the antenna and switched it on, checking the dials and the lights and the battery capacity. Noting that the battery was still in good shape, he counted the spares he had brought and saw that three were still left. If they weren't enough to see them out of this, then it wasn't going to matter anyway. If things went reasonably well, there wouldn't be a need for a radio after tomorrow afternoon. Right now, the radio was infinitely more important to this effort than were their weapons.

He sat down next to the radio and pulled out his map of the area. Dalton saw him do it and came over and sat next to him. Together, they began to compose a situation report.

Liam Callahan sat with his back up against the wall of the stairwell and wished he had a beer. His legs ached from carrying the lieutenant up the ladder to the roof, but at least they'd quit trembling from the exertion. On either side of him sat the rest of the small group, speaking quietly and waiting nervously for the helicopter to come and snatch them away.

The roof was hot. The intermittent sunlight, now in full force, was heating up the tar, and Callahan could see waves of heat shimmering just above the surface. He was thirsty and sweaty and nervous. Many times in his years in Vietnam he'd felt exactly like this, but those times had always immediately followed some hair-raising brush with the enemy. Callahan figured he must be getting old when the mere effort of climbing a ladder could get him in such a state.

He listened to the clamor from the streets below the building and realized that the noise was much different from the usual sound. Normally, the shouts and traffic noises became nothing more than background, like the wall behind the painting. But today there was a frantic edge to it—the shouts were more strident and the replies more shrill. The horns of the vehicles sounded louder and more insistent. In the distance the thumps and rumbles of battle sounded more distinct. In all his years covering events like these, there had always been a sort of preparatory hush before the cataclysm began in earnest. It was odd, he thought, how this one seemed to be preceded by an increase in volume. Maybe that, too, was because he was getting old.

Callahan reviewed his own situation here in Saigon. He'd have to leave it permanently very soon, certainly in the next twenty-four hours. Standing at the Presidential Palace waving his press credentials was probably not going to prevent at least a brief stay in jail or worse. He had seen time and time again how the NVA and their idiot children, the Viet Cong, or PRG as they now called themselves, had treated prisoners. It had never mattered much in the end whether the prisoner was an actual combatant or merely someone who was not one of their own and whom they didn't understand. The results were always the same—pain and sometimes death.

Nothing was left here in Saigon for Callahan. Everything of value had been shipped home long ago. He had only a few easily replaceable things in his office and even less in his rooms. He had a safari jacket that he liked a lot, but that wasn't something he'd risk his life for. No, it was better to head for the fleet offshore with the Marines when they came. He could get a couple of good pieces out of the evacuation, wire them to the magazine, and then go on to Bangkok.

He loved Asia, and Bangkok was as good a place as any to reestablish his headquarters. Thailand was the most politically stable country left in Southeast Asia and would be a good vantage point to observe the imminent paroxysm of horror that was going to befall Vietnam. Callahan figured that among other things, he was getting far too old to be a war correspondent. He'd used up a lot of his body and most of his luck in stomping around the boondocks and little villages trying to tell the world what he saw. In Bangkok, he could be one of those sage types who could hang around at the elegant hotels and embassy parties and speak and listen. He would then be able to pontificate in monthly articles on the machinations of Asian politics. Maybe he could even hire on part-time as a stringer for one of the networks. Maybe he could sit down on "Patio Beach" and write a book about the war, perhaps about the young air cavalrymen he'd known all those years before.

The magazine would make it official and create a desk for him there—they owed him that much and they knew it. They also weren't crazy enough to try to assign him to a stateside job—that had already proven a bad idea. Nope, it was Bangkok or bust for Liam Callahan.

Callahan was lost in Thailand when he heard the dull rhythmic thumping of a Huey growing gradually louder. In all the concrete of the surrounding buildings, the sound was diffused as it always had been when it had come over the trees in the boonies. He waited thirty seconds or so to make sure that the sound continued to grow in volume, then got to his feet. Standing under the lean-to, he looked out across the city toward the northeast and saw the small dot of the Huey approaching. He waited until it had flown overhead to make sure that it was an Air America helo and not one of the VNAF birds that were beginning to fly around the city like disturbed bees. As it pounded by well overhead, he could see the silver-gray colors and two men in the open door in the back looking down at the rooftops. Boyle and Santy had come through. He stepped out into the open and began waving his arms.

Boyle steepened the bank and flew by from east to west. He looked down at the small building. Except for the clotheslines, the roof was empty, and other than the door leading to the stairwell lying open, there was no sign that anyone had been there at all. At this altitude and speed, he couldn't see the roofs of the adjacent buildings too well. Boyle was about to turn for another, lower spotting pass when he heard Santy's voice over the ICS, or intercom system.

"Tim, I think I see them. They're on the roof next door. There's somebody waving. I think that's Callahan, but I can't tell for sure."

"Roj. Okay, we'll make another pass down low. I'll slow it as much as I can. Stand by."

Boyle lowered the collective and banked the Huey around again, this time flying generally up the street at about fifty knots. Out of the corner of his eye he looked for someplace to land if the engine quit as he lined up with the taller building. Other than trying a landing in the middle of the crowded street, there was nowhere for him to go if the engine failed. Boyle, like all helicopter pilots, hated the feeling.

Boyle looked away from the street at the rooftop. There was going to be plenty of room for a landing, and the departure was going to be to the east, toward the river. He looked for something to give him a sense of where the wind was and saw that a flag atop one of the buildings down the street was showing a north wind of about ten knots or so. Looking back at the rooftop, he saw a figure standing next to the stairwell waving both arms.

"Okay, Tim. It's Callahan all right. Looks like he's got Tran's family there, too."

"Okay, everybody, listen up. Admiral, I'll be looking outside mostly, so keep your eye on the gauges and let me know if you see any caution lights. Make sure you're strapped in. In the back, you guys recheck your gunners' belts. Mike, lean out and look aft. Make sure the tail is clear. Here we go."

Boyle glanced at the three-item landing checklist on the instrument panel and pushed his shoulders forward in the straps to make sure his harness was locked. He bumped the button under his left thumb to increase the engine rpm slightly and wiggled his butt in the seat. He lowered the collective and eased the Huey into a long descent toward the rooftop. He adjusted the nose attitude and slowed the descent, keeping the helo on a gentle glideslope from which he could easily wave off and fly it out if something went wrong.

As the helo approached the edge of the roof, Admiral Wallace took his eyes off the instruments and glanced down at the street below. Traffic had completely stopped and all eyes were looking up and watching the helicopter slide toward the top of the building. Just as he turned to look back into the cockpit, he thought he saw several figures dash up the steps of the building and run inside. He started to say something to Boyle, but when he looked at the pilot, he decided against disturbing his concentration.

Santy looked back and saw that Boyle had judged this well—the tail was well clear of any of the small obstructions near the edge of the roof. "Tail's clear," he said quickly into the ICS. Boyle grunted and felt the power decrease as the Huey moved over the roof itself and into ground effect. He stabilized the hover and gently eased the aircraft down until the skids were touching the roof. He reduced collective slowly and steadily, trying to feel for any give in the structure that would indicate that the Huey was on the verge of breaking through. In a few seconds or so, he had the collective on the bottom and all the weight of the helo was being supported by the roof. He breathed a sigh of relief and rolled the throttle back toward idle to keep the rotor wash from blowing things around.

"Okay, gents. We're down. Mike, you guys can load 'em up now. When we take off, I want one of you guys on each side so nobody falls out. Make sure your belts are secure. Okay?"

Hearing two clicks over the ICS in acknowledgment, Boyle watched as Santy and Lou Bonnett, the admiral's aide, jumped down and ran over to Callahan. Bonnett led a small group of women and children over and loaded them in. He climbed in with them and arranged them as best he could, trying instinctively to balance the load. Boyle cursed himself for forgetting to brief Santy and Bonnett on weight and balance. He looked at the people and hoped that they weighed as little as they appeared to.

Santy ducked under the lean-to and emerged carrying a man piggyback, but the man was so small that Santy apparently didn't even have to work hard at it. An old man whom Boyle took to be Tran's father followed, carrying several pieces of luggage.

When Santy got closer. Boyle noticed that the man he was carrying was missing both legs just below the knee. Boyle tried hard to remember who in Tran's family was supposed to be wounded, and when he couldn't come up with anyone, he began to suspect that he was about to try a takeoff with a far heavier load than he'd planned on. If he'd known about the extra passengers, he'd have dumped some fuel before he landed. Then he remembered that this helo didn't have a fuel dumping system. He cursed as he looked back over his shoulder trying to estimate the weight of the passengers. With all the other things he had to think about, the math got a little difficult, so he gave it up. If they couldn't fly, they could always dump the bags and try again. If that didn't work, it was going to be one of those "pull-up-and-hope" kinds of takeoffs.

Boyle hated them. He remembered one up on Yankee Station where he and his aircraft commander had bounced one off the water before they got it flying. The problem here was that all there was to bounce off was buildings.

It took only a few minutes more for everyone to get themselves loaded and the bags arranged. Santy and Callahan were still standing on the roof next to the Huey when the door to the stairwell flew open and three men emerged holding M-16s. They spotted the helo and began to run toward it, pointing their weapons at Boyle in the cockpit.

Out of the corner of his eye, Boyle saw Santy spin around and drop to one knee. He carefully aimed the Air America pistol he had pulled from under his jacket and began firing at the three men.

Two went down immediately, but the third pointed his rifle at Santy and opened fire. He had gotten off only a short burst before Santy's bullets found him and spun him around, dropping him next to his two friends.

Boyle heard two distinct impacts in the aircraft and quickly checked his instruments to see if anything vital had been hit. The gauges were still okay, so he looked back at Santy, who was trying to lift Callahan into the rear of the aircraft.

He rolled the throttle back on and checked the engine instruments. Everything looked good so far.

Santy's voice came over the ICS. "Everybody's in! Get us out of here, Timmy! Callahan's been hit and I'll bet those assholes have friends." Boyle heard the thump from the left side as Bonnett slammed the cargo door on his side closed.

Boyle took a deep breath, and just as he began to lift the collective, he heard Admiral Wallace's calm voice. "Clear left, Tim. Gauges are good. Let's go."

Boyle nodded and pulled the collective up, but the Huey almost staggered under the weight it had to lift. Boyle saw the rotor rpm decreasing and he could feel the rudder pedals losing their effectiveness. The Huey began to settle back onto the roof, and it was all he could do to keep it pointed in the right direction as it touched down.

Wallace looked over with a completely calm expression. "We all right?"

"Yeah, but we're heavy as shit. Everybody hang on. Watch the engine temp for me, Admiral. Mike, heave out some of those bags."

Santy turned and reached for the nearest of the luggage, but before he could pick it up, the older of the Vietnamese men took it and heaved it onto the roof. He grinned and shoved several more of the ones close at hand. Santy looked up in time to see the door to the stairwell fly open again and two more men charge through it. They stood rooted for a moment as they saw their predecessors lying about bleeding. One shouted to the other and both raced to pick up their comrades' weapons. "There's more of 'em, Tim. We gotta go *now!*"

Boyle thumbed the engine governor, or "beep," switch forward to increase the rpm. He took a deep breath and pulled the helo up off the deck again, watching the torque gauge as the needle barely touched the bottom of the red line.

Beside him Wallace called out the engine temperatures. "Five eighty, Tim. There's six twenty. Coming up on the red line. That's six forty!"

" 'Kay." Boyle lowered the nose and held the collective steady. He was getting everything the engine and rotor system could deliver, but he wasn't sure that it would be enough.

The Huey nosed over and began to pick up speed but very slowly. It began to settle again and Boyle could see the low wall around the roof coming at them. He raised the nose a little, regained a little rpm, and nosed it over again. The Huey cleared the wall by inches, and Boyle dumped the nose to get just a few more knots of airspeed.

The aircraft settled below the level of the roof as it flew over the street, and Boyle felt the helo shudder as the rotors gained enough efficiency to stop the descent and stay in the air. Wallace looked down and saw dozens of people staring at the helicopter so close over their heads.

Boyle saw the torque gauge begin to decrease away from the red line and heard Wallace tell him the engine temperature was headed back into the normal range. Boyle thumbed the beep switch back until the engine rpm was again at 6,600 and rechecked all the other instruments, sighing in relief when he was sure he hadn't hurt anything by taking it that close to the limits. Boyle let the Huey climb slowly at first and waited until he had enough speed to be comfortable before easing into a gentle right turn.

"Okay, Mike. We're flying. That one won't make the textbooks though. What's happening back there?"

"Callahan took a round in the calf. Tran says he's okay, and judging from the cursing he's doing, I agree. Tran's getting the bleeding stopped and everyone else is fine but scared. Including your faithful crewman, me."

"Don't feel alone, pal. I think the aircraft took a couple of hits, too, but it's flying fine and everything looks good on the panel."

Boyle leveled the Huey out heading south and headed down the river. He'd pick up the evacuation corridor and follow it out to sea. For now, they were safe unless some gomer popped up and fired a missile at them. Boyle thought about that and took the Huey down lower so the missileers would have a more difficult shot at them. He reached into his shirt pocket and took out a cigarette. He replaced the pack and lit up.

To his left, Admiral Wallace keyed the ICS. "Want me to fly it awhile, Tim? I think I can keep us from hitting the water."

Boyle smiled and took his hands off the controls. "You've got it, sir." He watched for a few moments to make sure that Wallace could indeed drive the Huey, and when he was satisfied, he began to set up the navigational radios for the trip out to the fleet.

★ 34 ★

Monday, 28 April 1975

LIAM CALLAHAN SAT WITH HIS BACK UP AGAINST THE AFT END OF THE pilots' center console. Tran sat cross-legged on the deck of the passenger compartment using whatever supplies she could find in the Huey's little first-aid kit to treat the bullet wound in his calf, her unlined brow furrowed in concentration and the tip of her tongue sticking out just a little from between her lips. The general sat on the other side of Callahan's leg doing what he could to help his daughter, which seemed to consist mostly of holding things she handed him and putting away whatever wrapping she discarded.

Callahan shifted his rear end a little and reached down and put one of the small tie-down rings that was jabbing him back in its depression in the deck. Now that the pain was becoming less sharp and burning, he looked away from Tran's ministrations and inspected the faces of the people whom the Huey had plucked off the roof.

Santy and Bonnett, the admiral's aide, were staring out the windows at the ground, doing their jobs as the "crewmen" and trying to spot groundfire or the deadly little heat-seeking missiles the enemy carried with them. Their eyes never stopped and they completely ignored what was happening only two or three feet behind them in the rear compartment. It was easier for them that way because no one wants to look at the wounded and be reminded of what can happen to him in the next moment.

The women were either doing their best to calm the children or staring out the window at the diminishing miles of their home-

273

land. Callahan would have given a lot right then to know what thoughts lay behind their expressionless faces.

The legless lieutenant was staring at the deck—could he be thinking of the many other times he had ridden in the back of a Huey on the way to a battle? Callahan wondered. Could he be thinking of his last ride into the LZ on the day he was wounded? Could he be thinking of the ride in the medevac that day, as he bled through his bandages and writhed both in the agony from the wounds and in the horrible imaginings of what would become of his body? Perhaps he was wondering what would become of him now that all he had was his family and the clothes on their backs.

The lieutenant looked up and met Callahan's eyes. He pointed at Callahan's leg and smiled reassuringly as if to say, "No matter how bad that wound is or how much it hurts, there are greater pains and more permanent wounds. Look at me." He looked into Callahan's eyes for a few more seconds and then went back to staring at the floor. Something Tran did shot a fresh lance of pain through Callahan's leg and he arched his back, trying to get away from the pain.

In his seat, Boyle caught Callahan's movement. He looked down at the newsman and then reached over and squeezed his shoulder. He held up both hands and flashed all the fingers twice and then one hand once. Twenty-five minutes to go, he was saying. Twenty-five minutes until they would be aboard the ship and Callahan's Vietnam War would be over forever.

Boyle looked at the lined face of the newsman and saw the oily sheen of sweat renew itself as the jolt of pain slowly subsided. He looked back out the windshield and uttered a small prayer that Callahan's leg wound was the worst they had received. He heard Santy's voice over the ICS.

"I wonder who those guys were?" The question came quietly, almost ruefully, but there was no apology in it. It was just a simple question from a warrior. But there was an undertone in his voice, perhaps a wish that it hadn't had to happen the way it had.

"No idea, Mike. Maybe they wanted to take over and get a ride out. Maybe they were NVA types looking to be heroes."

Wallace looked over at Boyle. "Just as we were coming over the edge of the roof, I thought I saw a couple of people run into the building. They weren't armed so I didn't say anything. Maybe

I should have, but you looked to be busy.'' The admiral's words carried a subtle apology.

"Don't worry about it. No way you could have figured they'd come at us shooting, Admiral. I'm just glad we had Wild Bill Hickok along with us."

"Not funny, Tim."

There was a pause. "You're right, Mike. Sorry."

Boyle watched the last bend in the river go by on the right and consulted his chart. "Okay, Admiral, ease it left to about one ten. That'll take us over the mangrove swamps and avoid most of the enemy-controlled areas." He shook his head. "I mean, the ones that have a *lot* of the enemy in them. At the tip of this mangrove peninsula is Dong Ha. We'll pass that by to the left and that'll keep us clear of Vung Tau, too. If we stay on that course, we'll eventually run into the fleet. Or maybe Australia."

Boyle was rewarded with chuckles from both Santy and Wallace. He reached forward and matched his barometric altimeter with his radar altimeter. "Let's go ahead and climb it up to fifty-five hundred feet. According to the plan, that route's called Ohio and the inbound one at sixty-five hundred is called Michigan."

Boyle watched Wallace smoothly increase collective and adjust the nose attitude for climb. There was only a little wiggle as he compensated with the rudder pedals. Boyle was impressed—most jet aviators forgot the rudders when making control inputs. Jets rarely required rudder corrections, while helos did for nearly everything that happened. Boyle once heard a student pilot complain that he had become convinced that helos needed rudder movements even when they were parked.

Twenty miles east of Boyle's Huey was the huge Marine Corps CH-53D of 1st Lt. Bob Dunn. He was the flight lead of two 53s that were bringing in a small security force to Tan Son Nhut made up of a lieutenant, a sergeant, thirty-six Marines, and two nurses. Dunn's aircraft carried the lieutenant, half the Marines, and the nurses. He was at sixty-five hundred feet and was not at all comfortable. On the rear ramp and in windows on either side, crewmen were positioned with Very pistols with magnesium flares to decoy heat-seeking missiles. The word for a missile firing was supposed to be "Cadillac," but Dunn figured that if anyone saw one, he should just yell "missile" rather than the unfamiliar code word.

As they passed by Cap St. Jacques on their right, Dunn's copilot tapped him on the shoulder and pointed down and to the right of the nose. A helicopter was headed toward them on the opposite course. "Who do you figure that is?"

"I don't know. We weren't briefed on any scheduled traffic. Let's wait and see if they call us. Heads up in the back. We've got an unident helo passing on the right. Keep an eye on him." Dunn heard acknowledgment from all three men.

Tim Boyle followed Wallace's pointing finger and saw the big helo high and to the right. He spun the radio selector to the Guard frequency that was supposed to be monitored by all aircraft in addition to the frequency they were normally using.

He keyed the radio. "Marine 53 south of Vung Tau, this is Air America 181 on Guard." He waited for fifteen seconds or so and repeated the call. This time the answer was instantaneous.

"Air America 181, this is Nighthorse 33. Go ahead."

"Roger, Nighthorse, 181 is at your two o'clock low. We're a single Hotel-one outbound from Alamo to USS boat, um, Quebec Delta. Request freq."

"Stand by."

Boyle hoped the message had been clear enough. Since he didn't have the fleet's card-of-the-day, or "carte du jour" in pilot jargon, he'd tried to use a simple code to confuse the enemy listeners. *Hotel-one* meant "H-1," *Alamo* was "Tan Son Nhut," and *Quebec Delta* was short for "November November Quebec Delta," or NNQD, which were the international call letters of the USS *Concord*. A Russian "trawler" was probably just hanging around the fleet out there, passing on everything that happened to the NVA, so disguising things was pretty much an exercise in futility, but old habits die hard.

"181, Nighthorse."

"Go ahead."

"You know that big road that goes from Jacksonville to Los Angeles?"

Must mean Interstate 10. "That's affirm."

"Okay. Multiply by thirty and add twenty-six point four."

"181 copies times thirty plus twenty-six point four."

"Roger. Contact Slug 771 on that frequency now."

"Roger, Slug 771. Thanks, Nighthorse, take care."

The Marine clicked his mike switch twice in acknowledgment.

Boyle looked down at his kneeboard. Doing mental math, he wrote down 326.4, dialed that frequency into his UHF radio, and set 1200 into his IFF transponder. "Slug 771" was the E-2 early-warning and radar-control aircraft orbiting the fleet.

"Slug 771, Air America 181's with you outbound from Alamo, level five point five, squawking 1200."

"181, Slug. Radar contact. Squawk 3323 and say intentions."

Boyle set 3323 into his transponder. "3323, Slug. 181 is a single H-1 headed for Quebec Delta. We have a U.S. Navy Code 5 aboard and one wounded civilian. We also have ten RVN Nationals, and one will need a stretcher, too." Code 5 was the designation for a rear admiral (upper half, equivalent to a two-star general). Few things piss off carrier air bosses and air-station operations officers more than having a surprise visit by a very senior officer like a Code 5.

"Slug copies. Stand by."

Wallace, the Code 5 in question, was still flying the helo and keeping his eyes straight ahead. Even though what Boyle had just set up was not of particularly legendary difficulty, it simply added to what Wallace had already discovered about the young man. He had handled the landing and takeoff from the roof with calm professionalism, while other pilots would have hesitated or made sure to let everyone else in the crew know how difficult it had been. Boyle simply did it. He didn't get rattled when those three men had started shooting at him, and he had approached every facet of this flight with perfect logic and calm. Wallace wouldn't have felt more secure on an airliner back in the States. And the group of pilots Wallace had ever felt that way about was pretty small.

Boyle's voice came over the ICS. "Mike, can you give me a rough condition on our wounded Irish comrade? Ask Tran, not Liam—he'll have us arranging a hero's funeral down O'Connell Street in Dublin."

"Isn't it Dublin where they make Guinness?"

"Yep."

"Hell, if we get to go to his funeral, I'll shoot him myself. Stand by a sec."

While Santy consulted Tran, Boyle looked down at Callahan,

who saw the conversation and looked up at Boyle. He gave the pilot a thumbs-up and a wink.

"Tim, Tran says he's got a single bullet wound in his left calf. The bullet passed through and doesn't appear to have done as much damage as it could have, so he'll be as good as new in a couple of months. She says she's seen a whole lot worse."

"I imagine so." Boyle remembered the bullet wound he'd received two and a half years before. It hurt like hell for a while and it hadn't done any permanent damage, but it had given him a good-sized scar as a conversation piece on the beach. That one, too, could have been a lot worse.

"Air America 181, Slug."

"181."

"Roger, come left to one oh seven and expect landing aboard Quebec Delta on arrival. Say condition of wounded civilian. Interrogative his nationality."

"Roger. The wounded pax is a U.S. national. He's got a through and through bullet wound in his lower left leg. His condition's pretty good, considering."

"Slug copies. We'll pass it on. Your pigeons to Quebec Delta are one oh seven for thirty-two. Father channel is plus thirty-six."

"Click-click."

Still using the number code he'd worked out with the Marine helo, Boyle reached down and switched the TACAN ("Father") to Channel 46 and watched the needle swing around a couple of times until the receiver found the signal from the transmitter aboard the ship. When the needle steadied out and pointed, he rotated the switch one more stop and the small window in the dial indicated thirty-one miles to the ship.

"Okay, Admiral, TACAN's up. I'll take it back when we have the ship in sight. You're doing fine."

"Thanks." Wallace wiggled his fingers on the stick. That bit of praise from a man twenty years his junior made him feel strangely good.

A little over fifteen minutes later, the E-2 called again. "Air America 181, Quebec Delta's on your nose for seven miles. Contact the tower this freq now."

"Roger. Thanks, Slug."

"Click-click."

Both Boyle and Wallace peered ahead, trying to see the gray ship in the gray haze, which oddly seemed to get progressively more opaque the farther they got from shore. Finally, Wallace said, "There she is. You have the aircraft." Wallace waited until Boyle grabbed the controls and then took his hands off. He reached down and checked that his harness was locked.

Boyle went through the three-item landing checklist and keyed the radio. "Tower, Air America 181's with you at five miles."

"Roger, 181. Expect a landing on the bow straddling Catapult One. Are you familiar?"

"That's affirm." Boyle had spent a large chunk of his life flying off this ship—damn right I'm familiar, he thought. But then the air boss in the tower had no idea who was flying this helo.

"Roger. Come up the starboard side and slide in, 181. Wind's down the deck at ten knots."

"181."

Boyle told everyone in the back to get set and brought the Huey up from astern the carrier. Off to the right the plane-guard helicopter, an H-3, was on the outbound leg of its D-shaped, mind-numbing orbit, and Boyle didn't see any jets in the landing pattern.

When he was a mile astern, Boyle eased the nose back a little and lowered the collective to slow the Huey down. He waited until he was even with the fantail, then slowed still further, matching speed with the giant carrier as if flying formation with her, and positioning the helo directly to the right of Catapult 1 on the starboard side of the bow. Without coming to a complete stop, he eased the Huey over the deck and came to a low hover. He followed the signals from the LSE, or landing director, and brought the Huey down gently astride the long catapult track.

Bonnett slid back the left-hand cargo door and jumped down as Boyle reduced the rpm and rolled the throttle to idle. Several yellow-shirted sailors appeared and reached in to help the Vietnamese out of the aircraft. Boyle smiled a little when he saw a huge American sailor gently holding one of the small brown children and hunching his shoulders over as he walked away protecting the child from the considerable blast of air the Huey kicked up, even at idle power. The other Vietnamese were handled equally gently until they were all out except for Tran, who was still tending to her patient.

As the Vietnamese were led away with several blue-shirted

plane handlers, two teams of stretcher-bearers appeared at the door, led by the flight-deck doctor. The doctor climbed in, took a quick look at the legless lieutenant, and gestured for the stretcher-bearers to take him out. Before they had done so, the doctor was squatting over Callahan with his head bent toward Tran, who was speaking loudly to him over the noise of the aircraft. Inspecting Callahan's bandages, the doctor nodded several times as she spoke. He waved to the remaining stretcher-bearers, who instantly climbed into the helo and carefully placed Callahan into a Stokes litter, a sort of wire-mesh stretcher.

The stretcher team lifted Callahan out and carried him back toward the deck-edge elevator, followed by the doctor and Tran, who, it appeared, was not about to let her patient go until she was certain of his treatment. Santy caught Boyle's eye and grinned as she walked out from under the rotor arc. "She'll be okay, that one."

"Yeah, that she will." Boyle reached for the book of checklists. "Okay, you guys. Either get back in your seats or go stand with the LSE. I've got to shut this thing down. Admiral, if you want to get out, now's the time."

Wallace took the book out of Boyle's hand and found the place among the many steps in the checklist. "The flight isn't over until the aircraft is shut down. I'm still your copilot, right?"

Boyle smiled. "Yes, sir."

Santy and Bonnett disconnected their headsets from the aircraft and walked forward to stand behind the LSE, well outside the rotor arc. Boyle flipped the side position lights to flashing bright and waited for the LSE to radio the tower. He vaguely heard the air boss's voice over the flight-deck loudspeaker system: "Head's up on the bow; disengaging the rotors on Air America 181. Stand clear of the helo."

The LSE gave Boyle the signal and Boyle performed the items and answered as Wallace read them out.

"Radios and nav aids?"

"Off."

"Radar altimeter?"

"Off."

"Throttle?"

"Comin' closed." Boyle depressed the release button and rolled the throttle completely closed.

"Main and start fuel?"

"Off."

"Inverter?"

"Off."

"Lights?"

"Holding."

"Rotor brake?"

Boyle waited until the rotor had slowed to 100 rpm and pushed the rotor-brake handle forward. "Rotor brake's on."

When the rotor stopped completely, Wallace closed the book and placed it on the console. "Battery?"

"Lights are off; battery's comin' off."

Boyle flipped the last switch and pumped the collective four strokes to release the accumulator pressure. He left it in the down position, pulled off his headset, and unfastened his harness.

"Well, Admiral, we're here."

"Yes, we are indeed. Thank you, Tim. Nice job. I like the way you handled all that stuff." Wallace ran his hand over his face. "Now I've got to go see what the hooraw is about. I want to get back in there before sundown. Where'll you be?"

"Either in flight-deck control or in the helo squadron's ready room. I want to have somebody look the aircraft over to make sure those hits we took didn't do anything permanent. I also want to get the frequency cards and find out what the big picture looks like."

Wallace opened the door and stepped out. "Okay. I don't think we'll be less than an hour, but get her ready to go as soon as you can. I have a feeling things are going to start moving really quickly now."

Boyle started to say "yes, sir," but the admiral was gone, trailed by Lou Bonnett, his aide and Boyle's late crewman.

⭐ 35 ⭐

Monday, 28 April 1975

LT. CDR. KEVIN THOMPSON TESTED THE LOAD OF HIS PACK AND TIGHT-ened the straps a little. The supplies he and Dalton had given the tribesmen had lightened their loads considerably, but Thompson knew that within a couple of hundred meters the load would be forgotten in the concentration required to move through enemy-held territory.

Thompson looked around the small area and saw with satisfaction that Butler's tribesmen had sanitized the place, eliminating any trace that they had ever been there at all. If they were moving on, certain that they were never to return, a lesser job would probably have sufficed, but the tribesmen had to traverse this area on their way back to their homes and might need to hole up here again. It would not do to have the enemy waiting here for them.

Dalton finished packing up the radio and swung it onto his back. He folded the map, replaced it in its plastic bag, and shoved it into a pouch on his harness. He looked carefully around the little spot where he'd set up and then walked over to Thompson.

"Did you get it through?"

Dalton nodded. "Yeah. According to their message, they don't know how much longer they'll be in business. Things are apparently happening pretty fast in there, but they did say that there's a helo standing by to come get us, and all they're waiting for is our call. The last thing in the message was, and I quote, 'Don't stop to smell any roses.' "

Thompson chuckled. "All I can smell around here is bad guys."

"Yep."

Thompson looked around the campsite once more and saw the

expectant faces of the tribesmen. They were squatting on their heels in the timeless way of their people just waiting for the next little episode of their lives to begin. Or end.

Butler was standing by the head of the little trail that led downhill with a hand on the shoulders of each of his sons. He looked at Thompson and nodded. Turning to his men, he spoke softly and they stood up and began to move quickly and silently down the trail. Butler fell into the middle of the line, followed by Dalton, then Thompson, and then the rest of the tribesmen.

In less than a minute, the little group had disappeared into the vastness of the jungle.

First Lt. Bob Dunn watched as the last of the Marines hustled out the rear cargo ramp and dashed over to the side of the building and then moved out of sight around the corner. He had been directed to land his helicopter in the parking lot of the commissary at the DAO compound, now known as Alamo. On the way in, the landing-zone controller had curtly told him not to bother with contacting the Tan Son Nhut tower and that all guidance for the helos would come from him.

Dunn had kept one of his radios tuned to the tower frequency but had heard no answer to any of the calls coming from other aircraft. The airport, once the busiest in the world, was now operating exactly like any one of the small grass airports back in the States. The FAA would call it "an uncontrolled aerodrome," and for Dunn, that was a more chilling sign of the Vietnamese disaster than the huge columns of smoke rising around the city.

To the left and slightly to the rear of Dunn's CH-53, his wingman was apparently having trouble with his ramp. It had come down partway and stopped. Then it had gone back up and come down again only to stop in the same place.

Dunn smiled as he saw the ramp bounce a couple of times, for he knew that the crew chief was jumping up and down on it trying to jar it loose. He always enjoyed seeing the American love of high technology reduced to anger and the implementation of brute force when it failed. Except of course when it happened to his aircraft.

"Nighthorse 33, Alamo."

Dunn keyed the radio. "Go ahead."

"Roger, we'll be loading some evacuees aboard. It'll take a cou-

283

ple of minutes to get 'em out here. We've been trying to organize them into sticks, but we haven't had the bodies available. Those troops you just brought in are over there now helping out. Stand by.''

"Roj."

Sticks was Marine jargon for the lines of people who would march up the ramps and sit on the nylon web seats along the sides of the helo. It sounded impersonal, but then much of what the Marines did was impersonal and necessarily so.

Dunn turned his attention to his wingman. The crew had apparently given up on the ramp and were now trying to manhandle the equipment they'd carried along, with the Marines, out the personnel door. The lieutenant was standing there with his arms crossed, glaring at the cockpit of the helicopter. Dunn knew that, in addition to being thoroughly pissed off at the balky ramp, the pilots were enjoying seeing the grunt lieutenant equally angry. The lieutenant, in addition to being pissed at the goddamned Airedales and their stupid helicopters, was probably enjoying getting to be a lieutenant and ordering people around. So Dunn philosophically chalked the whole thing up to valuable occupational therapy for all concerned.

From around the corner of the building came a pathetic procession of evacuees. All Vietnamese, they carried small bags and bundles of personal possessions slung over their shoulders or on their heads. Many were either carrying small children or dragging them by the hand. Most of the adults were young in the characteristic Asian way—they could be anywhere from twenty to fifty. In among the sticks were several old people, denoted by their shambling walks and their stooped shoulders. On either side of the sticks were Marines in full battle dress, their weapons pointing up and out, giving the Vietnamese at least the impression that they were safe in American hands.

The two lines split off—one heading for the rear of Dunn's helo and the other heading for his wingman's. Dunn turned and looked over his left shoulder into the rear of the 53 and watched his crewmen guide the people to seats. The crew began to try to fasten the narrow little seat belts on some of them and wound up having to do it for nearly all. After a minute or so Dunn got a thumbs-up and a shrug from the crew chief, who told him over the ICS that he thought they were all set.

Dunn turned and looked out at his wingman, who was just getting the last few Vietnamese through the passenger door. Dunn saw the rear ramp move up a few inches and stop again. He keyed the radio.

"Lead's set."

There was a pause. "Dash Two's ready. The goddamn ramp's stuck again, but we're set."

"Roger. Frito, Nighthorse 33 and flight are ready to lift."

"Roger, Nighthorse, you're cleared to lift and depart to the southeast. Request you pass on to whoever that communications will be with Frito vice the tower. This will be the primary control frequency."

"Will do. Nighthorse is lifting."

"Click-click."

Dunn pulled up on the collective until the huge 53 was hovering fifteen feet above the ground. He glanced at the gauges, heard his copilot confirm that everything was good, and climbed the helo up and away from the LZ. He heard his wingman call, "Two's comin' up," and told his copilot to take over the controls.

As the helicopter banked right to head for the coast, Dunn glanced back and looked at the landing zone he'd just left. He hoped fervently that he wouldn't have to use that one at night.

Tim Boyle handed the roll of "thousand-knot" tape to the metalsmith. The two were working to cover up the damage done by the rifle rounds that had hit the Huey on the roof back in Saigon. There had actually been four hits instead of the two Boyle had originally thought. Two of the rounds had passed harmlessly through the tail boom, doing nothing more than tearing up some of the sheet metal. Another had nicked the tailpipe of the engine, and the fourth had destroyed the motor for the rescue hoist.

Boyle had gotten the maintenance officer from the carrier's helicopter squadron to canvass his men and find a couple whose shore duty had been at HT-18 at Ellyson Field in Pensacola. HT-18 was the Navy's advanced helicopter training squadron and was equipped with TH-1L and UH-1D Hueys. When sailors left HT-18 to go back to sea duty, many of them wound up in H-3 squadrons aboard the carriers. Now, two of those men, the metalsmith and a jet-engine mechanic, were working on Boyle's helo.

The nick in the tailpipe caused nothing more serious than some jagged edges, which were easily ground down. The hoist motor was more serious but meant only that there would be no hovering pickups—Boyle would have to land the aircraft to load passengers, but since he had no trained crewmen to operate the hoist anyway, he had the metalsmith remove the entire assembly. The holes in the tail boom were easily covered up with the tape, which was reputed to stay on even in a thousand-knot airflow. Boyle remembered many other holes in helicopters he had flown that had received combat damage and been temporarily repaired in this same way.

The metalsmith, who had once been in Boyle's old squadron, HC-17, and dimly remembered him, pressed the edges of the tape over the last hole and straightened, stepping back to inspect his work. "Well, that ought to do ya, Mr. Boyle. I'd say you were pretty lucky. A couple of inches higher and you woulda got hit in the tail-rotor driveshaft. Then y'all would have been in some serious shit."

Boyle smiled and nodded, remembering his flight with Mickey Harris only—what?—a week ago yesterday? Boyle shook his head to clear away the intrusive memory. Now was not the time to be feeling that way.

He turned to the metalsmith. "Do you guys have a hand pump I could borrow for a couple of days? We're going to need to refuel when we get back in to Tan Son Nhut, and I don't think the fuel farm is going to be very reliable."

The metalsmith scratched his chin and nodded. "I think I saw one in the line shack a while back, and knowing the line chief, he's probably got another one stashed away somewhere. Let's go find out."

Mike Santy walked into his squadron ready room and smiled at the familiar sights and sounds. He walked over toward the coffee urn in the back but had only gotten a few steps when the duty officer, "Snake" Mitchell, spotted him.

"Look out! There's a civilian in the room. Eat the classified!"

All heads turned, and in a second, Santy was surrounded like the quarterback who has just won the Rose Bowl. There were so many questions that he could only grin and shake his head helplessly. Finally, the CO, Cdr. Nick Taylor, broke through the mob and stepped up.

"All right, all right. Me first. I *am* the goddamned skipper around here, you know!" He stuck out his hand. "Welcome home, Sandman. Planning on staying long?"

Santy caught an odd note in the CO's voice. "Well, sir, at least long enough to get a decent cup of coffee. Unless you guys have sold my cup for a souvenir."

Taylor grinned. "We'd never do that, Mike. We might throw it over the side, but we'd never sell it. Why don't you grab some and step into my office." Taylor walked to the front of the room and sat in his chair.

Santy filled his cup and tasted the coffee. He was firmly convinced that in all the world, no one, but no one, knew how to make coffee like the U.S. Navy. He took another sip, topped the cup off, and walked up to the front of the room. Pulling over the ammo box that held the squadron's crypto material, he sat down in front of Taylor. By now, the XO and most of the other pilots had gathered around.

Taylor looked his young pilot over from head to foot. The change in Santy was dramatic—he was pale and had dark circles under his eyes. He looked completely beat. Taylor forced a smile. "So, how're you doing? Are you back for good?"

Santy sipped his coffee as he thought. "I'm doing pretty good, Skipper. We're still busy as hell in there, but I don't think that'll be for very much longer. Two days, maybe. And no, I'm only here with Admiral Wallace. He's come out for a meeting of some sort and we're waiting to go back in in an hour. Tim and I will probably be coming back out here for good when he does. Which should be pretty soon."

"Are things really as bad as we're hearing?"

"Yeah. It's getting to be a real zoo."

"What are you doing in there? I mean, what's your job?"

Santy looked up and started to speak. Before the words came out, he realized that Taylor would go ballistic if he knew that Santy and Boyle were planning on flying out to retrieve Thompson. "We're basically doing all the gofer jobs that the admiral needs done. We mostly hang around the DAO compound and run messages." That was completely true as far as it went.

Taylor caught the hesitation but let it pass for the moment. The other officers gathered around and pestered Santy with all sorts of questions ranging from the availability of single women in Saigon to the number of SA-7 missiles the enemy was supposed to

287

have. Santy answered as best he could, but before he could finish any one answer, two more questions were always waiting. It didn't take long for an hour to pass, and the session could have gone on all evening if the duty officer's phone hadn't rung. He answered and stood up.

"Excuse me, you guys, but that was the aide. Mike has to get up to the flag spaces on the hop. Admiral Wallace needs to see him."

Santy looked at his squadronmates and shrugged apologetically. He stood. "Well, when the admiral beckons, us lieutenants come arunnin'. I'll see you guys."

Taylor stood also. "I'll walk you down there, Mike."

"Sure." Santy walked to the back of the ready room and replaced his cup on the board with all the others. He pulled the stack of mail out of his box and separated out all the letters, stuffing the rest of the papers back in. He didn't really care about the newest changes to the A-7 flight manual, but he couldn't wait to read the letters from home.

Once out in the passageway, Taylor stopped and stood in front of the young pilot. "Okay, Mike. What are you really doing in there? That bullshit line you gave us in there fooled most of those guys, but you've got to remember, I taught you most of what you know about pulling the wool over people's eyes. Let's have it."

"Skipper, what I said in there was true. That's all we're doing." Santy stopped and searched Taylor's eyes, which were staring levelly right back. "Okay, okay. Admiral Wallace has Tim and me standing by to fly out and pick up a couple of spooks who are still up in the back country. One trip out and back. That's it."

"You and Boyle." Taylor sighed and ran his hand over his face. "You and Boyle. Why am I not surprised?"

Santy looked at the floor and then back at Taylor. Santy shrugged.

"Mike, I could probably get you kept here on the ship. I could revoke your temporary assignment. I really don't want any of my guys involved in stuff like that. I told you to stay out of it when you went in the first time, didn't I?"

"Yes, sir. You said something like that. But it's not that easy. There's nobody else available, and if those guys get stuck and we can't get them out, they'll be there forever. They'll never get home. We *have* to go, Skipper."

Taylor cursed under his breath. "All right, Mike. But I'll tell

288

you this: I don't like it and I don't want you to get your ass in a sling where nobody can get you out of it. This really and truly pisses me off."

"Skipper, to be perfectly honest, I wish there were another way. But there isn't. And one more thing, if I have to go into a place like that in a helicopter, there's not another man on earth I'd rather fly with than Tim Boyle. If he says we can do it, then we can do it."

"You're pretty sure of him, then. You're willing to bet the hacienda on that."

Santy nodded slowly. "Yes, sir."

Taylor sighed. This one wasn't covered in the book. He wished it were. "Okay, Mike." He stuck out his hand. "Please be careful. If it doesn't look right, it probably isn't—give it up and get the hell out. Okay?"

Santy took the hand. "Yes, sir. We will."

Santy opened the door into the Flag Conference Room and tried to make his entrance inconspicuous. Admiral Wallace, leaning over a large map spread on the table, saw him. "Mike, come on over here."

Santy edged his way over to stand next to Boyle, who was across the table from Wallace. "Sorry I'm late, sir."

Wallace dismissed that with a wave. "No problem. As I was just telling Tim, I won't be going back in there with you. The orders are going out for the evacuation to begin sometime tomorrow, so there's no need for me to go in and sit around waiting to leave again. But there are some, ah, details to be worked out, and for that you two will go back in this evening and wait until tomorrow. If your mission is not set to go by noon tomorrow, you will fly that aircraft out here to the ship. At that time, noon tomorrow, you will consider yourselves under my direct orders to leave the country. Do you understand?"

"Yes, sir." The two spoke in chorus.

"Fine. Now, you will ensure that the remaining members of our staff embark on the first available helicopter out. You may tell them that that is also a direct order from me."

"Yes, sir."

"All right, get going. There will be an Air Force C-130 and our own E-2s airborne so any messages can be passed through them. Good luck."

Boyle and Santy looked at the admiral, muttered a couple of semisincere "aye, aye, sir" 's, and left the room.

As they climbed onto the flight deck, Santy stopped and turned to his friend. "Timmy, that's the second heavy who's laid that sort of speech on me in the last fifteen minutes. First, Skipper Taylor, and now the admiral. I'm getting the feeling that we're walking into something."

"I got the same thing from the helo skipper." Boyle looked out across the water at an accompanying destroyer. "Okay, Mike. The deal still holds. If either one of us decides that enough is enough, we both leave. Right?"

"Right."

⭑ **36** ⭑

Monday, 28 April 1975

IN THEIR OFFICE IN THE DAO BUILDING, THE TWO GENERALS, LEW ALEXANder and Ted Toone, were sitting in two large desk chairs pulled up to the large picture window that looked out across the airfield. On a small table between them sat an ashtray with several cigar stubs, a couple of packs of matches, and a half-empty bottle of Jack Daniel's.

Behind the generals was a large color television, which was carrying the voice of "Big" Minh, a general who was assuming the reins of power in South Vietnam. Minh had been speaking for nearly twenty minutes now, and both generals, fluent in Vietnamese, had quickly realized that this change of governments was the final twitch in the tail of the dying nation. So they'd broken out the bottle of medicine that was prescribed in these parts for the periodic end-of-civilization-as-we-know-it moments and were looking out across the runways and taxiways at the waves of rainstorms that were crossing the vast expanse.

The rain lashed the aircraft across the way and created little streams in the middle of the streets. The ramps where hundreds of aircraft once parked were now nothing more than shallow lakes. There weren't enough airplanes out there now to drip enough oil to make even the smallest slick on the water, Toone thought glumly.

Behind them, Minh's voice droned to the conclusion: "Citizens! My brothers! In these last days you have wondered why so many have calmly deserted their country. I want to tell you, my fellow citizens, that this is our beloved land. Take courage, I beseech you. Stay here and accept the fate decreed by heaven. I beg you: stay here and stay united. Rebuild an independent South Vietnam,

291

democratic and prosperous, so Vietnamese may live with Vietnamese in fraternity."

Toone sipped his drink. "Well, that certainly sounds encouraging. 'I know we're fucked, y'all, but hey, let's all stick around and die like good little peasants.' Christ, Lew, how did they survive this long with leadership like that?"

Alexander shrugged. "I don't know. Maybe the question is why did we allow them to keep putting people like that in power? I mean, we could have de-rigged at least one election, couldn't we?"

"What do you think the PRG is going to say to that speech?"

"They'll probably tell Minh to go piss up a rope. Unconditional surrender and your eldest daughters—something like that, I suppose. Hell, if I was them, I wouldn't even bother with a reply. Hand me the bottle, will you?"

Toone leaned across the small table and handed his boss the whiskey. "Here you go." He sat back in his chair and put his feet back up on the windowsill. "When do we leave, boss?"

"Anytime, Ted. We've burned the files, turned the president's picture to the wall, and shut off the stove. We're done. I guess the embassy will be giving us the word tonight."

"We're getting too old for this shit, Lew."

"Yeah, I know. It wasn't like this when we first met in the Old Army, what, twenty-four years ago?"

"Twenty-five, if you count infantry school."

"I think I'm gonna retire."

"I know. Me, too. After they make us go through all the obligatory postmortem bullshit, I'm going to walk out the damn door, go sit on my ass out in Louden County, and grow radishes."

"Is there still some land available out there?"

"There was last time I looked. Quiet, too."

There was a pause as Toone poured another finger of whiskey in his glass. He leaned back and stared out the window again. "It'll be good to get home."

"That it will, old friend. We'll have that cookout we've always talked about."

While the generals were listening to Minh, Tim Boyle and Mike Santy were making their final approach to the taxiway next to the Air America ramp. They'd made several calls to the tower and were only answered when they were less than a mile from the airfield. The tower had only given them the altimeter setting and the surface winds and remained silent. Boyle assumed that he had clearance to land, but it didn't really matter much. By the time anyone got around to filling out a flight violation, there wouldn't be a government to send it to.

Off to the west of the airfield, the blue-white flashes of another approaching thunderstorm lit the ground eerily. The one they'd just skirted had left the field wet and shimmering in the evening gloom, and the wiper was fighting a losing battle against the hundreds of persistent droplets on the windshield. There'd been a little turbulence and some strange wind shifts, but the Huey had come through.

Boyle remembered another thunderstorm he'd been caught in once back in advanced flight training. The turbulence had been so rough that it had torn off his helmet, and the visor had cut his face under his right eye. He still bore the scar as a reminder to stay the hell away from thunderstorms. But sometimes you couldn't avoid them and then all you could do was try to minimize the danger.

Off to the right, Boyle could see the lights inside the Air America hangar burning brightly in their oddly yellow way. He flared the Huey a little and flew a shallow approach to the taxiway and transitioned smoothly into a fast air-taxi over to the ramp. He landed the helo as close to the hangar as possible and quickly shut it down, trying to beat the next wave of rain.

Three mechanics in coveralls trotted out and put on the ground handling wheels and a tow bar and waited for another to drive the tractor out. Within two minutes the Huey was safely parked in the hangar and the fuel truck was topping off the tanks.

Santy climbed out of his seat and stepped down onto the hangar floor. He pointed to the fuel truck. "They'd shit a brick in the Navy if they saw you refueling inside a hangar."

Boyle laughed. "They'd shit a bigger one if you did it outside in a thunderstorm. Come on, we've got to scare up a couple of fuel drums."

"Why?"

"When we have to go out after Thompson and all tomorrow, there won't be any gas stations around, so if we carry a couple of drums with us, we can fill the tanks and then ditch the drums. We'll have full tanks for the ride home."

"How about the weight?"

"One hundred and ten gallons at six and a half pounds each comes out to a little over seven hundred pounds. We had more weight than that aboard coming off that roof."

"How're we going to get the gas out of the drums and into the tanks?"

"I tried to find a long-range internal tank, but nobody has one. So I cumshawed a hand pump from the helo guys out on the ship. It'll be a little slow, but it'll get the job done."

"You mean one of those things you have to crank?"

"Yup."

"Who gets to do the cranking?"

"Since I am the pilot in command and you are the lowly crewman, you get the honor."

"That's what I figured."

"You can always get Thompson and Dalton to help. Tell 'em it's their cab fare."

"Good idea. SEALs are always bragging about how strong and in shape they are. We'll give them a chance to show off."

"There you go. Now, let's go find out what's happening."

It was just past six P.M. when Boyle and Santy walked out of the radio room at the DAO building and into the damp evening air. They'd caught up with Thompson's position reports and had double-checked the coordinates of the pickup point. All they needed now was a call from Thompson and they could be ready in an hour or so.

"Think we can scare up something to eat, Mike?"

"I hear the Marines have got something over near the commissary."

"Sounds good."

The two had just rounded the corner and were walking alongside the ramp when five small aircraft appeared in formation over the airport. Boyle looked up at the unfamiliar jets. "What the hell are those?"

Santy squinted. "They're A-37s. The VNAF uses them as light attack aircraft, but they're basically a variant of the Air Force T-37 trainers."

"I've never seen one before. They're kind of little, aren't they?"

294

"Yeah, well, so are Vietnamese pilots."

"Good point."

The two Americans watched the jets fly around the field a couple of times. "Hey, Mike. I know the tower's a bit slow tonight, but don't you think those guys should have gotten their landing clearance by now?"

"Should have." Santy watched for a few more seconds. "Tim, there's something strange about those guys. They still have bombs under the wings and they're not in any kind of landing pattern I've ever seen. Either they completely suck as pilots or they're not here to land."

Just as Santy finished saying that, the little jets broke away from each other and began diving on the various installations on the airport. Boyle and Santy stood openmouthed for a couple of heartbeats and then sprinted for one of the bunkers that were scattered around the area. As they ran, the first gouts of yellow flame and black smoke mushroomed on the far side of the runways.

The two dove headfirst behind the blast baffle in front of the bunker and crawled as quickly as possible through the main doorway. The ground shook and trembled as the bombs burst nearly everywhere on the airfield. Several times, one of the jets flew overhead strafing the area, and at least two of the bombs landed close enough to the bunker to bounce the two pilots clear of the floor where they lay.

"Christ, Tim! There's no triple-A going up at them. Those guys are just cruising around, taking their time. I just hope they run out of bombs soon."

Suddenly, gunfire erupted all around the area. Rifles and heavy machine guns began blazing away at the A-37s. In the distance, the heavier thumps of serious antiaircraft weapons began to open up. "That's better," Santy observed.

In only a few more minutes, the bombing stopped and the sound of the jet engines died away. Santy picked himself up and moved to the door. Boyle got up and dusted himself off.

"Mike, maybe we ought to be real careful about walking around for a while. There's probably some trigger-happy folks out there right now."

Santy nodded and eased his way to the blast baffle and peeked out. "Holy shit, Tim, look at this."

Boyle came up behind his friend and looked cautiously around the corner. All over the airfield were burning aircraft. At least four C-47s were on fire, as were several AC-119 gunships. Scattered around among them were well over a dozen destroyed VNAF helicopters.

"What a mess."

"Yeah. Well, we can't do anything about it, so let's just wait for everybody to calm down."

"Okay." The two stood in the doorway and watched the crash trucks and ambulances rush around trying to do their jobs.

After twenty minutes or so, the sporadic gunfire around the airport died down as the shaken ARVN troops realized that they were not under direct attack by North Vietnamese paratroopers. Boyle and Santy left the safety of the bunker and walked carefully back to the Air America hangars where they found the place filled with men moving quickly but deliberately around the half dozen or so helicopters parked in the building.

When they walked in, they saw that a great deal of the activity was centered around their helicopter, which had been parked next to the wall that faced the airfield. The side of the aircraft away from the wall looked fine, but as they went around to the other, they found that a small portable platform had been pulled over and four men in grease-stained coveralls were working feverishly on the engine. Frank Wheeler was standing on the ground watching.

Boyle walked up and looked at the engine. It had been badly hit: the combuster section had several large holes and the entire tailpipe had been blown off.

"What happened, Frank? I didn't see any bomb craters outside."

"Nope. This is from machine-gun fire. Our heroic guardians in that emplacement out there shot up the place trying to hit the A-37s. They kept on shooting when the jet went by and stitched this side of the hangar pretty well."

"Is everybody all right?"

Wheeler smiled. It was just like Tim to ask about the people before he asked about his helicopter. "Yeah. The biggest casualty is my underwear. Those bullets flying around in here scared the hell out of me."

"Can you guys fix this thing?"

Wheeler stepped back and wiped some stray oil off his hands on a rag. "Yeah. The only real damage is to the engine. The transmission is okay and everything else survived. The cowlings got chewed up some, but that'll be the easiest part, that's just cosmetic. We have a spare engine in the back, but it'll be fresh out of the can so we won't know if it's one hundred percent until we turn it up." Wheeler fixed Boyle with a steady gaze. "That might not be until right before you guys get ready to go. If the motor doesn't work, we won't have a chance to do much tweaking."

Boyle nodded. "I know, but if that's our best shot, I don't see that we have a choice. The engine that's in there now sure isn't repairable."

"That's for damn certain. Oh, I noticed that there's some fresh tape on the tail boom. What did you do, fly through a formation of moths?"

"No. We picked some people off a roof earlier and took some hits. The tinbenders on the ship fixed it up for us."

In reply to Wheeler's upraised eyebrow, Boyle told him the whole story of his flight earlier in the day, including the part about nearly overtemping the engine.

"Well, I'm glad you made it, but maybe a new engine will help you tomorrow. Okay, now go get something to eat. We'll take care of the Huey. We've got the best mechs in the Far East here. We'll call you if we need you."

"We'll be over at the DAO area. The Marines ought to be good for some chow."

As the two walked outside the hangar, Boyle looked across the field at the destruction. "Who were those guys?"

"Probably NVA pilots led by that deserter who tried to bomb the Presidential Palace last week. If the fucking gomers have got airplanes down here now . . ." Santy let the thought lie.

"Yeah," was all Boyle could say.

In their office, Alexander and Toone reassumed their positions next to the window. They'd spent the past half hour in the normal staff frenzy of trying to get information on what was happening. Very quickly after the A-37s had done their work, things calmed down, and the two generals found that there were no American casualties and that while numerous aircraft had been damaged or destroyed, much of the equipment was undamaged or, like the Air America helicopter, was repairable. The largest problem was the panic among the three thousand or so Vietnamese civilians waiting patiently for the helicopters to come. It had taken a while but the Marines calmed things and everyone settled down into a long night of waiting.

Toone flipped on the radio and turned it to the BBC World Service. The calm voices of the British announcers were just the thing to soothe frayed nerves and demonstrate that somewhere in the world were places that were tranquil and quiet.

At the top of the hour, the bells of Big Ben sang out and the announcer read the news. Toward the end the announcer said:

"In response to Vietnamese president Minh's inaugural speech, Radio Liberation, the official voice of the Communist People's Revolutionary Government said: 'After the departure of the traitor Nguyen Van Thieu, those who are replacing him, namely the clique Duong Van Minh, Nguyen Van Huyen, and Vu Van Mau, are holding fast to their war, to keep their present territories while calling for negotiations. It is obvious that this clique continues stubbornly to prolong the war in order to maintain American neocolonialism. But they are not fooling anyone. The fighting will not stop until all of Saigon's troops have laid down their arms and all American warships have left South Vietnamese waters. Our two conditions must be met before any cease-fire.' "

Alexander leaned his head back in the chair. "I told you, Ted."

"Told me what?"

"I told you the gomers would tell Minh to go piss up a rope."

⋆ PART 4 ⋆

The
Final Days

★ 37 ★

Tuesday, 29 April 1975

THE SOLDIERS GATHERED THEMSELVES IN THE PREDAWN GLOOM AND SHUF-*fled by squads and platoons and companies to their assembly points. Their sergeants screamed at them and their officers exhorted them. Their colonels watched them and their generals ignored them. Their comrades waited with them and their enemies dug in and prepared to kill them.*

But for most of the soldiers, it was simply another long night that followed a longer day of movement. First by truck and then on foot. Then by truck again and finally on foot once more. They'd sat and waited and they'd double-timed and halted. All the while the city moved closer.

Several times they'd had to move off the road while columns of tanks passed them by. Occasionally they would pass a regiment of antiaircraft guns and would smile and wave at the pretty girl gunners under their ridiculously large helmets. They'd been fed a meal and another an hour later, and then they'd waited nearly ten hours for the next one.

The rumors were rampant among the soldiers this morning. Their old enemy, the French Army, was back to hold Saigon. Saigon had surrendered. The government had decided to stop the advance and negotiate. The Americans were coming back. The bombing of Hanoi had resumed. A squad of sappers had captured the Newport Bridge. A squad of sappers had been wiped out trying to capture the Newport Bridge. A squad of sappers was trapped on the Newport Bridge. The Newport Bridge had collapsed into the river. Every passing half hour brought another story heard

301

from someone who had talked to another who had gotten the story from somebody else.

What the soldiers knew for certain was that no one had ordered them to stand down. The guns to the north and west had not ceased firing. A huge barrage was to begin in just a few minutes against the airport. The heavy artillery and the tanks were still moving toward the city. And the officers who passed by them still wore expressions of grim determination.

After a while they were called to fall in once again and they moved into formation. A colonel in an open-topped car stopped in front of them and read a proclamation from Hanoi praising the troops for their rapid progress and large territorial gains over the past several days. The proclamation further directed the troops to drive with great zeal and determination straight into the heart of the enemy's final lair. With burning eyes, the colonel reverently folded the proclamation and replaced it in his case. He studied the soldiers for a moment and sat back down in his seat. Without a word being spoken, the colonel's driver ground the gears and roared off so the proclamation could be read to the next unit in the line of march.

The soldiers glanced at each other briefly and quietly fell out of formation and into small groups.

As the time passed, the soldiers began to loosen their equipment, and finally they sat down on the wet ground alongside the road. Some dozed, some talked, and others stared off into the middle distance, lost in the thoughts soldiers had been thinking for uncounted hundreds of years.

★ 38 ★

Tuesday, 29 April 1975

THE LAST FULL DAY OF THE EXISTENCE OF THE REPUBLIC OF VIETNAM began with an almost desultory sunrise—the low clouds permitted sunlight to the land only grudgingly. In the jungle where Butler, Thompson, Dalton, and Butler's tribesmen rested, moisture steadily dripped from leaf to leaf and finally to the ground. Even though the air was fairly warm, Thompson felt chilled.

The gloom within the jungle had inexorably dampened whatever optimism either of the American SEALs might have felt after meeting Butler's group and setting out on what was supposed to be the last leg of their journey. Only a few minutes ago, Dalton had sent a position report to the listeners in Saigon and was told that they would "try" to pass the message to the pilots of the helicopter.

Everything was falling apart, Dalton was told. The enemy was at the very gates of the city, and the ARVNs were erecting sandbag barricades in the streets. The orders were going out soon, possibly within minutes and certainly within two or three hours, for the final evacuation to begin. The radio operator did not know how much longer he would be able to maintain the listening watch; it would be very soon, he said, that the word would come down to destroy the equipment and haul ass. He was sorry as hell, but that's the way it was.

All Dalton could do was repeat that they were presently only one hundred meters from the planned pickup spot and were ready anytime the helo got here. They would wait until twelve hours after the listening watch no longer answered and would then try to escape some other way. Just what the other way was going to be was what was now occupying everyone's mind. The several alternatives were all equally unappealing.

Tim Boyle was shaken from his fitful sleep on the battered leather couch in Frank Wheeler's office. He sat up quickly and looked around, trying to get his bearings, listening to the sounds of several Hueys taxiing by the building. He looked around and saw Santy across the room, looking out the window.

"What's going on?"

"The Air America guys are heading down to Can Tho. Apparently, there's a bunch of CIA guys who need to be evacuated right now."

Boyle checked his watch, surprised that it was nearly eight in the morning. He had been able to sleep a little earlier in the evening, but at four A.M. a huge artillery barrage had driven everyone to the bunkers. They'd huddled and cursed and sweated while uncounted shells rained down on the airport.

The enemy even used their massive 130mm guns on the runways and installations. A C-130, one of several American Hercules that had made one final run carrying ammunition for the ARVNs, had been hit and abandoned, its crew now waiting at the DAO building for evacuation. The other 130s had managed to get out safely carrying about 180 Vietnamese each, but the burning C-130 was the end of any attempt to reopen the fixed-wing airlift out of the city. It was now to be helicopters only. There could be no further deliveries of supplies to the ARVNs.

Boyle had no idea how long he'd slept, but the last thing he did remember was Frank Wheeler and a group of Air America pilots quietly discussing the plan for today. It must have been somewhere around five-thirty A.M. when he put his head down on the couch and drifted off through the drone of the pilots' voices. He was so exhausted that the sound of the guns was no longer sufficient to generate enough adrenaline to keep him awake.

He got to his feet and moved over next to Santy. "Is everybody going?"

"Damn near. They're leaving seven helos and crews behind including us. The others are supposed to start ferrying people from the rooftops to the airport here."

"That leaves only six to move all those people. It must be quite a clusterfuck at Can Tho."

"Frank told me that the reason they're taking so many helos down there is that they'll have to run a shuttle out to the ships. Bringing the CIA people here would just add to the confusion."

"Did he say when they'd be back?"

"No. But he did say that it would be a while."

Boyle watched the helos take off in pairs and head across the field to the southwest. "Are six Hueys going to be enough to get the people off those roofs?"

"They'll have to be. Those roofs aren't big enough or strong enough to take anything bigger than a Huey. The Marines'd never be able to find them anyway, and the VNAF are pretty useless right now. All they're trying to do is find their own way out."

"Mike, I almost hate to say this, but you're starting to think like a rotorhead. Maybe I could get you a helo transition and you could be in my squadron."

"Nice thought, but my mom would disown me. Come on, we've got work to do. I'll go over to the radio room and wait for something. You go check the helo out. They should be almost done with the engine change."

Marine 1st Lt. Bob Dunn sat in his seat in the extremely hot and unair-conditioned ready room aboard the USS *Madison*. For about the twentieth time in the past few weeks, he and the rest of his squadron were being briefed on what was now called Operation Frequent Wind. Up until just a few days before it had been known as Operation Talon Vice, but it had leaked to the press and been referred to all over the world. The name had been changed, which had fooled nobody. The plan had remained the same, which had fooled Dunn. It had been a sound plan from the start, but he'd figured that some genius would decide that since the name had been changed, the plan must therefore be impossible to accomplish. As if you were going to be able to hide half the big green helicopters in the Marine Corps flying down Main Street.

The squadron was tired. They'd been on and off a one-hour alert status for the past four days—they'd be called to the one-hour status and then stood down to a six-hour alert. Usually, the explanations for the change either way were not forthcoming—all

305

it took was for somebody in the chain of command to decide that something might possibly be in imminent danger of perhaps looking as if it were going to happen, and the pilots would be called away and would dash up to the flight deck to get their aircraft ready to go. The lack of sleep and the constant emotional pendulum began to wear the pilots down, and the maintenance men and the enlisted crewmen were in similar shape.

Another difficulty was the attitude of the captain of the ship. Captain Guy showed no signs whatsoever of accepting the Marines, and his attitude seemed to have percolated down through much of the ship's company. Deprived of his normal attack-carrier air wing of fighters and bombers, Guy acted like a child and begrudged the Marines everything. It had been hoped that as the evacuation grew closer, he would ease off or at least become somewhat neutral, but it hadn't happened yet. Dunn did not envy Colonel Miller, the Marine CO, his daily dealings with the captain.

Colonel Miller now stood in the front of the ready room and pointed to the blowup of the aerial photographs of the DAO compound. He pointed out the planned landing areas, mainly the newly razed tennis courts and the parking lot of the commissary. He showed a photograph of the lawn at the embassy and noted the large tamarind tree, which the ambassador still refused to cut down. The point of all this, Miller said, was that the huge CH-53s could not land at the embassy and so were to go only to the airport. The CH-46s from one of the other Marine helo squadrons would do all the lifting from the embassy roof. It was going to be tough, he told his pilots, to keep this whole thing organized, but if everybody stayed cool, remembered their training, and kept their heads on a swivel, they could pull it off.

He finished the briefing and put down the wooden pointer. He looked at his hands for a few seconds and then at the pilots. "The go announcement will be 'Deep Purple' over the ship's PA system. When you hear that, come arunnin'. I want you all to get some rest. As soon as the chow lines open, get something to eat. Don't wait for the chow lines to shorten because by then you may have to be gone. Okay? Any questions?" He looked around the room and saw no hands—they'd heard it all before. "Dismissed."

Lt. Cdr. Kevin Thompson stared through his field glasses at the small field they had planned as the LZ. Ten minutes earlier a small group of NVA troops, fifteen in all, had come out of the tree line on the far side and moved to the middle of the field. They'd dropped their packs and proceeded to set up camp, gathering wood, arranging themselves and their equipment, and sending out men in several directions, probably to forage.

They had given no indication that this was to be a permanent camp, but a delay of even two hours increased the danger to the plan for the SEALs' extraction. But as Thompson watched, another group, about equal in size to the first, walked carelessly out of the trees and joined the camp.

Thompson slid backward deeper into the brush, and when he was sure he was invisible to the NVA, he stood and moved more quickly back to the rest of his small force. He knelt and spread his map on the ground, pointing with his knife.

"The enemy are all over that field. We'll have to find another place."

One of Butler's men looked over his shoulder in the direction of the field. "Can we take the field away from them?"

Thompson shook his head. "No. There are too many. Even if we did kill most of them, someone would escape and report to somebody. From the way they moved, I think they are part of a larger force." He jabbed the knife into the dirt in frustration. "They looked like two squads or so, which means that there are probably more of them in the area. We can't take the chance of being found. We have no reinforcements to call on like they do."

"Can we wait until the helicopter is nearby and then attack? We could surprise them and drive them from the field long enough for the aircraft to land."

"That would put the helicopter in greater danger. The enemy would concentrate their fire on it and would probably shoot it down."

The man grunted agreement. It was true that their greatest asset now was not firepower but stealth.

The group studied the map for a moment and discussed the various options. Few areas on the map were as clearly marked as was this field. They could stumble around out here for days and not find another suitable spot at all. Even if they did find one, it would be difficult on such short notice to communicate the coordinates to Saigon and the pilots. No, what they needed was a plan that would be independent of the radio room in the DAO compound. They couldn't count on Boyle and Santy's being able to arrange an aircraft radio relay.

Finally, Butler pointed to a small ridge nearly seven miles to the northwest. "We can go there."

Dalton nodded. "It's what, nine hundred and fifty feet at the top? If we can get there, we can climb it and they can get us off."

Thompson looked at the area between where they were and the ridge. "Can we make it in ten hours? The sun sets by then and I don't know if the helo can get us off at night."

Dalton looked up. "Do we have a choice?"

"No. I don't think we do."

Thompson looked at Butler and the rest of the tribesmen. Butler looked up from the map. "If we are to do this, we'll have to get going."

Dalton was already unpacking the radio. "Make sure everybody eats something while I phone this in."

Mike Santy listened through a headset as Dalton reported the situation, then waited a few seconds for the radio operator to acknowledge the report. Santy consulted his copy of the frequency plan, passed on the relevant parts to the SEAL, and set up a couple of times for further communications. Through a special effort, Santy had been able to work out an arrangement with the airborne C-130. The important part, the call signs of the 130 that could be used for relay, he repeated twice, receiving an equally careful readback.

Santy gently took off the headset and placed it down next to the operator's console. "Thanks. If anything more comes in, I'll be over at the Air America hangar."

The operator nodded as he lit a cigarette. "Okay, but I can't promise much. When the time comes, we'll have to destroy all this equipment and beat feet. Check in with us periodically."

Santy smiled. "I will. Thanks for your help."

"De nada."

Boyle rubbed his face and looked at the new engine that had just been installed in the Huey. As soon as Mike got back here, they'd pull the helo outside, turn up, and check it out. Boyle hoped that the worst they'd have to do was to make a couple of minor adjustments. He'd never seen an engine work exactly right straight out of the shipping can.

He was closing up the cowling when he heard a nasty voice behind him. He turned around and saw Bailey and France. If he hadn't still been thinking about his helicopter, he would probably have laughed at their appearance.

Both were dressed like some sort of commando. They had on military load-bearing harnesses complete with two canteens on the belts along with what looked to be one of the wicked-looking K-bar fighting knives. Each had a shoulder holster with issue .45-cal Colt automatics under their left arms and a pouch carrying extra magazines under their right arms. The only thing missing, Boyle thought, was the Sten gun.

He stood, deciding to let the get-ups pass. "G'morning, Commander. What can I do for you?"

"You are assigned to this helicopter, right?"

Boyle glanced around the hangar. "Yes, sir. We're on standby to fly a mission for Admiral Wallace."

"That mission is canceled. At eleven A.M., you will take me and Mr. France out to the ship."

"If I may ask, sir, why at eleven?"

"The evacuation order will be given then and our work will be finished. Since we will have no further responsibilities, we are under orders to leave immediately. Your helicopter will be the most immediate means of transportation."

Boyle walked over and sat down on the deck of the rear compartment with his legs dangling out the door. He saw that Santy had come up behind the two men. "Who canceled our mission?"

"Admiral Wallace."

"And when was that, Commander?"

"When he left me in charge upon his departure."

"May I see the message, sir?"

"I am acting under his verbal direction. I am the senior officer from the staff present, and I'm giving you your orders now. Have the helicopter ready to go at eleven."

Bailey spun around and marched out of the hangar. France hesitated. He glanced over his shoulder at Bailey's retreating back and looked at the ground. "Tim, look, I'm sorry the commander's been so hard on you guys. I've tried to get him to ease up but . . ." He glanced at Santy and started to speak again but was stopped by

Bailey's voice calling him from the hangar door. He shook his head and followed the commander.

Boyle noticed, idly, that France's canteens gurgled. He should be smart enough to keep those things filled, Boyle thought. Never use your canteen when other sources of water are available. That advice from one of his survival instructors had been of immense help to Boyle in his time on the ground in North Vietnam.

Santy flopped down on the deck next to his friend. "You know, I kinda feel sorry for him, having to be with Bailey all the time. It must make the day go by like an ice age."

"Yeah, well, it was his choice. But maybe there's hope for him yet."

Santy scratched his jaw. "Amazing outfits, weren't they?"

Boyle laughed. "They were ready for anything. Probably even an Indian attack."

Santy waited for a few seconds, and when Boyle continued to stare at the hangar floor, he broke the silence. "Well?"

"Well, what?"

"What are we going to do about Bailey's commandeering us?"

"Ignore him, of course. As far as I'm concerned, the admiral's order to us yesterday still stands."

"Uh-huh."

"I can't imagine Wallace calling us off with those guys out there unless he had a real good reason. And I'm pretty sure he'd make sure we were cut in on the thinking."

"Okay. And what do we do if Bailey and his Boy Scout show up before we leave to get Thompson?"

"We go get Thompson."

"All right. And what will Bailey do if he gets here and we're gone?"

"I sadly fear that he'll have to get on one of the Marine helos with the rest of the commoners. His private taxi will be unavailable."

With an evil grin, Boyle turned and looked at Santy. "Then again, we could always take him out there with us."

"And leave him, maybe?"

"No. I think the Geneva Convention has a rule against doing something like that to your enemy. We could take him along and give him some professional broadening."

"I'd like to broaden his ass." Santy pulled a sheet of paper from his pocket. "We just got a message from Thompson. They have to move to another area because there's bad guys all over the place."

Boyle looked at the paper. "How long is that going to take?"

"Ten hours minimum."

"That'll make it after sunset."

"Yeah, I know. But we can either make a try at night or wait until first light tomorrow."

"Mike, I really don't want to go motoring around out there at night. Not with the lousy nav gear in this thing, and I'm not sure that this place will be here in the morning."

"Then we'd best hope those guys are good distance runners."

Boyle sighed and stood. "I found a couple of drums we can use for fuel. Let's go fill 'em up."

"Okay, but how are we going to keep people from stealing them?"

"I don't know. Maybe we can paint 'Raw Sewage' on the sides or something."

★ **39** ★

Tuesday, 29 April 1975

Gen. Lew Alexander drew the last of his working files out of his desk drawer and leafed through it. The file contained a list of supplies due in under the military support program the United States was still bound to by the agreements made back in 1973 right after President Nixon declared victory and withdrew the country completely from any combat role in the war. He smiled at some of the items due to arrive in the next few weeks. A contract had been signed only twelve days ago for twenty-five-thousand ponchos for a quarter of a million dollars or so. Alexander doubted that there were that many soldiers left in the entire South Vietnamese Army.

The contracting office had been shipped out at the end of the previous week, taking with them most of the paperwork, but several of the staff remained, and last night one of them was trying to figure out how to find 300 million piasters to help balance the books. He'd come to Toone, and with uncharacteristic restraint, Toone had directed him to the embassy.

Alexander sighed and closed the file, throwing it on the small stack on the corner of the desk. He called into the outer office, and one of his aides, Maj. Steve Fixx, came in. Alexander shoved the stack of files across the desk. "Take these, Steve, and burn 'em with the rest. No sense letting the gomers know all our secrets. I'd hate to have them hold our delivery schedule for uniforms and underwear up in front of the world as another example of our insidious plot to destroy freedom in this part of the world."

Fixx picked up the pile and laughed. "General Toone just found one in the bottom of his drawer that had to do with replacing

312

Huey gunships with the new Cobra. That only happened eight years ago or so." He shook his head as if in wonder at the bureaucracy. "Anything else that needs doing, General?"

"No, that's it for now, Steve. Are you all set to go?"

"Yes, sir. When the time comes to head for the helos, don't slow down or you and I will be *real* friendly." Fixx carried the files away.

Alexander smiled and looked at his watch. It was just about ten A.M. Not much more time, he thought. Not much at all. He spun his chair around and looked out the window. He was just thinking about how lousy the sky looked when the telephone rang. He heard Fixx in the outer office pick it up.

After a few seconds' pause Alexander heard Fixx's voice from the doorway. "General? There's a phone call for you on line two. It's the embassy again."

Alexander sighed wearily. He turned and picked up the receiver. "Alexander," was all he said. When you're a general, you no longer have to worry about correct military telephone procedure.

He listened for a few minutes, said "okay" and "uh-huh" a couple of times. With a final "I'll see what I can do," he hung up and looked at Fixx consideringly.

"Steve, see if you can find those two pilots Admiral Wallace left here. Santy and Boyle. They're probably hanging around the Air America hangars. Ask them to come see me. Like real quick."

"Yes, sir. But those other two from Wallace's staff are just down the hall. Will they do?"

"No. I don't think so. I need helicopter types. Get going."

Mike Santy let the small hand truck down gently. The heavy drum of JP-4 jet fuel rocked forward onto the concrete floor next to the other two. He shoved the drum and slid the flat part of the hand truck out from under. As he moved out of the way, Boyle rolled a couple of empty drums forward to hide the full ones.

"That ought to do it," said Santy.

"Hope so. Okay, let's go get somebody to tow the helo out and we'll turn it up."

They walked over to the little office where the maintenance supervisor watched over his flock of helicopters and got two men to help move the Huey out onto the ramp. Once they had positioned it, Boyle untied the main rotor and did a fast walk-around. Just as he was finishing, one of the senior mechanics came over towing a fire bottle.

Santy volunteered to stand fire guard, so Boyle climbed in while the mechanic acted as the plane captain. Pulling out the pilots' handbook, Boyle carefully went through each step of the special postmaintenance checklist. Once he had everything set, he gave the signal to the mechanic and pulled the starter trigger, uttering a small prayer that the damn thing would start in the first place.

He listened to the welcome whine as the engine wound up and saw the rotor blades slowly begin to swing overhead. When the engine temperature began to rise, he started to count the seconds, and at 40 percent rpm, he released the trigger. Like an old veteran, the new engine accelerated until it was running at idle power with all the gauges dead in the center.

Boyle ran through the checks and carefully lifted into a two-foot hover, rotated ninety degrees to the left and back to the right, finally sliding the helo from side to side and backward and forward. He ran through the other hover checks, and when everything stayed normal, he landed again and shut it down.

Once the rotor blades had been stopped, Boyle closed the rest of the switches and unstrapped. Stepping out of his door, he looked at the mechanic and grinned.

"Work good. Last long time."

The mech smiled at the old saying. "Hover checks okay?"

"Perfect. I figure if it'll do okay in the hover, it'll do just fine in flight." Boyle looked across the airfield. "I don't suppose that we could get clearance for a test flight anyway."

"You got that right. Do you want to bring it back inside?"

Boyle looked at Santy, who shrugged. "No. We'll leave it out here. We might have to go flying in a hurry and you guys have other things to do. Listen, um, nice job with the engine change. Thanks."

The mech smiled. "No problem. I'd rather you got a new engine than us leaving it in a can for the gomers. When we put the old one back in the can, we marked it 'RFI' so that'll at least fuck up their inventory. The little bastards might even be stupid enough to install it in one of the helos they capture. Who knows."

Boyle and Santy laughed as the mech walked away. *RFI* meant "ready for issue," which indicated that the engine in the can was in working order. The one that was in there now was definitely not.

Boyle pulled the rotor tiedown from the rear compartment and put the hook through the eyelet on the end of one of the blades. He pulled the blade around and tied it to the tail boom. He and Santy both went up and removed the ground handling wheels, dragging them inside the hangar and stowing them behind the door.

Santy wiped his hands on a rag. "Okay. What do we do now?"

"Well, there's no good movies showing in town and the bars are closed. So I guess we go sit in Wheeler's office and wait."

"Great. My favorite pastime—staring at a telephone. Reminds me of college waiting for girls to call and ask me out."

"Good. Then you're used to long waits."

They'd made it halfway across the hangar when Fixx came around the corner and spotted them. "Hey, Boyle!"

"Yes, sir?"

"General Alexander wants to see you guys. He said like right now."

"What's up?"

"I don't know. He got a phone call and sent me to find you."

Santy looked at Boyle and shrugged. "So much for boredom."

As the three were walking down the hall to Alexander's office, they heard a voice calling them from one of the others that lined the long, dark passageway. Boyle turned and saw Commander Bailey step out and stand squarely in front of them. France came to the doorway but hung back a little. They'd at least taken off the combat harnesses, but the pistols were now in holsters on their hips. Apparently Bailey expects NVA sappers to burst forth from the file cabinets at any moment, thought Santy.

"Yes, sir," said Boyle in his most noncommittal voice.

"What are you doing here?"

"I don't know yet, Commander. General Alexander sent for us."

"General Alexander? I didn't know he'd sent for you."

Boyle said nothing and Bailey looked at Fixx. "Why did the general send for my officers?"

Fixx shrugged. "I suppose he wanted to talk to them, Commander. They're a little too senior to be carrying his bags."

Bailey stiffened. "Very well. Let's go see what General Alexander wants with members of *my* team."

Fixx only just managed to keep a smile from crossing his face. "Whatever you say, Commander."

Alexander was reading a sheaf of message forms when the small group entered the room. He looked up and smiled wearily. Santy was surprised at how tired he looked since they'd seen him only a couple of days before in the hotel.

The general gestured to some chairs against the wall. "Good morning, gents. I'm glad Major Fixx found you so easily."

Bailey spoke up. "I had directed them to stay close by their aircraft, General." His tone carried a gentle reminder that it was he who was supposed to be in charge of the two pilots.

Alexander looked directly at Bailey. "Excellent thinking, Commander." His words very deliberately failed to carry the irritation that was in his eyes. He turned back to the pilots. "Gentlemen, I know that you've been directed to stand by to go get our wandering gypsies, but we have a problem. With a bunch of the Air America helos dedicated to Can Tho, we're a little short on assets here. At Can Tho they're coming under repeated attacks from the gomers, so we need a lot of speed down there. But we can't spare any more helos from here and the fleet can't help out."

Alexander bit the end off one of his cigars. "We have only about a half dozen Hueys available to move people off the planned LZs on the roofs. The surface evacuation plan, using buses and cars, will probably go completely to shit, so many of the people we need to get out of here won't make it. The fucking State Department has run our ass out of time, so we'll have to do a lot more of the people movement by helicopter. Frankly, we need you to help out. Are you familiar with the roofs we've designated? There's thirteen of them."

Boyle nodded. "Pretty much. Mickey Harris showed them to me, but I haven't landed on most of them yet."

"All right. Now, as to your other mission. We will maintain the communications watch for you downstairs as long as we can. When we close down, you can still use the airborne C-130; call sign will be 'Cricket.' He's got radios out his ass and he's been informed that your other mission is still on."

Boyle smiled a little. "Okay, General. When do we start?"

"I'm not sure exactly, but it'll be pretty soon. But I want to emphasize this: if the call comes to go get Thompson's party, that will be your priority. Break off work with the evacuation, top off your tanks, and go."

Alexander nodded his dismissal and the small group stood up. As they turned to go, Alexander called to Bailey. "Commander, stay a minute. I've got something for you. Close the door please."

Once out in the main passageway and headed for the exit to the building, Boyle looked at Fixx, who this time couldn't help smiling. "I think my boss is about to explain the facts of life to your boss."

Boyle grimaced. "He ain't *my* fucking boss. At least not permanently, thank God."

"Whatever. Do you have everything you need?"

"I could use a crewman. When we go get Thompson and all, it won't be a problem since they've all been in helos before. But if we're going to be picking up a bunch of civilians who don't know anything, there ought to be somebody back there who at least understands how to close the doors and fasten a seat belt. I'd hate to drop somebody over downtown." Boyle looked back at Alexander's office door. "That's not true in *all* cases, of course."

Fixx smiled again. "Tim, I don't have anybody to give you. How about Air America?"

"We can ask. But they all seem to have lots of other things to do."

"I'll go."

All three turned. Joe France was standing in the doorway to his and Bailey's office. Boyle and Santy looked at each other and back at France, who stepped farther into the hallway.

"I mean it, Tim. I've been in the airplane-loading business my whole career. I even know how to drive and operate a fuel truck."

Boyle still couldn't get over his surprise. "But why?"

"I'll explain it later. You need help and I'm available."

Boyle glanced at Santy, who simply raised an eyebrow. Boyle turned back to France. "You understand that *I'm* the aircraft commander. I'm not going to have any bullshit about who's senior and who makes the decisions."

France looked at the floor. "Fine. I think I've already pulled that on you a bit more than I should have."

"Okay. Can you get Bailey to turn you loose?"

Fixx spoke up. "I believe that when I explain your need of a crewman to the general, and he explains priorities and stuff like that to the good commander, things will be most clear all around."

"Okay, Joe. Meet us at the hangar as soon as you can. We'll go see the Air America people and get the plan."

Aboard the USS *Madison,* 1st Lt. Bob Dunn reached up and flipped the external light switch on his CH-53 to "steady-bright." All the preflight checks were down, and except for a few items on the takeoff checklist, the 53, call sign Nighthorse 10, was ready to go. Dunn looked ahead up the flight deck and saw that his flight leader, Nighthorse 12, was still getting set.

Behind Dunn's aircraft two more 53s were turning up. The four were to go over to the USS *Tarawa,* an amphibious carrier, pick up the first members of the ground security force, and fly them into Tan Son Nhut airport. Dunn realized with some sadness that the arrival of the GSF at the airport would certainly be the last helicopter insertion of combat troops in the Vietnam War. Which, of course, had ended two years earlier, he thought wryly.

Dunn saw the lead's lights go to steady-bright and asked the crew chief how the two helos behind were making out.

"Looks like we're all set, Lieutenant."

"Okay, make sure you're strapped in."

"Click-click."

Dunn watched the yellow-shirted sailor standing ahead of the lead's aircraft spread his arms and signal the 53 to lift off. The rotor blades formed a shallow cone as the pilot lifted the collective, then the blades changed pitch and began to take a larger bite out of the air. The big machine peeled itself off the deck and jumped quickly into a hover. It stabilized for a few seconds, and when the yellow-shirt circled his arm over his head and pointed outboard, the 53's nose dipped and it began to climb away, banking left to enter the rendezvous pattern.

When his own yellow-shirt signaled him to lift, Dunn called for the last items on the checklist, checked the instruments once again, and pulled the helo up into a hover. When the copilot reported everything looking good, Dunn watched the yellow-shirt point outboard and eased the helo into a climb away to the left. The copilot raised the landing gear and Dunn searched the sky for his leader.

In only a few more minutes, all four helicopters were joined up and heading for the *Tarawa,* to pick up a hundred fifty or so young Marines, who in most respects were no different at all from the other young Marines who had first come ashore at Danang nearly ten years earlier.

When France walked into Frank Wheeler's office, Boyle and Santy were bending over a map of the city of Saigon with three Air America pilots trying to make some sense out of things. The Air America pilots were pointing out several LZs and describing the safest routes in and out of them. These were new ones Boyle had not yet seen, but he was at least familiar with the general geography of the city, so it wasn't completely hopeless.

France saw the coffee urn in the corner and walked over and got himself a cup. It had obviously been made some time ago because although it was nice and hot, it also had the consistency of mud, which suited France nicely. He walked over to the desk and sat down, listening to the small group.

After ten minutes or so the discussion broke up. The Air America pilots left to get their flight gear, and Boyle and Santy turned to France.

Santy sat at the desk. "Well, Bailey decided to let you go, huh?"

"Let's just say he didn't pitch a fit about it."

There was a silence for a few minutes. Santy stood up and took the map. "I'll go put this in the helo. See you two out there."

France watched him leave and sighed. "Look, Tim, I'm not trying to be a hero. If you don't want me to come along, just say so."

"Joe, I don't have a problem with you as a crewman. I need somebody and like you said, you know how to manage loads. But what I don't understand is the sudden change of heart. Although I noticed that the last time or two I saw you before today, you seemed a little different."

France sat up. "I know you think I'm an asshole, and I have to admit that I've been a pretty good one sometimes. Commander Bailey told me that coming along on this trip would be good for my career, so I came. But when we got here to Saigon, I started to see things differently. For example, I started to understand that not every job in the Navy is there to be a stepping-stone for promotion or just a way to get a ticket punched. These people are hurting and we can do something about it. Not much maybe, but something. I'd like to help."

"Fair enough. You ready?"

"Yeah, but there's one more thing. The other night when we got shit-faced and you put us to bed, well, that taught me something else. I had treated you pretty badly and yet you still did it. You made sure I was okay. Then when Commander Bailey got assigned that investigation and he treated you and Santy like shit even after what you had done for us, it made me feel like some sort of scumbag. I don't want to be like Bailey if that's what I've got to be like in ten years." France stood up and stuck out his hand. "Look, Tim, I'm sorry."

Boyle shook his hand. "Okay, Joe, forget it. I believe I've said some not-too-nice things about you, too. But right now I need you thinking about weights and loads and looking out for bad guys, so let's get going before Santy wanders off somewhere."

✬ **40** ✬

Tuesday, 29 April 1975

THOMPSON AND DALTON LEANED AGAINST A TREE IN THE JUNGLE AND stared off into the middle distance, which was about fifteen feet in the green thickness they'd been traveling through. They were as physically worn-out as either man could remember having been in a long time.

A few minutes ago, after nearly three hours of traveling, Butler had called the second halt in the march, and the SEALs had simply collapsed in place. They'd drunk sparingly from their canteens and leaned back, feeling the increasing deadness in their legs. Neither man would speak of it to the other, but the march to the ridge was going to be just about all they would be able to handle—if they couldn't be picked up from there, they would not have the strength to go on to somewhere else. Both knew, too, that if they didn't make it this time, it wouldn't matter because there would be no other pickup point. They would have to attempt to get to the coast somewhere and steal a boat or march clear across Cambodia to Thailand.

Dalton put his canteen back in its pouch on his belt. "I'm getting too old for this shit."

"Me, too. But this is what happens when you sit on your ass behind a desk for a couple of years."

Dalton looked at his watch. "Seven hours to nightfall."

"Yeah."

"I'm beat, boss."

"So am I, but we'll make it."

"Yeah."

After another couple of minutes, Butler walked over and sat

321

with them. He pulled Thompson's map out of the case at his side and unfolded it, but only enough to reveal their route of march and a kilometer or two on either side. He pointed to a spot about a third of the way to the ridge. "I make us about here. This is the stream we crossed a while ago, so we must be at least this far beyond it. We're making pretty good time."

All three knew that their pace would necessarily slow as they used their reserves of energy and the land began to steepen.

Thompson refolded the map. "How are the boys doing?"

Butler smiled. "They're doing all right, but we've had to carry the little one sometimes. The older one will need that, too, pretty soon. They are tough and strong."

"Like their father."

Butler shook his head. "No. Like their mother," he said gently.

Dalton sighed and took out the radio. "Let's see if there's still anybody left in the DAO."

Butler stood. "Make sure you eat something. We'll start as soon as you finish sending your message."

Santy hung up the phone and turned to Boyle. "That was the communications watch guy. Dalton just called in and they've still got a little over seven klicks to go. They might make it by sunset, but they don't know."

"How far is that in miles?"

"About four."

"Shit." Boyle remembered his own trek through the jungle toward the coast of North Vietnam. He could imagine what the SEALs were going through, and according to his pilot's chart the terrain was more difficult for them than it had been for him. On the other hand, the SEALs were better trained at land navigation and escape and evasion, or E&E, than he had been. Which really had been not at all, but no matter how he ran this through his mind, it was going to be close at best.

Boyle stood up and stretched his back. He would love to get a good night's sleep in a real bed. He couldn't remember when he'd had eight straight hours to do that. Soon, he thought. He turned to Joe France, who was still poring over the chart that had chronicled Thompson's trek. When Boyle and Santy had filled him in on what the mission, which Bailey had so officiously told them was canceled, truly entailed, he had been appalled, but not at the mission.

What appalled him was that first of all, for all his self-importance, it was obvious that Bailey had not been cut in on very much of the big picture. Secondly, Bailey had refused to even consider that there could be something of greater importance than his own small concerns. France shared none of this with Boyle and Santy—not his surprise, nor the several conversations, lectures really, he had had with Bailey as he had presented his view of things in Saigon, nor even the cold way in which Bailey had schemed for official recognition.

France had just kept it to himself and had done what he could in the past hour or so to get himself up to speed on both the mission planning for the rooftop evacuation and on what he would need to know to be an effective helicopter crewman. That, he believed, was the best he could do for now. Later on, he told himself, once he was safely back in Hawaii and his old job, would come the careful reassessment of his career in the Navy. If he was to stay in instead of taking one of the airline jobs that he had been idly considering, he would have to do things differently. Hitching his professional wagon to a star like Bailey had gradually, but certainly, become repellent to him. He wasn't sure yet that feeling this way was professionally smart, but at least he felt better about what he was doing. And that was a move in the right direction.

As France was looking at the chart, one of the Air America pilots came into the office. "Tim, the word has just come down. The evacuation is on, commencing immediately. 'Execute Option Four' was the way we got it. We're going to start ferrying people to the airport as soon as we can get airborne. You guys ready?"

Boyle nodded. "We're ready."

"See ya." The pilot was gone.

First Lt. Bob Dunn slowed his helicopter and let his flight leader get a little farther ahead than he had been during the flight in from the ship. In the back, the Marines craned to get their first glimpse of the city about which they'd all heard stories from their veteran sergeants and majors. Most of them had still been in early high school when the American combat presence had ended and had been in third or fourth grade when the Marines first came ashore in 1965.

Dunn listened to the Marine officer who acted as the LZ controller give the wind direction and estimated altimeter setting to the lead and then clear him in for a landing on the tennis courts. Dunn slowed a little more and set up for his own landing slightly behind and to the left of the lead. He kept his approach coming and touched down a few seconds after the lead had landed and reduced the collective and thus the downwash blowing across Dunn's landing spot.

As soon as he had Nighthorse 10 on deck, the crew chief signaled to the GSF Marines to get out, and they stood and rushed out the rear ramp, assembling off to the side with those from the other 53. Over his shoulder, Dunn could see the Marines and some other Americans leading "sticks" of people out to both his and the lead's rear ramps—men, women, and children of all ages, carrying pathetic bundles of personal belongings. The people climbed in, guided by both the crewmen in the back.

Dunn turned around again and looked out the windshield. His job was to fly, and it was the crewmen's job to get everybody organized in the back. He watched the people climb aboard the lead's aircraft and waited for his crewman to call him on the ICS, resisting the temptation to look back there for himself.

"Okay, Lieutenant. We're loaded. Ramp's up and we're ready to lift. I'll get you a head count once we're airborne."

"Roj." Dunn's copilot completed the checklist while Dunn keyed the radio. "Dash two's ready."

He heard the lead's slow drawl. "Roger. Break. Alamo, Nighthorse 12 and 10 are ready to lift."

The Marine on the commissary roof answered, "Roger, 12, Alamo. You're cleared to lift and depart. Call clear."

"Click-click."

Dunn watched the lead's helicopter lift and climb vertically until it was clear of the buildings and then nose over and fly off.

"Comin' up," he said over the ICS as he pulled his helo straight up and then nosed it over, turning to make a running rendezvous with the lead. Behind him he could hear the other two 53s from his original flight of four call for takeoff from the old ball diamond at the DAO compound.

Out ahead in the distance, Dunn could see several formations of helicopters heading in with the rest of the GSF. Dunn looked at the countryside around the city. There were supposed to be sixteen divisions of NVA troops out there—about 160,000 men. He shook his head. Aside from the columns of smoke, he could see nothing of the enemy. Here they were actually attacking in conventional formations and he still couldn't see the bastards.

"Alamo, Nighthorse 12 and flight are clear to the southeast. Traffic in sight." Lead was letting the controller on the ground know that he didn't have to worry about warning them about conflicting traffic. It was one less thing for the guy to deal with.

The helicopter formations passed by high and to the right. At least eighteen more CH-53s and a dozen tandem rotor CH-46s were heading in with the rest of the GSF, somewhere around 840 Marines, Dunn had been told at the morning briefing.

Dunn gave control of the helo to his copilot and slid his seat back on its rails. He flexed his fingers and pulled a cigarette out of the pack in his sleeve pocket. Lighting it up, he placed the pack and his lighter on the frame of his side window. He called the crew chief. "You guys got a head count back there yet?"

"Yes, sir. We got seventy-eight souls back here counting babies. Some of these folks had guns on 'em, but we managed to get them to hand them over. They're in the tie-down box up forward. Everybody's pretty quiet back here though."

"Thanks. Seventy-eight pax. The GSF people are supposed to be frisking these folks for weapons, but don't take any chances. Keep searching them when they get aboard. I'll call lead and tell them to do the same."

The lead had had the same problem with weapons and decided to call ahead to the ship to make sure that somebody was waiting on deck to disarm the refugees. It chilled Dunn a little when he heard his lead dispassionately discussing the problem with the ship. He had a mental image of gunfights breaking out on the ships between the refugees and the crew.

It was going to be a big enough zoo out there without the guns.

Tim Boyle set up for his approach to the first rooftop, a building in the southern part of the city near the racetrack. Off in the distance he could see the other Air America helicopters making their approaches to other buildings.

325

As he had flown over them, Boyle could see that the streets were even worse than they had been the day before. The crowds were immense and vehicular traffic was either nonexistent or completely immobile. He couldn't see how the buses were ever going to get a single soul to the airport in time to be evacuated. The evacuation order had been given less than forty minutes ago, and it already looked to him that the entire plan was breaking down.

"Okay, guys. Here we go. Clear the tail, Joe."

"Roj."

Boyle eased the Huey over the edge of the roof and touched it down gently on the tarred surface. Off to the right, a large water cistern dominated the roof. But this one was wide open compared to most. Once the skids were firmly planted, France jumped out of the cargo door and ran over to the stairwell. He cautiously pulled the door open, peeked in, and disappeared. In just a few seconds, he reappeared leading eight Caucasians, presumably Americans, to the helo.

The passengers climbed in and seated themselves, some sitting on their luggage. France quickly scanned the group, moved a couple of people around, and fastened his gunner's belt around his middle. He closed the cargo door and pushed the ICS button.

"Okay. We're set back here. I think I've got the load balanced, but be careful—some of these bags looked pretty heavy."

"Okay. Comin' up."

Boyle lifted the Huey into a five-foot hover, checking his engine instruments carefully. They all looked good and the helo felt pretty stable, so he increased collective and flew it off the roof. It only settled a little when it passed over the edge and lost the cushion of air between the blades and the surface of the roof. The chuffing sound and the shudder as the helo passed through translational lift lasted only a couple of seconds, and the Huey began to climb away easily.

Santy grinned in his seat. "Well, that was nice. I'd like to thank you for not scaring the shit out of me like you did yesterday."

"Kiss my ass, Mikey."

"What happened yesterday?" asked France from the back.

"Tim here tried to take off with half the population of Vietnam in this little bitty helo. It was a good thing we started out high

326

because if we'd been at ground level, we'd have bottomed out in China."

Boyle grunted. "We're on China's side of the world over here, you asshole. We'd have ended up in Maine. Didn't you learn anything in school?"

"Maine's nice," France observed.

"Anywhere's nice compared to this," said Boyle. "How many people are there in that building, Joe? Any idea?"

"No. The stairway is pretty full. Wait a minute. I'll ask one of these folks."

There was a pause. "Nobody seems to know for sure how many are supposed to go from there. This guy back here says that the word was put out that there were thirteen buildings and you were supposed to go to one of those. He says that they only started playing the signal song, 'White Christmas,' on the radio a half hour ago, so he expects more to show up as the day wears on. He says with the streets the way they are it's going to take longer than anyone figured."

"Yeah. Thanks." Boyle keyed the radio and got clearance to land at the little area near the DAO compound, clear of the bigger landing zones designated for the Marines.

He checked his fuel. If consumption stayed where it was and each trip took about the same length of time, he could probably make a total of eight trips to that building and back before he had to get some gas. He wished the other helos would get back from Can Tho pretty soon. Seven Hueys weren't going to cut it.

General Alexander watched another pair of Marine CH-53s touch down in the parking lot. These two arrived empty, which meant that the GSF was now all ashore. As he watched the sticks of people walking quickly to the rear ramp, he could see two more helos climb out of the tennis courts and fly off with their loads.

The phone rang in the outer office and he heard Fixx pick it up. A moment later, the major stuck his head into the office. "Phone, General. Line one."

The general sat in his desk chair and picked up the instrument. He wondered idly what bad news or what problem this was going to be. "Alexander."

The voice on the other end was one of the ambassador's assistants. "General, we've got somewhere between five and ten thousand people in the street outside. The marines of the embassy guard detachment are just about overwhelmed. Can you spare any troops from your security force to help out?"

"Let me check. I'll get 'em over there as soon as I can." Alexander hung up and walked into the outer office. "Steve, go track down General Toone. Tell him to get with the Marine GSF commander and tell him that I'd like a couple of platoons of his men sent over to the embassy most skosh. Apparently, they're about to be overrun. If he needs to use helos for that, tell him to go ahead."

"Yes, sir." Fixx left the office on the double.

Alexander was back standing at the window again when Fixx returned. "General Toone has one hundred and thirty Marines on the way over to the embassy, General. He says it's been a hell of a long time since anybody used him as a company runner."

Fixx was pleased to see his boss laugh heartily for the first time in days.

Kevin Thompson carefully let Butler's smaller son down from his shoulders and lifted him up to the waiting hands at the top of the streambed. The boy was hoisted all the way to the top, and Thompson followed, pulling himself up by grabbing a couple of small bushes that hung over the edge.

He turned and helped up the others in the column. They all waited for a few minutes until Dalton, who was covering the rear, entered the streambed and helped him up, too.

Now on reasonably level ground again, Thompson sat on the trunk of a fallen tree and pulled out his canteen. He rotated his neck, trying to get the stiffness out of it. He remembered the last time his neck had hurt this way, when he had allowed his nephew to sit on his shoulders at an air show. The little boy had loved seeing the Navy's Blue Angels perform, but after about ten minutes of the thirty-minute show Thompson's neck had been on fire, and he was never so glad to see anything end as he had that performance.

Dalton crawled over and flopped next to him, pulling out his own canteen. "Christ. How many more of these little fucking streams are there?"

"Damned if I know. None of the last three has been on the map. I'm gonna have a chat with the Defense Mapping Agency when I get home."

"Make sure you tell 'em I said to go take a flying leap, will you? Better yet, shoot a couple of them for me." Dalton sat up. "How much farther do you think we have to go?"

"Maybe a little under three klicks."

Dalton sighed. Better than halfway there, but if they ran into many more of these streambeds, it would take them until July to get to the ridge. He got to his feet.

"Give me my namesake. It's my turn to carry him."

Thompson placed the boy on Dalton's shoulders and took the radio, which he slung over his own back.

★ **41** ★

Tuesday, 29 April 1975

TIM BOYLE WATCHED HIS FUEL GAUGE MOVE SLOWLY BACK TOWARD THE fifteen. The gauge would continue to move for a few seconds after the fuel-truck operator released the handle and pulled the nozzle out of the filler neck. When the tanks were full, holding their 242 gallons, the indicator should be just beyond the mark that indicated fifteen hundred pounds.

He and his crew had made nine trips to the downtown rooftop and flown over sixty people to the marshaling area at the DAO compound. As near as France had been able to tell, at least the same number of people were left to go.

Brief radio conversations with other Air America pilots had told him that they would all be at it at least until nightfall and probably for several hours after that. The good news was that the buses were beginning to get through to the airport and the embassy. Each bus could carry nearly eight times the load of an H-1. If the buses could continue, there was a chance, Boyle thought, that the people waiting in the buildings might just make it.

He had overheard a brief radio conversation between one of the Marine CH-46s and the orbiting Air Force C-130 control plane, known as Cricket, that the estimates of people left to go was somewhere in the neighborhood of ten thousand. Santy had looked across the cockpit at Boyle and said, "Timmy, the U.S. military doesn't have enough helos in the whole goddamned world to move that many people."

"Ours is not to reason why, Michael, me lad."

"Terrific. Just what I need—Tyrone Power."

"Errol Flynn, I believe."

"Whatever."

Santy stuck his head out his door and looked back. The refueler was dragging his hose back to the truck. He shoved the nozzle into its holder and pulled the lever that wound the hose back onto the reel, using his foot to guide the coils back onto the reel evenly. He pulled out a small clipboard holding the billing forms, consulted the meter, and wrote in the number of gallons on the top form. Smiling pleasantly, he walked up to Santy's door and handed him the clipboard. Santy pulled a pen out of his pocket, scrawled his name on the proper line, and handed the clipboard back.

"Okay. We're good to go."

Boyle checked the switches. "Is the truck clear?"

"Almost." A pause. "Okay, now he's gone. You're clear on the left."

Boyle looked out his side. "Clear right. Starting."

He pulled the trigger on the collective and the engine began to wind up. Within five minutes, they were airborne and headed back to the rooftop LZ.

France came out of the stairwell leading only four people this time. He arranged them in the back and plugged into the ICS. "That's it, Tim. These folks are the last of 'em."

"What happened to the rest?"

"These folk said a bus finally got through while we were gone getting fuel. They said the others all figured we might not come back, so they went for the bus. These four figured that they'd rather wait for us than risk a bus trip to the embassy. They've heard that there is a huge mob over there, and trying to ride a bus through it was a scary idea."

"Okay. Everything all set back there?"

"Everybody's strapped in and your tail is well clear."

"Comin' up."

Boyle lifted easily off the roof and climbed out for the airport. He waited for a break in the radio chatter and keyed the mike. "Alamo, Air America 181."

"Go ahead, 181."

"Roger. 181's inbound to you from LZ Seven. This is the last load from that LZ. The rest took surface transport."

"Okay, 181, when you make this drop, head for LZ Four. There's apparently a good-sized backup over there."

"181 copies LZ Four."

"Click-click."

Santy pulled out his chart and found LZ Four, which was another rooftop well to the northeast of the one they'd just come from. He folded the chart so that the only part facing out was the route to and from LZ Four.

"Once we're off the airport, Tim, head about oh six five. That'll get us in the area."

"Okay." Boyle started a gentle turn to line up on the place on the taxiway adjacent to the DAO compound where he would drop off his passengers. He was beginning to raise the nose to slow down when he saw a large black-brown geyser of dirt erupt from alongside the taxiway. An Air America H-1 was just lifting off, and three more dirt geysers grew less than an aircraft length behind it.

"This is Alamo on guard. The outer LZ is under fire. All aircraft stand clear. Alamo out."

Boyle hauled his aircraft up and to the right, following the Huey that had just departed the LZ. He cut inside the other Huey's turn and eased into a loose cruise formation on the outside of the turn. He looked over and saw the side number 176 and noted several holes in the tail boom, but they were all on the underside, well away from the important parts.

"Air America 176, 181's joined on your left. You've got some holes in your tail. How's she flying?"

"Fine. I didn't know anything was wrong until the nose tucked under all of a sudden."

"That was probably the concussion. One of those rounds was real close."

"Do you see any damage other than the holes in the tail boom?"

"Stand by." Boyle eased the Huey back and up. Crossing well above the rotors of the other Huey, he settled into a close parade on the right side. Aside from a few exit holes matching the holes on the other side, the only damage was about a foot of buckled metal on the horizontal stabilizer. He told the other pilot what he saw.

"Okay. Thanks, 181. I'm going to press on here. I'll have the crewman check it out when we land."

"Roj. 181's breaking away."

Boyle pulled the Huey around and headed back toward the airport. He set up an orbit well clear of the Marines' flight patterns and waited for Alamo to call him in. He asked France to fill in the passengers on what was happening.

After fully ten minutes, during which no one in the crew saw any further mortar attacks on the DAO side of the field, Boyle called the controller. "Alamo, 181's holding south. It looks like the gomers are shooting somewhere else now. Request clearance."

"Roger, 181. You're cleared. Break. All light helos. You are cleared to resume landings at Tan Son Nhut."

Boyle eased the Huey down and came to a low hover over the taxiway. He had to slide the aircraft well off the pavement to find a spot that had not been chewed up by the mortar rounds. France got the passengers out and escorted them to the waiting Marines from the GSF. He dashed back and jumped in.

"Okay. All set back here."

Boyle flew the helo away and headed for LZ Four. Boyle gave control to Santy, who by now was becoming a fair straight and level helicopter pilot. He looked back into the cabin and saw France looking out the open cargo door and smiling. "Are you having fun back there, Joe?"

"You're not gonna believe it, but I am. It beats the shit out of sitting around and listening to Commander Bailey give his semi-hourly assessments of the situation. Or revising that goddamned accident report."

"What did he come up with?"

"After interviewing every American within ten miles he concluded that the VNAF helo fucked up and rammed Hickerson's helo."

"That's what we told him."

"Yeah, but you're only helo guys so you don't know jack shit about flying."

"Oh. Well, I'm sorry to have wasted his time."

"No problem. If you hadn't wasted it, he'd have found somebody else to bother."

First Lt. Bob Dunn looked over his shoulder and saw that the other 53 was still hanging out there in formation. Dunn was now the flight lead because he had lost his own leader.

On their second trip into the DAO compound, the lead was carrying some equipment for the GSF. Dunn's empty helo had been loaded quickly before the lead's had been unloaded. As he watched the equipment being laboriously carried down the cargo ramp, the LZ controller had called.

"Nighthorse 10, Alamo. Depart the LZ."

"Negative. I'm waiting on the lead."

"Nighthorse 10, depart now! Incoming!"

"Go, 10."

The last, from the lead, was an order. Dunn hauled up on the collective and flew out of the tennis court. He'd wanted to wait for the lead to complete his unloading and loading, but once Dunn was airborne, he was in the stream of aircraft headed out and he couldn't just pick a spot and orbit. At the many briefings he'd sat through, that point had been stressed—get in, do what you have to do, and get the hell out. There was far too much potential danger from NVA triple A and missiles to take chances.

That was the last time he'd seen his leader, but they had passed each other at least twice on the routes to and from the ship. Most of the other pairs had also been broken up. So whenever two helos found themselves ready to go, they joined up in a new pair and went about their mission. It was obvious to all that hanging around and worrying about flight integrity was not something they had time for today.

So they loaded up and went, and when they arrived at the ship, Dunn was surprised at the number of other vessels that had closed in seemingly from everywhere. He'd known that a large force was out here, seventeen miles from the coast or so, but when they had all closed in, the sheer number had amazed him. He'd never seen this many ships in one place in his entire career.

Surrounding his armada was what from a distance looked like a huge swarm of bees. Not only were there nearly forty Marine helicopters coming and going along with countless Navy helos moving around the fleet, but it seemed that Vietnamese pilots had commandeered everything that would fly, were loading them to the gills with family members and such, and were flying out to land on whatever ship they could find despite warnings, threats, complete ignorance, or rather complete disregard of any semblance of safety. Dunn remembered reading about the huge number of Washington civilians who had gone to watch the First Battle of Manassas in the Civil War. After the Union Army had been defeated, the civilians' wild flight had turned whatever orderly retreat the army could have made into a wild melee on the various roads leading back to the capital. Ambulance wagons, senators' carriages, shattered regiments, cavalry units, picnic baskets, had all smashed into each other all the way back to the city. No one had been able to restore order until the last straggler stumbled into Washington. The difference here, Dunn realized, was that shoving matches were certain to result in a rain of burning body parts and shredded aluminum.

While awaiting clearance to land aboard *Madison,* Dunn had watched several VNAF Hueys simply come up the wake and land on the ship, once directly in between two CH-53s, scattering refugees and ship's crewmen, who frantically tried to get out of the way of the whirling rotor blades. Dunn had gritted his teeth, fully expecting to see the Huey collide with one of the Marine helos and smash onto the deck in a fireball. He could only imagine how the 53 pilots must have felt sitting there, strapped in and completely powerless to do anything to save themselves, their crewmen, or their aircraft and watching this idiot drop out of the sky only feet from their rotor blades.

Dunn watched one VNAF Huey land on the fantail of the carrier, disgorge an amazing number of people, and then take off again. At first, Dunn had thought that this guy was going to head back in for another load, but he took the helo out to the port side of the ship and rolled it into the water on its side. Just as the rotor blades first hit the water, the pilot popped out of the cockpit and landed several feet from the aircraft.

The Huey bobbed for a few seconds and then sank. The pilot surfaced and was quickly picked up by one of the many motor whaleboats from the ships. The whaleboat crew parked the pilot on a seat and resumed their patrol.

Dunn looked across at his copilot, who was staring open-mouthed at the scene. He realized he was doing the same.

"Do you believe that shit?"

"My dad always said that if you live long enough, you'll get to see about everything. He was right. This is fucked up."

Far to the west of the flying circus that Dunn was part of, Thompson and Dalton were sitting in an almost clear spot in the thickest jungle they'd yet encountered. There had only been three more streambeds, but once out of the last one, they'd encountered a shallow valley that seemed as if it were some sort of botanical garden of the gods. Every species of plant that grew anywhere in Southeast Asia seemed to be growing here and within an inch of every other one. The tribesmen and the SEALs had each been taking turns at the head of the little column hacking a path with machetes. At first, the SEALs had been hesitant to use the machetes because of their ingrained aversion to noise when in the field. Butler brought up the point that there was no other choice— it might take days to find a way around this valley, which like the streambeds was not marked on the map. It was also obvious that any enemy in the area would have just as much difficulty and would also have to hack their way through equally noisily. That was the final argument.

The main result was the small band was slowing down and was burning energy at a prodigious rate. The hacker at the point could only keep it up for fifteen minutes or so before his arms became almost useless and he would have to be replaced by someone else. But since the going was so slow, the boys could keep up and did not have to be carried. The only danger was losing them in the brush, which was so dense that it was impossible to see anyone on either side of the path more than ten feet away. The boys would have been even more difficult to find had they become separated from the group. So now, instead of carrying them, the group assigned a man to watch each of the boys until it was his turn to take the machete and the point. Only when he was personally relieved would the boy's watcher leave and go to the front.

It seemed now that their last halt had come at least half a day ago, but in fact it had only been an hour. Dalton broke out the radio and attempted contact with the radio room at the DAO, but there was no answer. The SEALs hoped that it was not their radio that was at fault but rather the confusion and chatter that seemed to be on every frequency they tried. Finally on their second try through the list of frequencies, they heard the new and strange voice of a controller in the back of the airborne C-130.

"Cricket" had told them that the DAO radios were still in business, but apparently their antennas were unable to pick out the increasingly faint signal from the SEALs' small one-man radio.

Dalton gave them a position report that was more hope than certainty and asked that it be passed to the DAO people and set up a time for further contact. The controller in the aircraft had them repeat the last part of their message twice and advised them that their signal was fading. Dalton's reply went unheard until he used the mike switch to break the carrier wave using Morse code. The controller acknowledged and wished them luck. Time was getting short, he told them. The evacuation was well under way, and no one knew how much longer Cricket or a relieving aircraft with the same call sign would be on station. He could see the ring of smoke pillars rapidly closing on the city.

Dalton packed up the radio and muttered to himself that he'd rather have a couple of fresh batteries for the radio than the good wishes. Only one unused battery remained in his pack, but with the heat and humidity he knew that it would be drained quickly when it replaced the one in there now. It struck him as strange that here in the middle of terrain that had been unchanged for several thousand years his biggest concern was the little bit of electricity left in his remaining battery. Then he realized that it was no more strange than the fact that he and Thompson were walking around in this place, voluntarily no less.

Butler had come up and sat with them while Dalton reported. He listened carefully to what Cricket had to say, chewing his lower lip in thought and looking around at the small group of men who were suffering much to help him and his sons.

He wondered whether there would be men like them for him to live with back in the States. Thompson and Dalton were such men, but Butler knew that once the official inquiries were over, it was unlikely that he would be able to remain in the SEAL teams. He would have to endure whatever it was that the Navy would deal out to him. He believed (or was it *hoped?*) now that the SEALs themselves would understand his actions, but the official system would have to do something, if only to demonstrate its power.

But whatever was to happen to him back in America, there was no chance of his ever being able to live among such friends as he had with him here and now and waiting back in the larger tribe.

Butler looked at his sons, sitting quietly and apparently unafraid by a tree in the gloom. He knew that they were confused by what was happening to them and understood only vaguely that it was happening *for* them. He sighed and got to his feet.

The others followed his lead and struggled up, readjusting their equipment. Without a word, Butler took the machete and moved into the brush. The others silently fell into column and followed, making sure that the boys were placed in the center.

★ 42 ★

Tuesday, 29 April 1975

ADMIRAL WALLACE TOOK HIS COFFEE CUP AND STEPPED OUT INTO THE CAT-walk just aft of flag bridge aboard the USS *Concord.* Now that he was back at sea he could breathe the clean air, free of the smells of Saigon and relatively unpolluted by political turmoil as well. On the other hand, out here he also felt a bit like a third wheel.

His direct boss, CINCPAC, or commander in chief, Pacific, was aboard his flagship, USS *Blue Ridge,* below the western horizon. Wallace could only catch glimpses of her when her racetrack-shaped holding pattern swung to the easterly leg and *Concord* swung to the west. Here aboard *Concord,* Wallace was no more than a guest. The ship already carried an admiral and his staff, who was known by the title Carrier Task Force 77, or CTF-77. The incumbent was a man several years junior to Wallace both in age and in rank, but he had the job and therefore was in command. Wallace, very much like an exiled prince of a defunct nation, was a passenger who was consulted on operations and plans and whose counsel was sought. But CTF-77 made the decisions.

Wallace ran his hand gently along the top of the rail overlooking the flight deck and watched the sailors prepare the deck and the jets for the next launch. In about forty-five minutes, the deck would be filled with the incomprehensible thunder of twenty or so jet aircraft, fully combat loaded and eager to drop their weapons on the enemy. But that wouldn't happen today unless the NVA suffered a massive brain fire and seriously attempted to interfere with the evacuation. What would most probably happen was that the jets would launch and check in to their stations off the Vietnamese coast. There the pilots would reduce their throt-

339

tles to "max conserve" settings and would spend their allotted hour and a half flying around in their own racetrack patterns. Their rear ends would soon grow painful from the hard seat pans and the ache would gradually extend from midthigh to halfway up their spines. They'd squirm and wriggle and adjust the seat, but within a minute or so their butts would be killing them again. Those fortunate enough to have someone along in the aircraft with them, the radar intercept officers in the backseat of the fighters or the bombardier navigators in the A-6s, could at least talk to someone and bitch and complain about the pain and the plan and the whole situation. Those in the single-seat A-7s would have to content themselves with speaking to the sky or the wind or the airplane or themselves.

But they would all stay off the radio and keep their bitches within their cockpits because naval aviators are supposed to be disciplined and you could never tell when you'd get lucky and be ordered to go drop your bombs on the bad guys. But Wallace knew, as did the pilots, really, that they wouldn't get lucky today. The war was over and only in the most extreme circumstances would the orders be given. And then only in consultation with the baggy-pants crowd in Washington who were even now risking all in the comfort of the situation rooms.

No, what would happen was that the aircraft would stay up there and at the end of their cycle would be relieved by a similar group of airplanes whose pilots' asses didn't hurt yet. Then they'd jettison their weapons except for the truly expensive ones, such as the Sidewinder and Sparrow missiles, and return to the ship. In a few hours, they would again man their jets and do it again. Wallace looked at his watch. It was just after four P.M. here and a little after four A.M. in Washington. He hoped the sons of bitches had missed their dinner. Better yet, he hoped their coffee was cold.

Staring across the gray sea, Wallace recalled the days when he was CTF-77. It had been very near the end of the American combat involvement in the Vietnam War, and he had commanded his force of two and sometimes three attack carriers and dozens of smaller support ships from this very bridge. He'd seen the jets launch against the enemy and return with their arming wires dangling from the now-empty bomb racks. He'd seen the deep lines caused by aching fatigue and soul-searing terror around the eyes of the pilots. He'd seen their triumph when the target was destroyed, and he'd seen their pain as a friend went down to the guns and missiles. He'd seen much, he thought, maybe too much.

He looked out to the west where *Blue Ridge* should be. In the nearer distance, a couple of destroyers steamed, like bodyguards for the carrier. He knew that there were many of these cocky little ships off to the west as well. As he looked, a large ball of smoke on the horizon climbed majestically upward. Whatever ship was under that cloud was still hull down below the horizon, so he turned and walked a few steps forward into the enclosed flag bridge.

Adm. Dale McNamara, who was CTF-77, was standing next to his chair with a large set of binoculars focused on the smoke. Behind him several officers of his staff, or "McNamara's Band" as they were widely known behind their backs, were holding headsets and trying to get someone to tell them what the hell was going on. McNamara had once been CTF-77's chief of staff in the days when Wallace had the job. He had been a very good man to have on your team.

Wallace found a spot out of the way against a chart table where he could watch and listen. There was no sense asking about things and being a pain in the ass because whatever information anybody found out was sure to be broadcast across the bridge. He'd find out as soon as McNamara did.

One of the staff officers held a radio handset in one hand and a pen in the other as he scribbled on a sheet of paper. He acknowledged the transmission and put down the handset. He turned to McNamara and read from his notes. "Admiral, we just got an initial report from *Blue Ridge.* They have a crash on deck. Casualties are unknown but believed to be light at worst. The ship has gone to general quarters and firefighting teams are working on it. The problem is confined to the flight deck and there are no reports of damage, fires, or casualties below decks. Apparently, they had one VNAF helo on deck and another one ignored all the signals and flares and tried to land, too. The second one landed mostly on top of the first and rolled over. They're requesting that we have medical teams and helos rigged for medevac standing by. *Blue Ridge* says that the accident seems to be just that. There was no apparent intention to damage or disable the ship. That's all they sent for now."

McNamara cursed. "Okay. The ship's company should already have that under way, but double-check for me anyway, will you, George?"

"Yes, sir." The chief of staff picked up the handset that connected him with the ship's bridge one deck up. Even though McNamara commanded the entire task force, the ship's captain was directly in charge of the carrier's operations. The chief of staff spoke for a moment and grinned as he hung up. "The medical teams are already mustering and the helo crews will be briefing in less than five minutes. Captain Grant says it'll be a cold day in hell before he lets us staff pogues get the jump on him."

Wallace smiled to himself. Captain Gant was a brilliant officer, well liked by both his superiors and his juniors. What was truly astonishing, however, was the high regard in which he was held by his peers.

McNamara shook his head, turning to Wallace. "Do you believe this shit? I'm amazed that we haven't had more flight-deck accidents with all these maniacs trying to land on anything gray and flat out here. Christ, over on *Madison,* they're taking VNAF helos aboard, unloading the people, stripping off whatever they have time for, and then shoving the damn things over the side. So far they've managed to completely strip nine Chinooks and God knows how many Hueys."

"I know, Dale, but we can't shoot the bastards down."

"Well, sooner or later they're going to have to run out of aircraft to fly out here. I just hope we don't get some good sailors hurt because of sheer stupidity."

"I hope the Vietnamese don't discover us. We've got enough problems providing air cover without serving as a heliport to boot."

"Well, we can move a little farther out to sea. What do you think?"

"I dunno." Wallace shook his head. "There's all those other ships between us and the beach. The Vietnamese will go for them first."

"Probably so. All right, we'll stay here unless it gets bad."

Wallace picked up an extra set of binoculars and stared across the sea at the column of smoke. As he watched, it thinned and then disappeared, leaving only the smudge of black dissipating in the wind. The fire was out and damned quickly, thought Wallace. The lessons had been learned.

The officer with the handset suddenly began taking notes again. When he was finished, he turned to his boss. "Admiral, *Blue Ridge* says that the fires are out. There were no serious casualties. Two men with minor burns and a Vietnamese pilot with a broken leg. There is only minor damage to the superstructure and no impact on the ship's ability to operate. As soon as they can get the wreckage cooled, they're going to shove it over the side. It'll take a while to clean everything up, but they say the deck will be back in battery in a half hour."

McNamara nodded. "Send 'em an acknowledgment and repeat our offer of assistance just so they'll know we give a damn."

Wallace headed for the door. "Well, Dale, you seem to have this part of the world pretty well in hand so I'm going down to sick bay and check on our wounded newsman and his nurse."

"How are they doing?"

"Let's see. The general is in his glory running around on a carrier. He and his lieutenant have been adopted by the chief's mess so they're having a good time—you'd think they'd been aboard for months instead of since yesterday. Tran and the women and children are stationed in sick bay, and the corpsmen are having a ball with the kids. Tran is taking care of the women pretty much and has made Callahan her own pet project."

"And Callahan?"

"Hell, he's promised everyone down there that he's going to write a series of articles on his experiences and put all their names in it. They can't do enough for him." Wallace pulled the door open. "I'll see you, Dale. And by the way, I'll bet I had a hell of a lot more fun when I was sitting in that chair."

McNamara nodded. "As I recall, you did."

"Why not? I had you to do all the worrying for me."

Thompson and Dalton struggled out of the last of the heavy vegetation and collapsed alongside Butler's tribesmen. For the past hour or so the land had been slowly rising as the small group passed the bottom of the valley and climbed out the other side. Going down one side had been sheer hell, but the thick brush was even worse when the fight had become uphill.

The group was almost completely spent—they lay there without even the strength to rejoice that they'd broken through or to curse at the ordeal. Butler struggled to his feet and walked over to his sons. He sat down between them and hugged them to his sides. He spoke softly in their native tongue, and neither Dalton nor Thompson could make out what it was he said, but after a moment the younger one giggled and the older smiled. Butler was silent then, simply sitting there both enjoying his sons and supporting them.

One of the tribesmen stood and moved off into the now much thinner brush to scout ahead while two others broke out some smoked meat and, after breaking it into small pieces, handed them to the others. Butler made sure each of the boys had a piece and then began to chew his own.

Dalton removed the radio from the pack and switched it on. Thompson sat up but Dalton spoke. "Don't worry, boss. Receive only. I just want to make sure there's still somebody to hear us if we call." He listened for a few moments and shut the radio off. "They're still at it back there. I just heard that Cricket tell somebody that the number still to go was over two thousand."

"That's a comfort. Now all we have to do is find that ridge and then climb it in the next hour and a half. Simple."

Dalton paused in packing up his radio again. "Shape up, Kevin. We've got a hell of a lot more behind us than we do ahead of us. We have to be almost there by now."

Thompson sighed. "Yeah. You're right, Mark. I'm sorry."

Dalton grunted his acceptance as he reached for his last full canteen. He got up and walked over to Butler and his sons. Kneeling, he offered some water to each of the boys and finally took a small drink himself. He reached for Butler's canteen and shook it. "You've been saving this and giving it to them, haven't you?"

"Yes."

Dalton poured some water from his canteen into Butler's. "You need to keep yourself going, too, you shmuck." As Dalton put his canteen away, Thompson grabbed Butler's and poured some of his in there also.

Butler looked up and grinned. "Thanks."

Thompson shook his head. "No. Thank you." He turned to walk back to his equipment, and the scout almost burst from the brush. He moved to Butler and began speaking rapidly in the native language. The two SEALs, even with the past few days' refresher in the language, could only catch snatches of what the man was saying, but judging from the animation on his face and the brightness in Butler's eyes, the news had to be better than it had been for the past eight hours or so.

Butler nodded and smiled, clapping his man on the shoulder. He turned to Thompson. "It seems that we are at the foot of the ridge." He gestured at the thick jungle they'd just left. "In the middle of all that we couldn't see it. We have only about a half mile to go. It's all uphill, but it's fairly clear."

The news seemed to lift everyone's spirits, and they set about preparing for the last leg with a will. Suddenly, Butler paused and looked at Dalton. "Do you think we should tell the helicopter to meet us, say, in ninety minutes? We should be able to make it to the top or at least to a safe landing zone by then. If we called them now, we wouldn't have to wait while they traveled all the way out here."

Dalton pulled out his pack. "All right. But the battery is weak. I'll try to get a short message through and save what's left for when the helo gets close."

The controller in the C-130 turned off all the frequencies he was monitoring except one and pressed the earphones of his headset as close to his ears as he could. The call was faint, but whether it was from a dying radio or from sheer distance he couldn't tell.

". . . contact DAO and have the helicopter launch for our . . . Over."

The controller fiddled with his receiver controls and keyed his mike. "Station calling Cricket on two three point eight six megacycles Fox Mike, say again, over."

The controller next to him leaned back and looked at the radio panel. He switched off all his frequences, too, and set his FM radio to 23.86. He turned up the knobs.

". . . -cket. Request you call DAO this freq and have them send the helo to prebriefed . . ."

"Their radio's going, Jack."

"Yeah, I know. I think I know what they want. Let me try something here."

He fiddled some more with his receiver and keyed the mike. "Station calling Cricket. I will attempt to figure out what you're saying. Break squelch twice for affirmative and once for negative."

345

"Station calling Cricket, are you the team requesting helo pickup? Call sign Walker?"

He heard the carrier wave broken twice as the operator keyed his transmitter.

"Roger. Understand affirmative. Are you requesting helicopter be sent now? Over."

Two more clicks.

"Roger. Understand affirmative. Are you at a prebriefed position? Over."

Two clicks.

"Roger. Understand affirmative. Are you in contact? Over."

One click. At least they weren't being shot at.

"Roger. Understand negative contact. Break. Walker, we will contact Alamo and pass your message. We will contact you on this freq in three zero mikes. Do you concur, over?"

Two clicks.

"Roger. Understand affirmative. Cricket out."

The controller turned and told his partner to take over his frequencies. He would call the DAO radio room and get the helo moving. He looked at his watch. The team in the woods would turn on their radio again in thirty minutes and he'd better have some good news for them.

Boyle was just approaching the rooftop at LZ Nine when he heard his call sign on the radio. "181, Alamo."

"Stand by." Boyle eased the helo down onto the rooftop and lowered the collective to the bottom. France jumped out and headed for the group of people waiting to board. This was the third rooftop they'd worked from after clearing the other two of evacuees. Unfortunately, the number of people waiting seemed to be growing rather than diminishing. At this rate it would take all night. Boyle keyed the radio.

"Alamo, 181. Go ahead."

"Roger, 181. I pass from Walker. They are in position and awaiting pickup. Cricket picked up a signal from them and passed it to me. Say your posit."

"181's on deck at LZ Nine. Estimating landing at Alamo in nine mikes."

"Roger. Understand. When you drop off this load, you are released from my tasking and cleared to proceed on own mission."

"181 copies. We're gonna need fuel. Can you set it up?"

"Roger. We'll have the truck standing by at your hangar."

"Click-click."

Boyle dropped the passengers off near the DAO tennis courts and taxied the Huey clear of the landing area. He set it down on the blacktop and looked around for the fuel truck.

"See the truck, Mike? Joe?"

"Nothin' here on my side."

France walked clear of the rotors and looked back down the taxiway. He turned to face Boyle and shrugged. Boyle keyed the radio.

"Alamo, 181. Were you able to organize a fuel truck for us?"

"Negative, 181. There's only two still running and they're both over on the Vietnamese side. They're not answering our calls. We've got a couple of guys from your company out trying to find one that works. I have no idea how long that'll take, pardner. I'm sorry."

"181 copies. Thanks."

Boyle looked at the fuel gauge, which showed less than seven hundred pounds remaining. That was not going to be enough.

Santy leaned forward and tapped the gauge. "Well, Lindbergh, what do you think?"

"I think we've got a problem. We've got enough to make it out there and we've got enough to make it to the ship, but we don't have enough to do both. We can shut down and wait for somebody to find a fuel truck, which may not happen for hours, or we can go get those fuel drums, load 'em aboard, and go get Thompson."

"You mean pump the gas out in the boonies?"

"Yeah. Or we can pump it here, but that'll mean we won't get out there until just before dark. And that won't give us a lot of time to look for them. If we wait until tomorrow, we won't make it at all."

"Where's the fuel farm?"

"There's two. One's at the bottom of that cloud of smoke over there, and the other is the one being held by the ARVN deserters. They're selling the gas, and I'll bet they don't take credit cards. Even if they were giving it away, we can't land close enough to pull a hose out."

347

"Then how are the Air America guys going to get their trucks filled?"

"They'll probably pay in piasters, which will be worthless this time tomorrow anyway. I don't have any Vietnamese bucks on me, do you?"

"Shit."

⋆ **43** ⋆

Tuesday, 29 April 1975

THE SOLDIERS LOOKED UP FROM THEIR TRUCKS AND SAW THE AMERICAN JETS fly overhead under the overcast. The older ones felt a corrosive knot of fear at the sight, but when their brains took over and they remembered that American F-4s were no longer a threat to them, they relaxed and calmly watched the two fighters bank to the left and arc around to make another pass at them.

Suddenly they heard two dull thumps followed by a whooshing sound. Two streaks of gray smoke rushed skyward from a truck farther back in the convoy. The soldiers stared openmouthed as the two little SA-7 missiles streaked toward the jets. Several soldiers cursed and shouted at the missile shooters. The younger ones let out with a ragged cheer when they saw the missiles go, but the older ones got to their feet and prepared to jump from the trucks if the jets decided to shoot back.

Up above, the fighters must have seen the missiles launch because they broke in different directions and twisted through the air in an effort to evade the missiles. They rolled until their wings were pointing straight at the ground and pulled their noses toward the tiny streaks coming at them.

The missiles tried to follow the maneuvers, seeking as hard as their tiny little brains could for the tremendous swath of heat coming from the jets' tailpipes, but the turns they had to make to follow the heat were too much for them, and one following the other, they tumbled out of control and into the jungle far from the road.

The jets reformed and peeled off, aiming their noses at the convoy of trucks. They leveled their wings and quickly grew larger in the sky.

349

Gerry Carroll

Many of the drivers had seen the missiles fired and watched the jets for their reaction, holding their breath. When they saw the jets turn to come at them, they jammed on their brakes and jumped from the cabs. The drivers who had remained oblivious to the drama above were unprepared, and the slower among them rammed into the tailgates of the trucks ahead of them, spilling soldiers and equipment everywhere.

Soldiers jumped from the vehicles and dove for cover as far from the road as they could get.

High above, the Phantoms each released a missile that drove straight into the trucks in the middle of the column. One missile exploded among a group of men trying frantically to get themselves clear, and the other detonated in a truck that was carrying ammunition.

The explosion threw bits of debris and parts of soldiers for hundreds of feet in all directions. Some close to the blast were burned by the flaming gasoline or shredded by the flying pieces of the truck.

After a moment, save for the screaming of the wounded, all was quiet and the soldiers raised their heads and searched the sky. The jets had resumed their orbit overhead and were apparently watching the column for further acts of stupidity.

When they were certain that the jets were not going to make another run at them, the soldiers got to their feet and looked around for their friends and comrades. In less than thirty minutes, the column was again under way, but every eye spent more time looking up than it did looking at the road ahead.

There were no more missiles fired.

Overhead, the implacable jets continued their orbit.

★ 44 ★

Tuesday, 29 April 1975

TONY BUTLER PULLED HIMSELF UP THE LAST FEW FEET AND ROLLED ONTO the top of the ridge. He got to his knees and scanned the area slowly and carefully for any sign of the enemy. The light from the sun, diffused in the low cloud, cast few shadows, but there was a narrow band of clear visibility beneath the clouds, and Butler could see the lush green lands in the distance. But within forty minutes or so, the sun would be setting and the light would rapidly fade.

The plateau Butler found himself on was at least a quarter mile square with an open area at the edge he'd just come over and a treeline that ran completely around the clearing, touching the edge both to Butler's right and left. The grass in the clearing was marred by only a few small clumps of bushes scattered haphazardly around.

The bluff they'd just climbed had been far less difficult than it had appeared from the bottom. Little ledges slopped this way and that across its face almost as if someone had cut paths in the side of the ridge. It was well, Butler thought, that the bluff had been no more difficult, because none of the small group was in any shape for mountain climbing.

Butler watched and waited for several minutes for any sign of human activity, but all he saw were several of the small native deer grazing on the far side of the clearing, at least two hundred yards away. He relaxed, for if anyone had been lying in wait in the tree line, the deer wouldn't be feeding so calmly.

He turned and looked down at his companions, who were waiting just below the lip of the clearing with their weapons pointing

351

upward, waiting either for Butler to reappear or gunfire to erupt. When they saw his head looking down, they visibly relaxed, and Butler could hear the snicks as the safeties of several weapons were placed back on.

Butler extended his hand to the next man. "Come on up. It is better than we had hoped."

Soon Thompson and Dalton were staring around approvingly as the tribesmen secured the area. They fished out a smoke grenade to throw out in the grass when the helo appeared and got the radio ready to transmit. After the difficulty they'd had getting their message through to Cricket forty-five minutes or so earlier, neither man wanted to use up the few remaining bits of electricity the battery still held.

The tribesmen returned from their search of the immediate area and reported. Butler translated to make sure that the SEALs got the picture exactly right.

One scout gestured to the extreme northwestern side of the clearing. "There is a road which passes by the foot of this ridge, but I saw only one trail which leads directly up here. But it is hard to see and overgrown. If an enemy wants to find us, they'll have to climb through the forest and they won't be able to do that quietly. Especially if we post a picket on that side at the top of the hill."

The other scout nodded his agreement. His side was much the same except that the road was much farther away from the base of the ridge and the climb would be steeper. So the obvious way for the enemy to come at them was from the northwest, especially if they were not completely familiar with the area.

Butler scratched his chin and turned to Thompson. "When will the helo come?"

"It's been nearly an hour now since we called for it. The flight time should be forty minutes at most, but it depends on how long it took for the message to get to the crew."

Butler looked at the ground. "Are you sure they will come?"

Thompson bit off a sharp answer. He forced himself to remember that Butler had spent long years getting the shaft from people who were supposed to be there to support him. It was a natural question from a man who had suffered much and been disappointed more times than was fair. He placed his hand on Butler's shoulder.

"They will come. If I am certain of anyone or anything, it is those two men. They are what we were once."

Boyle landed the Huey as close as he could to the Air America hangar. He shut it down and followed France and Santy into the large building, which, with all the aircraft gone, had an air of abandonment about it. Lights were on only in one office, that of the maintenance chief, but all the equipment was carefully stacked in the center of the building as if awaiting packing for shipment.

Boyle pointed to the pile of equipment. "You guys get the fuel drums. I'm going over to maintenance control. There's a couple of things I want to scrounge."

"Okay, but don't take too long." Santy walked over and dug out a hand truck from the pile and pulled it over to the steel drums placed in the corner. He pulled aside the empty ones and moved the truck up next to the ones he and Boyle had stashed. He and France pushed the first drum up on one edge slightly and slid the base of the hand truck underneath it.

France sniffed. "Are these things okay? There's sure some heavy fuel fumes right around here."

Santy let down the drum and moved around it to the two others. He shoved them and tested their weight. One was full, just as they had left it, but the third drum moved as easily as the ones they had hidden it behind. Santy looked at the floor behind it and saw how wet it was. The stream of fuel had flowed toward the hangar wall and gone through a gap between the wall and the concrete floor. Santy looked at the side of the drum and saw several large and jagged holes in it that matched several holes in the hangar wall.

"Goddamnit. A mortar round or something must have hit outside and punched these holes. The fucking thing is just about empty." Santy looked up at France. "That's one-third of our fuel gone."

France cursed and looked around. He found the hand pump hidden between two other drums and looked it over carefully. "Is this our pump?"

"Yeah. Why?"

"Look." France held up the hose, which had been sliced along a ten-inch length. "This ain't gonna work."

353

"How long is the good piece?"

"Not more than three feet."

Santy spun and kicked an empty barrel. The echoing boom sounded across the hangar. "Shit. Shit. Shit! We need more hose than that to reach the fuel filler port. Shit!"

"Just hold on a minute, Mike. Let's get these drums aboard and then we'll work on the pump." The two struggled with the drums and finally got them in the cargo compartment. France climbed out and stepped back a few feet. He looked up at the rotor head and down at the drums. Nodding with satisfaction, he climbed back inside.

Santy rooted through the "cross-country box," which normally contained all the small, easily lost items that a crew always needed when they operated away from their home base. "What were you looking at?"

"I was checking to see that the drums were as close to directly under the rotor mast as possible. That's the center point, and I don't want to have a bad CG." If the center of gravity was too far forward or too far aft, the aircraft could be difficult and sometimes impossible to control in flight. The problem didn't necessarily show up in a hover but always did just about the time the pilot was committed to flight.

Santy shook his head. "I hadn't thought about that. But we've got another problem—no cargo tiedowns."

"No sweat. We can always use rope for that, but let's go work on that hand pump."

The two walked over to the pile of equipment and began rummaging through it. They quickly found some tiedowns and threw them off to one side. Down near the bottom, France found a length of hose, but it was obviously smaller in diameter than the hose on the pump. "This'll do," he sid. "Now we have to find some tape."

No matter how hard they looked, there was no tape at all in the pile. Santy stood up and stretched his back. "Let's try maintenance control."

Across the hangar, they ran into Boyle, who was dragging a large cart behind him, which was filled with all sorts of equipment. There were three five-gallon cans, a couple of boxes with red crosses painted on them, and lying on top of the stack were four M-60 machine guns. Santy and France looked at each other and back at Boyle.

Santy picked up one of the M-60s. "What the hell are you going to do with these?"

"Well, if we go down, they'll be handy to have. Our pistols aren't really worth a shit in a jungle fight. With these we can really do something."

"Are you serious? Us?"

"Sort of. If we need them, we'll have them, but we can give them to those tribesmen. We can also give them some medical stuff. That'll always come in handy."

"Timmy, don't be offended, but if we go down in the weeds, those things are only going to slow us down when we're running our asses off. Just remember our little sprint last time we were down in the weeds."

Boyle shook his head at the memory of his and Santy's brutal run through the bush to get to the coast of North Vietnam. He remembered the pain, the fear, and the exhaustion. Santy was right—if they'd had to carry a single pound more, they might not have made it. But this time if they went down, they would be sixty or seventy miles from the coast and rescue. Running for it wouldn't work.

"Okay. We can always throw them away if we need to, but we'll bring them along just in case."

Santy couldn't argue with that. "So what's in the cans?"

"Water. If they don't need it, they can dump it out, but they've been running through some nasty-looking boonies and I'll bet they could use this. At least we know it's clean."

"Where's the ammo?"

"There's another cart through the door loaded with it. The Air America guys were going to have to destroy it. You guys can bring that."

"I'll get it. Joe here needs to go into maintenance." Santy told Boyle about the fuel drum and the pump.

Boyle looked at France. "Do you think you can fix it?"

"Yeah. I was an enlisted man before I went to OCS. I worked on a flight line so jury-rigging is in my blood. But I'm going to try the easy way first."

"What's that?"

"I'm going to ask the maintenance chief if he's got another pump that works. But do you think that two drums of fuel will be enough?"

"Yeah, if we don't have to do a lot of looking, we'll be fine. But we won't have a lot of time to screw around when we get out to the fleet. Twenty minutes or so."

"Are we going to shut down out there?"

"Yeah. Running the engine while that slow pump works would cut into the margin. Plus, the noise of the rotor and the engine'd also provide a good locator for the bad guys."

"Okay. I'll see if I can scrounge an extra Nicad in case we have to run the radios or something. It'd be a bitch to have to stay in Vietnam for ten years or so because of a dead battery."

Boyle looked at Santy and back at France. "Joe, you've been a great help today. But you *don't* have to come out there with us."

France smiled a little. "Yes, I do." He turned away and walked toward maintenance control.

Gen. Lew Alexander stood in the doorway of his office. He let his eyes wander slowly around the room that had for so many years served the man who was responsible for the war in Vietnam. A lot of history was here in these walls.

In this room decisions had been made that brought the young men from the cities and the farms and the college campuses of America and placed them in camps and firebases and jungles to fight an enemy few knew anything about before they arrived, lonely and frightened but outwardly brave, ten thousand miles from home. In this room the hours and days of the siege of Khe Sanh and the brutal times of the Tet Offensive were seen through. From here was commanded the first engagements of a new concept in warfare, air mobility. From here the plans and ideas and orders were sent to the sweating and exhausted troops in the field. In here sat hundreds, perhaps thousands, of visitors, from Bob Hope and John Wayne to the latest delegation of nosepickers from Congress.

Incumbents of this office had gone on to fame and prominence in the history books. But, for Alexander, little of that would happen. He was the man who had to preside over the death of a free nation, such as it was. He was the man who had to finally switch off the light at the end of the tunnel. None of the renown nor the promotions nor the parades nor the speaking engagements lay in

Alexander's future. But that was all right, he thought. At least I tried. At least I answered the bell.

The general switched his briefcase into his left hand and placed his hat on his head. He reached for the doorknob and gently, almost reverently, pulled the door closed.

He walked the few steps down the hall and entered his deputy's office. Toone's brow furrowed when he saw that Alexander had come in the front door instead of through the connecting one between his office and the greater, more powerful office next door. Then, suddenly, he understood.

He got to his feet and picked up his briefcase. "It's time, huh?"

Alexander nodded. "Yeah. Let's go. Fixx has the car waiting outside."

Toone turned and pushed his desk chair under the desk and carefully recentered his blotter on the polished surface. He stood erect and unconsciously squared his shoulders. "Okay, then," he said quietly, and followed his old friend.

The Marines in the courtyard of the embassy looked up as another CH-46 came in to land on the embassy roof. They were almost finished cutting down the huge tamarind tree that had stood for so many years in this courtyard. The Marines wouldn't understand it that way, but this had been for the past few days a symbol of the conflict between the political and military objectives that had been such an integral part of the war. The military planners wanted to cut the tree down to create another helicopter landing zone in the embassy parking lot since the big CH-53s were far too heavy to operate from the roof. The diplomats had refused permission to cut the tree down, believing that its removal would send the wrong signals to the Vietnamese people.

They didn't want to do anything that would cause the Vietnamese people either to panic or to begin to lose faith in their government's ability to negotiate a peaceful settlement.

The military saw the streams of refugees coming into Saigon ahead of the advancing NVA and the huge fires and smoke pillars rising from the lost battles around the city, and they heard the thunder of the guns growing louder as the days and hours passed. They saw the frightened faces of the civilians and looked at the situation maps and pressed for the removal of the tree to help them get their job done. But the diplomats stubbornly refused to see the truth, believing as they always do that there is nothing on earth that cannot be negotiated if only the other side would see reason and the proper leverage was applied or the right carrots offered.

The military, having to use their expertise and skills in the field as opposed to a cocktail reception, knew well that sometimes the only leverage was firepower and force and that the stick was quicker and more effective than the carrot. They knew the old disciplinarian's aphorism, that the quickest way to a kid's brain is through his ass, often applied to governments, too.

But now the goddamned tree was down and the first CH-53 would soon be landing to pick up its first load of evacuees.

The Marines looked uneasily at the huge crowd gathered in the streets surrounding the embassy on three sides. Every once in a while, some of the Vietnamese would try to scale the wall and would be pushed back. At the gates, in an effort of timeless parental love, families were attempting to hand their children to the Marines manning the gate so as to get them, at least, on a flight out.

But not everyone was struggling to leave. Occasionally, from some of the surrounding buildings, small-arms fire would cross the wall and send everyone diving for cover. South Vietnamese troops or Saigon police or, less often, a small unit from the Marines themselves would have to enter the building and cautiously clear it of the snipers.

The Marines stood amongst the chaos and organized the people into small groups, waiting with them and finally loading them onto the helicopters. Others tried to shut out the screaming and wailing from the thousands of people who were not going to get to go. When they had time, they wondered how this operation could have gotten so fucked up so fast. Who was at fault didn't really matter to them much. They just worked and sweated to get their job done as quickly and safely as they could.

For the helicopter pilots, the mission was getting progressively more dangerous. The low clouds were getting lower and lower— they could no longer fly anywhere near the planned altitudes. Visibility was deteriorating steadily, but fortunately the routes between the city and the sea were generally over flatlands, so there was still room between the clouds and the ground. The aircraft were being flown up to and sometimes beyond the limits in the manuals. In the pilots' minds, the flights were beginning to run together, and both man and machine were beginning to wear out.

But no matter how many trips the helos made or how furious their pace, the number of people left to go wasn't shrinking at all.

✴ **45** ✴

Tuesday, 29 April 1975

TIM BOYLE LIFTED THE HUEY INTO A HOVER AND TAXIED OUT CLEAR OF
the hangars.

"Alamo, 181."

"Go ahead."

"Roger, Alamo. 181's departing to the west. We'll maintain contact with Cricket."

"Alamo copies, 181. Good luck."

"Thank you."

Boyle scanned the gauges and keyed the ICS. "You guys ready?"
Two "Yeah" 's.

"Once we're airborne, Mike, see if you can get in contact with
your E-2. Maybe they can keep a better eye on us than Cricket
can. He sounds awful busy."

"Okay."

Boyle eased the nose over and pulled in some collective. The
Huey moved forward slowly at first but rapidly accelerated. He
kept it low to the ground for as long as was comfortable and then
raised the nose into a gentle climb.

France spoke from the back. "Everything's secure back here. I
just rechecked the tiedowns and there are no fumes or leaks."

"Roj." France's security report was textbook. It reminded Boyle
of all the crewmen he'd had in his last squadron.

Santy spun the frequency selector on the UHF radio. "Slug, this
is Air America 181."

The E-2 orbiting high over the fleet answered almost immediately. "181, this is Slug 772. Say your squawk."

"Presently 1200. We are off Tan Son Nhut headed two eight oh. Level one point six."

"Okay, 181. I have several contacts in the area. Squawk mode three, code three four four six."

"Three four four six." Santy spun the dials on his IFF, or identification friend or foe, transponder to 3446. He looked up at Boyle. "You know this is really a bastard rig."

Boyle grinned. The radio suite in this aircraft was a mixture of sets from both earlier and later models of the H-1. It still had most of the original UH-1E systems, but as newer systems came into the military supply system, they had apparently been stuck in, replacing the originals. The IFF set that Santy had just set up was at least an entire generation newer than the one listed in the flight manual. "Oh, well. The price was right."

"181, Slug has you in radar contact. Say intentions."

Santy pressed the radio foot switch. "181 is outbound for pickup of U.S. nationals. Request radar following."

There was a long pause. "181, understand outbound for U.S. nationals?"

"That's affirm. Posit is eleven twenty-four north and one oh six twenty-three east. Request radar following."

"Slug copies eleven twenty-four and one oh six twenty-three." It was obvious that the E-2 had a lot more going on, and being asked to keep an eye on one civilian helicopter was asking a lot.

"Slug, be advised. The copilot of 181 is Condor Eleven." Santy gave the E-2 his "rocket number" or his place in his squadron's seniority. The squadron call sign was Condor, so the E-2 now knew that one of the men in the Huey was not only a shipmate but someone from his own air wing. That got the point across—the E-2 controller now had an almost personal stake in the safety of the Huey. Santy smiled as he imagined the confusion on the E-2 officer's face, wondering what the hell one of the A-7 guys was doing swanning around Vietnam in a goddamn helicopter.

"Slug copies." There were a few moments of silence. "Okay. Condor 181, take up a heading of three three oh. Estimating, um, forty miles."

"181, roger. Three three oh for forty." Santy looked over at Boyle. "I guess we've been adopted. We're now a Condor."

"That sounds better than Air America."

Boyle banked the helo to the right and headed 330, or generally northwest. He glanced down at his instruments, figuring that they ought to be overhead in twenty-five minutes. He looked at the clock and shook his head. In twenty-five minutes, it would be past sundown, and given the cloud cover, darkness would follow quickly.

Cdr. Nick Taylor was sitting in the Combat Information Center aboard the carrier *Concord,* listening to the various radio transmissions coming in from the ships in company and the various aircraft around the task force. At all times since the evacuation order had been given, either Taylor, his executive officer, or the squadron operations officer had been sitting here in CIC listening. The only time Taylor had left this room was to fly his own mission and to eat dinner. Right now, the ops officer was in an A-7 orbiting ten miles east of the ship, waiting for the call to go provide air cover for the helos. The XO was in the ready room briefing for his mission, which would relieve the ops officer's small formation after the next launch.

Although dozens of voices filled the air in CIC, Taylor was most interested in the chatter to and from the C-130 over Saigon and the E-2 over the task force. The first would give him an indication of how things were going in-country and would alert him to any calls for air support. The chatter on the E-2's frequency would give him the earliest indication of the aircraft that would be dispatched from their stations in response to the requests for support. Since half of the A-7s that flew from this ship belonged to his squadron, Taylor had a large stake in what was happening ashore. But the stakes also included a flight that had nothing to do with A-7s or the designated mission of the squadron.

Last evening, in company with the air wing commander, or CAG, he had been called to see Admiral Wallace, the deputy CINCPAC, and after getting over his initial apprehension at being called into such an august presence, he had listened more than attentively as Wallace described with some admiration Santy's performance in Saigon. Wallace had then cleared his throat and told Taylor the full story of the mission to retrieve the SEALs, including what bare-bones history generals Alexander and Toone had been able to provide. Characteristically, Taylor had been furious, and it had taken a harsh word from CAG to calm him. He took a few deep breaths and, in measured but unmistakably angry words, had let the admiral know that if he had known that this would be the result of Santy's temporary assignment to the admiral's staff, he would have refused.

Wallace fixed him with a steady gaze. "And if I'd taken him anyway?"

"Then you'd have been short one A-7 commanding officer."

Wallace nodded slowly as he considered Taylor's blazing eyes. "I see."

The admiral stood up and began to slowly pace the room. "Commander, if I had any choice in the matter, not only would those two young men not be going out into the boonies, but the two whom they're going to bring back wouldn't have gone out either. I wasn't consulted. But given that in my opinion the mission is necessary, I saw no option but to allow"—he held up a hand—"yes, *allow* those men to go.

"It was their choice. They were not ordered to go at all. I understand why the SEALs went and I understand why Boyle and Santy went after them." The admiral put his hands in his pockets and shrugged. "To be completely honest with you, Commander, I'm not certain whether I could have ordered them *not* to go. I don't think I'll ever know if I could have done that, but for what it's worth, I honestly wish that this mission had not been necessary." The admiral turned and looked straight into Taylor's eyes.

"One more thing, Commander. You have one young man in that aircraft. The other one belongs to me, and you can bet your ass that I care about him very much. And just so's you'll know, as far as I'm concerned, Santy is one of mine, too."

Now sitting in CIC, Taylor was listening for anything that would let him know what was happening to Santy and Boyle. He knew that three men were now in the aircraft since Commander Bailey had returned to the ship and gone straight to the admiral informing him of Lieutenant France's irresponsible behavior in volunteering to go along. Wallace had immediately called Taylor to tell him that he could now increase his worry by 50 percent. Taylor was not told what Wallace had to say to Commander Bailey, but those who overheard it would later speak of it only in respectful tones.

Taylor was reaching for his coffee when he heard the E-2 call a "Condor 181."

He looked over at the CIC watch officer and asked him who the hell was Condor 181. The watch officer picked up a radio handset and called the E-2 on another frequency. He listened for a few moments and turned to Taylor. "The hummer says that 181 is an H-1 out of Tan Son Nhut headed out to pick up some Americans. Says the copilot is one of yours. Who's Condor Eleven?"

"Mike Santy. Look, can you ask the E-2 to consider that helo one of our own air wing aircraft and keep us informed about anything, anything at all, that has to do with it?"

"Sure, Commander. No problem." The watch officer spoke into the handset and then called over one of the chief petty officers. The chief nodded and walked over to the huge clear Plexiglas status board. In one of the empty spaces he wrote in "Condor 181. H-1. Santy."

Taylor sat back and strained to pick out any transmission from the E-2 to the Huey. He wasn't sure whether he was more afraid for them now that he knew that they were airborne or before when he was dreading hearing their call sign over the air control frequencies.

Mike Santy looked up from his chart and out through the windshield at the land ahead. He had been pretty much able to follow their track over the ground mostly by the various roads they'd crossed and the villages they'd had to arc around. Santy had easily been able to warn Boyle of the various places to avoid—the Huey covered the ground at about one-fifth the speed his A-7 did, and low-level navigation was almost a piece of cake for him.

The only problem he had was that he'd never felt this lonely and exposed before in his entire life. He looked over at Boyle and was glad that they were together out here, but knowing that they were the westernmost and most exposed aircraft in the American inventory was frightening.

He looked at the ridge rising in the distance and used his pencil on the scale at the bottom of the chart to get a rough estimate of how far ahead it was.

"Tim, that's gotta be the ridge up ahead at about twelve miles."

Boyle glanced down at the fuel gauge. It was well below three hundred pounds and within a few minutes the 20 MINUTE FUEL caution light would come on and that would be all the time they had left in the air. He hoped that they would be able to find

Thompson before then. The sooner they found him the more fuel they would have for the flight out to the ship.

Boyle looked up at the ridge ahead. "Mike, try 'em on the radio."

Santy checked his transmitter selector and keyed the mike. "Walker, Condor 181 is estimating ten miles out now."

It seemed like an eternity before they heard the weak reply. "181, Walker copies. We are in a large clearing at the top of a high ridge. I'm pretty sure it's the highest one around. Do you have it in sight?"

"Roger, Walker, we got the highest one on our nose. We're now at, uh, nine miles. Request you pop a smoke when we pass overhead."

"Walker, wilco. Be advised that we have seen no sign of unfriendlies in the immediate area. The LZ is cold."

"181 copies. Standing by for the smoke."

In the gathering dusk, 1st Lt. Bob Dunn turned his CH-53 eastward and headed out to sea. In the back were 102 evacuees, which Dunn was certain was a record for the biggest number of people ever crammed into one of the helicopters. He was about to mention this to his copilot when the crewman stationed at the rear ramp called on the ICS. "Dash Two's going down!"

There was a moment of stunned silence in the helo before Dunn could muster a reply.

"What the fuck do you mean he's going down?"

"He's headed for the ground real fast. He's at our eight o'clock low."

Dunn's copilot banked the 53 left and craned back to try to pick up the other aircraft, Nighthorse 03, which was the wingman, or "Dash Two," in the flight. "I don't see him. Do you still have him in sight?"

"Negative, sir. I lost him."

Shit! thought Dunn. He keyed the radio. "Nighthorse 03, lead."

"Lead, Nighthorse 03 got hit with something. We're okay, but we have to land to check it out. We're headed for the beach at the tip of the cape."

"Roger, 03. We don't have you in sight." Dunn called the crewman. "Sarge, was there any fire?"

"No, sir. He just pointed his nose at the deck and dropped like a rock."

"Nighthorse 03, my crewman observed no fire on your aircraft."

"Roj. It's flying okay, but we really need to check it out."

"Still don't have you in sight."

"We're at three hundred feet. There's a field behind the beach. We're heading for that."

"Roger. Break. Cricket, Nighthorse 10."

"Go ahead, 10. Cricket copied 03."

"Roger, Cricket. We're gonna need a Snake over here for cover. 10 is fully loaded with pax and has, um, one point five on the fuel."

"Okay, 10. We're working on it."

With that it suddenly seemed that nearly everybody who had access to a radio transmitter was yelling for updates on the status of Nighthorse 03. There were so many calls that they were overriding each other and the piercing screech of conflicting transmissions destroyed anybody's ability to communicate. It wasn't until Cricket came up on the Guard frequency and none too gently told everybody to shut up that order was restored. Even then a couple of people got huffy and demanded that Cricket answer them first— one even threatened the C-130 controller. Dunn almost laughed as Cricket told them that under no circumstances were they to use the frequency until specifically called by Cricket.

Dunn's copilot had taken the aircraft down to five hundred feet and was searching the beach for any sign of their wingman. "I don't see him."

"Me either." Dunn unconsciously leaned forward in his seat, scanning the area. Nothing was there but bushes and grasslands. They were turning around for another pass when the crewman in the back sang out, "I got 'em! They're at our six o'clock and a half mile behind some trees."

The copilot rolled the helo the other way and headed in a little closer to the beach. Neither pilot spoke of it, but they were both nervously looking for the enemy as much as they were for their fellow Marines.

"Nighthorse 03, 10 has you in sight. How're you doing?"

"Don't know yet. The crewmen are checking it out now."

"Nighthorse 10, Cricket. There's a pair of Cobras inbound to you. ETA five mikes. His call sign is Bandit 44. What's going on?"

"Cricket, 10 has Dash Two in sight. He's safe on deck and

checking things out. We'll let you know. 10 is orbiting off the beach on the western tip of the cape. Request you find another 53 to stand by in case we have to abandon 03."

"Roger. How many pax does 03 have aboard?"

Dash Two broke in. "Cricket, 03 has one two seven souls on board."

There was a pause. "Understand one two seven souls?"

"That's affirm. One two seven."

"That's gotta be a record, 03."

"I believe it is."

Dunn shook his head. Nighthorse 03 had to have loaded every midget in Saigon to get that many.

"Nighthorse 10, Bandit 44 has you in sight. And, um, we believe we also have 03. You are relieved and you're cleared to detach and head on out. We'll take care of him."

"Roger." Dunn watched as the deadly looking AH-1 Cobra gunships broke apart their already loose formation and passed over the beach. They quickly did a fast search of the approaches to 03's position and then set up a protective orbit over the downed 53. "Nighthorse 10's departing."

Dunn listened as the C-130 assured everyone that 03 was in good hands and they could all get back to their jobs.

Dunn watched the altimeter wind up as the copilot took the 53 back up to altitude. He lit a cigarette and tried to imagine being the pilot of 03. The thought of being down in the weeds in enemy territory scared the hell out of him. He keyed the ICS. "I don't know what happened to 03, but let's keep a sharp lookout, okay?"

The crew chief's east-Texas drawl came back. "Lieutenant, if I move my head and eyes any faster, I'll burn out the bearings and then where you gonna be?"

Thompson sat a few feet back in the brush and watched several deer move cautiously across the far side of the clearing. Every so often they would raise their heads and peer around, nervously looking for predators. Thompson knew exactly how they felt. He looked at his watch and saw that it was exactly two minutes later than it had been the last time he'd checked.

Beside him sat Dalton, fingering the strap of the pack that had held the radio, which he had arrayed on the ground in front of him. Between the two lay a smoke grenade with the safety pin straightened.

Suddenly all the deer across the way raised their heads together. Their ears twitched this way and that as they listened for the cause of some strange sound. Their noses jabbed the air as they tried to get the scent. In the blink of an eye they were gone, ducking back into the trees, fleeing from some vague threat that the humans could not yet sense.

Thompson nudged Dalton and the two SEALs silently got to their knees and brought their weapons forward. The tribesmen saw the movement and followed suit.

Butler moved forward until he was at Dalton's shoulder. "What is it, Mark?"

"'I don't know. Something spooked the deer and they hauled ass."

"Where did they go?"

"Into the trees on the far side."

"Then the danger is on this side. The deer would not run *to* it."

"There's nothing on this side but that drop behind us."

"And we have watchers on the other sides."

The little group fell silent, each pair of the tribesmen's eyes scanning the area for the enemy. After so long on the dodge, their senses had become far more acute than either Thompson's or Dalton's.

They felt the sound before they actually heard it. It was a low, rhythmic pulse too dim for their ears. In a half minute or so the pulse became audible. It was now a thumping sound that neither increased nor decreased in frequency but only in volume. Ten seconds later the sound became almost distinct as the trees caught it and spread it around, making it impossible to tell from which direction it came. Every face in the group relaxed a little and there were even a few smiles.

It was a sound they'd all heard so often that it had become as common as the chirping of the birds. It was the sound of a Huey's rotor blades pounding the air.

Dalton flicked on the radio and put on the headset. Thompson picked up the smoke grenade and removed the safety pin, still carefully holding the spoon against the side of the cylinder.

★ **46** ★

Tuesday, 29 April 1975

"181 SEES YOUR RED SMOKE."

"Roger, red."

Boyle brought the helo low over the trees from the east, effectively masking his landing area from the road on the far side of the ridge. He and Santy had had only a brief look at the road, but they hadn't seen any traffic. Boyle had flown off to the north as if he were headed somewhere else, then made a wide sweeping turn back to the east. Once he was a couple of miles away from the clearing, he dropped to treetop level and turned back directly for the ridge.

As he approached the ridge, he asked Thompson to pop his smoke grenade and used the smoke as both proof that the voice on the radio was in fact the Americans and not an English-speaking Vietnamese and as an indicator of the wind direction. What little wind there was was coming from the northwest, so when Boyle burst over the edge of the bluff in a sharply nose-high and decelerating attitude, all he had to do was skid the aircraft slightly and come to a no-hover landing between the smoke and the edge of the bluff.

Once the skids were firmly planted in the grass, Boyle rolled the throttle to idle, waited only fifteen seconds for the engine to stabilize, and shut it down. He applied the rotor brake and unfastened his harness while Santy turned off all the electronic equipment except the UHF radio.

Boyle keyed the mike. "Slug 772, Condor 181 is safe on deck. No indication of enemy presence. We will give ops-normal reports every thirty mikes."

"Roger that, 181. We'll be here." Santy shut off that radio, too, and both pilots climbed out.

Thompson was the first to greet them. "Thanks for coming, Tim. Hello, Mike. I was worried that you all might be gone before we could get ourselves clear."

Boyle introduced France and rubbed his face. "If it had taken you another twelve hours, Kevin, we *would* have been gone. The evacuation is going full steam, and I don't see it going much past six or seven tomorrow morning." Boyle looked around the group of tribesmen. "Where's your man?"

"He's out guarding a trail. Those are his sons over there." Thompson briefly filled Boyle in on Butler's story.

Boyle looked at the small boys sitting quietly near the edge of the clearing. Nobody had said anything about having kids along. Not that it changed anything.

Thompson looked at the Huey as Santy and France began unstrapping the fuel drums. Several tribesmen quickly moved over to help. Boyle followed Thompson's look.

"When your call came, we were ferrying people to the airport and were getting low on fuel, but we couldn't get any at the airport so we brought it along in drums. We'll have to pump it here."

Thompson walked over to the Huey and looked at the treasure trove that Boyle had managed to stuff in there. He pulled out one of the M-60s. "Nice. Planning on going hunting?"

"No. We thought they would come in handy if we had to set down somewhere nasty. If we didn't, we thought these tribesmen could use them. Besides the ammo for the weapons and a couple of cases of grenades, there's also some rations, some first-aid stuff, and fifteen gallons of water in there."

Thompson rolled his eyes. "You'll never know how important that water is right now. We were just about out."

"That's what I figured. I remember when I was on the run through the weeds. Water's the first thing I had a problem with."

"Yeah. How long is it going to take you to transfer that fuel?"

"I don't know, Kevin. The pump we brought took a hit from a mortar round and Joe fixed it as well as he could. We tried to borrow another, but nobody had one. Even at its best that thing is pretty slow."

"No way to get out of here before dark?"

"Nope. And I'm not sure I really want to try to fly back in the dark."

"Why not?"

"We'd have to fly too high to avoid hitting something. That would put us right in the middle of effective range of small arms. There's all sorts of NVA units between here and Saigon, and I'd hate to fly directly over one."

"You're going to run the same risk tomorrow."

"Yeah, but the Huey is a comparatively shitty instrument aircraft. I don't want to have to make some wild-ass evasive maneuver in the dark. It's been a while since I've flown anything, much less one of these, at night. Honest, Kevin, I could easily roll us up in a ball." Boyle looked around the clearing. "How secure is this area?"

"About as secure as any we'd be able to find. We'll have plenty of warning, if that's what you mean. There are only two ways in here, the way we came and an old trail over there. We've got pickets out on both of them. Either way they come, the gomers would have to make a lot of noise. These tribesmen have been hiding from them for years, and what we have here are the survivors. They may not look like much, but I'd put them up against anybody."

"Okay. I can have that helo airborne in less than three minutes if I have to. That's all the warning we'll need."

"Even in the dark?"

"Especially in the dark. When I'm scared."

Thompson smiled. "All right, Tim. You get your fueling done and I'll distribute the Christmas presents."

Boyle walked over to the fuel drums, which Santy and France had maneuvered onto the grass under the fueling port. France was turning the handle and sweating. He was also rhythmically cursing. "How's it going?"

"Slow as hell. This damn thing is about on its last legs. It's no wonder those helo guys gave it to you."

Boyle looked closely at the hose that France had been able to attach to the pump. France followed his look. "Yeah, I think one of the reasons it's so slow is that the only hose I could scrounge was a smaller diameter than the original. You remember, when you decrease the diameter you increase velocity, but you also increase back pressure. Or something like that. Shit, I don't know. All I can say for sure is that this is one limp-dick pump."

Boyle shook his head. "Probably has something to do with physics or fluid dynamics or some other goddamned thing that wasn't included in my English degree."

France rotated his shoulder, trying to ease some of the pain from the constant effort. "Thanks. That makes this easier to deal with."

"Think nothing of it, my man."

Santy took over the pumping. "My turn. Don't go anywhere, Tim. You're next."

In the darkness of the late evening, 1st Lt. Bob Dunn slowed the CH-53 so as to come into a hover a little over one hundred feet directly above the landing zone in the parking lot of the embassy. He'd been holding in an orbit with several other helicopters of different types, waiting to get in for another load of people. The CH-46s with the call sign of Lady Ace were holding in a different pattern a little to the west and were taking turns using the LZ on the embassy roof. Everyone was trying to keep the interval between one helo departing and another landing to an absolute minimum. This was all being coordinated by two Marine pilots in an AH-1 Cobra helicopter gunship known as Frito 26 Alpha, orbiting at three thousand feet about a mile south of the airport. "If there were ever two pilots busier than a one-legged man in an ass-kicking contest," Dunn's copilot muttered over the ICS, "it's those guys in 26A."

Dunn watched the 53 ahead of him climb straight up from the LZ until he was higher than the tops of the surrounding buildings and then nose over into forward flight. He heard the pilot report his departure using the call sign Nighthawk, which was from one of the U.S. Air Force special-operations squadrons. Christ, this really is an all-hands show, thought Dunn.

He brought the 53 to a stop and reduced collective, beginning his descent. He tried to force himself to keep his eyes moving constantly—in-out-down, in-out-down. He let his eyes see the gauges, looked out the windshield to make sure he had no sideward or forward drift, and then glanced down to judge his rate of descent. His eyes were moving so quickly that his brain was merely cross-checking the information, occasionally sending an order to his hands and feet to make some minuscule correction. So quickly that if he had taken time to be conscious of everything his eyes saw, he would never have been able to make the two or three hundred movements per minute that kept everything under control.

Dunn could see the LZ illuminated by the automobile headlights and the ugly green lights installed on the outside of the building. Out of the corner of his eye, he noticed some winking yellow lights in the windows of the buildings across the street. "You're taking a little small arms from the buildings," called the controller on the ground.

No shit, thought Dunn. But all he said was, "Roger," as he continued to bring his helo down, knowing that getting shot down and crashing into this particular LZ would close it, certainly for hours and probably forever. In addition to killing everyone on board and many others standing around the LZ, it would also reduce the evacuation capacity from the embassy by about two-thirds.

The big helo kicked up a cloud of dust as the wheels touched the ground and bounced just a little. Dunn dumped the collective all the way to the bottom, and the crew chief began directing the refugees into the back of the helo. It took less than a half minute before the crew chief called that everything was "set aft" and Dunn began raising the overloaded helo back into the air. The rotor rpm drooped toward the minimum and the rudder pedals lost some of their effectiveness, but the Sikorsky did its job well. It continued to climb to a point where Dunn could safely nose over and gain some flying speed.

"Frito, Nighthorse 10's off the embassy. Be advised there's somebody taking potshots at us."

"Roger, 10. Depart southeast. Break. 03, you're next for the embassy. Be advised—small arms in the area again."

"Click-click."

Dunn flew over the New Port area of the city on the Saigon River and turned right for the coast, waited for the crew chief to give him the tally of passengers, and passed it on to Cricket, invisible in the dark sky above. The radios were full of aircraft calling each other, trying to find out where lost wingmen were, advising each other of conflicting traffic. All the while the controllers in Cricket labored to keep the entire operation running smoothly. They even patiently fielded the periodic stupid questions. At one point, Cricket even got Dunn and his crew laughing.

One aircraft called for directions along the route to Tan Son Nhut. "Cricket, this is Bruno 11 dash 1. Request route in use to Alamo."

"Roger, 11. Fly direct from Hope on the three four oh radial to Wishbone, then direct to Keyhole. At Keyhole, contact Frito 26 Alpha this frequency."

"Cricket, Bruno 11 dash I copied direct to Keyhole contact 26 Alpha. Say again all else."

The Cricket stayed very calm. "Bruno 11 dash 1. Fly direct to Hope. From Hope fly three four oh to Wishbone. From Wishbone fly direct to Keyhole. At Keyhole, contact Frito 26 Alpha on this frequency. How copy? Over."

"Bruno copies route. Say again who to call. Understand 'Frito'?"

"Roger, Bruno. As in Bandito. Cricket out."

Tim Boyle slapped at another of the 50 or 60 million little insects that had apparently taken serious offense at the Americans' presence in the clearing on the top of this ridge. Even in the sporadic light rain, the little bastards kept at it, siphoning tiny loads of blood from the humans. Even liberal application of the insect repellent Dalton had given him had done nothing at all to stop the assault.

He looked at the luminous dial on his watch and saw that it was just about eleven-thirty P.M. He stood up and walked over to the Huey and climbed into the copilot's seat. Turning on the battery and inverter switches, he heard the whir of the system. He turned on his ARC-52 UHF radio and put on the headset.

In a little while the radio warmed up and he listened to the Air Force C-130's end of most of the conversations. He could pick out little bits of chatter from some of the other aircraft, but only those that were at a high enough altitude so as to be in line of sight of his antenna. He listened as Frito 26 Alpha directed helos here and there and could hear many of the helicopters check in and out of the landing zone.

He soon had a feel for how things were going. The pilots' voices were calm and disciplined, but he could also get a sense of their frustrations. They had been flying now for nearly nine hours, most of them, and were getting tired. There was also an acceptance of the fact that many people were certain to be left behind when the last helicopter had gone.

Boyle realized that he was listening to these transmissions as a kind of mental life raft. All he needed to know really was that there were still American aircraft operating in and out of Saigon. Anything else was using up his battery, which not only had to provide power to the DC side of the ARC-52 but also had to drive the inverter to provide the AC current that the radio also required. Well, he thought, let's get it over with.

"Cricket, Condor 181."

"Go, 181." He must be busy. Either that or he's been at this too long.

"181, ops normal. Next report twenty-four hundred local."

"Roger, 181. Be advised that Alamo communications are secured as of this time—permanently. Also be advised, GSF retrograde from Alamo is currently under way. Embassy expects evacuation to cease at oh six-thirty. Cricket will expect your call at twenty-four hundred local. I wouldn't wait a whole lot longer if I were you, 181."

Boyle clicked his mike switch and switched off the radio, the inverter, and then the battery. He gently placed the headset on the center console and climbed out of the cockpit. Carefully closing the cockpit door, he stood staring out into the darkness, now oblivious to the flying insects.

"What's up, Tim? What did they say?" Boyle turned to find Santy and Thompson standing behind him.

"The DAO's gone. They're pulling out the Marines from the airport, and the Embassy will be gone by oh six-thirty. The 130 said we shouldn't wait much longer. When's first light, Kevin?"

"About oh five-thirty. Give or take."

"Okay. We'll take off then. Next report, I'll tell Cricket."

Adm. Keith Wallace sat on the couch in the captain's in-port cabin aboard the USS *Concord*. The cabin was really a beautifully appointed three-room suite, which the captain of the ship used only when his ship was either in port or engaged in operations that did not demand his instantaneous availability to the bridge. Operation Frequent Wind and the huge number of aircraft and ships motoring around out here did not allow the captain to go far at all from his other, much smaller and more functional cabin directly aft of the bridge high in the island structure. Since Wallace was a flag officer, he was extended the use of this cabin.

Wallace was rereading a transcript of the message from the C-130 informing them that Boyle and Santy were still safe, or had been fifteen minutes ago, and summarizing the information that had been passed to the helo crew. He looked up at his aide, Lt. Lou Bonnet, who had hustled down here as soon as it had been received.

"Better pass this to Commander Taylor."

"I already did, Admiral. I ran into him on the way here. He said to ask you whether your fingernails were as far gone as his."

"Damn near, Lou."

Bonnett pulled a can of Coke out of the small refrigerator and sat on the other end of the couch. He closed his eyes and slowly rolled the can across his forehead.

"When's the last time you got any sleep, Lou?"

"I don't know, sir. Night before last, I think."

"You mean the night we spent ducking artillery shells?"

"That's the one, sir."

"This is an order, Lou. Go to bed. Now." Wallace saw the expression on Bonnett's face and held up a hand. "I swear I'll wake you the minute I hear something."

Bonnett got slowly to his feet and walked to the door. He started to say something and shook his head. "G'night, Admiral."

"Good night, Lou. You've done a hell of a job these past weeks. I appreciate it."

Bonnett smiled. "Thanks, Admiral. That means a lot."

First Lt. Bob Dunn landed his CH-53 on the parking lot at the DAO compound. All around the area the buildings were ablaze, probably set by the DAO personnel as they pulled back to the LZ. Ahead and to the right sat the helo of the squadron CO, whose original wingman, like Dunn's original flight lead, was now somewhere in the seemingly endless stream of green, white, and red position lights and flashing red anticollision lights that extended, with a short break here and there, all the way out to sea and the ships waiting there.

The CO and Dunn had unloaded and finished refueling at roughly the same time last trip so their crewmen buttoned up the aircraft and away the two helos went. They had expected to go to the embassy, but Frito 26 had diverted them to the airport for one last load. They'd had no problem either finding their way or seeing their landing spots in the light of the burning buildings.

Dunn watched the flickering shapes of the Marines running toward the CO's helo and looked back into his own cargo compartment to see several dozen of them dash up the ramp accompanied by quite a few men in civilian clothes. He looked back at the CO's 53 in time to see three more Marines dashing from the door of the commissary and up the ramp. The last ones had to be those who had been directing traffic all day from the commissary roof. If they were going, no more helos would be landing here.

As Dunn waited for the crewmen to report all secure, he looked around at the burning compound. He remembered the pictures on television of this place back when he was in high school and college. It had always been full of ramrod-straight American soldiers confidently going about the business of war back then when it was known as MACV Headquarters. He wondered briefly whether he would ever again have that image when he thought of this place. He knew, somewhere deep down, that he would not. His image would now be of yellow and red flames, collapsing walls, running shadows of men against the flames, and the wild confusion of fifty aircraft all on the same radio frequency.

"Comin' up, 10."

Dunn watched the CO lift the big helicopter into a hover and then climb straight up into the night sky. He waited until he saw the nose lower against the flames, then lifted his own aircraft into the air to follow. In just a few minutes the cockpit was again dark except for the dim red light on the instrument panel. He gave control to his copilot and slid his seat back, rubbing his hand over his face.

"10 from 01. How many do you have aboard?"

Before Dunn could ask, his crewman gave him the totals. Dunn keyed the mike. "01, I've got forty-eight GSF and eleven U.S. civilian employees of DAO."

"Okay. Forty-eight and eleven U.S."

Gerry Carroll

Dunn listened with half his mind to the CO reporting to Cricket and then answering the same questions three times from the various people out on the ships. He had no control over what he would remember of this night, but he wished his last sight of what was once a beautiful country was not going to be the flames of burning buildings.

★ 47 ★

Wednesday, 30 April 1975

BOYLE WAS DETERMINEDLY TRYING TO DOZE WHEN ONE OF THE TRIBESMEN who had been posted as a picket came hustling up to the small group spread out near the helicopter. Boyle looked at the luminous hands on his watch. It was just before five.

"There are trucks with soldiers on the road below! They stopped at the foot of the trail that leads up here!"

Boyle jumped to his feet and made to move toward the pilot's compartment of the Huey. Thompson called him back. "Hold on, Tim. Let's get a little more info first."

Boyle chuckled in the darkness. "You're the Indian fighter. I'm only the chauffeur. You get the information and I'll set the switches and get the limo ready."

He climbed into his seat and pulled out a small penlight. Shielding the red beam with his body, Boyle quickly went over the panels, checking once more that they were all in the proper positions. Thompson turned to the scout. "Tell me exactly what you saw."

"There were two large trucks which came down the road and stopped near the foot of the small trail which leads up here. Their officer got a group of soldiers, maybe twenty of them, out of the trucks. He lined them up alongside the road and began sending them into the brush on this side. It won't be long before they find the small trail."

Thompson knew that the camouflage that Butler's men had placed to hide the mouth of the trail would not hold up for long. Camouflaging the trail had been Dalton's idea, and he had led the men who did it. Using the grenades Boyle had brought in, he had

379

also sown the trail with as many trip wires and booby traps as he could in the ninety minutes after the helicopter had arrived before it had gotten too dark to see. They were in no immediate danger up here because it would take a while for the enemy to climb the side of the ridge, especially after a few of them had been killed or wounded by Dalton's little surprises.

"How did the soldiers look to you? Were they experienced?"

The tribesman thought for a second. "The soldiers could be, but their officer is not. He made a great show of getting his men organized. He was shouting and blowing his whistle."

That was good. The officer would probably make more noise coming up here than all his men combined. Thompson found himself hoping that the officer would not get himself killed early on. Bad leadership of good troops on the enemy's part would work in the Americans' favor. But if the officer got killed, command would devolve to the next senior man, who would likely be an experienced sergeant, and that would be a problem. "Good," said Thompson. "Where is Butler?"

Butler's voice came from the darkness behind Thompson's left shoulder. "Right here, Kevin."

"How long do you figure it will take them to get up here?"

"A half an hour if they do it right. If they do it wrong, an hour."

"Let's bet on thirty minutes. They'll probably hear the helicopter start up and then move faster. But when they do that, they'll run into the booby traps. How are your men going to get out of here?"

"We'll go back down the way we came and hide in the bush for a day. If what the radio has been saying is correct, the enemy should take Saigon sometime today. It will take them a few days to get organized, and by then we will be back in the mountains."

Thompson was silent for a couple of heartbeats. "You said *we,* Tony. Don't you mean *they?*"

Butler sighed. "No. I mean *we.* I'm not going back with you."

"What the fuck do you mean, Tony?" Thompson hadn't heard Dalton come up to them.

"I mean I can't just fly away and leave these people."

"We came all the way out here and *now* you decide not to leave? That sucks, Tony!"

"Mark, up until tonight, I intended all along to leave with you. I didn't deceive you. It's just that now that the time has come, I can't do it. I can't walk away from these people. They have sacrificed too much over the years, and they have sacrificed more to see that me and my sons got here to meet you. I think they'll be better off with me than without me. I just can't leave them."

Thompson sighed and looked into the black sky. "Do you think you can make a difference? You know that the gomers will spare no effort getting rid of you now that the war is over. You will be an embarrassment to their revolution. They'll hurt you down and they'll kill you."

Thompson could almost hear the grin in Butler's voice. "They haven't caught us yet. I don't think they're good enough."

Dalton spoke. "Jesus Christ, Tony. What about your sons? What chance will they have compared to what they'd have in the States?"

"What chance will they have with me in Portsmouth?"

Dalton stopped himself from explaining that Portsmouth Naval Prison was closed and the inmates transferred to Leavenworth. The point seemed irrelevant.

"They'd at least have a live father!"

"When they got older, they would not understand why their father was in prison for doing what was right. I would rather they never have to understand that. If I go to prison, the state will take them and they'll be just another couple of half-black, half-Asian kids bouncing from foster home to foster home like I did." Butler cleared his throat. "I'd like to ask that you take them with you. And keep them with you."

There was a long silence as Thompson and Dalton considered that. Finally, Thompson broke the silence. "Are you sure about this, Tony?"

"Yes, I am."

"How will you tell your sons?"

"I have already told them. They are too young to understand it all, but they will in time. They . . ." His voice broke.

Dalton let out a long sigh. "All right. We'll take them to the States. We'll look after them for you. I'll make you one promise, though. They will not grow up to be SEALs."

Butler placed his hands on his friends' shoulders. "Thank you, Kevin. Thank you, Mark. You'd better be going. I'd like to be gone, too, before the enemy gets up here. We have about ten minutes."

"Okay." Dalton turned and called Boyle. "Tim, we're leaving. Start her up."

"It'd be better if I did that with everyone aboard. It'll limit the time we're sitting here making noise."

"Right. I didn't think of that."

Boyle walked around the aircraft checking things as best he could in the lousy light of his red-lensed pilot's flashlight. Joe France was struggling to do something in the small battery compartment on the left rear of the aircraft while Santy held the light. "We're about to go, guys."

Santy spoke without looking up. "Yeah. We heard. We're just about done here."

"What are you doing?"

France spoke with his head inside the compartment. "I just put the fresh battery in. I wasn't sure how much juice you'd used talking on the radio, but I figured we'd need to be sure we got started on the first try."

Boyle continued around the aircraft. He made sure that all the ration boxes and ammo cans and grenade cases and other things that could be picked up by the rotor wash and blown into the aircraft and people standing around were secured. He noticed the fuel drums were missing and called to Santy.

"What happened to the fuel drums?"

"Joe and me and a couple of Butler's guys rigged up a little surprise for the gomers."

"What? How?"

"Well, there was a little fuel left in the bottom of them which the pump couldn't reach, so we poked some holes in the sides and left the tops off the drums to get some oxygen in them and then taped a grenade to each one. If it works, when the gomers get here and move them—*blammo!* The grenades light off the fuel fumes and up they go. Pretty neat, huh?"

"Terrific. My future brother-in-law is a mad bomber."

"Well, one way of looking at it is that the gomers won't have to worry about carrying the drums down to their village either."

"Great. Get in the damn aircraft, you maniac. Where's Joe?"

"Right here, Tim."

"Okay. Make sure everything is tied down tight and everybody is strapped in. We may have to do some evasive maneuvering."

"No problem. We'll also have two of the M-60s with us. Butler says that his men would shoot up the ammo twice as fast if they had four guns instead of two. I kept a can of ammo for each gun. It isn't much, but it will make some noise."

"Joe, I've had crewmen who'd been at it for years who weren't as good as you. I'm glad you came."

France was obviously pleased. "Thanks, Tim. That means a lot."

"All right, load 'em up."

Boyle made sure the main rotor blade was turned so that it was perpendicular to the long axis of the Huey and climbed into his seat. Beside him Santy had fastened his harness and was adjusting his headset. "You all set, Mike?"

"Uh-huh. Whenever you're ready, sir."

"See that you keep that respectful attitude in the future, Mr. Santy."

Boyle turned and watched Thompson and Dalton climb into the rear compartment. France took their gear and stowed it carefully where it was out of the way but would also be near at hand. The two small boys climbed in and were seated on the bench across the rear of the compartment and strapped in. Thompson turned and looked at Boyle. "All set."

"Where's Tony?"

Thompson shook his head. "He's not coming, Tim. I'll explain later. We're all set back here."

Boyle gave Thompson a long look and turned back to the front. He stared out through the windshield and concentrated for a moment on remembering the way the immediate area had looked in the light of yesterday evening. He knew for sure that the clearest way out was to head due west—he could do a normal takeoff that way because no tall trees were in that direction. If he headed any other direction, he would have to be careful to climb to at least a hundred feet just to be safe. That meant more power, which meant more fuel used. It wouldn't be much, but every bit counted.

Just as Boyle was reaching for the battery switch, a dull explosion came from the eastern side of the clearing, followed by the distinct flat sound of AK-47 fire. Boyle glanced in that direction and saw that although he could hear the gunfire, he could not see the muzzle flashes, so the enemy was still below the crest. He flipped on the battery switch and quickly went through an abbreviated start checklist. Within two minutes, he had the main rotor coming up to speed and the instruments were almost stabilized.

He wished that it were daylight so he could go without worrying about the attitude instruments. At night, if the instruments were off just a little, it would be easy to fly the Huey into the ground.

Boyle glanced to his right again and saw several muzzle flashes now, but over the engine and rotor noise, he couldn't hear the gunfire. Santy reached down and pulled the knob to align the radio compass indicator with the magnetic compass. He had just finished and was resetting the knob when a hole appeared in Boyle's Plexiglas side window and the magnetic compass exploded into small flying parts.

"Shit! Let's go!"

Boyle nodded and lifted the Huey into a hover, but just as it cleared the ground, he felt two jolts from somewhere in the upper part of the aircraft. He quickly checked his instruments and pulled the collective up still farther, watching the radar altimeter increase steadily toward one hundred feet, and without the hover indicator that other, more sophisticated helicopters had, he could only hope that he was holding it steady and not drifting over the ground too much. When the altimeter reached the hundred-foot mark, Boyle lowered the nose and climbed the aircraft straight ahead. He felt the shuffling as the Huey passed through translational lift and raised the nose a little to get the maximum climb rate. Once at fifteen hundred feet, he lowered the collective and trimmed the controls for forward flight at ninety knots. Since Santy's curse on the ground, not a word had been spoken by anyone in the aircraft. They all understood that the last thing Boyle needed during his takeoff was distraction.

Boyle took a long breath and let it out slowly. "Everybody okay?"

France spoke on the ICS. "Yeah. Everyone's okay in the back. But we took a couple of hits around here somewhere. I don't see any leaks or anything, but I'll keep looking."

Boyle looked at Santy. "You okay?"

"Yeah. But I'm scared. We lost the magnetic compass. Does that mean anything?"

Boyle glanced down at the MA-1 radio compass panel. The white indicator was still centered in the window. "I don't think so. The RMI is still aligned and centered, so we should be getting good information from it. The magnetic compass is only a backup and isn't much of a loss unless the RMI fails. Then we could be in trouble. I'm more worried about the hits we took back aft. I could feel them in the controls."

Santy shook his head. "Let me guess. That's another one of the twenty-seven million bad things about helicopters, right?"

"It ain't good, Mike."

Santy spun the dials on the UHF radio and waited for it to warm up. The communications gear had not been on Boyle's abbreviated start checklist. The old saw he'd learned in Pensacola about flying priorities, "Aviate. Navigate. Then, communicate," seemed to fit.

"Slug 772, Condor 181."

There was a moment of silence as Santy waited for a reply. Finally, "181, Slug, go ahead."

"Roger, Slug. 181's airborne headed oh nine oh for the water. Level, um . . ." Santy looked at the altimeter which showed fifteen hundred feet. "181's level one point five."

"Roger, one point five and oh nine oh. Say your squawk."

Santy looked down at the IFF panel—he'd forgotten to turn it on. "Slug, stand by on the squawk."

"Roger, 181. When able, squawk 3424. I think I have you. Are you about thirty west of the city?"

"Something like that. We're west of it anyway."

"Roger, 181. I pass from Guntrain: 'Is the pickup complete'?"

Santy looked at Boyle and then over his shoulder at Thompson. Both were looking straight back at him. "That's affirm, Slug. Pickup's complete. We've got everybody."

"Roger. We'll pass it on."

Back aboard the carrier *Concord*, Admiral Wallace, or "Guntrain," leaned back in the chair in CIC and stared at the ceiling. Since early yesterday evening, he had not been able to spend a minute without his mind wandering back to the crew of the Huey.

He had haunted CIC waiting for the half-hourly ops-normal reports, which were passed on from Cricket to the Slug E-2 overhead the ship and then down to the Combat Information Center. Wallace would close his eyes momentarily in relief that they were still all right out there, then would walk out of the room and attempt to return to his cabin.

But each time he neared the cabin, he would turn right and walk outboard, carefully stepping over the "kneeknockers" in the ship's frames where the passageways were cut through. He would make his way to the short ladder that led up to the catwalk below the flight deck on the starboard side under the island. He would lean against the railing and stare out over the sea.

Behind him on the flight deck the sailors would walk past on their way to an aircraft or their work space or just to get a cup of coffee. He'd hear their voices and sometimes their laughter vaguely, but it wouldn't truly register. He could clearly hear the rush of the waves displaced by the hull of the ship as it passed slowly through. He could hear the moan from an old bearing as the huge search radar antenna high above him rotated persistently.

But Wallace could also hear his own voice as he tried to explain to the families of the young men aboard that helo what had happened, and why, should something go wrong and they not return. He tried to find the words he would have to use if that came to pass. After a few minutes of trying to force himself to consider other things, he would find himself back in the passageway leading to CIC so as to be there when the next report came in. He would listen to the seven or so words of the verbatim repetition of Boyle's words and would clench his teeth at the sheer inadequacy of the mandated format of the report.

All it told him was that nothing had gone wrong. There was no place in the report for any comment on what was going well or what the crew was actually doing or what they thought might happen next. There was no place for them to say what it felt like to be sitting on a dark hilltop waiting out the night with the enemy all around. There was no place for them to tell the admiral that the mission he had sent them on, even though they had volunteered, was a good mission. There was no place in the report for them to tell him that his decisions that often risked the lives of his men were the right decisions.

This time the report had been different. They were airborne and on their way out. At least something was happening that was driving for a conclusion, no matter how slowly. The helo was headed this way, and in a little over an hour, whatever happened, the mission would be finished.

Wallace stood and walked out of CIC and headed once more for his cabin. He was certain that this time he would actually get there, but in less than two minutes he found himself standing in the catwalk and staring into the darkness in the west.

★ **48** ★

Wednesday, 30 April 1975

"HEY, MIKE. I'M STARTING TO GET SOME FEEDBACK IN THE CONTROLS. ONE of those hits we took might have gotten the hydraulics."

"Do you want to slow down?"

"No. The book says that below fifty knots this thing will be a bitch to control. I'm gonna keep it at ninety or so."

Santy cursed. "It's not like we've got a lot of emergency landing fields around here even if we could see them."

"Yeah. We're still okay. It's just that we have to be real careful if we have to do any hard maneuvering. How 'bout calling the E-2 and letting them know what's going on. You guys in the back hearing all this?"

France spoke. "Yeah. We're all fine back here. These kids look like owls staring out the windows. I'll bet this is their first ride in an aircraft."

Santy keyed the mike. "Slug, this is Condor 181."

"Go, 181."

"Roger. We're estimating fifteen miles west of the city. Are there any reported areas of groundfire? We're having some control problems here."

"Understand control problems. Be advised, 181, that there are no safe landing areas left short of the fleet. The last lift out of the airport was a little after midnight, and we only have the Lady Ace 46s working the embassy and from the roof only. The parking-lot LZ is gone. I suggest you fly directly over the city and join the evac routes the Marines are using. We had a couple of Phantoms get into a missile duel late yesterday just northeast of the city, so watch for Grails."

387

"We understand. Our intentions are to head for the fleet, but we would request that you have one of the SAR helos rendezvous with us over the beach. We have two kids aboard who I don't think can swim."

"Roger. Expect an H-3 to join on you feet wet."

"181, roger. Thanks."

Boyle looked out to the horizon and could see the light of the city in the near distance. To the right, he could see the huge fires burning at what should have been the airport, and off to the left, near where Bien Hoa should have been, was another group of even bigger fires. He keyed the radio.

"Cricket, 181. You still up there?"

"That's affirm, 181."

"Be advised that my self-navigation gear is not going to get me through to the coast. Can you describe the route?"

Before the C-130 could answer, Boyle heard another voice. "181, this is Lady Ace 25."

"Go ahead, 25."

"Okay, 181. Do you have the city in sight?"

"Affirm."

"Head slightly to the north of the lights and pick up the river. Fly about one six oh until the river gets real wide and then head due east. Do not overfly the airport or the north and east banks of the river. The gomers will shoot at you if you do. And be advised we still have several 46s working the embassy. If you can find one of us, just follow."

"Roger, 25. 181 copies all."

"Click-click."

Santy listened to the exchange and then looked over at his friend. "Feels better not to be alone, doesn't it?"

Boyle chuckled, not particularly surprised that Mike could figure out pretty much what he'd been thinking. "Yeah. I didn't like it much spending most of a night in the weeds."

Boyle made a turn slightly to the left and felt the cyclic stick shudder a little in his hand. He rolled back out just in time to see the master caution light in the upper center of the instrument panel come on. He looked down at the panel by his left knee and saw that the HYD PRESS #2 light was also on.

"Dammit it. I knew that was going to happen. Mike, turn off the accumulator switch there on the panel."

Santy leaned forward, flipped the switch, and reset the master caution light. "So what does that mean?"

"Right now, not much. Number one and number two systems are separate. The only common point is a manifold back there. If that's what took the hit, then we're going to lose number one, too. That ain't good."

"Will we still be able to fly?"

"Yeah, we should be, but it'll be a bitch and it won't be pretty. The real problem will be landing. We'll have to do a run-on to one of the bigger ships. We get to slide down the deck a ways with no brakes since these babies don't come with 'em."

"Terrific."

Thompson's voice came over the ICS. "Still beats walking, Mike."

Santy sighed. "Kevin, somebody told me once that helos are aeronautical impossibilities. I'm beginning to think he was right."

First Lt. Bob Dunn watched the enlisted signalman indicate that the main rotor blades were folded into their stowed positions and pulled off the throttle, listening to the diminishing whine from the engine as it wound down. Reaching up with a leaden arm, he unsnapped the chin strap and pulled off his helmet. He couldn't remember being this tired after a flight. Looking at the eight-day clock on the instrument panel, he noted the time.

Comparing it with the original takeoff time he'd written on his kneeboard, he saw that he'd been strapped into this seat just shy of eighteen hours. He reached down to his lap and unfastened the harness, throwing the shoulder straps over the back of his seat and allowing the lap belts to drop to the deck.

Dunn looked at his copilot, who was sitting with his helmet in his lap simply staring out the windshield. Dunn turned and looked back out across the deck at the Marines who were escorting the last few evacuees out of the CH-53s onto the deck ahead of his aircraft.

The Marines were frisking each person and checking through the bundles of personal belongings. They were doing it gently but thoroughly, trying to strike a balance between military necessity and respect for the people's dignity. Occasionally a Marine would find a weapon—a pistol or a carbine or a K-bar fighting knife—and toss it on the surprisingly large pile on the deck.

Other Marines were taking armloads of weapons from the pile and tossing them over the side. Once through the weapons inspection, the refugees were led to one of the hatches in the island structure and then below decks to whatever part of the processing waited for them there.

Dunn watched the squadron's maintenance flight-deck coordinator step down from the helicopter up the deck and walk quickly to Dunn's personnel hatch. He climbed in, spoke for a moment to the crew chief, and then came up to the cockpit.

"She fly okay, Lieutenant? Any gripes?"

"She did good, Sarge, real good. The only gripe I have is that these seats suck. My ass is numb between my knees and my armpits."

The sergeant laughed. "Well, sir, that's five straight aircraft that have bad seats. I'll write to Mr. Sikorsky and tell him to get on the stick. So the bird's up and available?"

"Yup. As far as I can tell, she'll be ready to fly a hell of a lot sooner than I will."

"Great, sir. Good job. The colonel said you guys lifted almost three thousand people out of there. He said he's proud of us." The sergeant's face clouded for a second. "There are some new holes in a couple of them, though. You guys get hit?"

"I don't think so. If we did, they didn't hit anything important."

"Good, Lieutenant. Real good."

Dunn smiled. "You maintainers did a hell of a job, Sarge. Thanks."

The sergeant grinned and patted Dunn on the shoulder. He turned and headed for the next aircraft in the line. Like most maintenance men, he didn't really care about the details of the mission. All he wanted to know was did his aircraft do its job and how badly did the pilot damage it in the doing. Telling him that not only did the job get done but also that the plane needed only normal servicing to be ready for the next mission was almost as good as handing him a letter from home.

He must be in heaven today, thought Dunn. The squadron had flown all its aircraft for three-quarters of a day virtually nonstop, and at the end of it, all the helos were home and in one piece.

"You ready?"

Dunn looked over at his copilot. "Yeah. I guess so. After you."

The two men climbed out of their seats and groaned at the stiffness in their legs and backs. As Dunn leaned back into the cockpit to make sure he hadn't left any of his gear in there, he heard his copilot muttering, "I'm definitely getting too old for this shit."

Just as Boyle began his right turn to follow the Saigon River, the controls stiffened in his hands and it took at least double the effort to roll the aircraft out of its bank. He was about to say something when the master caution light came on again. Boyle glanced down at the panel by his knee and saw that the HYD PRESS #1 light was now on.

Santy reached forward and reset the master caution light. "This is bad, right?"

"Yep. You'd better phone it in. And turn off the accumulator switch on that panel there."

Santy looked for a moment, found the switch, and turned it off. "Slug 771, this is Condor 181. We've just had a complete hydraulic failure. We're presently passing east of the city level at fifteen hundred."

"181, say your intentions."

Santy looked at Boyle, who told him, "Get us radar following out to one of the carriers. Tell 'em we'd like as much room as possible to land. We'll need to slide it on, and that might take a couple of hundred feet of clear deck."

Santy told the E-2 what they wanted and received a curt "Wilco." He looked over at Boyle, who was now gritting his teeth in the effort to keep the aircraft under control. "You okay, Tim? Need some help?"

"No, we're all right, I think. Just do the talking and make sure your harness is locked."

"Okay."

France spoke up. "We're all set back here. Everything is tied down and the kids are still having fun."

Boyle found that keeping the Huey flying at ninety knots kept the control forces at a minimum. There was still tremendous feedback in the stick and collective, but the less movement he made with the controls the less the forces acted against him. He lowered his left hand and tightened the collar on the collective friction. Santy watched him do it and Boyle explained.

"With a complete failure like this, you can still move the stick and the petals, but the collective would be impossible. So there's an accumulator in the system which is supposed to give you four full throws before it bleeds off and the damn thing locks in place. The collective is the up-and-down parts of the controls, Mikey, so I don't want to waste any movement I've got."

Santy grinned. "The up-and-down part, huh. I'll bet you were a whiz in ground school."

"Well, I passed."

"By how much?"

"You don't want to know. But look at it this way: If the minimum wasn't good enough, it wouldn't be the minimum."

"Condor 181, Slug."

"Go ahead."

"Roger, be advised that all decks close in to the coast are fouled at this time. There doesn't seem to be much hope that any of them will be clear within the next hour or so. Every time they get them clear some VNAF clown lands without clearance and fouls them again. The only one with a chance is Guntrain, which is twenty miles further out. They're currently launching the air cover and still have to recover the last launch. They estimate a ready deck in thirty minutes."

"Okay, Slug. Guntrain'll have to do. Advise them that we'll need the entire angled deck forward of the wires. We'll have to come over the fantail very flat and drop it on."

"Slug copies."

On flag bridge of the USS *Concord,* known as Guntrain over the radios, Adm. Keith Wallace picked up the handset of the radio tuned to the ship-to-ship frequency. He called the command center aboard the USS *Blue Ridge* and asked for General Alexander. He waited for a few minutes and then heard Alexander's voice on the frequency.

Wallace told him that his SEALs had been picked up and were on their way out. He then explained as best he could the difficulties the Huey was having and promised to keep him informed. He gave him the estimate of the landing time, about thirty minutes away, and signed off.

On the *Blue Ridge,* Alexander looked at the handset for a moment before replacing it in its cradle. He turned away from the console and faced General Toone.

He looked into his friend's open face but couldn't muster the energy to put on the smile that he ought to be wearing. "They got 'em, Ted. They're on the way out. Ought to be crossing the coast in about ten minutes or so. But the aircraft has got some bad problems with the controls. Apparently they had to leave the LZ under fire and took some hits."

"What ship are they going to?"

"*Concord*. She's got the biggest deck and the Vietnamese haven't discovered her yet."

Toone shook his head. He wanted to be there when Thompson and Dalton arrived. He also wanted to meet their friend, the one who was worth risking so much for. Alexander read his mind.

"We'll see them soon enough. Keith Wallace will let us know as soon as they're safe on deck."

In the cockpit of Salty Dog 732, Lt. Cdr. Frank Holtz scanned the sky above and in front of his SH-3D Sea King. He was from the helicopter antisubmarine squadron aboard the *Concord* and had been dispatched to meet and escort Condor 181, a Huey flying from Saigon to the ship. Holtz hadn't received any more information than that when he was called away from his normal plane guard rescue holding pattern on the starboard side of the ship, and he was intensely curious as to why the helo would be using a call sign reserved for one of the A-7 squadrons from his carrier and air wing. He knew he wouldn't get an answer to that question until after he landed, and if it was a classified mission like the many others he'd seen in his three other deployments to Vietnam, he might very well never get an answer.

His copilot, who was only a lieutenant (junior grade) and was therefore younger and with better eyes, pointed high and to the right to a flashing red anticollision light. "There he is."

Holtz looked up and keyed the radio. "Slug, Salty Dog 732's got the Huey in sight. He's at my two o'clock high."

"Roger, that's him. He's at fifteen hundred and doing ninety knots."

"Roger. Break. Condor, 732's at your two o'clock low. We'll be joining port."

"Click-click."

Holtz pulled up the collective and traded some of his airspeed for altitude. He flew a long curving approach and slid into a loose formation well above and behind the Huey.

"181, Salty Dog's joined."

"Roger. We've got a complete hydraulic failure and ninety knots seems most comfortable."

"Ninety it is. Try channel seventy-four."

Santy switched his TACAN receiver to channel seventy-four and watched the needle swing around several times before it stopped and pointed ten degrees left of the nose. He switched on the DME switch and saw the mileage indicator stop at thirty-three.

"There she is, Tim. Left ten. How're you doing? Do you want me to fly it awhile so you can get ready for the landing?"

Boyle steadied out on the new heading and looked over at his friend, realizing how hard it must be for him to sit there in the seat of an essentially unfamiliar aircraft in emergency conditions and do nothing but talk on the radios and sweat it out.

"Okay, Mike. You have the controls. Be gentle with it and don't make any sudden moves. Keep everything where it is." He watched Santy take over the controls and let his hands drop away. He flexed his fingers and rotated his wrists trying to loosen them up. They were nearly frozen into position from the constant struggle to keep things straight and level against the heavy control forces. He placed his hands on his knees so they would be close to the controls just in case and looked out the windshield.

The sky to the east was beginning to lighten. The sea below was still shrouded in darkness, but in only a few minutes they might even be able to see the deck clearly. If they were lucky.

When Santy took over the controls, he was surprised at how much effort he had to put in to make the tiny movements to keep everything in balance. Boyle had been fighting these controls for nearly forty-five minutes now and had never said a word. Santy looked across the cockpit at Boyle and saw him staring fixedly out the windshield as if willing the sun to come up faster.

✫ 49 ✫

Wednesday, 30 April 1975

CDR. NICK TAYLOR STOOD JUST INSIDE THE HEAVY ARMORED DOOR OF Primary Flight Control high on the island structure of the USS *Concord* and waited to catch his breath. When he'd been told that "Condor" 181 had checked in, he'd sprinted for the long series of steep ladders that led up here to Primary, or the "tower" as this room was almost universally known.

Taylor straightened up and walked the few steps past the coffee urn and the sailors who sat facing aft and kept track of the settings on the arresting gear. He approached the two elevated high-backed chairs that were assigned to the air officer, or "air boss," on the left and his assistant, or "miniboss" on the right. The only occupant of the little area this morning was the boss, who was standing in front of his chair, craning to see the mad ballet of men and airplanes on the flight deck below as the preparations for launch went forward. Over his head the speakers that were set to the various radio frequencies used in the aircraft traffic patterns buzzed and hissed and popped. It was the mark of a good ship–air wing team when an operation as dangerous and complex as this could be done with the absolute minimum of chatter on the radios.

Taylor stood well out of the way between the chairs and looked down at the deck. On the bow catapults, F-4 Phantoms were getting set to go, followed by a group of A-7s and A-6s from the waist "cats." Taylor was careful not to interrupt, wisely waiting for the boss to notice him.

The 19MC, or silver "bitch box," at the boss's left elbow bel-

395

lowed before the boss could turn down the volume. "Primary, Conn. You have the deck."

The boss adjusted the volume knob and pushed the small talk switch. "Primary has the deck." He caught sight of Taylor and motioned him into the empty miniboss's chair.

"One of these days I'm going to kill that guy."

"Who?"

"That new lieutenant shmuck from the Navigation Department. Every time he stands the bridge watch he thinks we can't hear him unless he screams into the damn 19MC. I guess he doesn't understand the concept of sound amplification. Dumb bastard."

Taylor smiled but didn't answer. He knew the boss was just filling empty air as he nervously waited for the ship to finish her turn into the wind and steady out on the launch and recovery course.

The bow of the carrier finally stopped swinging, and the inclinometer showed that she was steady into the wind. The boss watched the clock, and when the time was exactly right, he pushed the button that lit the green launch light hanging outside several feet below his window.

Instantly the Phantom on Catapult 1 went to full power, and in a couple of seconds the bright flames from its afterburners lit the deck all around the aircraft, and the jet blast blew sheets of water back down the deck from a rain shower the ship had passed through minutes before. Taylor saw the lighted wand of the catapult officer swing down, touch the deck, and raise back up to the horizontal, pointing forward. The twin flames of the Phantom streaked down the deck, and when the catapult released the big fighter, it eased to the right in a clearing turn. Before the first F-4 had steadied out on its departure course, one of the A-7s had launched from the waist, and the F-4 on Catapult 2 on the bow was in full afterburner.

Taylor could see the outlines of the aircraft below and looked aft of the ship where the dark sky was definitely beginning to brighten. In a little while, it would be that time of the morning when there is light but little definition. He knew the day would be gray and overcast again, as yesterday had been.

The launch continued for fully ten minutes as aircraft after aircraft left the ship and climbed away to relieve the other fighters and attack jets in their stations along the coast. In the break between launch and recovery, the boss grabbed a cup of coffee and made sure his radios were set to the approach and landing frequencies. He flopped down in his seat and glanced up at the small television screen to see if the cameras had picked up the first in the line of aircraft descending toward the ship.

The boss watched the lights on the visual landing-aid system on the far deck edge flash as the landing signals officer tested them. He turned to Taylor.

"I hear you have a new aircraft in your squadron."

"Yeah. We got it on sale. Santy's taking it for a test ride."

"Last I heard they're about thirty-five miles out. They ought to be coming aboard in about twenty minutes."

"How many aircraft do we have in this recovery?"

"Fourteen. We ought to make it. If we don't, we'll land the helo anyway, get everybody out of it, and shove it over the side."

Taylor looked down and saw the big yellow forklift positioned off to one side of the landing area directly below the tower. That ought to do it, thought Taylor.

"181, Salty Dog."

"Go ahead."

"How's the flying?"

Santy glanced over at Boyle, who was still trying to get the stiffness out of his hands. "Sorta like an eighteen-wheeler with seventeen of 'em flat."

Santy heard the chuckle in the H-3 pilot's voice. "That sounds about right."

Boyle glanced down at the DME and saw that they were now twenty miles from the ship. He looked down at the sea and for the first time could make out the surface of the water. It wasn't much, but it would get better.

"181, Slug. Tower advises there are eight to go. Expect clearance on arrival. Be advised there are rain showers in the area. Switch button fifteen."

"181, switching." Santy looked over at Boyle, who was fishing in his pockets for the frequency card he'd gotten when they brought Callahan, Wallace, and Tran out to the ship. He found it, looked up channel fifteen, and set in the frequency. Santy listened for the channelizer tone to stop and keyed the mike.

"181's up fifteen."

397

"732."

"Tower copies, 181 and 732. How do you read, 181?"

"Loud and clear."

"Roger. Set up for a long straight-in. Base recovery course is two eight oh."

"Understand BRC is two eight oh. 181 will arc around to the south."

"Okay, 181. Call a ten-mile final."

"Roger."

Santy eased the Huey into a gentle turn to the right. The carrier, in order to get the proper winds over the deck for the launch and recovery, had had to steam westward, which put her course directly opposite the Huey's. In order to line up with the stern, Santy had to fly a wide arc around to a point five miles behind the ship to begin his approach, but he couldn't cut any corners because the air around the ship was filled with other aircraft, and in the poor predawn visibility, the dangers of midair collisions were never far away.

Santy wiggled his butt on the seat. "Tim, listen, if the deck is wet, it's going to be real slick. The nonskid is worn almost down to nothing, and there's probably a lot of oil and grease on what's left. The boss may not remember to tell you."

Boyle nodded and watched the needles on his navigation instruments until he saw that the Huey was directly south of the ship. He took a deep breath and let it out. "Okay, Mike, I'll take it." He took over the controls and saw Santy release them. He grinned when he saw his friend try to loosen up his arms and hands.

Santy smiled. "That's a bitch. The last time I felt controls that stiff was in an A-4 when I had to disconnect the control boost."

"Yeah, well, we've only got about fifteen minutes left."

Boyle asked France if everything was set in the back. "Yeah. I've got the boys padded as well as I can. We've got everything else tied down, and when you give the word, I'll pin the doors."

Boyle cursed himself silently—he should have remembered the doors. "Okay, Joe. Go ahead and get the doors."

France slid back both cargo doors in the rear of the helo and inserted the pins that would hold them open in case of a ditching. Boyle had forgotten for the moment that if he hit the water, those in the back would never be able to get out if the doors were jammed shut on impact as sometimes happened. "Okay, doors are pinned."

Boyle continued the arc and aimed for a point a little outside ten miles so he would have some extra room to maneuver to the final approach course. He wanted to keep the turns shallow so that if the aircraft decided to do something strange, it wouldn't happen at a steep bank. He glanced over his shoulder and saw that the H-3 had eased over to a wide position on the starboard side.

Boyle felt oddly comforted that the H-3 was out there. It is a lonely thing to be in a crippled aircraft and be unsure whether or not you are going to get it down safely. Even though someone else flying your wing can really do nothing but offer encouragement, it still helps just to have him there. If that other aircraft is also a capable rescue helicopter and has a well-trained and equipped crew, it goes quite a way in minimizing the many things the pilot of the aircraft in trouble has to worry about.

All of which is fine until the pilot remembers that there are passengers aboard who are completely unfamiliar with the ways of getting out of a rapidly sinking aircraft. Then, when he remembers that two of the passengers are children who probably can't swim at all, the rescue helo flying out to one side serves as a reminder of the price of failure.

Admiral Wallace came in and stood behind the chairs in the tower. Taylor noticed him and started to get up to give him the miniboss's seat, but the admiral pushed him back down.

"I've been sitting on my ass for the past two days, Nick. I'll stand." Wallace gestured with his thumb toward the stern where Boyle and his crew would cross the deck. "How are they doing?"

"They're almost set up for a straight-in. They should be calling ten miles anytime."

Wallace nodded as an A-6 intruder roared over the fantail out of the predawn gloom and slammed down on the deck, its exhaust blowing more sheets of water along the deck. The arresting wire ran out and the pilot pulled his throttles back to idle when the aircraft stopped. The admiral watched as the jet's tail hook dropped the wire and the pilot goosed the throttles forward again to taxi clear of the landing area. The arresting wire was drawn back down the deck until it was again stretched across the little "fiddle bridges," which kept it suspended a few inches off the deck. The next jet was already less than a quarter mile behind the ship.

"How many left?"

"Five, Admiral. We had a couple of foul-deck wave-offs, but they're both aboard now."

"Tower, Condor 181's at ten miles. Out of fifteen hundred for five." Boyle's tight voice on the overhead speakers stopped all conversations in the room. Another A-6 slammed down onto the deck.

"Roger, 181, four to go. Call five miles. Be advised that the deck is wet. Plan on it being slick."

"181."

Wallace looked aft of the ship and could make out several aircraft lined up in the long line headed for the deck. Ten miles, he thought. Another six or seven minutes.

Boyle had allowed the Huey to pass through the final approach course and leveled the wings so as to stay parallel with it. He told Santy to turn the accumulator back on and eased the helo into a gentle descent toward five hundred feet. Because at ninety knots he was far slower than the jets were, and because he wasn't sure they'd be able to see his silver-gray helicopter against the equally gray dawn, he wanted to be well below the altitudes and slightly offset from the glide path that the jets used.

He lowered the collective gently and allowed the rate of descent to build up to three hundred feet per minute, and once he reached it, he eased the collective back up to keep it there. He wondered how much of his accumulator pressure that had cost him. He knew that once it was gone it was irretrievable, and his chances for successfully landing this aircraft were decreasing with every bit of dissipated pressure.

Santy looked out to the left and watched an A-6 pass by on the final approach course. The aircraft had green rotating anticollision lights instead of red—it was a tanker version of the intruder bomber, and the tanker was usually the last aircraft to land. He was about to tell Boyle when the radio came to life.

"181, Tower."

"Go ahead."

"Roger, 181. The tanker at your eleven o'clock is the last one. The deck'll be yours on arrival."

Boyle glanced at Santy with a half-smile. At least he wouldn't have to do a spacing turn before the approach. "Roger, Tower. 181's at six miles. We'll try to float over the wires and drop it abeam the lens."

"Roj."

The boss watched the A-6 tanker cross the rounddown and catch the wire. In far less than a minute, the intruder was clear of the landing area and the wires were back in place. The boss picked up the handset of the flight-deck loudspeaker system, or 5MC. "On the flight deck. Stand clear of the landing area. We have a helo inbound with no hydraulics. Clear the catwalks on the port side. Paddles, clear the platform."

Across the deck, Taylor watched the LSO, or "Paddles," and his white-shirted assistants hurriedly close up their console and duck into the hatch that led below decks. Most of the other people on deck moved quickly behind whatever solid object they could find. Earlier in the cruise, a helicopter had crashed on deck and the sailors had seen what happened when the rotor blades struck the deck, sending large chunks of metal in all directions.

Taylor found himself standing in front of the miniboss's chair anxiously staring aft to find the one speck against the gray clouds that would be the Huey. Out of the corner of his eye he could see Admiral Wallace, peering between the two sailors sitting at the arresting-gear consoles. Suddenly, the bitch box erupted with the officer of the deck's voice. "Primary, Conn. Can you hold off that helo until we make a turn? We're running too close to the beach."

The boss turned and stared ahead of the ship. There was nothing out there but water. He could see no sign of land or conflicting ship's traffic at all. He couldn't even see any of the ships that were stationed closer in to the coast. Taylor saw the look in the boss's eyes when he took in the situation. Even though he'd known the man for years, the look sent chills through him.

The boss pushed down the switch on the bitch box and nearly spat the words into it. "Conn, Primary. We have a goddamned helicopter with seven souls on board inside four miles. The helicopter has a dual hydraulic failure, which means he is having trouble flying the fucking thing. If you turn this ship one fucking degree off the present course before he is safely on deck, I will

401

personally come up there, rip off your head, and shit down your neck. Do you understand me?"

There was nothing but silence from the bitch box. Admiral Wallace broke the moment in Primary by clearing his throat. "Well, Boss, I'd say that was pretty clear. But maybe you should quit pulling your punches and tell the young gentleman what you *really* think."

Despite his worry about the Huey, Taylor couldn't help but laugh at the air boss's outraged expression, which soon colored with embarrassment. "Sorry, Admiral."

Wallace grinned as he turned and looked aft again. "Don't be, Boss. I couldn't have said it better myself."

Tim Boyle looked out at the ship about a mile and a half ahead of the Huey. He scanned his instruments quickly and saw that aside from the hydraulic-pressure lights, everything was still all right. Reaching down, he locked his shoulder harness and wiggled his butt up against the seat. "Okay. We're about a mile and a half out. Brace yourselves, and when we get on deck, stay strapped inside until I get the rotors stopped. Mike, call out my airspeed. Call it every ten knots until we get down to fifty and every five after that. I want to touch down as close to twenty knots as I can. Everybody set?"

France took one more look around the cabin and rechecked the boys' lap belts. He smiled at them and was rewarded with smaller ones in return. He braced his back against the rear bulkhead and his feet against the pile of equipment behind Boyle's seat. On the other side of the boys, both Dalton and Thompson did the same. "All set aft."

Santy reached down, unlocking his harness. He leaned across and double-checked Boyle's and then relocked his own. He sat back in his seat and watched the ship get closer.

At three-quarters of a mile, Boyle called the tower and received clearance to land. He looked out and saw the yellow light, or ball, which gave him a visual indication of his position on the glideslope. He was a bit high so he eased off a little collective and increased his rate of descent slightly, and looking back at the deck, he began to raise the nose to decelerate. He heard Santy call out eighty knots and then seventy and felt the controls begin to stiffen even further and the feedback from the massive dynamic weight of the rotor system increase. He could feel the beat through the cyclic stick in his right hand and found himself fighting to keep up with the rhythm instead of chasing it and adding to the oscillations. He knew that if he got behind the feedback, he would certainly lose control of the aircraft.

"Sixty knots, Tim."

" 'Kay." Boyle raised his nose a little more and crossed over the deck edge just as Santy called out fifty knots.

He pulled up on the collective and stopped the descent about ten feet over the deck, still gradually decelerating.

The Huey crossed the first arresting wire at forty-five knots and the last one at forty. Boyle looked forward and with a sickening feeling in his gut saw the end of the angled deck coming up fast. He raised the nose slightly more and pulled just a little more collective, feeling it stiffen as the accumulator began to lose the rest of its pressure.

"Thirty-five knots, Tim. Now thirty."

Boyle held the nose up for another few heartbeats and then lowered it smoothly to a level attitude.

"Twenty-five!"

Boyle pushed down on the collective and felt it move a little and then stiffen even further. "Mike, push the collective!"

With his left hand, Santy instantly put as much force on the collective as he could, and combined with Boyle's efforts, that moved it down.

"That's good. Stay close, Mike," grunted Boyle. He held his breath as the Huey dropped the last few feet to the deck.

Santy never took his eyes off the airspeed. "Twenty knots! Deck edge is comin' up!"

When Boyle felt the skids begin to scrape along the deck and heard the screech of metal on metal, he yelled, "All the way down. Now!"

The two pilots shoved the collective all the way down and Boyle shoved in the right rudder pedal to correct a slight yaw.

In the tower, Taylor found himself gripping the windowsill as he saw the Huey come over the deck. He had never flown a helicopter but could see that this was going to be close. The helo floated over the wires so low that he thought the tail rotor was going to dig into the deck and spin the thing out of control. But the pilot held it steady, and once past the wires, he allowed it to drop the last several feet. As the metal skids scraped along the rough deck, long plumes of sparks flew back. Taylor remembered something from physics that the sparks represented dissipating energy, which meant losing speed. He quickly glanced forward and saw that the helo was headed straight for the end of the angled deck and a seventy-foot drop into the sea. He knew that the pilot would never be able to get the Huey flying again and that the shrinking strip of deck was all the time he had left.

Boyle pulled the stick back to get all the decelerating force he could from the rotor system. The pedals were useless now and the collective was not going anywhere without two or three men pulling on it. All there was to do now was to hold on and hope.

Santy felt a sudden knot of fear as he saw the deck edge coming. As an A-7 pilot, he would either have shoved his throttles forward in an attempt to go around or pulled the ejection handle to get himself clear of the aircraft as it dropped into the water. He reached with his left hand for his emergency door release and put his right hand on the buckle of his harness, forcing himself to take deep breaths to stay calm. He reminded himself that all they had to do was get clear of the wreck and tread water for a few minutes and they would be picked up by the rescue helo that had followed them down. He told himself to remember the kids.

Boyle felt the helo rock up on one side as it slid slowly over the end of one of the waist catapult tracks and lost its last few knots of speed. The Huey rocked back on an even keel, gracefully rotated ninety degrees to the left, and stopped less than twenty feet from the white and yellow painted stripes at the end of the angled deck. Automatically, Boyle rolled the throttle off and shut off the switches. He reached up for the rotor brake and threw it on, hearing the grinding sound as the brake slowed and finally stopped the main rotor. He let his hands drop into his lap and stared at the water passing by seventy feet below.

"Je-sus Christ," was all he could find to say.

Admiral Wallace let out the breath he'd been holding when he saw the Huey yaw to the left and finally stop sliding. He watched the rotor blades come to a quick halt and several groups of men run over to the aircraft and begin securing it to the deck with chains. The crash truck drove up and aimed its foam nozzle at the wisps of smoke coming from the rotor-brake area on the top of the aircraft. All over the deck, men began to peek out from their hiding places.

The admiral caught the air boss's eye and shook his head. The boss nodded and pushed down the switch on the bitch box.

"Conn, Primary. Recovery complete. You can start your turn."

✷ **50** ✷

Wednesday, 30 April 1975

THE SOLDIERS RODE IN THEIR TRUCK THROUGH THE CITY AND STARED *around at what to them was as strange and magical as Oz. The months and years they had spent in the jungle and before that in the drab and lifeless towns and villages of the North had not prepared them for this. Only a few hours ago the Southerners had surrendered, and the soldiers had been rushed into these trucks and driven hastily across the Newport Bridge and into the city.*

They saw the shops and glittering signs on the fronts of the buildings and marveled at the sights. They didn't notice the people who stood outside the shops and under the signs and watched them with fear.

The trucks passed a huge and very ugly green statue of several ARVN soldiers and correctly assumed that it was a memorial to the Southerners who had died in the war. At the foot of the statue lay the corpse of an enemy officer with the pistol still in his hand and the side of his head gone. After all the death the soldiers had seen, the statue was more interesting than the bit of human wreckage at the bottom of its five short steps.

After the dirt roads and dust of the Ho Chi Minh Trail and the long country roads leading here, the drivers were unused to the close confines of Saigon, and they turned up this street and that trying to find their way through the strange city. The soldiers did not know their destination but were glad of the time to see the city.

After quite a few minutes, the trucks turned onto a wide boulevard and halted in front of a huge white building that was more splendid than any they'd ever seen. It could only be the Presiden-

406

tial Palace, built and kept with far more dignity than the relatively spiritless and austere edifices of their own government in Hanoi. A tall decorative fence of wrought iron surrounded the building, but the main gates lay twisted and bent, their hinges torn from the sandstone pillars.

The officers blew their whistles and the soldiers jumped down from their trucks and followed them into the courtyard. The soldiers walked cautiously around the NVA tanks that sat with their guns pointed outward at the streets and buildings of the city. From the flagpole on the balcony of the building flew a red and light blue flag with a yellow star in the center.

Only then did the soldiers loosen their grip on their weapons and look at each other in silence and then stare again at the flag on the roof. Only then did they realize that it was over.

1992

⋆ EPILOGUE ⋆

Still Fighting

☆ News Item (Friday, 2 October 1992) ☆

The United Nations is conducting a high-level operation to protect and rescue a lost army of Montagnard guerrillas who are still fighting against Vietnamese Communists over seventeen years after the Vietnam War ended. The 407 members of the United Front for the Liberation of Oppressed Races (FULRO) are the survivors of an army that once numbered 10,000 and are operating out of deeply forested areas of Cambodia.

FULRO, which is a loose organization made up of minority Christian hill tribesmen, has been making small-scale attacks on Vietnamese forces in an effort to secure an autonomous homeland around Pleiku and Ban Me Thuot in the Central Highlands of what was once South Vietnam. During the years when American troops fought there, the tribesmen, chiefly Montagnards, were trained by and fought alongside American Special Forces units against Viet Cong insurgents and later against North Vietnamese Army (NVA) regular troops.

Decimated by combat losses and by disease, a few FULRO fighters in remnants of uniforms and carrying old and worn but well-maintained weapons contacted UN peacekeeping authorities at a border monitoring station in an attempt to send a message to U Thant asking for help. Thant, whom FULRO still believed to be the Secretary General of the UN, has been dead for years.

An American member of the UN peacekeeping force, Mark Butler, an Asian American whose mother was a

413

Montagnard tribeswoman, has flown in to deal with FULRO so as to ease the meeting between cultures and to avoid further massacres at the hands of the Vietnamese. As one UN officer said, "These people are in a very vulnerable position and we fear for their safety and security."

Butler is expected to meet with the leader of the FULRO fighters, who has remained in the mountain encampments. Local natives tell stories of the leader, who has successfully avoided capture by the Vietnamese despite a reward that's the equivalent of $100,000.

Local legend has it that the FULRO leader is a very dark-skinned man, fueling speculation that he may be an American left behind when the North Vietnamese army took over the country in 1975.

The time and place of the meeting between Butler and the FULRO leader have been kept secret in an effort to avoid Vietnamese search forces that are reputed to be in the area.

"Ave atque Vale"

★ ★ ★

Tom Clancy

IT HURTS TO SAY GOODBYE. IT WAS MY FIRST FUNERAL AT ARLINGTON National Cemetery, the expansive front lawn of a guy called Bobbie Lee by his blue-clad countrymen, the first time I had to listen to "Taps," the first time I had to console the widow and children of a close friend, and though I'd been lucky, I suppose, to make it so far in life before my first such event, losing one's best friend neutralizes all of that in a hurry. A thoroughly evil way to play catch-up ball.

He was supposed to be safe. Almost 5,000 hours aloft as a naval aviator, much of that combat time, floating around the sky in a vibrating mechanical contrivance a lot larger than a duck, but not much faster and a lot less maneuverable, full of jet fuel and human bodies, ever so well contrasted with a blue sky. Or peacetime flying, searching the surface of a stormy sea at midnight for the blinking light of a comrade, or doing an emergency rescue of a boater's family on the Chesapeake Bay, or doing a civil medevac, or lots of things, most of which he never told me about. His naval career ended in May 1990, a dignified ceremony at which there were about as many chiefs as commissioned officers. It was supposed to be safe after that. But it wasn't.

The official report is that Gerry's heart failed him. If so, he's

415

the only person whom that big heart ever failed, and perhaps that was really the reason, after all. There are thirty-eight "official" rescues on his flight log. There's a rule in the Navy. A rescue isn't a *rescue* unless at least one (1) person would probably have died if the helo-driver in question had not shown up. On the other hand, even if you rescue ten (10) people from likely death at the same time, it's still just one (1) event, and so the number of lives Gerry Carroll saved directly in his career is unknown to me. Not that it mattered. We're both products of a Jesuit education, of course, and one (1) is enough in the Great Scheme of Things. Metaphysics, you see, which was a frequent topic in our arguments.

Arguing with Gerry was a trip. Again, it was the educational background. We both believed in much the same things, thought in much the same way, searched for the same truth. One of us would find it first, and truth be told, the final score was about even, for he was a passionate man, and made small mistakes about as often as I did—and, truth be known, our disagreements were, in the main, about as artificial as plastic flowers. It was the discourse we engaged in that had the real value most of the time.

Gerry was a tad shorter, a little wider, and somewhat louder than I. He had a decidedly odd golf swing, but he never failed to whip my butt on the course—he cheated; his dad, you see, is a doc, and he started a lot earlier than I. That's how we spent our last day together, on a golf course, along with an Air Force one-star whose shoulder-weights were new enough to have the original shine, and Gerry took me aside to say that his new friend was the first USAF flag officer with whom he'd felt comfortable. So, yes, he was somewhat chauvinistic. He also regularly sang the praises of the U.S. Navy aviator, female, who checked him out in a fast-mover—but didn't think womenfolk needed to be exposed to combat.

So, who's perfect? I could fudge the details, but Gerry would wring my neck for that, and his imperfections merely give a brighter light to his real qualities.

I learned much from my friend, far too much to recount here, but the most important lesson of all, I think, was the nature of courage. That virtue can take many forms, but they all have the same beginning. The foundation of courage is always found in love. Courage means taking a risk with your life or your soul, or sometimes both, a risk that appears necessary only to the one who does it, to the onlookers who don't, and who does that except for something of great value? Most often that something is your fellow man. Whether a fellow warrior in danger, or a child who needs a hot ride to a hospital, whether dodging ground fire or thunderheads, Gerry risked his life for others without hesitation, because the lives of those strangers mattered to him. Why? If you asked him the question, you got a growl: "It's my job, Tommy!" Sure. Press the issue and you'd get: "Hey, somebody had to do it, right?" Except it's never "somebody." It's Gerry, or somebody very like him. Every single time.

Our society asks much of its warriors and gives little back, a fact of life too long-lived to be the shame to us that it ought to be. We very often don't even have the decency to ask. We just expect them to be there when they're needed, and out of sight when they're not. We examine their every action for flaws, and celebrate those for the world to see as though the people who wear our uniform were enemies instead of friends.

That was the particular burden of Gerry's generation of warriors, wasn't it?

But be it known that as the generation of our fathers put "paid" on the account of Adolf Hitler, so the generation of their sons put an end to the most malignant political movement of all of human history. While some members of our generation graduated from drug-experimentation to polyester suits, Gerry and his fellows were usually wearing greasy khaki or sweat-stained nomex, often out there at sea, beyond our sight, serving those who scarcely knew and hardly cared, standing guard for a nation still trying to find itself amidst the doubts, and then to like itself enough to recall that it really was, in Lincoln's words, "the last, best hope of mankind." Gerry loved us enough to care about what we were and what we would again become.

History will probably take note of what our generation has accomplished. But it wasn't all of our generation. It was actually just a few, many of whom, like Gerry, expressed their devotion in a hot, lonely place called Vietnam.

If you want to understand just how hard it was, just how deep was the hole they started from, and just how far they had to come, the place you have to start is at the end of the nightmare, because even there, they were what they were, America's warriors, serving an inconstant and troubled nation in the way that she deserved— whether she knew it or not. Gerry was there.

Gerry Carroll's Vietnam War/ Naval Aviation Trilogy

NORTH SAR

GHOSTRIDER ONE

NO PLACE TO HIDE

Afterword to

★ ★ ★

No Place to Hide

★ ★ ★

Tom Clancy

Thus ends the trilogy. Maybe it wasn't his heart after all. Maybe it was the demons who pursued my friend even after he'd defeated them, the memories of crewmen lost, the rescues not made, the windmills which his lance occasionally failed to topple. But if the demons think they've won, well, they're wrong.

I regret, even more than you, that this is the last tale of Tim Boyle and Mike Santy. Both are based on real people. Tim Boyle *is* and always will be Gerry Carroll. Mike Santy was Lt. David M. Santille, USNR, an A-7 pilot, lost in the Med in December 1975. The exploits you've read about them are, technically speaking, fictional.

But in a broader sense they really happened, and though Tim and Mike may not appear again on paper, their work is found every day you wake up and remember that your children will probably never be charged by their country with fighting a major war.

The only consolation for a life prematurely ended is the knowledge that the owner of that life made a difference. In the case of LCDR Gerald E. Carroll, Jr., USNR, that knowledge is certain. Your freedom is his legacy, even more than his three splendid novels which cover the nightmare from which Gerry's generation of warriors awoke. If you ever want to know how it came to be that you live in peace, read these books to remind yourself that it didn't happen by accident, nor without a price which in one case close to me was paid on a hot afternoon in Arlington, Virginia.

Rantoul Public Library
225 S. Century Blvd.
Rantoul, Illinois 61866